Expulsion

Gordon L. Thomas

Published by SellMyBooks

Copyright © Gordon L. Thomas 2016

The right of Gordon L. Thomas to be identified as author of this work has been asserted in accordance with sections 77 and 78 of the Copyright, Designs and Patents Act 1988.

A CIP catalogue record for this title is available from the British Library

ISBN 978-0-9956778-0-7

Cover picture: Gabriel Puig Roda, *The Expulsion of the Moriscos* (detail) 1894, Museu de Belles Arts, Castelló, oil on canvas 355x556 cm, photograph by Joanbanjo
Cover design by Rohan Renard (www.RenardDesign.com)

First published 2016

Printed in the UK by CMP (UK) Ltd

SellMy Books
(contact: www.gordonlthomas.com)

Gordon L. Thomas is retired and lives with his wife in London, England. He began his career lecturing in physics at King's College, London. He then worked in the UK Home Office as a scientist and also as an administrator. Latterly, his responsibilities were in police science and physical security. Since retiring he has become a keen writer and this is his third novel. For more information please visit his website www.gordonlthomas.com which you may use to contact him.

Acknowledgements

I want to express my grateful thanks to a number of people for helping me with the writing of this novel. First my darling wife, Janet, to whom the book is dedicated and who shared the triumphs and disasters I experienced in writing it. Janet also proofread the first manuscript and pointed out an embarrassing number of errors.

I also thank our son, Greg, who read it critically and made a number of suggestions for improvement.

A number of others read the first draft and commented. I am therefore also grateful to fellow authors, Loretta Proctor and John Chamberlain, my good friend Chris Forkan and my sisters-in-law, Kay Sinclair and Karen Teuber, all of whom gave me helpful feedback.

I am also grateful to our daughter Mel Hartley, her husband Guy and Greg's wife, Sue, for their constant encouragement and all for pressing me to complete this novel which sprung from the smallest of ideas.

Preface

This novel is a prequel to Gordon L. Thomas's first, The Harpist of Madrid, which is based on the extraordinary life of Juan Hidalgo de Polanco, a brilliant 17th century harpist and composer in the court of King Philip IV of Spain.

The protagonist of this novel is Juan Hidalgo's father, Antonio. In 1605, while working as a musician in Guadalajara, he learns from the daughter of an inn keeper about a Morisco plot to kidnap and ransom the king. What should he do with this dangerous information? Does he ignore it or report it to the authorities? What role could he play in the conflict between the state and the Moriscos? How does it end?

The novel is set in one of the most horrific periods of Spanish history when the aristocracy and church wanted to expel the Moriscos. These were those Moors who remained in Spain after the reconquest of 1492 and had converted to Christianity, were coerced into converting to Christianity or remained Muslim. Regardless of whether they had converted or not, they were treated with great brutality by the Spanish military, under the authority of King Philip III.

To Janet

Spanish Words

almalafa: Moorish garment worn only by women that covers the body from the shoulders to the feet

azumbre: unit of volume, about 4 pints

burdel: brothel

calle: street, road

cárcel: prison

cazuela: area in a theatre reserved for women

chorizo: spicy sausage

comedia: a play containing tragedy and comedy

Constelacíon de Orion: Constellation of Orion

corregidor: chief magistrate in a town, senior representative of the king

corrido: bull fight

cuchinillo: dish made with suckling pig

ducat: currency, 11 reales

encantado: greeting, delighted to meet you

fiesta: fair, festival

infante: prince

junta: committee

legua: league, five km or three and a half miles

libra: unit of weight, about a pound

mancibía: brothel

maravedí: unit of currency. 34 maravedís = 1 real

matador: bullfighter

milla: about a mile

Morisco: a Moor forced to convert to Christianity

pie: unit of length, about a foot

plaza: a square or market square

plazuela: a small square

policía: the police

pueblo: village

puente: bridge

puerta: door

pulgada: unit of length, about an inch

puta: prostitute

regidor: local official, alderman

real: unit of currency, 34 maravedís

señor/señora/señorita: mister/missus/miss

tercio: Spanish Infantryman

Tercio: regiment of infantrymen

tonelada: unit of weight, about a ton

vara: about a yard

zaguan: hall of a house

zarabanda: saraband, a fast, erotic dance

Part I

CHAPTER 1
The well-dressed man

'Good gal. With luck, I'll be stabling you here in a minute or two,' he said as he patted the old horse's neck and tethered her to the rail outside the inn. The mare looked around at him wide-eyed, appearing to know what he meant.

He lifted the latch on the heavy door and shoved it open. He eased his head back as he breathed in the cooler air that drifted from the inside, even though the smell of stale beer and sweat tainted it. He walked in. Several groups of men, some laughing, a number in heated argument and others looking half drunk, were scattered in the area reserved for drinking. One group shocked him into stopping: they were throwing a dwarf to each other and catching him as he fell after hitting the ceiling. The little man looked scared and tense, not seeing a way of escaping their brutality.

'Put him down! Now!' said the musician.

'Who the hell are you to tell us?' said one of the ruffians.

The musician turned, opened the door and shouted to the outside. 'Come here lads. I need help!'

With that the men carefully put the dwarf down. He quickly walked away, towards a table at the back of the room. The musician continued walking into the inn, smiling to himself.

He imagined that many of these men were robbers, vagabonds, pickpockets or some other form of criminal. Some might be earning a more honest *real* but he doubted it. Except for one, they all looked dishevelled with hats at awkward angles and clothes appearing as if they had adorned the backs of beggars. The musician thought he recognised the well-dressed man in the corner, lecturing a group of untidy individuals in such terms that they could be the man's employees.

The musician continued his anxious but expectant survey of the room. His heart leapt as he saw her, cloth in hand, wiping spillage from a table near the back. She knew how to attract a man. Her black hair fell in waves over the shoulders of her white dress, teasingly displaying a little cleavage and belted tightly to shape her waist. Her eyes had the sharp look of a vixen about to leap at its unknowing prey. She carried a look of pride about her and a knowing smile that drew men towards her whether they wanted to be or not. Most wanted to be.

'God, what a surprise, Antonio!' she said. 'You haven't been here in months!'

'Just dropped by to say, hello!'

'A lie,' she quipped. 'Not all the way from Madrid, just for that. Don't tell me… the "Wandering Chordsmen" are back in Guadalajara. For how long this time?'

'A few days. Maybe three. Depends.'

'On what? Not the weather. Looks like it'll be baking. This is the hottest September I can recall. And it's nearly October!'

'You're right, Jac. Lope's very latest *comedia* is playing at "The Coliseum". Certainly for two days, could be three. As usual, we're just the on-stage band. Me, Giant Carlos on guitar, Iago the Bad on dulcian and Josep on the harp.'

'What's the story in this one?'

'Come along and see!'

'You're joking! I've got work to do here. Father isn't well again and Mother can't do it all on her own, despite her guts. So tell me, what's the plot?'

'Later. Got other things to sort out now.'

Within a minute or so, Señor Antonio Hidalgo, second in charge of the band, had arranged to stay for up to three nights at the Guadalajara tavern. His body ached, even though he bore the looks of youth. The band had played nearly all day out in the blistering sun. He and the others had fiddled, strummed, plucked or blown and sweated their way through two performances. The audience, on the other hand, readily accepted the discomforts of standing in the heat in this makeshift theatre, there in the central square - The Coliseum indeed - and yelled with delight at this entertaining yarn. The long queues at the pay desk, for standing places only, could easily point the way to a third day, if only an afternoon performance.

Antonio had no reason to rush back to Madrid. Born in 1585, and by then a mature and independent twenty year old, he lived alone in ground floor rooms in a massive house, owned by the grisly old woman, Doña Marta, a few hundred *varas* down the right-hand side of the Calle de Toledo from the Plaza Mayor. He remembered well his mother's tears, not that many months before, as he climbed on his horse and headed from his parents' farm in Pedraza down the uncertain road to Madrid and a new start in life. His father Diego laughed as if pleased to see him go but he, too, would miss his hard working, only son who could turn a hand to any task on their substantial farm. They had tried to persuade him to stay, if only until he was twenty five. There were ways in which, while he was young and active, they still needed him, not just to work but to manage the labourers, male and female who worked their land.

Antonio had other ideas and, while he loved them deeply, realised that, if he stayed much longer, he would become indispensable and a farmer all his life. Not for him while adventure in the great if dangerous city beckoned. So he pulled on the horse's reins and galloped off, only to fall back to a trot when out of sight and earshot.

'I'll take the horse to the stables then. Usual rate, I suppose?'

'More if you want to sleep there, too!'

'Only if you sleep there with me!'

'I gave up hay romps years ago.'

'It'll have to be a bed then! Yours or mine?'

'Don't rush me. I'm still in shock at seeing you! I may not feel that way tonight!'

The banter didn't end there but end it eventually did and she and Antonio laughed as he went through the heavy doors again to fetch his patient horse and take her to the stabling.

'Sorry, gal. Thought I'd be quicker,' he whispered in her ear. The horse flicked its head. 'But I could strike lucky tonight. I'll let you know in the morning.'

The one thing she didn't like about herself was 'Jacinda'. She hated that name and could not forgive her mother for choosing it. She far preferred to be known as Jac. The family had always lived in Guadalajara, at least as far as 'always' went and that was for as long as she could remember. Not that long, for Jac was a mere twenty two years of age. Her mother possessed the strength of a bull in the *corrido*, both in body and in mind. Not so her father. His working life began in a copper mine not far from the town. While the job swelled his wallet, the constant hammering and dust had almost destroyed his lungs and hearing. So he spent as much time ill in bed as working at the inn and doctors paid him as much attention as he paid them in cash. Jac rode above it all and confidently held her own in working in the inn as cook, cleaner, bed maker and waitress as well has having some interesting relationships with her customers. She enjoyed the intimacy of several of them, and that included the handsome Antonio Hidalgo. But she knew how to protect herself.

'So what can I give you to eat tonight?' she said, in her role as waitress. He had arrived after most others in the inn so wasn't the first to be asked.

'Do you have fish?'

'Only something coarse from the river. I don't recommend it. And it may hang on your breath in a way I may not appreciate.'

He saw her concern about his ambient odour as a good sign. 'Do you have that meat pie you serve with green beans and artichoke?'

'You're in luck. No artichokes but will turnip do?'

'Fine, and some red wine?'

She nodded acceptance and turned towards the kitchen. His mind followed his eyes and stopped at the well-dressed individual in the corner, talking to that medley of ruffians who seemed to consider him their leader. Despite racking his brain, Antonio remained puzzled about who he could be. Yet he seemed so familiar. Antonio just sat there at the table until the smiling Jac arrived with a plate of steaming food in one hand and a generously poured cup of wine in the other. She carefully placed it in front of him and extracted a bone-handled knife and matching fork from the pocket of her pinafore.

'Maybe not the best meal to suit this heat but it's colder in this stone built palace than outside,' he said. 'It'll go down well. Want to join me for a drink? I'll buy it.'

'I'd love to but there's too much to do. Mother is at her wits end sorting out beds and preparing the food for tomorrow's breakfast. And father is none too well. Let's meet at the bar in an hour or so and we can chat then.'

'Accepted!' he said. 'I'm patient!'

'And it will be better for your digestion if I'm not sitting here distracting you!'

He took his time in eating the tasty fare. He enjoyed the pie and the wine slid down like an aging rioja from a rich man's cellar. She brought him a second cup and a plate of grapes for dessert. She uttered not a word, even while removing his empty plate.

While he relaxed in vacant reverie and all but dozed, she appeared and pulled up a chair at his table. 'I've finished,' she said. 'That's my work done for today.'

16

He struggled to interpret these words. She must know what occupied his masculine mind. Yet she gave no indication of what she wanted, at least not then. Somehow he needed to extract from her a less neutral statement. But how could he divine it? 'I think bed is beckoning me,' he ventured, chancing an off-hand rejection. One of them had to make a clear indication. He wondered about mentioning the word 'love' but that would be totally disingenuous, knowing that love played no part in this equation. He wanted nothing more than to make love to this attractive, friendly woman. Nothing more; and she'd mentioned his breath.

'Time we went up then,' he said, still an open statement but edging gradually towards his needs.

No reply.

So he decided to take control of the question. 'In that case, back to my original request: the one I made before I went to the stables. Your room or mine?'

'Not much subtlety in that. Surely a man of your talent can do better!'

He pondered for a moment or two. 'My dear Jac, I would delight in taking you to my bed. To make love to you. To give you the kind of pleasure you know I am capable of. Please indulge me. I am a desperate man.'

'That's better,' she smiled. 'But still clumsy. Actually, I'd prefer my room …in case I fall asleep! I'll go first and you follow after say, five minutes. I don't want this lot to know what's in store,' she said, nodding towards the others in the room, 'either for me or for you!'

By the light of the flickering candle he held by its holder, he climbed the narrow staircase and turned towards her room. His excitement rose at the pleasure he freely anticipated. He knocked on the door and waited. No reply. He stood there. He wondered whether to knock again. A full three minutes elapsed and still nothing. He placed an anxious ear against the door but could hear nothing, not a sound. Had she decided against a love encounter, he wondered. If so, she surely would have told him.

Then he heard a commotion from the floor above and the sound of footsteps rapidly descending the stairs. She shouted, 'Antonio, it's my father. He cannot breathe! He needs a doctor! Quickly! I'm sorry!'

'I'll find one! Go back and make him sit up… if he will.'

'I'll ask mother to help me. She's with him now.'

His mind rushed into an ordered chaos. He had no idea where to find a doctor, especially at this time of night. He entered the drinking room. By then only a dribble of men remained.

'Anyone know a nearby doctor? Jac's father's ill. He's having bad trouble breathing.'

'Not this time o'night, mate. You won't get one now,' said a crumpled individual sitting near the door by the stairs.

'No chance!' said another. 'He'll have to wait 'til tomorrow. Give him a drop of brandy. It'll either kill or cure.'

Antonio's mind spun as he despaired at these gratuitous remarks. He couldn't just wander the streets in the dark shouting for a medic. That would be stupid. Then it dawned on him. Jac would surely know of a doctor, one who had attended her father in the past. He'd go back up and ask her. He was about to turn around towards the stairs.

'Let's go! There's a doctor not far from here. He'll come out in an emergency. I know him well,' said the well-dressed man who was accompanied by only two of his followers.

The man grabbed an oil lamp hanging from the wall and led the way as Antonio followed. They ran out of the inn and down the road to the left. Dark cloud had all but obliterated the moon and after a few more turns and traverses of the narrow streets, Antonio realised he had no idea where he was. The well-dressed man stopped outside of what, in the almost total darkness, seemed a large house and knocked repeatedly on the door. They stood there for a few minutes. Then a woman, dressed in a full length nightgown and carrying a candle, appeared. Her puzzled features glowed in the yellow light. Antonio raised his eyebrows and leant forward at the exchange which then took place. He understood only the man's first sentence in which he gave his name as Hajib al-Asadi. The man and the woman conducted the remainder of the brief and rapid conversation in a strange tongue which Antonio imagined to be Arabic, the use of which had been banned in the whole of Spain for nigh on thirty years, since the uprising. So the well-dressed man and the woman were *Moriscos*.

Antonio suddenly realised where he had seen the well-dressed man. He had led a street march in Madrid, not many weeks before, protesting at the treatment of Muslims in the city. The march had ended in all but a riot in the Plaza Mayor. He'd seen this man arrested by the constabulary and taken off along with a gang of *Moriscos*. So here he was, free again and now, of all things, helping Antonio in his quest for a doctor.

The woman in the nightgown then turned and shouted something up the stairs, again fearless in using Arabic. A minute passed and a large man appeared, dressed in day clothes, topped by a tricorn, and carrying what looked like a doctor's bag.

'You lead the way, Pedro. I and your friend will follow.' Not more than five or so minutes later all three of them were back in the inn and being welcomed by a tearful Jac.

'Come this way, doctor. It's good of you to come. He's in a bad way. Up here.' Jac and the doctor disappeared behind the door to the hallway, leaving Antonio, the well-dressed man and a few others, including his two colleagues, in the drinking room. Antonio was panting after the late night expedition and so too was the well-dressed Pedro. Antonio had no intention of telling the man that he recognised him but thanked him profusely for his help.

'It's a pleasure, señor. Anything to assist in a situation like this. Least I could do. It was lucky that my friend the doctor lived so close by. Well, gentlemen, I'm off to my bed, now.' He bade his colleagues good night and went through the stair door. His two dingy workers uttered a few words to each other and went through to the street.

Antonio walked to the table where not long before he had consumed his meal. He decided to stay there at least until the doctor appeared again. He had barely settled when Jac and the doctor emerged. 'How is he now?' asked Antonio, with genuine concern.

'Much for the better. I made him sniff some strong salts and he's breathing reasonably well. I'll come back in the morning,' he said, turning to Jac.

'Thank you, doctor. You are kind turning out this late. Mother and I are so grateful.'

'Don't worry. Just keep him up as straight as you can. Put some more pillows beneath him if needed.' He then turned and went, leaving only Jac and Antonio in the room. Antonio realised immediately that it would be wrong and unfair to expect to share a bed with Jac then and although she apologised for the hiatus, they agreed to go to their separate rooms, at least for the night.

Antonio had left the window open and awoke with a fresh, cool breeze blowing across his face. The early morning sun beckoned so he decided to get up and go for a walk before it became too hot. He closed the inn door quietly and set off in the same direction which he and the man Pedro had taken the night before. He would try to follow the path to the doctor's seemingly impressive property. After several wrong turns and retracing his steps, Antonio turned a corner and there it was, facing him and about a hundred *varas* away, on the curve in the road he walked around before. He had been right: the house stood proud, exalting itself as by far the largest property in the street. A large oak front door sat between two large ground floor windows as three more large windows on the second floor overlooked the roadway. The angle of the sloping roof was less than he might expect but this served to accentuate the elegant façade. He stood outside for a moment simply admiring the property. Then he felt a hand on his shoulder.

'What d'you think you're doing here, mate?' said a voice from behind him.

'Minding my own business,' said Antonio, casually. 'Why don't you do the same?'

He then felt something cold on the back of his neck: the barrel of a gun. 'I'm telling you, chum. Clear off! It won't be good for you, if you stay. I might even put a bullet in your pretty throat.'

'You leave me little choice,' said Antonio coolly, but not turning towards his interlocutor, in case the man fired.

'Just walk away, in the direction you came and you'll be all right.'

Antonio did as the gunman demanded. He feared for his life as he managed to restrict himself to walking the hundred or so *varas* back to the street corner and turning into the adjacent road. Then out of sight of the gunman, he breathed a sigh of relief and ran back to the inn.

'Holy Jesus, what's the matter with you?' asked Jac's mother as he burst in through the tavern door, panting like a dog chasing a rabbit.

He could see nothing to be gained either in saying that he'd been to see the doctor's house or that he had been threatened by a faceless gunman. So, after a moment's thought, he came up with a reply. 'I decided I needed to exercise my muscles after sitting all day yesterday so I've been out for a run.'

'But you look scared and pale in the face. What have you been running away from?'

'Nothing. Really. I'm not scared at all. I admit, I did get lost but I soon got back on the right road,' he said with a forced laugh. 'Anyway, how's your man this morning. That's much more important.'

'He's much better, thankfully. We were really worried about him last night. Go and sit down. Jac or I will bring you some breakfast.'

Antonio sat at his table of the night before wondering about the gunman, what he wanted, why he was so anxious for Antonio to move from outside the doctor's house, why he couldn't manage this without threatening him with a firearm and what the consequences of going back there might be. Never before had he been threatened by a gun or felt his life to be in danger. He concluded that the gunman was for some reason guarding the doctor's house or some other adjacent property in that street. There had to be a *Morisco* connection but could not understand what it might be.

'What's going on in your head?' said Jac, while placing a plate of fried eggs, tomato and *chorizo* in front of him, along with a hefty chunk of oat bread.

'Just planning the day ahead,' he said, vacantly.

'You look troubled about something. Not just playing the fiddle.'

'No. Seriously, I was just thinking, another day in the raging heat of yesterday will be tough going. And I can't think of a way out of it.'

'You'll be fine,' she said. 'Now father is much better, tonight we may… Well who knows?'

Antonio beamed back at her. 'Let's hope so,' he said. 'But family comes first.' He didn't know whether he meant it or not.

'Enjoy your breakfast and leave your room key on the desk before you go. Is that all right?'

'Of course. I'll see you later.' He could see no one looking so he placed a surreptitious kiss on her cheek.

Antonio finished his tasty meal, packed up his things and went around the back to the stables and his waiting horse. 'Not so lucky after all, old gal. Maybe tonight!'

CHAPTER 2
The face in the crowd

Antonio rode to the central square in good time for the planned rehearsal which the four musicians had agreed upon the night before. By the time he and his horse arrived, all three of the others were there. Giant Carlos, standing with his guitar strung around his neck, looked up at him. Tall though he was, he still had to look up to Antonio who sat astride his horse. 'Holy Mother of Mary! What's the matter with you, Antonio? Have you seen a ghost?'

Antonio had not prepared himself for what he would say. So he thought for a moment and decided, rightly or wrongly, that he'd tell them exactly what had happened. Although they knew about his relationship with Jac, he'd steer clear of her.

'I'm amazed,' said Josep. 'Have I got that right? You just stood outside the doctor's house for less than a minute and you had the pistol barrel pushed against your neck?'

'Yes.'

'So what had you done, then?' said Iago the Bad, doubting Antonio's veracity.

'Nothing. I promise you. I just went back to the house where this character Pedro, or Hajib al-Asadi, had taken us for the doctor.'

Giant Carlos insisted that they break off discussing Antonio's frightening experience and start rehearsing. Antonio envied Carlos who played the guitar so well that, in his hands, the submissive instrument seemed to express every possible emotion. Love, laughter, joy and even jealousy and anger. Antonio had seen grown men reduced to tears at the intensity of feeling that Carlos could extract from his obedient guitar. He played individual notes with his finger nails so quickly and precisely he could make it sound as if two instruments were playing at once. He performed at his best as a soloist but as leader of the band could inspire them all into playing well as a quartet. He was the oldest of the group at twenty four and came from Segovia where his father painted landscapes and portraits of rich land owners for a living. He didn't say much about his past and Iago the Bad often speculated that he'd spent time in the *carcel* there, but not for anything more serious than affray and there was no evidence for that.

Iago the Bad epitomised the proverbial pot calling the kettle black. He had spent time in prison, in Zaragoza. At fifteen he had killed a soldier in a street fight and was sentenced to ten years for manslaughter. His father, a rich wool merchant, paid the court two thousand *ducats* for his release but by the time the court papers had cleared and the payment accepted, Iago had already served four years. His father and mother went to the prison gates to meet him, both hugged him, gave him fifty *ducats* in a leather purse and told him never to appear at their door again. So he never did.

He took his rejection quite well. Although fond of his mother he harboured an intense dislike of his father. He soon settled into life outside of prison and took up working as a street musician. He'd learnt to play a number of improvised wind instruments in the *carcel* and had a special talent for the recorder and the flute. But he played the tenor dulcian best of all and saved up and bought one in a shop in Segovia where he lived for a time. That is where, while playing solo on a street corner, Giant Carlos heard him and recruited him into the band. It was to Iago's disadvantage that he made himself the least popular of the troupe, mainly by talking behind the backs of the others and being the least flexible in reaching the compromises, which of course, were necessary to manage even a small troupe like this.

Josep learnt the harp in Madrid. He was the only one of the band who had benefitted from a formal musical education and consequently the only one of them who had been taught to read music. Funded by a bursary available only to poor orphans, he had attended the famous Imperial School in the Calle de Toledo and been inspired to play the instrument by one of the best harp teachers in the whole of Europe. He shone as a talented musician and taught his colleagues the basics of reading music. This gave them great flexibility as it meant that Josep could write down a tune and copy out the various parts for them to play.

They worked well together as a travelling troupe of players and were good friends. Like any group of men, they would mercilessly tease if one of them did something out of the ordinary, played a wrong note, or lost his place in a piece, but likewise were sensible enough not to do so when the potential victim could take such teasing badly. That is probably why they held back from chiding Antonio about his encounter with Jac when they saw he was clearly worried about something.

It must have taken several days for the team of constructors to build 'The Coliseum'. It stood at one end of the central square in front of a row of shops but far enough in front for the shops' customers to have access. The stage, on two levels separated by about three *pies* and connected by two sets of steps one at the back and the other towards the front, was covered by a large canvas tarpaulin suspended over a series of wooden beams. Actors could appear on the stage from either side, from behind curtains, from up the stairs at the front or even descend on ropes and pulleys from above.

Unlike in a conventional theatre, there was no special area for the women in the audience who were therefore compelled to stand in the same area of the square as their male counterparts. Seating was provided only to any actors who had to sit on stage or for Josep the harpist.

At that time of the morning, the troupe of musicians and a couple of scene shifters were the only theatre people there. Carlos led his men up the steps at the front of the stage and grouped them to the left, looking from the audience. He wondered, as would any responsible leader, how his group would perform that day. Early results were not good.

'Antonio, you are missing notes and hitting wrong ones. You are all over the place. What's the matter with you? And you too, Josep. Are you in sympathy with Antonio or something? You fingers aren't working. Thank goodness you are playing well, Iago!'

'Sorry, Carlos,' said Antonio. 'I don't know what it is. You are right though.'

'Could be having a gun barrel pushed into your neck,' said Josep. 'I have no excuse. Sorry all the same. I'll try harder.'

Iago kept out of the discussion but merely looked approvingly at Carlos, presumably for mentioning the issue. He had nothing helpful to say.

'I have an idea,' said Carlos. 'Antonio and I have spoken parts towards the end of the play and we'll rehearse them. Iago and Josep can comment.'

'Let's do that,' said Iago.

'Right, Antonio, I go first.'

Then followed the short, almost meaningless, dialogue:

'So then. What do we do now?'

'Haven't we got any other work?'

'Nothing until tomorrow night.'

'I'm going home to bed, then.'

'She's lovely.'

'Yes. Nice. I'm jealous, too.

'Ah well. Let's go,' Carlos concluded. 'Well, what do you think, Iago?'

'Not at all bad.'

'And you, Josep?' said Carlos.

'You are both overdoing it. Don't overact! Just be more natural!'

'Very helpful,' said Carlos. 'Take note of that, Antonio. I think Josep is right. Let's play again.'

This time, Carlos seemed much happier and broke into a beaming smile when, after the band stopped playing, the twenty or so people who had formed an impromptu audience gave the troupe a vigorous round of applause.

The actors turned up in ones and twos. They seemed a strange amalgam from the cheerful, plump lady who was to play Casita, the heroine, to the tall, wiry character given the part of Fernando, the manservant of the jealous commander. They were all on or near the stage with about half an hour to spare. However, a number had been gambling in a drinking house the night before and one of them had lost all his clothes, including his breeches, betting with a card sharp. He appeared dressed in a sheet with a hole cut out for his head. His face glowed red with embarrassment as his colleagues in the cast and members of the audience spotted his condition and pointed him out to others.

'Look at that idiot! He's naked under that white sheet!' said one.

'What's he done with his clothes?' laughed another.

'I said he was a small boy! He's more than proved it now!' said a third.

No one wanted to pay to get into these outdoor, moveable theatres. The many gaps in the fence panels which define the auditorium are an open temptation to slip through unnoticed. This is just too much for some townsfolk to resist. But not all of these attempts to deceive were successful.

'I'm bloody stuck,' yelled a plump woman carrying a small child as she marooned herself neither in nor out.

'You cheating cow,' shouted one of the patrolling constables. 'We'll get you out all right.' Three of them, each wielding wooden batons descended on her and together pulled her out, still clutching her child,.

One of the constables applied his baton sharply to her rear. 'Here's a touch on the ass for you, my dear. Maybe you'll come in through the proper entrance next time. Now clear off and take your kid with you.'

By the time the performers were ready to start, the delay had amounted to about fifteen minutes but that was fairly common for one of these shows which were not organised to start at a precise time. The band assembled on the lower part of the stage and the actors positioned themselves at the points on the higher part where they would start saying their lines. Iago played a fanfare, if you could call it that, on his dulcian and, after that, Carlos made three solid bangs on a drum. The manager of the acting troupe then appeared at the front of the stage and addressed the audience.

'Ladies and gentleman, thank you for coming here today. Special thanks are due to those of you who've paid, all four of you!' - a wave of raucous laughter from the crowd, then silence - 'You are about to enjoy Félix Arturo Lope de Vega y Carpio's very latest play, Peribañez. It is a love story which ends in a murder but you'll be glad to know, it's not mine. So let's begin.'

Carlos banged his heel on the stage, the signal for the actors to dance and sing. While playing the first few notes on his treasured violin, Antonio cast his eye around the audience, studying their reactions. Then he saw him.

CHAPTER 3
The meeting

King Philip III was sound asleep when Andrés de Prada, the royal secretary, stood up and walked the few steps from his desk in the outer office to knock on His Majesty's door. He knocked loudly and persistently but the king continued his slumbers. 'I'm sorry, Your Grace,' said the secretary, a senior civil servant, 'but I don't think I could have missed him going past me. He must be in there somewhere. He and the queen had a heavy lunch today and he's probably sleeping it off.'

'Get out of the way, fool. I'm going in,' said the Duke of Lerma, the king's principal adviser, the *valido*, the most worthy, to whom the freshly crowned king had delegated virtually all his powers. Francisco Gómez de Sandoval, 1st Duke of Lerma, appointed to the dukedom by Philip III himself only a few years before, was born into the powerful Sandoval family who originated in Seville. His father was the Marquis of Denia and his uncle the Archbishop. While Philip II relied little on the nobility in the administration of his government, the fact that the future Duke of Lerma became a favourite of the heir apparent was innocuous enough. But the late king gradually became troubled at this developing relationship and, given the *infante*'s propensity to indulge in the sin of sloth, could see potential trouble developing for the monarchy, when the *infante* became king. Philip II was right.

The duke knocked on the door, paused for a full three seconds, turned the door knob and walked in. He stopped, raised his eyebrows and thrust his hands on his hips. His face turned a frenzied crimson as he saw the king slumped across his desk with his bottom just about retaining its position is his high backed, wooden chair. He listened to the rhythmic, purring snore of the slumbering monarch. He leant over the king and, as he came nearer to his face, he could detect the smell of wine on his otherwise rancid breath. His eyes almost leapt from their sockets as he saw that the king had dribbled on the official document beneath his head. The black infusion of ink and spittle was still wet.

'For the blood of Christ,' thought the duke. 'Here we are in one of the worst crises Spain has ever had to face and here is the king, totally oblivious to the troubles of his fading empire. Just as well we don't rely on him.'

The duke put a hand to the king's shoulder and gave it a gentle shake. 'Philip,' he said. He never used a formal address when in the presence of the king and only the king. 'Wake up!'

The king jolted himself out of his reverie. 'Holy Mother of Jesus. It's you, Francisco. I was in the middle of an incredible dream. I was sitting with the Virgin Mary having dried tomatoes, bread and olive oil for breakfast when she asked me if I'd like to meet Her Son. After all, She said, I was the king of my domain and He was the king of his, so we ought to have the pleasure of each other's company. Is that blasphemy, Francisco? If so The Holy Inquisition of Toledo could drag me before them couldn't they? I could be burned at the stake.'

'Don't tell anyone else about this dream, Philip and you'll be all right. Believe me,' said the *valido* in such a flat voice it could easily be taken as contempt.

'Presumably, you want to discuss something, Francisco.'

'Yes. Something difficult which requires your full attention,' he said, stressing the word full.

'Oh? What might that be?'

'We need to think about moving back to Madrid.'

'Be more specific. Who are "we"?'

'"We" are you, your court, the Councils and your officials.'

'What's brought all this about? My first reaction is no. The court is working well and I can't, off-hand, see any reason to move back. We've only been here four years and we are all settled in. Surely, the reasons I accepted - which you gave me, I might add - for moving here in the first place - cannot be invalid.'

'There are sound arguments. Firstly, the expected improvements in the economy of Valladolid have not materialised. In effect, we have moved the ancient university to Burgos along with the chancellery so we could use the university buildings for your court. The huge increase in population caused by the move from Madrid has caused a large rise in house prices and consumables. The indigenous population cannot buy food for their children, let alone afford to buy property here.'

'I haven't seen evidence of any of that.'

'Maybe not but, with respect, you don't meet the people who may be suffering.'

'Maybe I should make the effort and get out there.'

'Secondly, Madrid is failing. Property prices have collapsed. The market for rented property is almost non-existent. Food prices have gone

28

through the roof because markets have vanished and farmers are not producing the food.'

'You aren't expecting a decision now are you, Francisco? It's all come as a shock. Shouldn't we set up some sort of *junta* to look into this? What you have said is inconclusive and, with equal respect, probably based on hearsay evidence. We need some sort of enquiry, don't we?'

'I'll think about that, Philip. Maybe we do. I could easily ask someone more knowledgeable than me to talk you about this.'

'The chief magistrate of Madrid perhaps and the Constable of Castile?'

'Maybe,' said Lerma, dismissively.

'Don't we need something written? Something we can sit here and talk about?'

'As I said, Philip, I'll go ahead and come up with some ideas.'

'Don't forget those I've mentioned.'

'Of course not. By the way, I ought to mention something else.'

'Go on.'

'The Moors, the *Moriscos* are becoming a problem again. Especially in Granada but also in other regions. We are going to have to think about what to do about them.'

'An interesting discussion, Francisco. Thank you for waking me up!'

CHAPTER 4
Accomplices

He was looking straight at Antonio. He stood with his arms folded over his chest, wore a white shirt, tied down the front with a leather lace, and tan breeches secured by a wide, leather belt. He wore an unusual style of hat but Antonio could easily see his face, even in the shade of the wide brim. Antonio felt a shiver rush down his spine as he realised that he was looking straight into the eyes of the well-dressed Pedro, or Hajib al-Asadi. Somehow the man looked different. Antonio was not sure how but he had a different air about him, a look which Antonio found threatening. Antonio, true to his profession, refused to be distracted and continued playing through these moments of discovery without the slightest hesitation.

The actors were soon playing Peribañez's wedding feast and began to dance so wildly that the audience felt compelled to join in. Men in the gathered throng grabbed the nearest woman, whether it was their wife or some other, and wheeled them into motion. The audience became actors in the play and threw themselves into it with abandon equalled by gusto. The actors became an audience as, while continuing to dance, they turned to witness this spontaneous burst of celebration. The town square became the scene of a boisterous party. One woman, larger than some of the others, fell laughing to the floor showing more of her friendly form than she meant to reveal. Three men, who had witnessed her decline, and delighting in what she had on display, slowly raised her to the vertical. Her dignity at least partially restored, she continued her uninhibited merriment.

These extraordinary scenes lasted no more than a few minutes and were interrupted by shouting and commotion off-stage. The noise struck terror into the audience who looked around them in fear of what might be about to happen. This was the introduction to the next scene in the play where Bartolo, one of the peasants, rushes in to announce that the knight commander of Ocaña is injured. The commander had attempted to capture a loose bull and had fallen badly from his horse. He is unconscious and is carried onto the stage.

By then the music had stopped so giving Antonio the chance to wonder what the man Pedro could be doing there. He suspected he was not just an innocent member of the audience. He turned towards Carlos and nudged him slightly.

'See that man with the odd-shaped brimmed hat, Carlos. Halfway back and right of centre,' whispered Antonio in Carlos's ear.

'Not sure,' said Carlos. 'Oh him, the one with the shirt laced down the front?'

'That's him!' said Antonio. 'He's the man Pedro I told you about earlier. He's the one who took me to the doctor's house. Where the gunman threatened me this morning.'

'Shut up, you two,' came a voice from the audience. 'We can't hear with you chatting!'

Antonio and Carlos looked at each other. Iago and Josep also looked towards them. 'Yes, quiet!' said Josep.

That didn't stop Antonio from wondering why the man Pedro was there. Something told him he was not there just to see Lope's play. Was he there alone? Antonio cast an eye around the rest of the audience. No, he was not alone. Some of the man's untidy companions were also there. They had distributed themselves in the audience, presumably not to be recognised. They were all there to cause trouble. He would try to thwart them but could not move until the interval after the first act.

The knight commander recovers his consciousness but is inflicted by a greater pain. He has fallen in love with Peribañez' new wife, the beautiful and faultless Casilda. The commander leaves with his manservants but not before promising the newlyweds that he will reward them for saving his life. His exit, punctuated by some improvised chords from the musicians, leaves Peribañez and his wife alone.

Antonio was becoming anxious in case he was too late to put his newly hatched plan into effect. He was counting the seconds.

Casilda asks Peribañez what makes a good wife so he takes her through an astonishing alphabet of wifely attributes. She does the same, alphabetically pronouncing a good husband's qualities which include, unsurprisingly, satisfying all her needs. He asks her to make a wish that he promises will come true. She asks him to take her to Toledo, a ten hour cart ride away, for the festival of The Assumption and to visit the Shrine of the Virgin. Peribañez grants it, promising her something expensive to wear which she can easily slip off when they are alone.

The knight commander asks his servant, Lujan, for advice on how he might gain the favour of Peribañez, as a step towards his seducing Casilda. Lujan suggests he buys Peribañez a pair of the finest mules and some gold earrings for her. The commander is delighted and instructs Lujan to make these special purchases.

31

By then Antonio was becoming even more restless. He wanted the act to finish but several scenes remained.

Casilda tells her cousin, Ines, how much she loves Peribañez, to the extent of describing the pleasure she takes from him in the hay in the stable and on the table in the kitchen. Peribañez interrupts this frivolous chatter and protests that their cart looks too plain and poor to drive it to Toledo. The couple decide to take up the commander's offer to repay the debt he owes them. Peribañez goes to see him and asks for some tapestries emblazoned with the Ocaña coat of arms and those of the commander's family. The commander is well prepared and not only gives Peribañez the tapestries but also the spritely mules and golden earrings for his wife.

The act concludes with the knight commander following the couple as they drive their cart, loaded with their family and decorated with the tapestries, to Toledo.

Antonio turned to Carlos. 'I am going to find one of the constables. I need to tell them of my suspicions.'

'Do it, Antonio. Go now but come straight back.'

Carlos' plea was justified. The band was to provide the entertainment in the interval and would have to manage without Antonio while he was gone.

'What's he up to?' asked Iago.

'I'll tell you later. We carry on until he gets back.'

'Gone for a piss?' said Josep.

'No,' said Carlos.

Antonio dashed from the stage into the audience. He looked around him but couldn't see a constable and thought they'd left and gone into the town. He almost gave up and thought of heading back to the stage. Then he saw them chatting and laughing together, the three constables who had pulled the fat, cheating woman out from the gap in the fences.

'Can I have a word?' said Antonio to one with a large mole on the side of his face and his baton tucked under his arm.

'What's up mate?' said the constable.

'I'm not too sure but I think trouble may be brewing.'

'Go on mate, tell us,' said one of the other two, shorter than his compatriots and leaning backwards to look up to Antonio.

Antonio told them how he was held up at gunpoint after he'd gone back to the doctor's house and about the well-dressed *Morisco* who had taken him there. He said that he recognised the man Pedro as the leader of a protest march a few weeks earlier in Madrid. He told them of the suspicions the man had raised when Antonio saw him in the crowd.

'What do you expect us to do about it?' said the third, the one who had hit the woman on the backside with his baton.

'You are the constables, not me!'

'How do we know that you've identified him as the *Morisco* leading the protest? Or that you've seen his mates here?'

'I suppose you don't. But what's to stop you searching him? He's going to do something and his mates will be involved too.'

'We'll think about it,' said the short one, again looking up at Antonio.

Antonio looked at them and shrugged his shoulders. 'I've done my duty. It's up to you now.'

Sounding vaguely more interested, the one with the large mole asked Antonio a question. 'How will we recognise him, mate?'

Antonio described the man and where he was. He wished them luck, quickly returned to the stage and climbed up to join his colleagues. His mind was racing. He was far from sure that the constables would speak to the man Pedro, despite what he had told them. He still felt that the man and his colleagues might do something bad but couldn't imagine what.

'Speak to a constable?' asked Carlos, looking anxiously at Antonio.

'Yes, but they didn't seem interested.'

'Not surprised. An odd lot. I wasn't impressed when one of them hit that woman. She'd done wrong but hitting her while she was holding her child was evil.'

'I've done my bit. It's up to them now,' said Antonio while lifting his violin from its case. He began to play again, re-joining his colleagues who by then were already deeply engaged in the interval music. The breaks in these performances are as important as the play and the audience enjoys them just as much. As well as the band playing, a variety of street vendors were mingling with the crowd and offering their wares. 'A mug of beer, señor? Brewed in the town here. Only two *maravedís*!' 'How about a pie, señora? Stuffed full of ham and fit for a king!'

Once again, members of the audience broke into a dance and wheeled each other around, continuing where they left off at the Peribañez wedding party. The dancing became wilder as the band speeded up the rhythm and played louder. A gypsy woman climbed on to the stage and sang the words to the tune they were playing. A huge round of applause burst from the audience as, with help from some nearby menfolk, she climbed back into the audience.

'See those constables, Antonio? They're moving around the crowd. What do you think they're doing? Are they looking for your friend?' said Josep.

'My friend, indeed! What a nerve!'

'Well, you know who I mean!'

He was right. The constables, still in a group of three, had moved from where Antonio had spoken to them and were moving around in the audience. He could see that they were gradually approaching the man Pedro. While bowing his violin at a frantic pace, he could see from the corner of his eye that they had reached him and were beginning to speak to him. Antonio smiled with satisfaction. He'd achieved something, if only to get the constables to speak to the man whom he could see was protesting to his interviewers. The man threw his hands in the air in apparent disbelief at what they were saying to him. Then one of them must have asked a crucial question. He shouted boisterously at the constables until one of them raised his arms and lowered them as if to encourage the man to calm down. The nature of that question became clear as one of the constables, the short one, searched the man's clothing, apparently to look for a concealed weapon. He bent down to pat his breeches, the insides of his legs and the outsides; then stood to explore his chest and underarms.

From the man's gestures and the expression on his face, the constables had found nothing. They said something to him and left him standing there, still looking annoyed and perplexed. Antonio wondered if the man suspected Antonio of being behind the interrogation with the *policia*. He hoped not. So Antonio's fears were apparently unjustified and the band continued supporting the audience in their celebration of the interval

'Looks like they've cleared him,' said Carlos.

'Either he's innocent or they've missed something,' said Antonio, still concerned.

'You've got no grounds to worry now, so just concentrate on playing and being part of the band,' said Carlos impatiently.

'I'll say no more!' said Antonio. But that would not prevent him from thinking.

After about twenty minutes of eating, drinking and merriment, the theatre group manager came again to the front of the stage to announce that the second act was about to begin. Four of Peribañez's fellow villagers were complaining about the decrepit state of the icon of San Roch, their patron saint. Their debate ended in agreeing that Peribañez, whom they had welcomed back from Toledo, should go back there to find an artist willing to restore the icon to its previous glory.

Peribañez accepts this important commission but realises that Casilda will not be pleased. In the meantime, the knight commander is colluding with his servant Lujan to devise a plot. The servant will attempt to seduce Casilda's cousin, Ines. The commander admits that he confessed in Toledo to following Casilda and telling her of his feelings towards her. While Peribañez is back in Toledo, Casilda is managing the harvest. The harvesters are exhausted and ready to sleep but Lujan is amongst them, disguised as a worker. He hears the signal that the commander is outside waiting his moment to seduce Casilda, and to have her, whether she wants it or not.

Iago provided the off-stage signal and blasted on a whistle. Then the knight commander bursts in. At that instant, four gun shots shattered the audience's rapt concentration. People were overcome by terror. Women screamed out and men and women dropped or fell to the floor. A number started to rush the exit, trying to escape from the makeshift auditorium. Fences fell in the panic and commotion. Some people were pushed over and trampled in the frenzy.

Antonio looked on, frozen to the spot, his violin secured under his chin and his bow in his hand. Each gunman had grabbed a woman by the hair and started to drag her through the crowd. They could not risk stopping to re-load their guns but the simple act of holding a hostage was enough to scare many in the audience. Most cleared the way for their departure but a few brave souls decided to take a chance. One of the gunmen was brought down and set on by his attackers who kicked and beat him. Another let go of the woman he had captured and attempted to make an escape. Some of the men pursued him. Antonio couldn't see the constables and the man Pedro had apparently vanished. But the gunmen had caused havoc and were those whom Antonio had suspected: Pedro's companions in the inn.

'How will this end?' said Carlos, resigned to not playing in this disturbance.

'No idea,' said Iago.

'Only when these gunmen have been caught,' said Josep.

Eventually, after men in the audience had stopped the gunmen, the three constables along with re-enforcements reappeared. They arrested the four gunmen and dragged them off, presumably to some place of detention. By then, apart from a few stragglers and some so terrified they had stayed fixed to the spot, the auditorium was empty.

The band and the actors had stayed on the stage during the commotion. The last thing they needed was to affect their ability to play which they protected by keeping clear. They had been intent on conducting another performance in the afternoon but that was impossible, if only because of the damage to the auditorium. The theatre manager decided that the later performance would be abandoned. That signalled the musicians' departure to a local tavern for a drink.

Most of the inns close to the theatre were already packed with the events' witnesses who were frantically discussing them. The band soon found one where they could all sit together.

'Well, what was that about?' asked Carlos, looking quite pale.

'Hard to say,' said Iago, with an air of indifference.

'Something to do with the *Moriscos*, I'll bet,' said Josep.

'I think you are right,' said Antonio. 'It's a protest like the one I saw a few weeks back in Madrid. But there are things I don't understand. Why did these people use guns when there was no way they could escape? They were outnumbered from the start and had no hope of getting away. They were suicidal. It must have been to draw attention.'

'But attention from whom? We cannot be sure they were *Moriscos*,' said Carlos.

'I can be certain,' said Antonio. 'I recognised the gunmen as companions of the man Pedro, obviously a *Morisco*, who took me to the doctor's house where I was threatened this morning.'

'The mere fact that you recognised them hardly makes it a protest,' said Josep.

'Wait until you see the news sheets in the morning,' said Carlos.

The four musicians were quietly chatting in the bar and drinking their second beer when two of the three constables appeared and walked across to their table.

'That's him,' said the one with the mole, pointing towards Iago. 'He's the one who started it.'

'I'll arrest him then,' said the short one, by then looking up into Iago's eyes.

Iago looked astonished. 'What's the matter? What am I supposed to have done?'

'You must know,' said the short one.

'We don't know what you're talking about,' said Carlos. 'I'm the leader of this troupe of players and if you want to arrest anybody, arrest me.'

Antonio chimed in. 'What exactly has our man done?'

'Several witnesses have come forward to say that you, the man with the whistle, gave the signal for the gunmen to fire. It was at the exact time you blew the thing!'

'You are wrong there,' said Josep. 'Yes, Iago blew the whistle but that's what's meant to happen in the play. It's in the script. The actor playing Lujan blows a whistle and that's the signal for the knight commander to come into the house where he is hoping to seduce Casilda.'

'You're making this up to get him off,' said the one with the mole. 'I've got a good mind to arrest all four of you. You three for perverting the course of justice.'

At that moment, the theatre manager appeared, along with two of his actors. He walked over to where the musicians were arguing with the constables, leaving his colleagues to find a vacant table. 'Good afternoon, gentlemen. To what do we owe the pleasure of the company of the town constabulary?'

'That's a loaded question,' said the short one. 'We are here to affect an arrest.'

'Just a moment,' said Carlos, smiling. 'Constables, do you mind if we ask this man a few questions… in your presence, of course? He's the manager of the troupe of actors who were playing when the guns were fired.'

'How's that going to help?' said the one with the mole.

'Give me a chance and you'll see,' said Carlos.

'Go ahead,' said the short one.

Carlos put his questions, just like a lawyer. 'Tell me, Andres, in the play we were performing, is there a whistle in the script? If so, at what point in the play is it sounded?'

'Yes, there is a whistle in the script. It is played to signal that the way is clear for the knight commander to enter the house and attempt to seduce Casilda.'

'There you are, constables. Andres here has explained everything!'

'Thank you, gentlemen. You have indeed explained it,' said the short constable. 'I have only one further question: could the gunmen have known about the whistle?'

'Yes,' said Antonio. 'Unless the timing of the gunshots was pure coincidence. Iago blew the whistle twice yesterday, once at each performance, and I imagine the gunmen were there at one of them and planned to shoot on the sounding of the whistle.'

'In that case there will be no arrest,' said the short one. He went up to Iago, apologised and offered to buy all of them another beer.

Iago beamed and waved his hands above his head, in celebration. 'Thank you gentleman,' he said, directing his comment at no one in particular. 'I didn't fancy spending the night in gaol. Yes, another beer please!'

CHAPTER 5
The fire

Antonio could not wait to get back to the inn. In his impatience, he rode his poor mare, despite the afternoon heat. Loyal to her master, she did not protest and managed the half *legua* at a canter. He took her straight to the stables and left her with a gentle pat on the neck. 'Bless you, gal. I'll tell you in the morning.' She looked around and flicked her head

'You're back early,' said Jac, smiling to greet him as he came through the back door of the inn. Her look of pleasure far outweighed her words.

'And how is the patient?' he asked, placing a kiss on her cheek.

'Much better! Mother and I are pleased with him. He's still weak but breathing easily now. The doctor came this morning and gave him some linctus to take. It's working well. Why are you so early? I haven't opened the kitchen yet so there is no food ready.'

'It's a scary story but I think you should know about it because danger could be lurking.'

'Go and sit at a table. I'll bring you a beer. I might have one myself.'

Antonio related the whole tale. He apologised for not telling her about his return to the doctor's house that morning and the gun the stranger had put to his neck; or about the well-dressed man who had taken him to the doctor's; or that the man and the doctor were *Moriscos*. He said that he felt she had enough to worry about with her father being ill. He said that after the events of that day she should be aware of these things, in case the man Pedro might cause her and her family any trouble. Her eyes betrayed her shock at the gun threat.

'Is the man Pedro staying here tonight?' Antonio asked, with a hint of fear in his voice.

She hesitated before speaking. 'Yes. He has reserved the same room, just two away from yours. But I can tell him there has been a mistake in the bookings and that the room is no longer available.'

'Don't do that,' said Antonio. 'Knowing that I saw him at the theatre, he may suspect that I am behind any decision to keep him out. No. It's best to let him stay. Otherwise, I don't know what he'd do.'

'Fine,' said Jac, taking a sip of beer. 'But do you think he will do anything to harm us?'

'I cannot think he will. Neither you nor anyone else here has upset him. And his mates won't be here because, as I said, they've all been arrested.'

'What about tomorrow? Will there be another performance?'

'The troupe manager wants to go ahead with one in the afternoon. That will give him time to get damage repaired and everything back in order. So I will stay here one more night, if that's all right.'

'Of course, Antonio. Fine.'

'I'm feeling a little tired after all today's activities and retiring late last night. Do you mind if I go to bed for an hour and, maybe, see you later, at dinner?'

'How can I object? You were so helpful in finding a doctor for my father, I owe you the early use of your bed. It's all made up and your room is clean.'

His mild hint that they might indulge in some afternoon love had passed over her like an unseen bat at night. 'I'll just go out to the old gal and bring in my violin then. All right if I use the back door?' he said, trying not to sound disappointed.

'Of course.'

Antonio said a few words to his horse, returned and, carrying his violin, was climbing the stairs towards his room. He'd had a quick look downstairs to tell Jac that he was on his way up but couldn't see her. He went to put the key in the lock but realised that the door was not fully closed. He stopped for a moment to think. Could this be some kind of ambush? Had the room been broken into? Was there someone in there?

He decided to enter, come what may. His anxious look turned to a smile. There lying on his bed was Jac. She'd slipped her dress off her shoulders to expose her elegantly beautiful breasts. With his heart suddenly beating faster, he said nothing until he had closed the door and put his violin on the dressing table.

'You had me worried, Jac. I looked for you downstairs and you were here all the time! You look so inviting and I can feel my heart racing!'

'Not too fast, I hope. You will explode! I almost carried on working but then I suddenly thought: this man should be rewarded for what he did last night. You've got half an hour.'

They both enjoyed each other's nakedness as they freely romped on Antonio's bed. They giggled and whispered cheeky words to each other as they moved, touched and embraced each other. 'There's something special about making love in daylight. And I did enjoy that,' she said, climbing back into her dress and doing up the belt which so nicely accentuated her waist. 'I must go now. There's work to be done!' She blew him a kiss and stepped out of his room.

Newly alone and freshly satisfied, Antonio lay there pondering the day's other events. He wondered whether the incident outside the doctor's house that morning had any connection with the gunshots at the theatre. The link could be Pedro, the *Morisco*. Even at his tender age, Antonio realised that the Moors had not enjoyed much favour in Spain, not since their final defeat in Granada in 1492, over a century before. Not only were they a different race but also a different religion, that of Mohammad, which was incompatible with the Church of Rome. In the early sixteenth century, Isabella I gave the Moors in Castile, and Charles V those in Aragon, a stark choice: either convert to Christianity or be expelled from the country.

Having known only Spain as their home for nigh on eight hundred years, expulsion meant adopting a totally foreign land and starting their lives anew. So, not surprisingly, hundreds of thousands took the offer of converting – becoming *Moriscos* – but the majority of them only pretended to do so, even observing the feast of Ramadan and praying to Allah in clandestine gatherings at secret mosques. Religious tension, envy, racial hatred and racial violence featured strongly, countrywide, and had done so since the battle for Granada.

So there surely was a connection between these events. They were, like the demonstration in Madrid, linked to the *Moriscos*. Whether the man Pedro was implicated remained a question. Within moments Antonio was asleep and dreaming uneasily of home.

'I need to speak to you,' said Jac, looking up to him as Antonio descended the stairs. 'Come into the store room. Mother is working in the kitchen.'

Antonio frowned, raised his eyebrows and followed her into the little room which was lined with shelves of fruit, vegetables and bags of flour. A number of wooden kegs, empty or full of beer sat like sentinels on the floor. He could only just see the features of her face by the light from the tiny window.

'What's the matter?'

'I'm scared,' said Jac. 'It's that man Pedro. I was cleaning the table in one of the drinking booths and could hear him talking to some of his colleagues. I heard him mention the king and curse his life. So I stopped and listened. I shouldn't have but I did. They couldn't see me because they were all sitting behind the partition. I heard more than I wanted to.'

'Just a moment. His colleagues were arrested and are in gaol awaiting trial.'

'No. There is one from the other night and three more. They are locals and I recognised them.'

'What did they say then?'

'They started by cursing the king and wishing him dead. Then they talked of plotting to kidnap, even kill him. The man Pedro asked for one of them to volunteer to go to Valladolid to find out exactly where the king's palace quarters were, where his guards were. And what other security he had. It would take several weeks and the man would go alone so as not to create suspicion. He would stay at a *Morisco* house. Pedro would explain where it was. When his man came back, they would work out a detailed plan to kidnap the king and hold him for ransom.

'I'm scared, Antonio. I feel better now I've told you. What should we do?'

'My God, Jac. I just don't know what to think. This isn't a demonstration, a protest. It's a serious threat. I'm concerned, too. We are the only two people who know this... other than them. We need to think about what to do about it. Leave it to me.'

'I must go, Antonio. I've much to do. And I don't want people to wonder what we are doing in here!'

Antonio began to shudder. He could hardly breathe, let alone think of what he should do with what he had heard from Jac. A simple violinist, working for an honest living and suddenly he learns of a plot against the state. He first tested her words in his mind. Could she have been mistaken in what she had apparently heard? Was she fooling him for some reason? Jac would never do that. They were only friends and lovers but he could trust her not to deceive him. If the men had been ordinary citizens of Guadalajara and just drinkers in the inn, he could see how she may, in some way, have misunderstood. But what they were planning fitted so well into what the man Pedro had already been involved in. So it was more than likely an accurate picture of what they had said. So he had to decide what to do with the evident facts that Jac had put to him. The king's life was at stake.

Antonio hardly slept that night. He'd taken his fill at the same table as the night before and eaten well. He'd supped a beer and a couple of glasses of wine but still he could not sleep. Try as he did, he failed to push those thoughts of the king's planned kidnapping and possible assassination from his mind. He collected his violin from his room and bade farewell to Jac after a filling breakfast. So pre-occupied was he with this awful knowledge, he almost forgot to tell his long suffering horse that he had made love to Jac.

Knowledge is danger. A danger he could not run from. It was like a disease. It had been transmitted to him. He carried it but knew no cure. He had to find one otherwise it could kill him. Those from whom the danger had been caught would kill him if they knew he had become infected. They would kill Jac, too, and any others, her mother and father perhaps, whom they might think possessed the same disease of knowledge.

'Not that terrible look again, Antonio. You had that yesterday and now you've got it today!' said Carlos, half laughing and standing alongside Andres Moreno while surveying the work a gang of men were doing on the broken fences around the auditorium and the damaged booking office. 'What's the story today?'

Antonio glared at Carlos in anger which he could hardly contain. He spat out the words. 'You may mock, but last night I heard a terrible story. I will tell you its full horror but only if you are prepared to listen without that sarcastic look on your face. Otherwise, I'll keep it to myself!'

'You win, Antonio. Let's go and sit on the stage over there. I promise to be fair!'

They sat facing each other awkwardly on the edge between the stage's two levels. 'I'm sorry, Antonio. I didn't mean to annoy you. It was just a bit of banter in front of Andres. Nothing more. Now tell me…'

Antonio related to him what Jac had said. He managed it without emotion but concluded by admitting his fear in knowing about the plot.

'The king will be well protected,' said Carlos. 'He will be in a secure part of the palace and will be guarded wherever he goes.'

'Are you saying I should forget about it and just see what happens?'

'Well, I didn't exactly say that. I'd have to think about what you do with what you've heard. Have you thought yourself?'

'Yes, Carlos, I have a plan but I haven't sorted out the detail. I intend to report this to the authorities here or in Madrid. I'm not sure which. Probably here because the man Pedro may already be known to them. They are more closely connected to the king in Madrid so I may decide to go there instead…or as well.'

'If you're asking me, I'd go to both. You already know that we'll be performing in Madrid next, in a week's time.'

'I may do that,' said Antonio.

The men eventually finished repairing the various parts of the auditorium but, by the time they had done so, there remained time only for an afternoon performance of Lope's play. Andres Moreno decided to put up some notices around the town to inform the population what was happening. But they were to little avail: the auditorium was only half full for the performance. The musicians and the acting troupe gave their best despite the poor numbers. They all looked at each other when Iago sounded the whistle in the second act but nothing happened. There would be no repeat of the previous day's disturbance: all four of the gunmen had been charged with affray and discharging a firearm in public and were locked up awaiting trial.

Antonio was still pondering what to do as he walked the old mare back to the inn. By then it was late in the evening, the sun had just about dropped below the horizon and the heat was beginning to go out of the day. He decided that he would go to the *corregidor*'s office the following morning, after he had left the inn. He'd ask the *corregidor* about seeing the authorities in Madrid. The mere fact of making the decision made him feel much happier so he greeted Jac with a broad smile.

'What's made you so cheerful?' asked Jac.

'I've thought hard about what to do with what you told me last night and I've made a definite decision. I'll tell you in case you have any objections.'

'No. That sounds sensible to me. But how will I know what the *corregidor* decides and what happens in Madrid? You must tell me.'

'If I'm not sworn to secrecy, I'll write to you.'

'I'd be happy with that. Now let me get you a meal. I've prepared something which will surprise you.'

Within moments, Jac was putting a plate of *cuchinillo*, his favourite dish, in front of him along with a cup of white rioja and some newly baked bread.

'It's to celebrate your last night here,' she said. 'There may be more to come,' she whispered in his ear.

That night, Jac and her mother had others to serve, too, not just Antonio. As he was tucking into the succulent, young pork and taking a sip of wine, he heard a voice from behind. 'Good evening, young man. Do you mind if I join you?'

Antonio cast a backward glance. It was the man, Pedro. He hesitated for a moment, wondering what might become of a conversation with an evident traitor. His first thought was to refuse and to dine alone. He quickly realised he knew more about this man than the man knew about him so the dangers were therefore minimal.

'Not at all. Sit down. I'm sorry that I'm already eating. Let me order you a beer.'

'Don't worry. There's one on the way. Did you perform today?'

'Yes but there were far fewer in the audience after yesterday's troubles,' said Antonio, wondering what the man Pedro's reaction would be. His response surprised Antonio.

'I couldn't believe that those men for whom I bought some beers the night before would cause a disturbance. They must have been mad. I saw and heard what they did. They were sure to be caught.'

Antonio decided to take a chance. He could be courting disaster but came out with it.

'Speaking for myself but not necessarily for my colleagues, I have strong sympathies for the *Moriscos*. They have been treated so badly. It's a wonder there hasn't been another insurrection on the scale of the riots of sixty eight. If I thought I could help them I would. But I guess there's no chance of that.'

'You're right,' he said. 'We rely on our own kind and you aren't one of us, unless I'm very much mistaken.'

Antonio took another step into the unknown. 'No. I'm not a *Morisco*. I'm a Christian but only in name. I'm one of those people who cannot believe in the resurrection, the Virgin Mary or the miracles. I believe in man, not God.'

'That is interesting' said the man Pedro. 'There cannot be many so called Christians who have such ideals, even fewer who are prepared to tell them to a virtual stranger.'

At that point, Jac arrived with the man Pedro's dinner, also a plate of *cuchinillo*. She looked astonished that he had joined Antonio for the meal. Antonio glanced at her but without changing his expression. The two men spent an hour or so chatting and covered many subjects of mutual interest, including the recent ending of the siege of Ostende, the virtual bankruptcy of the country, the loss of revenue from the Americas and the damage to Madrid caused by the transfer of the court to Valladolid. Philip III was doing nothing to improve the lot of the ordinary

Spaniard and Lerma was lining his own pockets at the expense of the impoverished taxpayer.

'We seem to have many views in common,' said Pedro, who by then had invited Antonio to call him by his first name. 'Why don't we meet in Madrid in exactly a fortnight's time? There is a tavern in the Platería called "The Silversmith". We can have another conversation… over a meal, maybe, and I'll buy you a glass of my favourite wine!'

'Agreed,' said Antonio, shaking Pedro's hand. 'I promise I won't forget!'

Antonio and Jac were lying in Antonio's bed. They had just enjoyed the most wondrous session of mutual satisfaction. 'You are one of my best lovers, Antonio. That milkmaid on the farm who gave you those lessons in love did a great service, to you and the women in your life.'

They laid there breathless for a few moments until Jac became overcome by curiosity. 'Come on then, what did the man Pedro have to say? You must tell me or you'll not make love to me again!'

'You mean not tonight, don't you?' laughed Antonio.

'No! Never!' chided Jac.

Antonio told her. 'What! You've agreed to meet him in Madrid? You could be arrested for that, especially if you carry out your other plan!'

'I feel safe enough. I can always fail to turn up!'

As they were lying there, Jac noticed a faint glow through the thin curtains. 'What's that, Antonio? Looks like a fire. Go and see.'

Antonio stood and peered out of the window. 'It's a fire all right. Looks like a house on fire. I'd better go to help.'

He got dressed, kissed Jac goodnight and left the inn. Within a few minutes he was standing right outside the scene of the fire. By then the fire warden had rung his bell to raise the alarm and a chain of helpers had assembled in the curve of the street to pass leather buckets of water from a pump to those trying to dowse the fire. The beautiful building which he had admired only two nights before was ablaze. Flames tens of *pies* high were leaping from the roof and licking the sky. One side of the building was verging on collapse. The fire warden shouted to warn his busy workers away. They looked up in amazement as the whole building suddenly crashed to the ground.

Pedro had reached this scene of devastation before Antonio. 'What's happened?' Antonio shouted above the sound of cracking timber and minor explosions.

'We know who did this, or we've got a pretty firm idea. People we know are jealous of the doctor's position. He's a *Morisco*, as you already know.'

'Where is he? Are the two of them safe?'

'Yes. He is over in that crowd, trying to comfort his wife. She is in a terrible state. She's only just stopped screaming. Their children left home years ago so they are safe but they've lost two horses. Their smouldering corpses are in what remains of the stable block.'

Antonio was shocked and ashamed. Shocked that anyone could commit this arson attack on the house of this distinguished citizen. Ashamed that the heartless people who had committed it called themselves Christians. He spent the next half an hour helping the water carriers. The doctor's house was a ruin but the other adjacent properties needed protection. He wondered what he would tell Jac about this awful event but tell her he must.

By midnight or shortly after, the fire had been reduced to a few smouldering fragments, well attended by the warden and a few of his colleagues who would keep watch on it until daybreak. A saddened Antonio returned to the inn.

'My God, Antonio! Did anybody die?'

Antonio did not hold back in describing it to her and the reason the man Pedro gave for it. She burst into tears. 'It's so bad. That poor man saved my father's life and look what's happened to him and his poor wife.'

'Yes, it's terrible. They have at least escaped with their lives. It makes you ashamed to be Christian.'

Antonio removed his smoke laden clothes before getting into bed. Once again, he could hardly sleep and wondered when he might. Eventually he did but woke at the break of dawn. He lay there wondering about the events of the night before but reached no particular conclusion.

He took a modest breakfast and spoke briefly to Jac. Again he promised a letter, if he was permitted to do so, and warned her of the dangers of the man Pedro and his friends. He hugged a tearful Jac, thanked her for everything, told her he liked her a lot and kissed her lips before bidding her farewell. Looking back towards her and giving her a gentle wave, he passed around to the stables to collect his horse. 'Not a good night, old gal. Now we're off to the *corregidor*.' The horse looked at him as if to say she hadn't slept well either.

CHAPTER 6
Back to Madrid

Antonio made an early start so as to arrive at the *corregidor*'s office before 9 o'clock. He knew it was situated somewhere in the town hall and tied up his horse outside the building as the clock struck the quarter hour before. He asked a guard on the main door whether the *corregidor* could be available to see him but the man did not know whether he would be in. He told Antonio how to reach the man's office which, the guard said, was situated on the ground floor, five doors from the main entrance.

'Should I go in and ask?' said Antonio to the guard.

'I don't see why not. Just go in and knock on the door. Somebody will answer.'

Antonio went in and counted the doors. He was reassured to see the inscription 'Alonso Guzman, Corregidor of Guadalajara' in gold, capital letters on the fifth one. He knocked and waited. An expressionless man, dressed in a black jacket, black pantaloons, which were just long enough to cover his knees, white stockings and shiny, patent leather shoes, opened the door.

'Can I help you?' he said, not even asking Antonio into the office.

'Yes, señor,' said Antonio, more than making up for the man's failure to use a mode of address. 'I would like to see Señor Alonso Guzman.'

'Do you have an appointment?'

'No.'

'He won't see you without an appointment.'

'How do I go about making one?'

'You tell me what you want to see him about and I make the appointment, but only if I consider the matter to be of sufficient importance.'

'I see,' said Antonio.

'So…?' said the man. 'What is it?'

'I have information about a plot to kidnap and possibly kill the king, señor.'

'Are you serious?'

'I am, señor.'

'Can you tell me more?'

Antonio was becoming impatient with this unpleasant and unhelpful official. 'If the matter I have mentioned is not sufficiently important, as you put it, then I'll go,' he said, turning as if to walk back along the corridor and thinking that if he couldn't get an audience with Señor Guzman, he'd go straight to the *corregidor* in Madrid, who would be more important and therefore more influential, and to hell with this one.

'No, no, señor! Please! I can give you an appointment at eleven thirty. Because you have such an important matter to discuss I will delay the current eleven thirty meeting until this afternoon. I'm sorry I cannot move anything before then.'

'At last,' thought Antonio. 'I'll go to a bar for a drink and wait there,' he told the official and that he'd see him later.

Antonio felt surprisingly calm considering the sheer importance of what he had to say to the *corregidor*. He wondered what sort of questions he would ask and whether he'd take him seriously. After a cup of grape juice, he walked back to the town hall, to the office and the difficult official.

'Just a moment. Our previous meeting is running just a little late. Please sit down,' the man said.

Within about ten minutes, during which Antonio was becoming gradually more nervous, the inner door opened and four men emerged from the *corregidor*'s office. One carried a sheaf of papers and seemed to be a secretary. Two looked as if they were town hall officials. The fourth seemed to be the *corregidor* himself. 'Thank you so much, señores. A very useful meeting. I'll pass onto the king what you have said and let you know his reaction. It'll take a couple of weeks, I imagine,' he said, smiling as if the meeting had gone the way he wanted. Antonio deduced correctly that this man was the *corregidor* and what a pleasant, easy going individual he seemed to be. So Antonio felt less apprehensive.

'Now young man, what can we do for you?' said the *corregidor*, rubbing his hands together in a gesture of satisfaction. He was a tall individual, dressed in what seemed like military dress with a brown leather jacket and matching breeches with leather boots up to his thighs. He wore a pointed beard and a moustache which curved upwards and had the most intense blue eyes. His hair hung loose over his shoulders and appeared not to be a wig. 'My name is Alonso Guzman, Corregidor of Guadalajara. And you are?'

'My name is Antonio Hidalgo.'

'I'm delighted to meet you, Señor Hidalgo.'

'It's my pleasure to meet you, señor,' said Antonio.

'My secretary has explained briefly what you want to discuss so come into my office and sit down.'

Antonio entered the elegantly appointed office. The *corregidor*'s huge oak desk dominated it. There were three matching arm chairs, upholstered in red leather behind the chair in which the *corregidor* invited Antonio to sit. The *corregidor*'s high-backed chair was carved in oak and crowned with the royal coat of arms. The red carpet matched the curtains which had been gathered to each side of a large window which overlooked the street. The furnishings and ambience were befitting of the office of the king's representative in the town.

Antonio, wide eyed at these sumptuous adornments, walked in, sat in the chair and shuffled into a position of comfort. The *corregidor* entered and sat in his chair. 'I hope you don't mind if my secretary takes a few notes,' he said, nodding towards the unhelpful official in black who had picked up some note paper and followed them in. He sat slightly behind Antonio, to one side.

'Well,' said the *corregidor*, still smiling. 'Tell me about this threat to His Majesty the King. Start from the beginning.'

Antonio related the whole story.

The *corregidor* asked some questions. 'Did you say you live in Madrid and that you visit other places to perform in your troupe?'

'That's right.'

'Do you ever play solo?' he said, thinking deeply, his fingers interlocked and his hands over his breast.

'Yes, that's how I started.'

'So, have I got this right? You know this Pedro is guilty of treason but you've agreed to meet him in Madrid?'

'Yes.'

'Why did you do that? I don't understand?'

'He asked to join me for dinner last night. I couldn't really refuse. So we sat and chatted. It seemed as if we had some views in common. He asked me if we could meet in two weeks' time in Madrid... I didn't ask him... And I couldn't see why I shouldn't agree. He did, after all, promise me a glass of good wine! He cannot know that Jac told me what she'd overheard, and therefore that we know he's a traitor. Jac would never tell anyone else what she'd heard, let alone tell him that she'd told me.'

The *corregidor* kept his hands in the same position as before but closed his eyes, as if in deeper thought. 'There is a weakness in what you say, of course. You've made a very serious allegation. It's what a court would call hearsay and not admissible as evidence but we aren't in a court. How reliable is Jac? Could she somehow have misheard this man Pedro?'

'She is reliable, in my opinion. You could ask her along and speak to her yourself, if you chose to do so.'

'Could you have misunderstood what Jac told you? Is that possible, do you think?

'No, señor.'

'What exactly is your relationship with Jac? Could she deliberately have misled you for some reason? Maybe to land this Pedro in trouble?'

'We are friends. When I am in Guadalajara, I always stay at her parents' inn. ...We are lovers, too,' said Antonio, blushing from the neck up.

'Please don't be embarrassed. That's helpful actually. It shows that, unless she was extremely devious, she'd have no reason to trick you. Sorry, Señor Hidalgo, but I have a few more questions. Do you have any sympathy for the plight of the *Moriscos*?'

Antonio found it strange that he had used the word 'plight'. The official view seemed to be against what they were and what they stood for. This indicated either that he had some sympathy for them or that he was testing Antonio about his views.

'My opinion about them is straightforward, señor. I am neither for them nor against. I have no strong religious views about them, even though I am a Christian. "Live and let live" is my motto.'

'Hmm. Very interesting. One final question, which may be hypothetical. If I asked you to stop playing with the Wandering Chordsmen for a while...let's say a year...and work solo, what would your answer be?'

'That would depend, señor. Mainly on what you would be prepared to pay me. I suppose I'm saying that I have a career to think about and I'm not exactly wedded to the troupe.'

'I have no more questions, Señor Hidalgo, you will be relieved to hear. I am now going to explain to you what I'm going to do. The four men who fired the gunshots are in custody awaiting charge and trial so we can put that incident to one side. While we suspect the man Pedro in its planning there are no grounds for apprehending him. I am aware of the fire at the doctor's house. He and his wife were lucky to escape with their lives. That was a blatant attack on a *Morisco* family and we are still investigating that.

'As to the allegation of a plot on the king's life, I have a plan. First, as I've said, we cannot arrest this Pedro on the basis of hearsay evidence. There are certain things we can do, however. My problem is my lack of authority. So what I am going to do is to write a letter to the principal *regidor* of Madrid and seek his views on my plan. He is my equivalent in your city. He can make the decision as to whether it should be executed. It is much more difficult to see him than it is to see me so I am going to write you a letter of introduction. You must go to him before you see this Pedro. I cannot overemphasise that. By then he will have the letter about my plan.'

'May I be party to your plan?' said Antonio.

'I'm afraid not. Without confirmation that the first *regidor* of Madrid agrees, such knowledge would compromise you, me and possibly him.'

'I see,' said Antonio when he didn't see at all.

'In conclusion,' said Señor Guzman, 'I am extremely grateful to you for coming to see me. You have warned us about something of possibly great importance and have shown considerable courage in reporting it. You could, of course, have dismissed it as not worth pursuing. What I'd like you to do now is to wait for a few minutes in the office outside as I write your introduction to our man in Madrid and my secretary here copies the letter for our files.'

The *corregidor* stood and so did Antonio. 'Thank you again for coming to see me. I hope we meet again,' he said, shaking Antonio vigorously by the hand.

Madrid beckoned Antonio for two reasons. His few rooms in Doña Marta's house provided his home and, while he loved his travelling job, he enjoyed being in Madrid just as much, if not more. He was always welcomed in some of the local taverns near the Plaza Mayor and Calle de Toledo, especially when he took his violin and offered to play. Madrid excited him as a city, despite the glaring poverty he could witness at every street corner, its thieves and vagabonds who made their living from people poorer than themselves, the ragged, long-haired beggars at the church doors who rattled their pots at everyone who entered. While he hated the stench of the human waste which flooded the streets in the morning, he loved the citizens of this struggling city, its theatres which performed every night and the outrageous behaviour of the audiences as the women in the *cazuela* teased the men, the open spaces around the city, littered with lovers and children watching them or merely at play.

But he felt the pain, too. The pain inflicted by the king when he decided to move his entire court to Valladolid. Madrid had almost died of poverty as a consequence.

He could feel the city's attractive pull even from those ten or so *leguas* away, much too far for his horse to walk or canter in one day. Two days later, after staying at a lodging house for the night in Alcalá de Henares, he pulled his sweating, aging mare to a halt outside Doña Marta's house. 'Well done, old gal. I knew you could make it.' He made sure she was feeding and comfortable in the stables before carrying his saddlebags, including the one containing his treasured violin, to his rooms.

A lady provided that second force of attraction. Her name was Catalina de Polanco. She was one of two sisters who lived with their mother and father just off the Calle Mayor, opposite the San Felipe Convent, so only a short walk from Antonio's home. She was a year or two younger than Antonio and lived in the most delightfully proportioned body, at least that's what Antonio thought. Her constantly smiling, sharp featured face gave way to a slightly long neck which took an observer's attention away from her small but firm breasts. She usually had her red hair up in a bun. Like Jac, she liked to wear a belt on her skirts, to display her attractively narrow waistline. Indeed, she and Jac were similar in a number of ways. The main difference was that while Jac seemed to cope with several lovers, Catalina preferred to focus her attention on one man at a time. Antonio, despite his frequent and prolonged absences from the town, was her one and only lover, at least as far as he knew. Her sister, Francisca was also an attractive, slightly fuller, dark haired woman but unlike Catalina, did not or would not, make time for men friends. She preferred to stay in the home and help her mother or go off to the daily market in the Plazuela de Selenque and chat or bargain with the stallholders. She had a couple of woman friends in the town whom she would occasionally visit for a drink and gossip.

Antonio cast an eye about the house to look for Doña Marta but to no avail. He assumed that she must be up at the market or out with some of her lady friends. So rather than unpacking his bags, he decided to walk up to Catalina's house in the Calle Mayor to see if she was at home.

'Antonio, it's you,' said Juana Díaz, [Note for the reader: women's surnames did not change on marriage] Catalina's mother, smiling from one ear to the other. 'You seem to have been away for ages.'

53

'Not at all, señora, only just over a week. How are you, your husband and the girls?'

'Very well, thank you. Señor de Polanco is playing in a group in Aranjuez and won't be back for a week. Only Francisca is in at the moment but Catalina won't be long. She's just popped up to the Selenque market. Come in and wait. I'll get you some beer. Go and chat to Francisca.'

Señor de Polanco was, like Antonio, an itinerant musician. He played the guitar and was as good as, if not better than Carlos. He was one of the best guitarists in Madrid and had even been invited to play in the royal court for the king and queen. Several of his sources of work had dried up since the royal court had transferred to Valladolid.

Antonio went through to the lounge where Francisca was sitting at a work table putting the finishing touches to some little leather purses she had made.

'Oh, it's you, Antonio. When did you get back?' said Francisca, barely glancing up at him. Antonio always found it difficult to converse with her and, try as he did, could never work out why. He could see no reason for Francisca to be jealous of Catalina or of him. If she made the effort, she could easily attract a man friend. All Antonio could think was that she knew that his relationship with her sister was strongly physical and she just couldn't cope with it. Her mother also knew but turned a blind eye.

'Only about an hour or so. I first looked for Doña Marta, so that I could pay my rent but I couldn't find her. So I decided to come here to see Catalina, and you, of course,' he said.

'I hope you worked hard in Guadalajara and didn't get into too much trouble,' Francisca said. If only she knew. Señora Díaz came in at that moment and put a jug of beer and a cup on the low table in front of him.

'There you are, my dear. You'll enjoy it after that long ride,' said the señora.

Antonio thanked her and took a sip. 'Excellent,' he said, smiling at her.

He continued the stilted discussion with Francisca. 'No, I stayed out of trouble and I wasn't looking for any. The performances went down very well, in fact. The audience loved Lope's new play.'

'Can you tell us what it's about?' asked the señora, as if to provide him with some respite from her daughter.

54

'You'll have to see it in the Príncipe,' he said. 'But I can give you a brief outline.' So he did.

'Sounds like a load of filth to me,' said Francisca. 'Anything to get intercourse onto the stage. Mind you, that's what people want these days and the dirtier the better.'

'No such thing,' said her mother. 'I've never seen that on a stage and I've been to a lot more plays than you. I think I can hear Catalina.'

'It's you, Antonio. I didn't know when to expect you but I thought it might be today or tomorrow, depending on how many performances you did. I'm so pleased to see you. Would you like something to drink or shall we go for a walk?'

'Let's go out,' he said. 'Your mother has given me a drink.'

The two of them made a pretty picture walking arm-in-arm along the Plaza Mayor and down the Calle de Toledo to Antonio's rooms. 'I didn't think you'd want much of a walk, Antonio. I've missed you in more ways than one!'

'I've missed you, too. You are the best lover of all my girlfriends and the best thing is you only live up the road!'

They could barely wait to get into Antonio's bedroom and close the door behind them. They tore off their clothes and jumped onto Antonio's double bed. Then they did it. Catalina liked it hard so he gave her what she wanted.

'That was wonderful, Antonio. You are some lover! Let's do it again before the night is out.'

'I hope I'm up to it! You'd make someone a crazy wife! I've never known anyone enjoy it that violent.'

'Wife? Not me. No. Not when I can get a man like you to do just what I want. Now we can relax for a while and you can tell me what happened in Guadalajara.'

So he told her it all, except that he'd bedded Jac.

Part II

CHAPTER 7
New work

The letter that Corregidor Alonso Guzman had given him had its desired effect. On reading it, the official in charge of the first *regidor* of Madrid's office made an appointment for Antonio to see him at 4 o'clock in the afternoon, four days later. The official said it could not be earlier because the *regidor* was at Escorial and would not be returning for several days. Antonio wondered just how important the king's life could be if the meeting could be delayed for that long. Couldn't they send someone to Escorial to tell the *regidor*?

Eventually, and after Antonio had played in nightly performances with the Wandering Chordsmen at the Príncipe theatre, he found himself waiting outside the *regidor*'s office. Catalina had told him not to show signs of nervousness and he did his best not to but could not help feeling apprehensive, given the gravity of the issue to be discussed. He even wondered whether he had reported correctly what Jac had heard which was becoming more clouded, given the time that had elapsed since she told him. He wished he'd written it down given that he was able to write, unlike many of his profession and age. However, he steeled himself to be confident and clear, just as he was with the *corregidor* in Guadalajara, and felt good as he walked into the principal *regidor*'s inner office.

With the formal introductions over, the *regidor*, began. 'Señor Hidalgo, you are aware of a letter that my opposite number in Guadalajara has written to me. And I can now tell you of its content. He proposes that the king engages you to help him thwart plots against his life. If you were willing to take up this post you would work direct to me, at least in the first instance. So I would engage you on behalf of the king. You would take directions from no other person than me. Do you have any questions about what I've said so far?' He smiled as he looked straight into Antonio's eye.

These few sentences struck Antonio dumb. Then he recovered. 'I don't understand. Here am I, a humble violinist, making an honest living touring the land, playing for theatre troupes and at *fiestas,* and suddenly I am being offered a job working for an important official in Madrid. A man who himself works for the king.'

'You could say that, Señor Hidalgo. And you would be right. Let me explain. The crucial thing you did to warrant my offer was to agree to see this man Pedro, Hajib al-Asadi, in The Silversmith tavern in two weeks. Without it I would not have made my offer. The meeting is part of the plan my colleague suggests. I give him the credit.'

'I am beginning to follow.'

'Good. This Pedro clearly likes you. He may have already sent someone to Valladolid. If not he might see fit to ask you to go.'

'But I couldn't do anything to harm the king.'

'You are not quite there, Señor Hidalgo. You would be working for me and I am not in the business of endangering the king. My job is to protect him and his interests. You would give this man the impression that you were cooperating with him to the full. To the extent that you would do anything, within reason, he asked of you. But you would report it all back to me. At some point, we would strike at him and his actual collaborators and that would be the end of his dirty game. Do you follow that? I'm sure you do!'

'I do, señor. But I need to ask you some questions. I don't want to give up being a musician so could I continue my usual work at the same time? And how would you pay me? I also sense danger and how would I be protected?'

'Whether you continued in your profession as a musician would depend on what you could negotiate with the man Pedro. You could suggest for example that an innocent violinist would create only little suspicion if he were to turn up at the king's quarters in Valladolid. The question of payment is simple. What are you paid now?'

'About three *reales* a day, maybe more if I am playing solo. This includes my time for travelling.'

'I will pay you a *ducat* a day plus your expenses. That is for giving me all of your time. Something else which may make the idea even more attractive is what you may call a "bounty". This would be a special payment in the expected event of your success on this particular mission. It could amount to fifty *ducats*. If we sent you on any other mission you would also be paid a bounty for its success. How is that sounding?'

'I am completely amazed, flattered and grateful. But unsure. The danger is worrying me.'

'Don't let it. We recognise there is a danger, in fact of being found out. What I am proposing is that we train you, say in the next week or so in the use of firearms. You will be trained by one of the best shots in

Madrid. We will also give you instruction in the use of a dagger and hand-to-hand fighting. All to enable you to defend yourself and take the initiative to attack.'

'How long are you giving me to decide?'

'We don't want you decide today but let me know after you've slept on it, tomorrow or the day after. We need to schedule your instruction in defending yourself. Have you ever handled a pistol?'

'No, definitely not. Another question, señor. Can I discuss this with anyone?'

'Yes, but there are some conditions. You may discuss what I've proposed with one person and one person only. But before you do so that person will have to sign a document swearing, on pain of death, that he or she will not mention it to a single soul. And you may go only as far as to say, a post in which you would be protecting the king, no more and no detail about your mission.'

'Would I need to sign a contract of some kind?'

'Yes, we would need to formalise any agreement we reached.'

Antonio still didn't know what to think about this incredible proposal. His head spun in confusion as he walked back to Doña Marta's from the *regidor*'s unprepossessing little office. What a contrast to the one the Corregidor of Guadalajara occupied. He loved playing his treasured violin, especially to an appreciative audience, and could see that slipping away. But the offer possessed some dimensions which excited him: the danger, the importance of the task and the money.

Clutching the document the *regidor* had given him, he needed to work out whom he would ask into his confidence. The obvious choice was Carlos, his current boss, but he had an interest in the decision. He could talk to one of his other colleagues but they too might think in terms of the effect on their troupe. Then he solved the problem: he'd discuss it with Catalina! She'd tell him frankly what she thought. He'd talk to her that night.

Catalina sat on Antonio's bed with her eyes wide open as she listened, occasionally putting her hand through her red hair.

'So you'd be a spy, Antonio. And you'd be away from Madrid. You'd be spying and reporting back to the *regidor* what you'd discovered. You'd have the protection of a spy, a pistol concealed about you, loaded and primed. If anyone suspected that you were spying on them, they'd kill you. Dead!'

'He never mentioned the word "spy" but, yes, I…I suppose you could be right. It's the element of danger that makes it attractive; and I would be helping to protect the king…and for good money! Nearly three times what I'm earning now!'

'The king's a lazy fool. Protect him…? Well, like him or not, he's still the king,' she said, almost resigned to Antonio deciding that he'd do it. 'But what would Carlos and the troupe think? They'd have to find someone else.'

'Yes. I couldn't do both jobs.'

'Did you like the man? What was he like?'

'Yes. I took to him. He was my height, not that tall, clean shaven, with his dark hair in a braid, and had a confident, relaxed air about him. He looked tidy, well dressed and reliable. He smiled as he spoke and seemed likeable. I'm sure I could work for him.'

'Antonio, all I can say is this: if you want to do it go ahead. But promise me you'll keep in touch. I don't want to lose a great lover as you sign a piece of paper!'

'I might have to come back to Madrid sometimes to report to the *regidor*. I'd call in to see you as well, of course. And I'll do my best to write to you. You won't be able to reply because you won't know where I am!'

'Antonio, you have my blessing. Go ahead! Now let's celebrate!'

'You're insatiable!'

Antonio's excitement rose like proving dough and he couldn't wait to get back to the *regidor*'s office. He was afraid that he might change his mind or offer the job to someone else. The private secretary, a doleful individual, expected him. The *regidor* was able to see him immediately and stood up to welcome him with a smile and a handshake.

'Good morning, Señor Hidalgo. What have you decided? I'm anxious to know.'

'I've decided to accept your offer,' said Antonio, smiling back.

'I can't tell you how pleased I am,' said the *regidor*. 'We need to complete some formalities. They are important but straightforward. I'd first like you to read this document. He handed Antonio a small, ornately written scroll which read:

30 September 1605
I, Antonio Hidalgo, of the Calle de Toledo, Madrid,
swear my allegiance to the King of Spain and will tell no other
that, from this day, I am a special agent of His Majesty. I further
swear that I shall report to the King's office or representative
any activities of which I become aware which may harm the
King or potentially affect his position as monarch.
I agree to report my activities in this post to the principal
regidor *of Madrid, as and when instructed to do so or by*
mutual agreement.
I accept a remuneration of one ducat *a day, while this post is my*
only employment, from and including this day, henceforth until
that amount is varied by agreement.
I shall be paid a bounty at the successful completion of any mission
assigned to me by the regidor.
Signed,

Antonio was surprised at the efficiency of the *regidor*'s office in having the document ready and dated. With his eyebrows slightly raised, he read it through three times. 'I'll sign it, señor. It looks fine to me,' he said as he took the quill pen the *regidor* was offering him and put his signature at the bottom of the page.

'Excellent, Señor Hidalgo. From now on we should be on first name terms. My name is Silva de Torres and you can call me Silva. It's not actually my first name but that's what I prefer to be called. Do you mind if I call you Antonio?'

The new spy felt happy with this friendly request which provided more reassurance that he could work for this pleasant, well-mannered individual.

'We need to make some arrangements now for your instruction in the use of a pistol and in the other means of self-protection.' Señor Silva de Torres went out of the office to ask his private secretary to take Antonio to the armoury and to ask the Head Armourer to see to Antonio's needs.

'I'll leave you in the hands of my assistant,' said the *regidor*. 'Before you leave the palace, I'd like you to return here for one final word with me. Another thing you must do, which is too sensitive to mention in our formal agreement. As a special agent, you must have the Habsburg coat of arms tattooed on your right shoulder. There is a tattooist in The Platería. Go there and have it done…as soon as you can.'

The private secretary led Antonio through the labyrinth of corridors to the Armoury, which was situated at the rear of the palace in the east wing, an area mainly occupied by the queen and her court before the transfer to Valladolid.

The entrance was protected by armed guards standing one at each side of a tall door constructed of thick iron bars which almost touched the ceiling.

'Can I help you, private secretary?' said the guard, wearing the uniform of a sergeant.

'Yes. The *regidor* has asked me to bring Señor Hidalgo along for some formal weapon training. He is our latest special agent recruit.'

'Follow me,' said the guard, lifting a set of keys on a ring the size of a dinner plate which dangled from a chain attached to the belt of his breeches. He inserted the largest key into the door lock, unlocked it and they went in.

They walked about forty *varas*, past open racks bearing long bows, staves, lances, pikestaffs with ornate halberds, rows of large bore cannons, harquebusiers, muskets and flails which Antonio thought could cause hideous damage in the hands of anyone strong enough to use them. There were several instruments of torture, including a rack and an apparatus for suspending a poor soul in the air, presumably over a pit or a fire: he dreaded to think. Eventually, they reached the armourer's office.

The guard knocked twice on the oak door and walked in. 'Private secretary from the *regidor*'s office to see you, major. Got someone with him.' The guard turned and went back.

'Good morning, private secretary. Have you brought him here for a gun or cannon, perhaps? Or maybe you'd like me to pull his fingernails out!' Antonio grinned.

'Very amusing,' said the private secretary, coolly. 'Something quite straightforward and which the *regidor* would like you to undertake personally. Señor Hidalgo is a newly signed-up special agent. He needs training in self-protection, in particular in the use of a pistol, and some self-defence teaching, too.'

'Leave him with me, then and I'll do it.' The secretary went. 'Well, Señor Hidalgo, I'm Major Rodrigo Gutierrez, Head of the Alcázar Palace Armoury. I'm very pleased to meet you. I'd be delighted to instruct you in anything you need,' he said, vigorously shaking Antonio's hand.

'I think the main thing is training me to fire a pistol.'

'That's easier to say than do, but of course I can teach you. We have a range here we can use. It's actually inside the palace not far from here but underground. You also need training in hand-to-hand fighting and the use of a dagger, from what the secretary says. What mission are they sending you on? It would help to know that.'

'It's very secret and I'm not supposed to tell anyone. Do you mind if I ask the *regidor* first?'

'You are new and I understand that you will want to make a good start with him so do ask him. In the meantime, we'll arrange for you to come again. How about tomorrow at 9 o'clock, say?'

Antonio appreciated this kind man's helpfulness and flexibility. 'Yes, that will be fine, Major Gutierrez. I'll go now and see you again tomorrow. I need to be at the Príncipe theatre tomorrow afternoon at 2 o'clock but that is the only constraint.'

'Tomorrow it is then. I'll take you back to the Armoury gate,' he said, not yet trusting Antonio to go back alone.

As Antonio reached the palace entrance, he realised he had to see the *regidor* before going. He returned, knocked on the outer door and went in. 'Ah, Señor Hidalgo, said the private secretary. I hope your meeting with the armourer went well.'

'It did, thank you,' smiled Antonio. 'The *regidor* wanted to speak to me before I went.'

'He's expecting you. Come in.'

The *regidor* stood up, came round to the front of his desk and shook Antonio's hand once again, almost if he'd been away on a mission. 'I have two things to deal with. First, let's sit down and I want to give you some advice. Call it an instruction if you wish! It's about meeting this Pedro character in the tavern off the Platería. If, as I suspect, he will be testing you and hoping to engage you, play a hard game with him. Don't agree when he first suggests it that you will work for him. Play him like a fish on a line. Enjoy teasing him. That will minimise any suspicion of you having *a priori* agreed to join him.

'Secondly, let me give you this. It's your first payment, along with twenty *ducats* for your expenses,' he said, handing Antonio a small leather purse tied with a lace. 'Do you have any questions?'

'Only two, Silva. I can't quite work out what I should say to my boss in the music troupe about this job.'

'I can only advise you on that. Don't say anything until you have a clearer idea of how you will interact with this Pedro and his cohorts. We can discuss this issue again after your meeting in the tavern, if you wish, that is. And the second?'

'The armourer said it would be helpful to know something about the mission. That way he could direct my training better.'

'Just tell him it's an infiltration. That should suffice,' he said, smiling. 'When do you see him again?'

'Tomorrow morning. At 9 o'clock.'

Antonio arrived at the gates of the Armoury with two minutes to spare. The guard took him to the armourer.

'Welcome back, Señor Hidalgo. I hope to take you back to the guard later today completely free of injury,' he laughed. 'But that depends on whether you shoot yourself in the foot or anywhere else for that matter!'

Antonio laughed, too. The armourer's frivolity made him relax but he could also see the potential danger of learning to use a firearm.

I've chosen a pair of snaplock pistols, one for each of us. We won't be duelling by the way. I'm going to take you to our subterranean firing range.'

Within five minutes or so, Rodrigo the Armourer was patiently showing Antonio the way to hold a pistol and steadying it on the forearm ready to fire. 'Never fire it with one hand, not if you can possibly avoid it. You'll miss your target and the recoil could seriously hurt you. 'This is a modern form of pistol. This is how it works. Now I'll show you how to load and fire it. See that skull, painted on that rock over there?'

Ridrigo placed the pistol in the firing position and aimed. He pulled the lever. The explosion almost deafened Antonio and he blinked hard. He opened his eyes soon enough to see a spark as the ball the Armourer had fired hit the image of the skull, midway between the eye sockets. The sound of the gunshot reverberated for a full two seconds.

Antonio applauded. 'Great shot! You made it look easy!'

'Now it's your turn. Load as I showed you. Use that gunpowder. That's it. Eyes on the target. Fire when you're ready.'

Antonio did as instructed and pulled the trigger. Again a loud bang. The ball ricocheted around the range, pinging the walls and ceiling.

'Missed!' chuckled the armourer. 'God knows where that went! Only did one thing wrong. You moved the gun as you fired it. Watch me again. Watch the gun!'

The armourer reloaded, fired and hit the skull on the right cheek. 'Not as lucky that time!' he grinned. 'See how steady I held it. Only moved after I shot!'

After about a dozen attempts, Antonio managed to land one on the target, just on the chin.

'Brilliant!' roared the armourer. 'See what difference a good instructor makes.' He hugged Antonio like a long lost brother. 'We'll make something of you yet!'

In the next dozen or so shots, Antonio hit the target three more times. The armourer and he congratulated each other three more times. They laughed at their success and laughed again as they heard their laughter reverberate around this catacomb of a firing range.

'We'll leave it there for today, but I tell you, you're going to be good. More instruction and plenty of practice. That's what you want,' he grinned. 'Come back tomorrow, same time.'

Antonio realised the importance of this coming encounter as he walked from Doña Marta's house to The Silversmith tavern. As he crossed the Calle de Guadalajara he looked back on the previous week's achievements and smiled inwardly with a satisfying sense of pride. He had, under the instruction of Major Rodrigo Gutierrez, and daily practice in that dark and subterranean cavern, reached the level of what the armourer called 'a damned good pistol man'. One of the armourer's men had taught him how to use a dagger and where to insert it, depending on what he wanted to do: kill, incapacitate or simply draw blood. He also taught him the art of defending himself without a weapon and that made Antonio feel more of a man.

With a degree of trepidation, he walked into The Silversmith. It seemed as if the man Pedro had been there all evening with his eye on the door. He looked straight into Antonio's eye as he entered. 'I knew you'd come, Antonio. Good to see you. How's our violinist?'

'Very well, Pedro. And you?'

'Much the same but very busy. Looking after the interests of my people. It's quite a responsibility you know.'

Not to miss an opportunity like this, Antonio leapt at him with a question. 'So what are you doing to protect the interests of your people? I suppose you are talking about the *Moriscos*?'

'That's a difficult question. I promised you a glass of my favourite rioja. Wait there and I'll get you one!'

Antonio sat at the table opposite Pedro's large glass of red wine and pondered how he could wheedle his way into the trust of this man. To Antonio, he seemed a shrewd individual who wouldn't part with a *maravedí* unless he had to, let alone some critical piece of information. Antonio could see two ways into this. He could get Pedro drunk and hope he'd blurt something out that he'd rather have not said. Or he could pretend great sympathy with the 'plight of the *Moriscos*', as the Corregidor of Guadalajara rather carelessly said. He'd follow the latter course and see where it took him.

Pedro returned holding two glasses, spilling over the top. 'Thought I'd get another for myself, now I've got the taste for it! There's boar on for tonight or we can have goose, so the waiter tells me.'

Antonio took a sip. 'You have good taste in wine!'

'And you have good taste in women. That lass Jac has really fancies to you!'

Antonio didn't want a conversation about wine or women so attempted to steer it more his way. 'Yes, she's a pleasant girl and knows a surprising amount about politics and the *Morisco* situation in particular. She seems quite sympathetic to their cause and hates the king and the bishops for ill-treating them.'

'I can't say I'm exactly in love with the king. He is too easily led by Lerma. He's not a friend of ours either.'

'You still haven't said what you are doing about looking after the interests of your people as you put it. I can understand you not telling me. This is only the second time we've met and I wouldn't expect you to give me any confidences.'

'There's a vacant booth below that window. Quick, let's go into it before that group over there realise it's free. We are less likely to be overheard from there.'

They each picked up their glasses. Pedro took his two as Antonio followed with his. The Madrid night was gradually closing in and the landlord was lighting the oil lamps on the walls and on the open ends of the booths. The tavern hummed with the chatter of the customers there but it was far from full.

'I have thought a lot about you since we met at dinner at the inn. You impressed me with your balanced, unprejudiced thinking about the *Moriscos* and your mature views about religion and politics. You are no bigot and I like that. I was thinking as we spoke then and I've thought about it since. I am looking for someone like you to help our cause. I wouldn't expect you to do anything which could put your life at risk but I might ask you to help me find out some facts, some information. You'd be ideal because, as an itinerant musician you could go virtually anywhere and you wouldn't raise suspicion.'

'I'm not sure where you are going, Pedro, but…'

'No! Don't stop me. Hear me out.' He stood up quickly and glanced over the partition into the next booth. 'No one there. Look into that one.'

Antonio looked over. 'No one there either.' How ironic that Pedro had not been so careful when he allowed Jac to overhear him.

'I'm going to tell you straight. You know that they are talking about expelling the *Moriscos*. To God knows where. Probably the Maghreb. It's pure religion and politics. Nothing else. Well, we want to kidnap the king and hold him up for ransom. The price will be to grant us our freedom of movement and religion in this country. We want to go back to what we had after the so-called re-conquest. Religious freedom, protection of our mosques, respect for our women… It's not asking for much. So that's the plan.'

Antonio raised his eyebrows at what that this man Pedro had so quickly revealed. 'Whose plan?'

'To be precise, mine. I'm the leader of this band,' he chuckled, knowing that Antonio played in one himself.

'I can't say that I'd want to do that. I'm not that keen on the king myself but I wouldn't want to be involved in harming him. And if they didn't deliver your ransom, I suppose you'd kill him.'

'No point in doing that. Mind you some in his court might want him dead,' he chuckled.

'I can see all sorts of trouble for anyone you got to do that.'

'That's where you're wrong. What I want is information about the guards at the palace, where the king will be at certain times, exactly where his apartments are in the palace… Things like that.'

'And I'd get that for you. Is that right?'

'Yes, you and the man I've already recruited, Esteban de Recalde?'

'Never heard of him. You are talking as if I should know him.'

'You do know him. You helped him out of a scrape. Out of trouble.'

'Now I'm completely fooled. That's not Jac's father.'

'No. Do you remember when you entered the inn, a group of roughs were throwing a dwarf up to the ceiling and catching him as he fell? You tricked them into letting him go. Well, the dwarf, Esteban de Recalde, is one of my men and he's going to Valladolid to get what I want. But I don't want him going alone. He's as strong as a mountain bear but small and vulnerable. Part of your job would be to protect him.'

'I'm still far from sure,' said Antonio, making it sound that he could be interested but that there might be a number of issues to settle. 'What about money? How would we manage? Would you pay us? How much?'

'Yes. I've thought about that. I'd pay all your living expenses and if you wanted any more, you'd have to earn it yourself, doing something else.'

'What?'

'Playing the violin, of course. And somehow, Esteban would help you.'

'How?'

'You'd have to ask him.'

'Where is he now?'

'Upstairs, in this tavern. Shall I go and get him?'

'Not so fast. I need time to think about all this. I'll have to give up work for my music troupe. They won't like that. I'd have to move out of my rooms. My poor horse. What would I do with her? She wouldn't survive a trip to Valladolid. It's nigh on forty *leguas* and the old gal won't do more than four or five a day. So it would take a week and more to get there.'

'I'm ahead of you there. My plan is that you go via Ávila and Segovia. Take up to three weeks if you like!'

'I'm getting cross with you! I haven't agreed to anything yet!'

He called Antonio's bluff. 'Let's forget about the whole thing then. We'll chat about something else over a meal.'

Antonio wasn't having that. 'I agree about the meal. We can continue talking and I'll let you know my decision afterwards. I have to admit, it's sounding quite an adventure. And I could ride my trusty old mare!'

Pedro smiled. He had captured his prey. Antonio was dangling on his hook; and he was dangling on Antonio's.

After the meal of spit roasted boar, an ale and a couple more glasses of Pedro's favourite rioja, Pedro was ready with the question. 'Well, what do you think, Antonio? Let's have it! Yes or no?'

'You may be surprised, Pedro. The answer is yes. I'm in!'

'That's the best news I've had since the old king died! I'll get Esteban. You must meet him!'

'Yes, I recognise him' said the small person, looking across at Antonio. 'Yes, he's the one! I'm sorry. I didn't thank you for rescuing me at the inn, so I thank you now!'

'It was a pleasure, señor. I just could not walk by!'

'My name is Esteban de Recalde and Pedro here tells me we'll be working together. Is that right?'

'It is indeed, Esteban, and I'm looking forward to it.'

'There is much detail still to be sorted out. I suggest we meet back here at seven o'clock in the evening in exactly two weeks. Does that suit you both?'

They agreed.

Antonio went straight back to his rooms. It was far too late to bother Catalina so he'd save his news for the morning. Awake bright and early, he decided to fulfil his obligation to return to the *regidor* to tell him his news.

'Congratulations, Antonio. Well done. You played the game well. I couldn't have done better myself. So you've met this man before, Esteban! What a coincidence. What did you think of him?'

'I hardly know him, but he seems intelligent. Dwarves find it difficult to survive against the prejudice they have to face. But he's managed up to now and he looks very strong with a wide chest and thick thighs. He's no wilting daisy. I'll get on with him well.'

'Just concentrate on doing what Pedro wants! You'll get on with both of them then. All we need to do now is to agree on how you will inform me about what's happening. I'm going to give you a codename. It's Diaspora. Mine is Algebra. Use these names when you decide to write. Just put Algebra, Madrid on the envelope and sign the letter Diaspora. The letter will find me, even though the postal service doesn't know I use that name. But only staff here, and nowhere else in Madrid, use codenames and that helps preserve our anonymity. If one of my officials, wherever he is, whenever he says he's from Algebra, you must give him what he wants. Is that clear?'

'What if I forget the names?'

'You must not! Repeat them a thousand times in your head but don't... I repeat don't... write them down.'

'There are a few other things I should tell you. If you have trouble with these people and think you are in danger, make your escape and return here. Do not hesitate to ask me for help or advice. If you need urgent assistance, go to another *regidor*'s office and give your codename. They will help you. Finally, always keep your pistol within easy reach.'

'Thank you, Silva. I can't think of anything else. Oh...I've just thought of something important. I have to tell my friends in the music troupe.'

'You are a sensitive man, Antonio. Tell them as soon as you can. You will be a solo travelling player now!'

'I'm grateful, Silva. Thanks again.'

The *regidor* stood. He wished him luck, they shook hands and Antonio started to walk back to Doña Marta's. He felt sure he was being followed.

CHAPTER 8
The road to Ávila

Pedro and Esteban were already enjoying a beer in The Silversmith tavern when Antonio arrived. From the look on Pedro's face, Antonio could see he was unhappy. He seemed reluctant even to greet Antonio as he walked over to the table where he and Esteban were sitting. Esteban spoke first. 'Hello, Antonio, what have you been up to?'

The question instantly put him on his guard. He hesitated but looked directly into Pedro's eyes. 'I've been at the Príncipe theatre. It was our last performance under our contract there and my last with the troupe. I've resigned. The leader was disappointed and tried to talk me out of it, but when I explained that I wanted to work as a soloist he seemed to understand. We went for a farewell drink and I promised to keep in touch with them all.'

'Is that all?' said Pedro.

'Well, yes.'

'Why didn't you mention your visit to the *regidor*'s office? What was that about?'

Antonio had an answer at the ready. 'I didn't think you'd be interested in my tax affairs.'

'What do you mean, tax affairs?'

'I owed some tax on my earnings. So I went to pay it.'

'Are you sure that's all it was?' said Pedro.

'Not sure. Certain! And, while we are on the subject, why were you following me?'

'I need to be able to trust you, so that was a test.'

'If you don't think you can trust me, I'll go now and we need never meet again.'

'No need for that, Antonio. I felt I had to do it, but I now admit I was wrong. I'll never do it again. Let's shake on that.' Pedro offered his hand to Antonio.

Antonio paused a second or two before taking it. '"Never" is what I'd expect. Once more and I'm out. This whole operation is going to depend on trust and trust alone.'

'I agree,' said Pedro, looking down at his shoes. 'Once again, I'm sorry. Now let me get you a drink. A glass of that rioja?'

'That'll do nicely,' said Antonio, by then more relaxed but still feeling bruised.

'We need to move to a booth to discuss our plan,' said Pedro.

'Where are we to start?' asked Esteban, sliding along a seat.

'Where we will end,' said Pedro. 'What I want you to bring back is this. I need an exact plan of the royal apartments at the palace in Valladolid. I need to know exactly where he sleeps, eats, bathes, washes and changes his clothes. I need to know what level of protection he has, exactly where the guards are positioned, how many there are. I need to know who else lives in the palace and where. Lerma lives there somewhere. I want to know where and whether he is guarded and to what level. Finally, I want you to develop a plan. How we can kidnap the king, when and with how many men and what other resources we may need. And how we escape with him, to where. Then the ransom. How do we tell the palace what we want? And when we achieve our aims how do we escape unharmed? Have you two got all that?'

'I think so,' said Antonio, 'but I can't speak for Esteban.'

'I'm fine with what you say. Let me be clear on the route we take and when we go,' said Esteban.

'I've told you that. You go via Ávila and Segovia. You, Antonio, use the cover of a solo violin player. And you Esteban are his assistant? Do you sing?' laughed Pedro.

'I suppose I could if I tried!'

'I can give you some lessons and teach you some songs,' said Antonio. 'We'll have some good times and the least you can do is have a collection pot as I play on street corners!'

'I'm giving you one full day to sort out your affairs, say your goodbyes, pack and be ready to go. We meet here at 9 o'clock in the morning, the day after tomorrow, and don't forget your violin, Antonio!'

Antonio rushed from The Silversmith tavern straight around to see Catalina.

'You're out of breath, Antonio. Do you want to come in?'

'I'd rather we walked around to my house. We've got one whole day together, then I go on my mission. I'll tell you more there.'

They were soon lying on Antonio's bed at Doña Marta's.

'What can you tell me?'

'I've spoken to Carlos, Iago and Josep and given my resignation. They've accepted it and believe I will be a soloist from now on.'

'How were they when you told them?'

'Quite shocked. Carlos said they'd have trouble getting a good violinist to replace me but luckily they have no specific work to do for at least a week. They did wish me well and we all went for a farewell drink.'

'Good work. So what is the exact plan?'

'I can't tell you but there will be two of us going to Valladolid. A dwarf called Esteban de Recalde and me?'

'A dwarf?'

'Yes, one I met in the inn I stayed at in Guadalajara.'

'Why choose a dwarf?'

'Quite a clever choice, in my view. No one would expect a dwarf and a violinist to be helping to protect the king!'

'I'm scared... for you, Antonio. What if you get caught by the people you are spying on? Just make sure the king's men don't shoot you when they arrest these people.'

'They never kill their own spies. Believe me. You can rely on that.'

'I'm not sure whether to be reassured or not, Antonio. I suppose I'll just have to hope you come back in one piece,' she said, resigned to whatever his fate might be.

'I don't want you to stay at home worrying all day. You must get on with life and, as I've said, if I can find time to write to you, I promise I will. I suggest we make the most of our time together. I've no idea when I'll be back.'

'Are you suggesting we make love?'

By then it was early November and he could feel the morning chill. 'We're going on a long journey, old gal,' said Antonio as he loaded his heavy saddlebag onto the horse's back. 'We're mainly taking clothing but there's water in there for both of us, my trusty violin, some cash …and my pistol!'

The unsuspecting horse looked at him as if she was wondering where she would be going. But within moments she was nodding her tail and flicking her head, with the pleasure of anticipating a run out of the town.

He kissed an emotional Catalina goodbye. He too looked sad as he climbed up into the saddle. 'Well, this is it,' he said looking down at her. 'I hope I'm not away too long.' He pulled gently on the reins and the horse trotted off in the direction of The Silversmith tavern.

Pedro was standing at the entrance. Esteban was already in the saddle and chatting to Pedro, presumably about the journey the intrepid horsemen were about to undertake. Antonio paused outside long enough to accept a purse from Pedro and his wishes for a safe and successful journey. All three gave each other a manly smile. Esteban and Antonio wheeled their horses around to shake hands with Pedro before they set off.

'Maybe we should have talked of this before,' said Antonio, 'but how far do you think we should go today?'

'I was looking at a map the other day and it seems like Valdemorillo might be in reach of a good day's ride.'

Antonio and Esteban were mutually wary, having hardly spoken to each other, since they met in Jac's parents' inn. So this first discussion gave them an opportunity to see how the other would react to being, albeit only modestly, challenged.

'I can't see us making it that far,' said Antonio. 'My old mare has hardly been out of the stables since I returned from Guadalajara and I don't want to push her too hard today. Your horse looks a lot younger than mine. How about aiming for Majadahonda? That's about half the distance.'

Antonio waited for a response. 'Hmm, I'm not so sure but if it depends on your horse, I suppose we'll have to accept it.' There seemed a slight reluctance in his voice which Antonio thought not unreasonable. Clearly, Esteban wanted to make good progress in the early days and that might not be a bad ambition. After all, they had no idea of what they might encounter on these robber ridden roads.

'Thank you. My horse will appreciate it,' said Antonio in a neutral vein. He didn't want to appear to have won any ground in this innocent exchange.

They walked their horses through the streets to the Puente del Parque. Riding their mounts and looking down at the denizens of Madrid, they could not fail to see the terrible state to which this once great city had descended. Apart from the overpowering stench of human waste that had been ejected, earlier that morning, from upper windows onto the streets and which they and their horses were trying to avoid, beggars were proffering their bowls at arms' length on every corner. On one, four or five were arguing loudly about which of them had the right to beg there, almost coming to blows, as their desperation erupted. A sad, quite well dressed woman, reduced to poverty, was lifting her skirt to display her intimate wares, hoping to earn eight or so *maravedís* from a passing, hopefully gentle encounter. Children, reduced to wearing rags, were scavenging the gutters for scraps of bread or a lost coin, hoping to find enough for what could pass for nourishment. The two riders were glad to cross the *puente*, away from the town's stench and the misery it shrouded.

Somehow, probably because of the freshness of the air and the cool of the morning, they were more relaxed with each other outside the town. 'Well, how are we going to earn our fortune?' Antonio ventured to ask.

'You said you'd teach me to sing. We can play as a duet then!'

'I'm game to teach you. I know some pretty dirty songs that'll make people stop and listen! And I know the words so I can teach you them as well!'

'I'm for it!'

Antonio felt then that he could have a constructive, friendly relationship with Esteban but it was still early days.

The amount of traffic using the road to Majadahonda was small. The two men discussed the fact and attributed it to the lack of economic activity in Madrid and the surrounding *pueblos*. No one was buying clothing, vehicles, horses, wine food or anything else transportable. However, the odd wagon and horseman was using the road for reasons only the riders knew. Just after they had been travelling for about two hours, something quite unearthly happened. While the sky was dull and dotted with high cloud, it suddenly lit up as a huge, fiery streak of light passed with a gentle roar right over their heads. They almost fell as their horses reared up in fear at what was happening above. Whatever it was, it scared the life out of every person and every animal on that road. Two horses pulling a wagon became so disturbed they pulled it off the byway and turned it over in a ditch. The horses lashed out with their hooves as they attempted to escape from the shafts to which they were tethered. Seconds after the streak of light appeared in the sky, an almighty explosion shook the ground the men and horses were standing on.

'Let's get to those animals,' shouted Esteban, over the eerily restored silence. They quickly tied theirs to a tree and went to help rescue the wagon in the ditch. It took six travellers to right it and untangle the panicking horses. The two men who had been driving the cart were still in shock, both at what their own eyes had witnessed and at their fall. After a few reassuring words from those who had helped them, they shook hands with all who had assisted, wished them an equally safe journey, climbed back onto the front of the rig and resumed their travels, stunned almost into silence at this extraordinary event. Another of those who helped and who had climbed off a white stallion came towards Antonio and Esteban.

'Tell me, where are you two going?' This inquisitive stranger was dressed in riding breeches, a loose jacket, boots up to thigh level and a wide brimmed hat, like a soldier's.

'I first thought you were a man,' said Esteban.

'Don't be deceived by appearances,' said the well-spoken woman.

'Well you certainly fooled me,' said Antonio. 'We are heading for Ávila but tonight we're staying at Majadahonda. What in the name of the devil caused all that light and the explosion?'

'I think that was a meteor,' said the woman. 'It must have been huge to generate all that light and sound. Pretty frightening.'

'It certainly scared the horses,' said Esteban. 'I'm tempted to go and find it. It must have landed over there, no more than a few hundred *varas* away.'

'It will have buried itself in the ground or smashed to pieces on the rocks.'

'Where are you heading?' said Antonio.

'Same as you. Ávila, eventually and I'll probably stop in Majadahonda, too. May I make a request?'

'Why not?' said Esteban.

'I thought I'd be safer dressed like this because a single woman travelling this road is vulnerable. May I travel with you?'

'Yes,' said Esteban. 'Don't you agree, Antonio?'

'Yes, it would be a pleasure,' said Antonio. He immediately wondered what a woman of her apparent breeding would be doing on a dangerous road like this. He ventured to ask.

'I cannot believe a woman, if I may say, a well-educated woman like you, would be travelling alone on this dangerous road.'

'It was a very difficult decision for me,' she said, climbing back on her horse. 'I heard only yesterday that my mother, who lives in Ávila, is very ill. She has asked to see me so I had to come. I had no choice, therefore, but to travel this road.'

Antonio and Esteban re-mounted their horses and all three riders headed towards Majadahonda. Each took an occasional glance at the sky from which, thankfully, no more unusual streaks of light appeared. Within a few more hours they were trotting through the gate to the town and looking for somewhere to eat and stay the night.

'You've got company, tonight, old girl,' said Antonio, settling his horse into its stables at a homely looking inn at the edge of the little town.

'I know it is an immodest thing to suggest, but should we eat together tonight or would you two prefer to eat just with each other?' said the woman, as they entered.

'Why not join us?' said Esteban.

So within half an hour, the three of them had unloaded their saddlebags, settled into their separate, albeit tiny rooms and were sitting and waiting for attention at one of the tables.

'So what do you two do?' asked the woman.

'We are travelling players,' said Antonio. 'Esteban is the singer and I'm the violinist. We are going to try the streets in Ávila and perhaps some inns there. Then maybe Segovia.'

'What a coincidence! I'm a singer, too. I often sing at the Príncipe theatre, sometimes at the de la Cruz. Occasionally I act.'

'It's a wonder I haven't seen you at the Príncipe. I've been performing there for the last fortnight with a music troupe. Accompanying the actors in one of Encina's plays, "Plácida y Victoriano". I didn't like the story line much but the actors in it were good singers!'

'I bet you do well, don't you?'

'Yes, but only if we sing ribald songs and there are plenty to choose from. By the way, I am Antonio Hidalgo and this is my colleague and friend Esteban de Recalde.'

'I'm enchanted, señores. I am Lupita de Pastrana. If you don't mind I'll retire now but before I do, may I have the pleasure… and the security… of your company tomorrow?'

'Don't see why not,' said Esteban, sounding less than enthusiastic about the idea.

The woman politely shook hands with each of them, bade them goodnight and went.

'You stupid fool!' said Esteban to Antonio.

Antonio couldn't believe his ears. Whatever had he done or said? He hadn't given anything away about the true purpose of their journey so what was wrong?

'I'm sorry, Esteban. I don't understand.'

'You should never have told her that I'm a singer. I'm not! You haven't heard me sing one note. And you took a great risk. What if she'd asked us to sing with her? Here in this inn. We'd have been completely exposed and made to look idiots. It would have been obvious we were lying and she'd be wondering … even asking… what we were hiding. Don't you dare do that to me again.'

'I think you are being too sensitive,' said Antonio. 'If she'd called our bluff we would have made our excuses. She couldn't make us sing.'

'That would have been even worse,' said Esteban. 'I'm going to my room.'

He turned his back on Antonio who suddenly felt sick and alone. He had to assume, despite this setback, that they would be capable of working well together. He remembered what Silva de Torres said about going back if he got into trouble. He thought this was hardly a reason to give up. Matters would have to be much worse. Whenever he felt down, Antonio could usually lift himself by playing his violin. So he got it from his room and played it in the drinking area. There were only a dozen or so customers, nearly all of whom applauded at the end of each piece. Within an hour he had put Esteban's remarks to the back of mind and went to bed.

'I apologise,' said Esteban as he arrived at the breakfast table where Antonio was already sitting enjoying a couple of fried eggs and some bread. 'I think I was still tense after seeing that strange object in the sky. I thought we were being attacked by the Christian God to stop our mission. And although he failed the first time, he might have another attempt.'

'Don't worry. No Christian God would do that. I apologise, too. I suppose I gave more away to Señorita Lupita than I should have. I didn't sleep well for worrying about what I said. We need to be friends if this mission is to succeed.'

'You are right,' said the diminutive man, looking up at Antonio. 'I'm certain we will be friends and very good friends at that.'

'But I'm sure we will have our disagreements,' said Antonio, by then smiling. 'And we must be frank with each other!'

'You must give me some singing lessons. That way that kind of problem can be avoided!'

'Tonight. In my room or yours, wherever we won't be overheard.'

Lupita arrived at that moment. 'Singing lessons, did you say?'

'Yes, I am teaching Esteban some new tunes which we want to try on the people of Ávila.'

'How far will we be riding today?'

'I'm sure we'll make Valdemorillo, even at the pace of Antonio's old horse.'

Within half an hour, the three of them had put their saddlebags back on their horses, had climbed on and were trotting away from the inn. It was difficult to speak to each other while riding, especially as the best way to travel on these narrow, uneven roads was in single file. Discussion at their afternoon stop turned to the subject of the *Moriscos* and religion.

'Tell me, you two, what do you think about the trouble we seem to be having with the *Moriscos*? A lot of people are complaining about them with very little evidence to support their claims. Or so it seems to me.'

'You are asking the wrong person,' said Esteban. 'I am a *Morisco*!'

'Well, I'm a *Morisca*,' said Lupita. 'I was only playing the Christian line because I thought you were both Christians! What about you, Antonio?'

'I am a Christian but with *Morisco* sympathies. I'll explain. I am officially a Christian and have been baptised into the religion but I am not a believer. I cannot believe in the virgin birth, the resurrection or the miracles. And I'm not sure about whether there is a God or not. If I made my views public, I'd be charged with heresy and burnt at the stake! So please keep that to yourself!'

'And what about the so called *Morisco* problem?' asked Lupita.

'I think the problem, as it's called, is about politics…by which I mean the king and the Duke of Lerma… They have made it a problem because the prestige of Spain has fallen in Europe and they think some a fight with the *Moriscos* may help to regain it. The Archbishop of Valencia, Ribera, is behind the religious problems. He is incapable of letting the Muslims worship their own god. He cannot understand that you can't just convert people to Christianity if they don't see a benefit. And he has many supporters, not least Fray Breda. That's why many *Moriscos* just pretend they are Christians and continue going to secret mosques to worship Allah.'

Tears welled in Lupita's eyes as Antonio spoke. 'You are a wonderful man, Antonio. I wish all Christians had the same views, especially those who lead the church. They are so bigoted and don't understand what religion is about. You can't simply change from one religion to another like changing your shirt.'

'I agree,' said Esteban. 'I don't know how all this will end. Ribera and his henchmen want us thrown out of Spain and it sounds like Lerma agrees. The king will certainly follow Lerma because he's a weakling with no mind of his own.'

'I'm scared at what could happen. I'm a single woman and I live with some other singers near the Mentidero. They know I'm a *Morisca* and I'd be thrown out with everyone else,' said Lupita beginning to sob.

'Now, now,' said Antonio. 'There's a long way to go yet. I can't see how this chaotic crowd could get rid of a galley full, let alone half a million!'

Antonio left it to Esteban to lead this part of the discussion. Neither intended to let this woman, *Morisca* or not, know why they were on the road.'

'Let's get moving,' said Esteban, or we'll not reach Valdemorillo in time to stay the night.'

'Come on then, give me that singing lesson,' said Esteban, as the two of them emerged from their rooms at a tavern in Valdemarillo.

'Let's see your room. Mine is overlooking the stables. We don't want to disturb the horses do we?'

'My room is next to Lupita's and she wants a sleep before dinner.'

'We'll use mine then.'

They stepped into Esteban's room. Antonio signalled him to sit on the bed. 'Right. What we are going to do is to learn a range of risqué songs that will cause a stir and some amusement on the streets. The first one is very simple. It's about a girl called Isabel who intends to go swimming but loses her corset so is going in naked. A boy friend tells her how pretty she looks without it.'

'I can't sing a song like that, not on the streets of Ávila!'

'Yes you can! You just take a deep breath and sing. You keep your clothes on, by that way!'

'I'll decide when I hear the song.'

Antonio put his violin to his chin and sang it, to his music:

'Isabel, Isabel,
You've lost your corset,
You need it for swimming
To go in the water
But do not regret it
You'll look better without it!'

'No. I can't sing anything as ribald as that,' said Esteban.

'Try this one then,' said Antonio, plucking the strings on his violin to tune it. Then he played and sang:

'I was going to my mother
To take her some roses
But I found my loves
Within the garden
Within the garden, I will die
Within the garden, they will kill me!
Within the garden, I will die
Within the garden, they will kill me!'

'You sang that beautifully, Antonio. I'll try that.'

'You stand by the bed and I'll play as you sing. What about the words?'

'I have a good memory and I learnt them as you were singing. The reason is that I can't read very well so I have developed a good memory because I can't take notes.'

'That talent of remembering so well could help us at the palace. We won't be able to take notes standing outside with the guards looking on!'

'Go on, Antonio, start me off!'

'One, two three, go!' Antonio accompanied Esteban through the song.

'You can do better than that.'

'What do you mean?'

'Only that you can do better! You have a good tenor voice and between us, we'll have you singing well! Let's try it again!'

They played it through again. 'That's much better! Now let's try "Isabel, Isabel". Go on!'

Esteban refused at first but Antonio persuaded him. The moment he hit the last note, Antonio slapped him on the back. 'Well done, my friend. That song and a few other ribald ones I know will make us a small fortune. Let's go down and join Lupita for dinner. Much longer and she'll be wondering what we're doing in here!'

The night before they arrived in Ávila, they stayed in a small roadside lodging house, owned by an older lady who explained that she had been widowed a few months before. Three robbers broke in through the front door as the couple were about to close for the night. They shot her husband in the face when he refused to hand over their money. That night, no one had stopped there to stay so no one could help her tend to her dying husband. It was only when she flagged down a passing carriage the following morning that she could share her plight.

'Now you know why I dressed as a man to travel this road,' said Lupita, as the widow, tears running from her eyes, concluded her sorry tale. 'You men don't know what fear is until you see what it's like to ride these roads as a single woman… it's next to suicide.'

The sad old lady soon put a tasty meal on the table and the three of them were conversing again.

'What I don't understand,' said Esteban, looking at Lupita, 'is why you live in Madrid when your mother lives in Ávila?'

'That's an interesting question. As you well know, the king and his court, at Lerma's insistence, moved to Valladolid in the January of 1601. My father knew one of the officials at the palace who knew the move was going to happen, before it became public. He was a neighbour of ours near the Plaza Mayor and they used go drinking together. My father suspected he knew more than he was willing to talk about. So father got him drunk one night and started talking about property prices. Then this *tio* told him in total confidence that the royal court, about twenty thousand staff, were going to move. He said he couldn't say where because that was a state secret. Well, my father owned nine properties in the town and rented them, mainly to civil servants, and predicted rightly a total collapse in the rental market when this many people moved out of town. So he did the clever thing and put them all, and the tenth house, the one we lived in as a family, on the market. He sold when the market was high and decided to buy our house in Ávila and three houses in Salamanca which is where he guessed the king and his court would go.'

'He was right over what was important,' said Antonio. 'Too bad that he guessed wrongly over where the king ended up!'

'Yes,' said Lupita. 'The tragedy is that Madrid is now in a far worse mess than anyone could have predicted. The irony is that Ávila was built to keep the Moors out and my family of *Moriscos* has moved in!'

'Why didn't you move with the family?' asked Esteban.

'The opportunities for singers in Ávila are limited. So I decided to stay in Madrid and share a rented house with some of my singer friends.'

'Do you have a man friend?' asked Antonio, always curious in such matters.

'No. Not now. I fell for an actor at the Príncipe a year or so ago but when I discovered from one of my friends that he was seeing all kinds of other women, including *putas*, I decided I'd finish with him. He then threatened to kill me but soon realised how stupid he'd been. He eventually apologised and asked to recommence our relationship but I refused. So I'm single now,' she smiled.

'Interesting,' thought Antonio and said, 'I'm sorry to hear that,'

'Can we change the subject?' asked Lupita.

'Yes, I understand,' said Esteban. 'What's our plan for Ávila, then, Antonio? Are we doing some street performances there? I'm quite keen, now I know these new songs!'

'The first thing you are going to do is to come to stay at our house. You two have been so kind, the least we can do is to put you up for a few nights. My parents will be delighted!'

'That's a very generous thought,' said Antonio,' but we wouldn't want to inflict a couple of common street musicians on your lovely family!'

'I insist!' said Lupita. 'My parents will be for ever grateful. You'll see!'

The sad, old widow's tavern was only a couple of *leguas* from Ávila and within a couple of hours of leaving the comforts of her lodging house, the three travellers were on foot and holding their horses' reins, walking them through the Alcázar gate of the ancient walled city. To the two strangers, Ávila seemed a bustling little town. As they walked up to the market square, they could see and hear the fevered voices of stall holders selling their wares and buyers bargaining with them. The town smelled sweeter than Madrid: less of the smell of human waste but more of horses, fresh fruit and even perfumes being tested by women at the stalls.

'Let's tie the nags up here,' said Lupita, pointing to a rail outside of her parents' house. Then follow me in!'

'How is mother?' said Lupita to her father who came into the *zaguan* to greet her.

'She is still very ill but improving. It must have been a very bad fever. She's lost a lot of weight but thankfully is eating again now. She's asleep in the bedroom at the back and I don't want her disturbed.' Her father was a dark skinned, stocky man with a distinct Moorish look about him. His round mop of black hair doubled the width of his face and, while a tall man anyway, made him look one or two *pulgadas* taller.

'Who are these vagabonds?' he said, glancing over Lupita's shoulder at the two men.

'They have been lovely to me, Father. They are so nice. They have accompanied me from just outside Madrid to our front door. They are travelling musicians on their way to Segovia. But they are planning to work in Ávila for a few days. Can they stay in our house?'

'Since you've been living on your own, you've asked for some odd things, like your soldier disguise and that white stallion. Now you're asking for two street players to stay here. Their mates usually sleep under the town *puentes*. What's so different about these two? And I'm not so sure about a dwarf.'

Lupita looked angry. 'Please father. I regard them as my friends, fellow musicians. There's nothing wrong with either of them... and your remark about dwarves is totally mistaken! Esteban has been very kind to me! The two have probably saved me from a fate worse than death on that evil road from Madrid. You should be grateful. Not abusive!'

'You've got a nerve, Lupita. Arguing with me in the hallway of my own house. And in front of these two. Come into the kitchen! Now!'

The arguing father and daughter made their way through while the two men just stood there. The kitchen door slammed. 'We could rob this place of everything worth taking now they've gone... if we were that evil!'

'I know,' said Antonio, 'but we're not. I think we tell them that we'll find somewhere else in the town, whatever he decides.'

Lupita and her father appeared smiling and the father spoke. 'I'm sorry, gentlemen. I spoke out of turn. I'd like to welcome you to our modest abode. Please come with me. We'll give you a room each.'

'Don't worry señor. We'll find an inn in the town or outside the walls. We won't trouble you here.'

'Please, please stay!' said Lupita. 'It would be a great honour for us and you can't just walk away because of a minor argument. I beg you to stay!'

'What do you think?' asked Esteban.

'We cannot let Lupita down over a matter of honour!'

'Agreed!' said Esteban.

Lupita hugged each of them in turn and kissed them on both cheeks. 'I'm so pleased! You've made me very happy!'

'Sorry, gentlemen,' said the father, as he led Antonio and Esteban along the spacious hall towards the elegant staircase in this mansion of a house. Neither had seen anything as opulent before, except when Antonio had stepped into the office of the Corregidor of Guadalajara, something he couldn't mention to Esteban. 'I was wrong to speak of you in such terms.'

Señor de Pastrana left each of them in their separate rooms unpacking their saddlebags. 'What's yours like?' said Esteban as he looked through the open door into Antonio's room.

'I can't believe our luck! Look at that bed. So high up and with a full canopy. All we need is a woman for the night!'

Esteban glanced around at the carved oak sofas facing the gilt painted fire place, the four poster bed and the green damask curtains hanging from their brass rail. 'Unbelievable but still not as good as mine,' he said.

Within moments the two of them were peering at the spectacular furnishings in Esteban's room. 'See! The paintings are of a better class than the ones in your room. I bet he paid a fortune for these.' Colourful oils of scenes from the Greek myths adorned every wall. The paint smelled fresh as if they were still new.

'Do we have to go to Valladolid?' said Esteban. 'Let's just stop here!'

Antonio put his index finger to his lips, pointed to the walls and then to his ears. 'I follow,' said Esteban, in a whisper.

'I'm coming with you,' said Lupita, as the two men prepared themselves to launch their career as a duet on the unsuspecting population of Ávila.

'What do you mean?' asked Antonio.

'We are going to be a trio today! I'll be the soprano and Esteban the tenor.'

'You don't know the words!' said Esteban.

'You'd be surprised. I know more ribald songs than many a male singer. And I can soon pick them up from listening to you! It'll shock our neighbours, to see me with you two and that'll add to the pleasure!'

At Lupita's suggestion, the three of them settled on a pitch in the middle of the busy marketplace. 'You are the leader of the band, Antonio. So you start when you are ready. We just need to decide on what to sing!'

'We'll start with "Roses for my mother". It's especially poignant for you. And Esteban knows the words. I'll play the tune right through, then you sing it, Esteban, and you join in on the third repeat, Lupita. Then we'll do the whole thing through again with me starting on the violin.'

Esteban put a collection bowl on the ground in front of them and Antonio counted down to start. Antonio played the brisk little tune at the high end of the range then dropped an octave for Esteban to sing. One or two shoppers stopped to listen. A bald-headed man with a dog threw a coin in their pot, their very first earning as a music troupe. Then Lupita joined in. Her trained and powerful voice carried all around the square. Before Esteban started on his solo for the second time, a modest crowd had gathered to watch and listen. A burst of applause sounded as the three of them bowed to their new audience.

'Now straight into "Isabel, Isabel" on three. Same order as before! One, two three!' Antonio started, then Esteban and Lupita at the third repeat. The crowd rocked with laughter at Lupita singing this song.

One of them recognised her. 'What would your father think of you singing that one?' the man, a red-faced, jolly looking individual with a pronounced limp, asked.

'He'd join in!' Lupita laughed back.

'Now we'll really get them going,' said Antonio. 'I'm going to attempt to sing to a dance tune. Listen and join in the second time I play it.' The song tells of a shepherd who came home to find his wife in bed with his brother. He goes round to his brother's house and gets in bed with his wife who is more than willing to oblige. The amusing lines, especially as sung by Lupita, caused much merriment as the crowd, by then grown to about fifty or more, were dancing with each other in front of the market stalls. By then the collection pot was running over.

'This is brilliant,' said Lupita. 'Why don't we do the same tomorrow?'

The three of them continued playing and became a popular source of amusement in the market square of Ávila and in the adjacent streets. Towards the end of a week of this enterprise, Lupita suggested that they try playing the following day at the Puerta de Carmen. 'It gets very busy up there,' she said. 'We'll do even better!'

As they were finishing a rendition of 'Juanilla, Juanilla', a small woman appeared and walked up to speak to Esteban. 'We could be related!' she said. 'My name is Carolina de Torres Madruga. I'm a musician, too. I just heard your soprano say you'd be performing at the

Carmen gate tomorrow. Maybe I could join you. I sing and play the guitar. Oh! And I dance and can act!'

Esteban raised his eyebrows at this impertinent suggestion and turned to the other two. 'Why not?' said Lupita, deciding for them.

'The four of us at the Carmen Gate at nine o'clock then!' said Antonio.

'Where is she?' said Lupita at quarter past. 'Nowhere to be seen.'

'We can't wait any longer,' said Esteban. 'These people are waiting for us to start.'

'I'm here! I'm here,' shouted the little lady as she ran up the road swinging a guitar that was almost as big as her. 'I'm so sorry! I overslept!'

'Not impressed,' whispered Esteban to Antonio, as if disappointed on behalf of all dwarves.

'One of those things,' said Lupita who had overheard him. 'Let's give her a big welcome and start up the band.'

All three applauded as she neared them.

'Let's do what we did yesterday except we'll start with Vásquez's "You have killed me, Maiden Fair".'

'Yes, I know that one,' said Carolina.

'And me,' said Lupita.

'I'll soon pick it up,' said Esteban.

They played this sad little refrain to a grateful audience. Then they played 'Roses for my mother', followed by the dance tune that Antonio chose the day before. Everybody there at the *puerta* started to dance, just as the day before.

'Time we played something a little risqué,' said Antonio.

'Such as?' said Lupita.

'How about "If you are going to bathe, Juanilla, tell me where?"'

'Brilliant,' said Lupita. 'I know that one, too.'

The audience loved the daring of this mixed group of players, especially when giving their version of a song usually reserved for drunken men in the town taverns. Laughter and applause burst from the crowd as the group of four took their bow, little Carolina almost knocking her guitar on the ground.

'I know, let's sing 'Woe is me, Alhama', not exactly a Christian song,' said Antonio but everyone knows it. You know it, Carolina?'

'Of course,' she said. 'Let's start then. Altogether?'

'Yes, on three,' said Antonio.

86

They sang the words:

The Moor king was walking in Granada
From the Elvira to the Villarambla
Woe is me Alhama
They wrote to say it was beaten
In a fire the bad news scroll he threw
And the messenger he then slew
Woe is me Alhama

Members of the audience stopped laughing and looked at each other. This group of players had the nerve to launch into a Moorish dirge on the fall of Alhama. How audacious; what an insult. At first this varied crowd were unsure. No one wanted to start. Their scowls and frowns gave the message. There were murmurings as their anger rose. Then, one by one, they reacted.

'Who do you damned people think you are singing that filthy *Morisco* ditty?'

'Yes in a city built to keep the Moorish scum out!'

'Clear off, you lot, and sing that to your *Morisco* brethren!'

Then the missiles started to land. Someone in the crowd threw an egg which broke on Lupita's dress. The yolk and white dribbled to the ground. Another egg smashed on Antonio's head and ran over his face. Someone kicked over the collection pot which scattered its contents. Then the mob started to jostle the players, coming yet closer and shoving them up to the wall. They chanted, 'Go now' 'Clear off'.

'Back to my place,' said Lupita, helping Carolina who had fallen to the floor. 'It's time we weren't here!'

The four of them dashed from the *puerta*, dodging other randomly thrown missiles, tomatoes, grapes, the odd olive and other detritus as they went.

'My God, I didn't expect that,' said Antonio, closing the front door after all four had rushed in.

'That's pretty obvious,' laughed Esteban. 'Otherwise I guess you wouldn't have suggested it!'

'I don't get it,' said Carolina. 'That song was about something which happened over a hundred years ago.'

'Yes, but the *Morisco* problem has raised itself again and is fresh in peoples' minds.'

'That's no reason to be thoroughly objectionable,' said Lupita.

'It's a wonder they didn't hit us,' said Carolina still afraid.

'Their children saved us. If they hadn't been there I dread to think what they'd have done,' said Esteban. 'And they don't like hitting us little people.'

'I hate to tell you this,' said Antonio. 'We will have to start for Segovia in the morning, like it or not. There will be riots in the street if we play here again. We'll be sad to leave you and the comfort of your parents' home.'

'They will understand,' said Lupita. 'We've had a wonderful time together and I'll always be grateful to you both.'

'You're going to Segovia?' said Carolina. 'May I come with you? I planned to go there by carriage but it would be better to travel with you men.'

'Give us a few moments to discuss the idea,' said Esteban.

'Come into the kitchen for a glass of juice,' said Lupita, leaving the men to talk.

'Well, what do you think?' asked Esteban.

'Tricky question, but what excellent cover. I'm sure Pedro would agree. But Carolina would be in the dark about it.'

'Yes. And an interesting trio! She's a good singer, too!'

'Why does she want to go?'

'I don't know. We'll find out soon enough. I'm taken with the idea. Don't let's put her off.'

Carolina hugged and kissed them as they told her the news. 'I love you both,' she said, on the verge of tears.

'Meet us here at seven o'clock sharp.'

CHAPTER 9
Death of the quarry

A shot rang out. He fell with a sickening thud. He twitched in a shattering convulsion that left him completely motionless on the ground. He was dead.

'Got the bastard,' he said, as he lowered the barrel of the harquebusier, smoke still pouring from the muzzle and the whiff of burnt gunpowder escaping from the stock.

'Great shot, Majesty. You've killed him all right.' There were others present then so the Duke of Lerma had to use a formal address, albeit an abbreviation.

Philip III and his *valido* loved to hunt. Far from the first time, they were hunting in the massive grounds of the duke's hunting lodge at Ventosilla, some fifteen or so *leguas* east of Valladolid, a property the duke had bought from his huge emoluments as *valido*. A horse starting a gallop at one end of this massive hunting ground would be totally exhausted before it could reach the far side. Not only did the estate stretch beyond the sight of an eye, it contained a huge range of terrain from the deep valleys of the Duero to the rugged uplands of Old Castile. A lame horse, loss of a sense of direction or an awkward fall could lead to almost certain death before reaching the safety of the isolated lodge. The Duke of Lerma and King Philip, accompanied by their entourage of helpers knew the terrain so well they were safe, apart perhaps from attack by a gang of local robbers who might outnumber and outgun them.

'I've wanted to kill that one for months. I'm sure it's him. I recognised the antlers.'

'We'd better get the ball out of him. It'll spoil the meat if we're not careful. Hey you!' shouted Lerma to one of the entourage. 'Use your knife to cut that ball out!'

'I'll do that, Your Grace. Right away!' The man jumped from his horse took a dagger from his belt and stabbed it into the side of the deer. He dug deep, right into the heart of the beast but soon had the ball in his bare hand. He held it above his head so the duke could see.

'You and you,' said the duke, pointing to a pair of unsuspecting companions. 'Give him a hand to lift it onto that cart.' The corpse landed with a crash on the floor of the wagon.

'Are you done, Majesty? Back to the lodge or would you like to hunt for longer?'

'I'm so excited to have killed that one, I could go on for longer. But I think we should go back. We don't want to risk being out here after sunset.'

'Blow up withdrawal,' said the duke to the head huntsman. The horn sounded and without a word being uttered the twenty or so men began to make their way back to the lodge.

The king and his *valido* usually dined together and with no one else present, other than those who came and went while serving them. His wife and consort Queen Margaret of Austria, his first cousin once removed, and daughter of Archduke Charles II of Austria and Maria Anna of Bavaria, was still suckling their baby son, the Infante Philip, heir to the throne. So she was indisposed and back at the Royal Palace in Valladolid. She and the king rarely dined together.

'I never know whether they gut a deer before they bury it, do you, Francisco?'

'They gut it first, clean all the blood and shit out of it, give it a good wash in cold water and then bury it for a fortnight.'

'I see,' said the king as he cut a mouthful of beef from a joint. He dipped it into some strong smelling, brown sauce, forked it straight into his mouth and began to chew. 'I was never very sure about that,' said the king, barely intelligible with his mouth overfull.

Lerma also carved off a piece, except he forewent the pleasure of the brownish concoction. 'Not a bad joint of beef,' he said. 'Tastes younger than some of the dog meat we used to get.'

'With all you've spent here, Francisco, I'm not surprised it's better. It's already giving me a stalk and I've nowhere to put it! Queenie's away and the boy's got her milky globes for tonight. All to himself,' laughed the king.

'It's probably the effect of the wine! I'll find you a chambermaid, if you want. If I went around this place and shouted, "Who wants to fuck the king tonight?" they'd all be fighting to get their clothes off and into to your bed. Some would probably die in the crush!'

'You are evil. The one thing I wouldn't do is to commit adultery. God would prevent me. You know that, so don't insult me.'

'In that case you'll have to resort to the method of Onan,' said Lerma, not wanting to drop the subject entirely.

'I won't do that either,' the king said, lowering his voice as if he could be tempted.

'Are you in the mood to discuss business, Philip?' said the duke, after a period of silence and concentrated scoffing.

'Only if you insist,' said the king, after taking a large gulp of wine from a slim stemmed, silver goblet.

'Just a couple of things,' said Lerma.

'I'm always suspicious when you start like that. You are going to tell me we're bankrupt, that the Pope has died or that the Dutch have over-run the Empire.'

'No, nothing like any of that. I wouldn't give a shit about the Pope though, despite his apparent generosity... and to me, of all his flock!'

'What is it then?'

'Whether we like it or not, we will have to move back to Madrid. There are all manner of objections to being in Valladolid. Madrid is becoming a place of untold misery. People are starving. There are fights on the streets for bread. Crime has never been higher. Property prices have collapsed.'

'While I trust you implicitly, Francisco, I still find it hard to appreciate what you say. Get some of the local Madrid nobility here to tell me themselves.'

'I'll do that, Philip. As soon as I can.'

'What happened to my idea of a *junta*?'

'Died in its tracks. Couldn't get the Council of Castile to agree the terms.'

'Oh,' muttered the king, pathetically. He'd lost to Lerma again but he didn't want to upset him. He needed him to run Spain.

'And what was the other thing you wanted to report,'

'Those damned *Moriscos*. They've dreamt up a plot to kidnap and hold you up for ransom. May even kill you, if we don't deliver.'

The king's eyes almost jumped from their sockets. He stood up. Lerma stayed seated. 'What? Kill me? What is going on?' Still glaring, he thumped his clenched fist on the table.

'I'm only telling you, Philip. The *Moriscos* are a useless bunch. They couldn't organise a cockfight in a hen house.'

'You can't dismiss it, just like that. It's not your damned life they're after. First, James of England and now me. I couldn't believe those treacherous swine were going to blow up the House of Lords with him in it. They foiled the attack on James. But what makes you so sure you'll stop these brigands from taking me?'

'Algebra has engaged a special agent to infiltrate the gang of them. A bright young spark who's a musician. They'll never suspect he's spying for us.'

'Engaged an agent? What d'you mean? Taken on some completely inexperienced novice? Surely, we need an accomplished master spy for a job as crucial as that. What's Algebra up to?'

'He's nobody's fool, Philip. You know that. The young *tio*'s best asset is that he's met the *Morisco* leader of the gang and has his confidence.'

'That's all very well, Francisco, but he hasn't got mine. What's the man's codename?'

'Diaspora.'

'Is that a joke?

'I did wonder. Algebra being clever.'

'And how many are involved in the plot?'

'Just the two. Diaspora and a dwarf called de Recalde. They're well on their way to Valladolid. Their leader stayed in Madrid. Algebra is keeping an eye him.'

'You'd better stay on top of this, Francisco. I want frequent reports.'

'I'll tell Algebra.'

'Well, I'm still in shock. Is that all for now?'

'Yes. Good night, Philip.' He left the king who sat back down at the table, as frightened as a man facing a smouldering death at the stake.

CHAPTER 10
The attack

None of them slept well that night. They still could not believe the crowd's reaction to 'Woe is me, Alhama'. The terror the crowd induced in them would take days to dissolve away.

'We're on the road again,' said Antonio to his aging mare. 'To Segovia and I won't work you hard.' The horse just shook her head in a gesture which puzzled him.

True to instruction, Carolina arrived outside of Lupita's as the cathedral bells struck seven.

'Where's your horse?' asked Lupita.

'I haven't got a horse!'

'You can ride as passenger on Esteban's!' said Antonio.

Esteban feigned a groan but manfully helped the tiny lady up so that she sat in front of him in the saddle. 'That's all very well but, we won't be able to ride quickly, not like this.'

'Not a problem,' said Antonio. 'It'll suit my old nag!'

Lupita was almost in tears as she bid the three of them farewell. They wished her the best and her mother a hasty recovery. She kissed them and stood back as Carolina and Esteban moved off.

When they were out of earshot, Antonio took two addressed envelopes from his saddle bag and handed them to Lupita. 'Please post these for me.'

'Of course. Who is Algebra?'

'Better that you don't know,' he whispered.

'Thank you for giving me your address, Antonio. I'll call in when I'm back in Madrid.'

He trotted off towards the others.

Esteban and Carolina looked an odd couple as they sat astride Esteban's horse. Antonio felt quite strange as he rode, slightly behind them. The small people usually made the minority he now formed. By then he was used to the ways of small people and had treated Esteban as an equal, different only in height. He would, of course treat Carolina similarly and as a lady.

Antonio had, he thought, made a good decision in writing a short letter to the *regidor*. He agreed before he came on this mission that he would report back when he had an opportunity and leaving Lupita's presented a good one. He wondered what Algebra would think about the group increasing to three, with the addition of Carolina. He said that they were leaving that day for Segovia, probably three days away. As an almost irrelevant diversion he mentioned what Lupita thought was a meteor; that she had joined them at that point; and stayed with them until Ávila. He told him that she and her family were wealthy *Moriscos*.

Lupita's father had fried them a healthy breakfast before they left and, as usual, they took plenty of water with them. They made good progress in the cool of the early morning and were well on their way before they took their first stop for a refreshment break.

'Tell me, how far do you think we'll get today,' asked Esteban as he slid down from his horse and started to help Carolina down.

'Hard to say but if we keep up this rate of progress we could well make Villacastín before nightfall. There's nowhere to stop for several *leguas* before so if we are going to get there today we'd better get moving soon.'

'Let's try it,' said Esteban. 'What do you think, Carolina?'

'You make the decisions. I'm only here for the ride!'

'Why were you so keen to leave Ávila,' said Antonio.

'That's an embarrassing question. I got into some trouble a few weeks ago and am due to appear in court there tomorrow. Someone says they saw me go into a shop and steal a bag but they are wrong. I did no such thing. So when you said you were leaving the town and heading for Segovia I thought...'

'You crafty wench!' said Esteban. 'So you're using us to escape from a possible prison sentence or worse!'

Carolina began to cry. 'Don't be unkind. I didn't do it... but the witness was a town councillor and which one of us would you believe?'

Antonio put an arm around her. 'Please don't cry, Carolina. You are one of us now and we'll look after you. Never fear!'

'Sorry,' said Esteban. 'It was wrong of me to say that. Stay with us and you'll come to no harm.'

'While we are resting the horses, tell us a bit about yourself, young lady,' said Antonio.

'I'm twenty six and my home town is Toledo. My father took us there from Madrid only because we suffered so much abuse. So bad in fact that my mother, also a dwarf, killed herself by jumping naked into the Manzanares and drowning.' She started to sob again so Antonio comforted

The landlady, a homely looking, rounded lady with her hair tied in a bun and wearing a cream coloured dress down to her ankles, recognised Esteban and greeted him as if he were her diminutive brother, even coming around the counter and bending down to give him a hearty kiss.

'It's wonderful to see you, too, Ángelita. You are looking well. We need three rooms, preferably close to each other and we'd like dinner here tonight.'

'So what brings you to Segovia this time?' she said. Antonio wondered what Esteban had been doing there before.

'We three are a travelling music troupe. Antonio the tall plays the violin, Carolina sings and plays the guitar and I sing.'

'You are joking, Esteban! You? Singing? Don't make me laugh!'

'Seriously! Antonio trained me and now we're all working together. Admittedly, we've only been at it for a few days. We made a small fortune in Ávila and we want to try our luck here for a few days before we head for Valladolid!'

'A very, very small fortune,' said Antonio.

'Valladolid?' said Carolina. 'First I've heard of that. I may just stay here.'

'Yes, we are heading that way,' said Antonio. 'I don't see why you shouldn't come if Esteban doesn't object.'

'I'll have to think about that,' said Carolina. 'I might have to buy a horse!'

'If you've got this band going between you, why not play here tonight?'

'In your tavern?' said Esteban.

'Right here,' said Ángelita. 'Some of the usual crowd are in tonight and they'd love you to entertain them. I'll put a couple of *maravedís* in the pot. That'll get you started!'

'Let's take Ángelita up on that, shall we?'

Carolina and Antonio, seeing an instant opportunity both agreed.

'Get us an early dinner and we'll be ready for your guests!' said Esteban, leading the way.

Within an hour, the three of them had enjoyed the meal that Ángelita had placed before them and were ready to perform in front of a motley group of about fifty men who had wandered into the inn in twos and threes and greeted each other as if they met there regularly. One of them passed a large jug around the group and each placed what seemed to be an agreed amount in it which would serve as the source of payment for the copious drinking on which they were about to embark.

'Where's this band you were on about, Ángelita. Are they here yet?' said one of the men, a swarthy looking character in a narrow brimmed hat.

'Here we are,' shouted Antonio. 'It's us three! Let's start with the "Roses for my mother" shall we, a little ballad to begin with. You play and sing, Carolina but I'll play a violin solo for the first verse. And you sing with Carolina from the first verse. One...two...three.'

The three of them fished to a tumult of applause and shouts of, 'encore, encore'.

'Now into "If you are going to bathe, Juanilla, tell me where". These lads will love you singing such a rude song, Carolina!' said Antonio.

'Let's do 'Woe is me, Alhama,' said, Esteban with a daring look on his face.

'We can't do that. We'll have a riot on our hands. There'll be broken jugs and glass everywhere!'

'Trust me, Antonio. As before: you and Carolina play the first verse as an instrumental and then Carolina and I will sing.'

Antonio had not expected this. Virtually every man in the house, the landlady and the waitresses joined in. Some of the men cried as they sang the second verse. Most knew every word, every intonation and felt every emotion of this poignant ballad. They worked their way through each verse, all twenty of them, until the triumphant last verse when voices were raised to such a pitch and strength that they could have raised the roof. The last note was greeted by a huge round of applause which must have lasted a full two minutes. One man, tears running down his face, raced to Antonio and hugged him. He held his violin aloft in a move of protection. Several others offered to buy the band a drink. Gradually, the audience settled and the group enjoyed a break.

'What did I tell you, Antonio? There was no risk of trouble here. To a man they are all *Moriscos*!'

Suddenly, several other things became clear: Esteban's wish to use this inn above any other and the effusive welcome the landlady gave him. She, too, was a *Morisca*. This was a *Morisco* community: a place where *Morisco* met *Morisco*; *Morisco* drank with *Morisco*; *Morisco* played cards with *Morisco* and even sung with *Morisco*. It seemed natural for a group of persecuted individuals to congregate in a place where they could relax and discuss issues of interest only to themselves.

One of the men who had shown the greatest emotion when the trio sang 'Woe is me' approached the players. 'I suppose you are all *Moriscos*, knowing and singing a song as Moorish as that.'

'No, not me,' said Antonio, wishing straightway that he had not made that admission.

'There's an Allah damned Christian over here, boys! Let's get him.'

Antonio left his fiddle and reached the exit to the hall before one of the men dived at his legs and brought him to the floor. Another burly individual kicked him in the thigh as another leant over him and clenched his fist ready to punch Antonio in the face. Carolina looked on in horror.

Ángelita suddenly realised what was happening and shouted out. 'Stop! Leave him alone. He's a friend of Esteban. Didn't you realise? Get him up!'

The swarthy *Morisco* thugs suddenly stopped their impromptu attack on Antonio and mumbled to themselves as they picked him up from the floor.

'Thank you, Ángelita,' shouted Antonio across the bar. 'These animals could have killed me.'

'If it hadn't been for her we might have!' replied one of the antagonists.

Ángelita imposed the last word. 'The first sign of more fighting and I'll have the constabulary in here to arrest you!' she yelled across the room.

'God bless her,' said Antonio as he re-joined his colleagues, gently put his trusty violin in its battered case and brushed himself down. 'I didn't expect that. Not after a performance they all enjoyed!'

'I'm sorry you were treated like that, Antonio,' said Esteban, after the men in the drinking area had left them talking in their own little group at the other end of the room. 'I feel responsible in not warning you that this is a *Morisco* enclave. This lot can be dangerous but only for those who are anti-*Morisco*.'

'That's what I don't understand,' said Antonio. 'They didn't even ask me what I thought of the *Morisco* issue or whether I sympathised with them. It was gratuitous violence against an innocent musician. They are thugs, Esteban. Don't apologise for them!'

'What if I had admitted that I was a Christian with gypsy blood? Would those horrible men have attacked me?' said Carolina.

'How can I know? I cannot speak for them. The one good thing is that only three attacked Antonio. The other fifty or so didn't.'

'But the others didn't stop them either,' said Carolina.

'Let's put this down to experience,' said Antonio, in a forgiving tone. 'They enjoyed our music and maybe they became a little too patriotic when they joined in "Woe is me".'

This mixed experience left the three of them puzzled. At breakfast the following morning their discussion focussed on whether they would stay there longer. 'I think we should stay,' said Esteban. 'I don't believe we will have another experience like last night. And we don't want to give the impression we are running away.'

'I've thought about this during the night and I agree. The one thing the incident teaches me is not to play, "Woe is me".'

Carolina and Esteban chimed in with Antonio.

'I'm not feeling well after that kicking last night. If we all agree, I'd like to stay here and rest but if you two would like to go out to perform without me, I wouldn't mind. I just feel sore and I've got a bruised shoulder. I've tried putting my violin there and it hurts. I'm sure I'll be all right tomorrow.'

'What do you think?' said Carolina, looking to Esteban.

'I'm willing if you are.'

'Let's give it a try. We might be able to find a good pitch that we can all use tomorrow if Antonio feels better.'

They wished Antonio well. The diminutive couple, Carolina, with her guitar slung over her shoulder, left to find a pitch near the cathedral market. Antonio did not feel good and, apart from resting his beaten limbs, felt he needed some time to think. This was his first mission as a spy but oddly didn't feel like one. In fact the feeling which predominated was that he was simply a member of a small music troupe that had met, certainly in the case of its latest member, purely by chance. He had never been trained as an infiltrator or given much guidance by the *regidor*. Perhaps he was the epitome of success in that Esteban, and certainly Carolina, had no idea of his subterfuge. He had to take some comfort in that. He wondered then what other missions he might be sent on when he returned to Madrid. Or would the *regidor* just thank him, pay him his dues and bid him farewell. Either way, he could cope. He played the violin well and could always work just as a musician. Inwardly, he hoped he would be asked to help on another, if unrelated task. Somehow he liked being a part of the intrigue, and the fact that the king was part of this added to the sense of mystery.

Then he thought ahead to Valladolid and how they would gain the information Pedro wanted. How could they, a troupe of itinerant musicians, discover where the king lived and worked in the Royal Palace? Although they would be able to see the guards outside the palace and how often they changed, they could surely not discover the whereabouts of those inside. Could they manage to find a means to enter, perhaps by breaking in or would they have to extract this information from some unsuspecting palace servant? But was that part of his job? He was the spy not the man with this mission. Then an idea struck him. He smiled inwardly and went up to his room.

He awoke to a gentle knocking on his room door. 'Antonio, are you there?' He recognised Carolina's gentle voice. He pulled on his breeches and went to the door.

'Antonio, what a handsome chest. I didn't expect to see that much of you,' she chuckled. 'Maybe I could see some more!'

Antonio beckoned her in. 'Carolina, you surprise me, if I have understood you correctly.'

'Antonio, I have taken a fancy to you ever since I first saw you in that market square in Ávila. You are one of the most handsome men I have ever set eyes on. But I cannot imagine you'd want to make love to an ugly freak like me, a dwarf.' She sat down on Antonio's bed and started to sob.

Antonio immediately felt sorry for her and the need to comfort her. 'My dear Carolina, how can you describe yourself in that negative way? You are a beautiful woman and I like you. You have a lovely strong personality which I find attractive. Not many women would have come out of the crowd in the way you did in Ávila. That took some courage and the three of us, including Lupita, recognised it. Of course you are a dwarf but that does not mean you are ugly: you are not! In fact I quite fancy you, too! In a very physical way! You are different from most people but, to me, that makes you even more attractive. I was hoping that at some point I would ask you to make love to me but you have beaten me to it! Where is Esteban? We don't want to make him jealous!'

'I left him talking to the landlady, downstairs at the desk in the hall. She's single, or so Esteban told me on the way back here.'

'Maybe they have more in common than we think!'

'What naughty thoughts you have!'

'We can enjoy each other now, if you want; or would you prefer another time. At night maybe, in the dark when we can each be more modest with the candles extinguished.'

'Let's do it now, Antonio,' she said, by then smiling and standing up to cuddle him. The little lady put her arms around his waist and rubbed her head into his muscular stomach.

'We'll do exactly what you want,' said Antonio. 'I've never done it with a little person before and I'm not sure how best to manage!'

'Are you implying that I know that?'

'Not at all!'

'Don't look so surprised. Yes, I have done it before and with a tall man, built much like you. The best way is for me to sit on top, facing you. Let's undress.'

They grinned at each other as they did so. 'Come and catch me,' said Carolina, running naked towards the door, her firm but tiny breasts moving up and down.

Antonio pulled her tiny buttocks as she grabbed the door handle. He didn't think for one moment that she'd disappear down the landing. He lifted her bodily into the air, pulled her close to him and sat on the bed with her on his knee. 'Is that a good start?' he said.

She eased herself forward and looked down between his legs. 'You'll need to do better than that if I'm going to enjoy you. Let me help. Lie flat on the bed.'

He did as instructed and Carolina sat on his upper thighs and started to do what was necessary. 'There,' she said. 'That's better!'

Seconds later, Antonio was lifting the little lady up and down, as she just looked into his vacant eyes and grinned all over her happy face. Then after a few minutes, 'Would you like to turn me around. Keep me on though. I'll stretch my legs out to make it easier to turn me around. I don't want to tread on anything! And not too quickly or it'll hurt you and me!'

Again Antonio did exactly as instructed and very slowly, assuming that if he couldn't feel any pain in this manoeuvre, nor would Carolina. They rocked and heaved at this gentle sport, the more so in the late afternoon with the sun peering through the window, enabling each to enjoy the sight of the other's shining nakedness. Antonio still could not believe that here he was, supposedly a spy, making passionate love to a good looking dwarf, while on a mission to save the life of our lacklustre king. Could this be a musician in a dream? It was not that long before Antonio reached that point where control is about to be overwhelmed by forces within. Then was a firm knock on the door. The pressure suddenly subsided.

'Quick, take your clothes and hide in this cupboard,' said Antonio, slowly easing her off him and standing her gently on the floor. He closed the wardrobe behind her, quickly pulled his breeches back on and went to the door.

'Is it you, Esteban? I was sound asleep.'

'I'm looking for Carolina. She wanted to go to the musical instrument shop in the Calle Centro. To buy a drum. Have you seen her?'

Antonio could do nothing but prevaricate. He could hardly let him in. 'No. Have you tried her room?'

'Yes. I'm sure she's not there.'

'Let me get dressed and we can go and look for her. I hate to think she's lost in the town somewhere. I'll be downstairs in two minutes!'

Esteban turned and went towards the stairs. 'He's gone, Carolina. You can come out now. We'll have to finish later! Did you hear what he said? I am to dress and look for you. You dress and slip into your room! Agreed?'

Within moments, Carolina had gone and Antonio had met Esteban in the drinking room. 'Where shall we start looking,' asked Antonio.

'Let's go back to the town square and see if she's up there.'

'Before we go from the inn let's have a good look around. She may be here and you could have missed her. You do the downstairs and I'll go up.'

Antonio knocked on Carolina's door. 'It's me, Antonio!' She opened it. 'Let's go downstairs. I found you in your room, right? And you'd been talking to one of the chambermaids who took you to around to the pump for some water.'

'That should be fine,' she said looking up and smiling. 'I hope he doesn't suspect…'

'Shh…'

They met Esteban on the stairs. 'Where were you, Carolina? I was truly worried.'

'I went with a chambermaid to get a drink of water. The rusty, old pump jammed and it took some time to free it.' That seemed to satisfy Esteban but neither Antonio nor Carolina was sure.

'What about the drum?' said Esteban.

'What do you think, Antonio? I thought if Esteban had a drum, he could beat out a rhythm and sing at the same time. We'd each have an instrument to play on then!'

Antonio thought it was a good idea and said as much. So Esteban and Carolina left for an instrument shop. They soon returned with a double drum: two small drums, one larger than the other, tied to each other by a strand of thick leather. By then, Antonio was sitting at a table having a drink in the drinking room. 'What do you think of this, Antonio?'

'Play it and I'll tell you!'

Esteban sat on the adjacent table and, with a pair of sticks, banged out a vibrant, noisy rhythm. Carolina improvised a tune and sang it to the drum sounds.

'That will make such a difference,' said Antonio. 'A drum makes a song more exciting. We'll make a fortune!'

At dinner, the three of them worked out their programme for the following days. Carolina decided that she'd like to remain with the other two until they reached Valladolid. She didn't say why but Antonio thought the afternoon on his bed may have influenced her. They agreed that they'd spend another five days in Segovia, mainly because they needed to make more money.

That night, before falling asleep, Antonio could not stop thinking about his love making with Carolina. She had surprised him with her willingness to indulge and the pleasure she took from this most intimate of encounters. He had enjoyed it too and wondered when they would have an opportunity to resume their activities and take them to a satisfying conclusion. He thought it important to keep their affair unknown to Esteban for two reasons. He did not know what influence it could have on Esteban and neither did he want it to affect his own credibility as a collaborator on this 'joint' mission. Nor did he want to make the little lady pregnant.

The following days turned out to be even more successful than the three expected them to be. Doubtless, their minor triumph was due not least to Esteban's enthusiastic playing of the drums. He had in no time at all become quite a virtuoso player on the two skinned instrument. Antonio's introduction of some fresh songs must also have helped. Members of the audience quietly sobbed at their soul wrenching rendition of 'Albuquerque, Albuquerque' and laughed raucously as they played

'You have killed me, maiden fair,' a humorous ballad about an unfaithful lover whose lady friend discovers his infidelity.

'How much do you think we've earned today?' asked Carolina who seemed to need it more than either of the others. Esteban was counting it discreetly as they looked on in anticipation while sitting in one of the snug holes of the main drinking room.

'Six *reales* and eight *maravedís*. Just a little more than yesterday. We must be getting better!'

'That'll more than pay the week's lodgings,' said Carolina, smiling gleefully. 'I think I'll go to bed now. What time should we depart in the morning?'

'We should start early, say eight o'clock after an early breakfast.'

'I agree,' said Antonio who at that moment caught the eye of someone on the opposite side of the bar, looking directly at him. When Antonio looked at the man, the individual averted his gaze. Antonio wondered who this person could be. He became curious to find out so decided to retire after Esteban so that he could be available to speak to the man, if that was necessary. If not, nothing would be lost, except a little sleep.

Antonio kept Esteban talking for another half hour or so. They spoke about where they might stay in Valladolid and how long it might take to return to Madrid. They spoke about Pedro. Esteban said he'd known him for several years and that he was a reasonable and responsible kind of person. Antonio lied his concurrence. They genuinely wondered what Carolina would do, once they reached Valladolid. Eventually, Esteban decided to retire, bade Antonio good night, suggested Antonio shouldn't stay up much longer either and finally departed from the room.

Antonio decided to leave it to the individual who had looked at him to make the first move, if there was to be one. Or was Antonio being unnecessarily suspicious? Apparently not for after about another three minutes, the man slowly walked over to where Antonio was sitting. Dressed in an expensive looking shirt with a wide, embroidered collar, and snug fitting, light brown, leather breeches, he looked like a property agent or banker. Surely he would not be asking Antonio if he wanted to rent a house or take out a loan.

'Good evening, señor. You're up late tonight. It's almost twelve.'

'I should go to bed soon. I have to be up and out early tomorrow with my colleagues.'

'May I ask where you are heading?'

'We are travelling musicians and want to try our luck in Valladolid. There's more money there than there used to be, now the king's court is there. And all those civil servants, dukes, consorts and other hangers on.'

'Does the name "Diaspora" mean anything to you, señor?'

Antonio looked stunned. He paused for a moment, looked around him and then spoke. 'I am known by that name, señor.'

'Then we have a need for a short discussion.'

'Who sent you here?'

'Algebra. I am from the *corregidor*'s office here.'

'Then we can continue.'

'Excellent. Let's move over to that booth. We won't be overheard there.'

They both picked up their drinks and slipped into the seats that the troupe had vacated earlier. 'I have some important news for you. The man Pedro, otherwise known as Hajib al-Asadi, is in Valladolid. This means his planned attack on the palace will take place while you and this Esteban de Recalde are there. That's why they sent you via Ávila and Segovia. So you wouldn't spot him and his other cohorts on the road. You must go ahead with the current mission and continue to collaborate with Esteban and find out what this Pedro wants. Or do your best to find it. Pedro will find you, we believe, and use the information you give him.

'Our aim is simple. He has no idea, as far as we know, that we are aware of his mission. We will intercept the whole gang as they are about to enter the palace. We think there will be about twenty. It could be dangerous for you to know more of the detail. And I myself do not know more. You can be assured that you will be safe. And so will your new colleague, Carolina. But make sure your pistol is always within easy reach.

'Algebra is grateful for all you've done and passes on his best wishes. You did well to write to him from Ávila. That letter was of great importance.

'Do you have any questions, Diaspora?'

Antonio was glad he had stayed in the bar for longer than he planned and spoken to this character. He couldn't get used to being called 'Diaspora' and laughed inwardly when the man said it. But this new information put him in a powerful position. He felt sure that Esteban didn't know that Pedro was already in Valladolid. That could only mean that Pedro had not brought Esteban fully into his confidence. This messenger was hinting that Antonio should take care to protect Carolina. He would have no difficulty with that.

'The only question I have is this. Will I learn more about Pedro's operation, his plans, while I'm in Valladolid?'

'Algebra has asked me to say that he will, by some means, tell you more about the man's plans when and if there is more to tell.'

'I have no more questions.'

'Then I will give you this and bid you goodnight.' The man handed Antonio a small fabric purse then stood up and left.

Antonio glowed with satisfaction. It became obvious to him, if there was any doubt, that the first *regidor* of Madrid was giving Antonio's interests and safety a high level of priority. He opened the purse. There were twenty *ducats* inside and a note, saying that this was a payment on account. 'Algebra' had signed it.

The three of them were ready to depart well before eight o'clock that morning.

'You take care on that road,' said Ángelita, as they were settling their accounts. 'It's a dangerous one.'

Esteban's eyes welled up as Ángelita bent over to hug him and kiss him goodbye. Both Antonio and Carolina thought there must be more to this relationship than it seemed. It surprised them that they made no mention of meeting again. They believed that they had made future plans in private.

'And you worry about him finding out about our little affair,' said Carolina when he couldn't overhear them.

'It's better that we know more about him than he knows about us,' chuckled Antonio.

Ángelita's warning prompted Antonio to conceal his loaded snaplock in front of him on the saddle. 'I hope I don't need this, old gal but better safe than sorry. At least I'm trained to use the thing,' he said while climbing into the stirrups.

They made good progress in the cloudy autumn morning. They stopped at about ten o'clock for a rest and sat by the side of the road talking.

'The usual question,' said Carolina. 'How far will we be going today?'

'I'm not sure,' said Esteban. 'This cold weather will help the horses so we may be able to do quite well, especially if we can trot them a little.

With a fair wind we could make El Carbonero. There aren't many inns before then and we don't want to sleep on the ground!'

'I agree,' said Antonio. 'Let's see if we can keep the pace up and make sure we reach El Carbonero well before sundown. My old nag can manage these conditions well.'

They made another stop around midday but confined themselves to a short break and were soon on the road again. They had been trotting along slowly but comfortably when Antonio heard horses galloping behind and gradually closing up with them. He glanced over his shoulder only to see the dust being kicked up by the rapidly approaching mounts. He thought there were two riders but possibly three from the cloud they were generating. As the horsemen came closer, he could see that there were three, each wearing black breeches and thick open-necked shirts. When they reached Antonio and the others the apparent leader shouted out.

'Stop in the name of the law!' Horror struck Carolina like a lightning flash. She wondered if she might be arrested and returned to Ávila to face the trial she had until then avoided. Antonio and Esteban just thought it odd that they were being stopped in the depths of the country for no obvious reason. The men were not wearing bandanas so were probably not highwaymen.

'We are from the crown constabulary in Segovia. Where are you going?' said the lead rider, pointing a heavy pistol in the air.

Something didn't seem right to Antonio. He wondered if they were highwaymen despite the lack of bandanas and as Ángelita had warned. So he turned the questioning on them. 'Do you have a warrant we can see? How do we know you are constables?'

The man lowered his gun and aimed it at Antonio. 'Don't shoot him!' shouted a terrified Carolina, looking around from the horse in front.

The gunman addressed Antonio again. 'Get down from your horse. Now or I'll blow your brains out and leave these two to clear up the mess.'

Antonio slipped his hand under the blanket roll and pulled out his gun, aimed it at the man's head and fired. With blood pouring from his face, the man fell off his horse and landed in a crumpled heap. The second man attempted to pull a pistol from a saddle holster. It got stuck so he jerked it out suddenly and fired it before taking aim. Antonio reloaded and fired at the second man hitting him full in the chest. The third man, seeing what he then had to face, including two probably dead colleagues, heaved his horse around by the reins and galloped back down the road. Two riderless horses chased after him.

Antonio climbed from his horse, his knife in his hand, and gingerly approached the two men on the ground. His heart pounded in his chest as he realised that he'd killed them both. He'd never fired a gun in anger before and at first felt disgusted and ashamed at what he'd done. But he quickly realised that he probably saved three lives, including his own.

'God that was terrible. I'm shaking like a freezing monk,' he shouted out to the other two. 'At least we can ride on in peace, unless the other one has gone for reinforcements.'

'Come quickly, Antonio. Help me off the horse. Can't you see? Esteban has been hit!'

Antonio dashed the ten *varas* to the horse. The stray ball the second man had fired had hit Esteban in the side of his right leg, below the knee. He was bleeding badly and in pain.

Antonio wondered for a few moments whether he should save Esteban or finish him off, there and then. This little man was, after all, a principal player in a plot to kidnap, and possibly murder the king. But to kill him in cold blood, having accompanied him thus far in the mission, would be wrong. Disposing of two highwaymen was one thing but to destroy the life of an apparent colleague was something he could not contemplate. He realised that, if he did kill Esteban, he could not explain such an action to Carolina to whom the two men appeared to be working together, as itinerant musicians and nothing else. Nor would he be able to explain to Silva the sudden termination of the mission. And, whatever the circumstances, except to protect his own or another's life, he could not kill a dwarf.

'Go to one of those bodies and tear off one of the shirts,' said Antonio, as he lifted Carolina from Esteban's horse. 'I'll get Esteban down so we can treat him.'

'I can't! I can't touch a dead body! What are you asking me to do?'

'All right. Give me a hand with Esteban and I'll get a shirt. We'll need something quickly or he'll bleed to death!'

'Thank you, Antonio. I couldn't, honestly.'

'I shouldn't have asked you. Sorry!'

They laid Esteban flat on the ground and Antonio used his knife to open the fabric of Esteban's breeches near the wound and tore it away. He could see some small bone splinters in the gash where the ball had hit. He held his leg at the knee and above the ankle. Esteban winced but the bone, while chipped, was unbroken. 'That's a relief,' said Antonio. 'You are still bleeding quite badly but we'll soon stop that.'

Antonio selected the corpse of the leader because his shirt was almost completely unbloodied. He used his knife to remove a sleeve which he tied as tightly as he could around Esteban's leg slightly below the knee. 'That will halt the blood,' he said, 'and it probably hurts.'

'It's not too painful,' Esteban said, manfully accepting his bad luck in being in the way of the stray ball.

Antonio stopped the blood flow and saved Esteban's life. Carolina looked on, still shocked into silence at the unprovoked attack and the highwaymen's deaths. Antonio could still not believe he had killed two men. He inwardly thanked the amusing Major Gutierrez for so skilfully training him.

Somehow, and inflicting unexpressed pain on him, Carolina and Antonio managed to manoeuvre Esteban onto Antonio's horse. They all agreed that it would be better for him to ride Antonio's and that Carolina and Antonio would ride the younger animal. Despite the setback, they eventually reached El Carbonero.

The landlord of the dilapidated inn they stayed at helped Antonio carry Esteban in and up the stairs into a small bedroom. He said he didn't feel like a meal and that he could manage to get himself into bed. So they left him to settle in for the night. Antonio and Carolina dined together on the simple fare the landlady provided which they helped down with a glass of a local wine.

'I'm not sure about you, Carolina, but if you felt so inclined we could finish what we started in my bedroom in Segovia.'

'I'm really not sure, Antonio. I still feel shocked at what happened this afternoon. I'm still shaking.'

'I'm not going to press you, Carolina. If you don't mind, I'll retire now. See you in the morning at say eight o'clock? On second thoughts, I don't want to leave you in the drinking room here, so I'll wait until you're ready for your bed.' He put a slight stress on the word 'your'. There were only a few other men in the drinking room: no women, other than the landlady.

It wasn't long before they both went up. Antonio bent over and gave Carolina a surreptitious kiss goodnight. 'I've changed my mind, Antonio. Let's do that finishing off. It'll settle us both and we'll sleep better for it,' she whispered. They each looked around as they disappeared into Carolina's room.

Around mid-morning of the following day, Antonio and Carolina helped Esteban, still in considerable pain, onto his horse. He agreed that the quickest way to travel would be with Carolina in front of him, provided she could keep clear of his wound. They were then on the final stage of their long, if eventful, journey to Valladolid. They decided to make for Cuéllar and, after playing for a couple of days there, attempt to reach Valladolid in one further day's travel. The stop in Cuellar would help Esteban's leg to heal.

CHAPTER 11
Valladolid

'You two saved my life,' said Esteban as he perched on the edge of a stool in the first tavern they encountered inside the city walls. 'If you hadn't staunched the blood from my leg, Antonio, I'd be as dead as a pickled partridge.'

'We only did it because you are so good on the drums,' Antonio said. 'If we only relied on your singing we'd certainly have left you there!'

'Take no notice,' said Carolina. 'Antonio can be really horrible!'

They raised their glasses to each other, drank up and went in search of an inn near the centre of the town. They agreed, for reasons Carolina found difficult to understand, to find one as close to the Royal Palace as possible.

'How long shall we stay here?' said Antonio as they stood arranging their reservation at an inn, the Queen's Head and Crown, less than two hundred *varas* from the palace main entrance.

'At least a week,' said Esteban. 'Let's book for a week and see if we need to extend it later. Does that suit you, Carolina?'

'I'm just hanging on to your shirt tails. Yours and Antonio's. There is a lot of money in this town and we'll see if we can collect our share!'

They were all tired that night, if elated that they had completed their terrifying and arduous journey. The two men were relieved when Carolina decided to retire to her bed. They needed to discuss their tactics for obtaining the information Pedro wanted.

'She will be a burden to us now, Antonio. We need to part with her somehow.'

'I'm surprised at you saying that. We can surely find what we want to find whether Carolina is with us or not. We don't have to tell her what we are looking for. I can see advantage in keeping her on board. We are a more convincing band as a trio. No one would suspect us of spying on the palace as such an odd combination of players! We might even persuade the palace that we should perform in there, in front of the king. I'm not afraid to tell her to go. Believe me. I wouldn't want to because I like her. But I think we should keep her. She is an asset to us. When she becomes a liability, we get shot of her!'

'Hmm,' muttered Esteban. 'I think you're right? Let's keep her in the group. That way she won't suspect that we are on a special mission. But we will need to meet regularly like this.'

'I agree. In the meantime, what will we do tomorrow? We need to start gathering the facts.'

'Let's set up near the palace, as close as we can. That way we might find out something about the guards and how often they change.'

'If we perform well, they might even ask us in!'

'I'll drink to that.' The two of them emptied a couple more glasses of beer apiece and, arms around each other's shoulders, made their clumsy way up the stairs.

The three nervous looking players looked an odd sight as they set themselves up to play at a pitch they had located right opposite the palace in the Plaza San Pablo. Antonio stopped on the paving stones and looked around at this irresistible building. Its simple symmetry amazed him with its twin towers, one at each end of the structure, perched aloft a classical façade with its windows looking proudly over the square. In some ways it reminded him of the *Morisco* doctor's house in Guadalajara that the arsonist's fire reduced to a pile of smouldering rubble.

At that time of the morning, the square, which the palace seemed to look down upon, swarmed with civil servants, lawyers, church officials, councillors and various sundry workers making their way into the palace, chatting and arguing with each other and gesticulating as they made their points. Madrid was never this busy, especially since all these people had transferred from that once great city to enhance the economy of this one.

Antonio wondered where in this vast structure the king and queen's apartments could be and how they might have to penetrate it to discover them. Would they be given access through the main gates; would one of them have to enter in some form of disguise; or would they have to break in at night to explore it while it slumbered?

He noticed that guards were checking the papers of some of those going in. He dare not mention the fact to Esteban with Carolina there. Eventually, the crowd diminished as those who entered the palace to work were presumably at their desks interrogating their in-trays or wandering off to join crucial meetings on the affairs of state. This lull in activity prompted one of the guards to cross the square to talk to the three intrepid players. He waited a few minutes until they had completed their hearty rendition of 'Albuquerque, Albuquerque' in front of a couple of street vendors and two women who could have been whores.

'Good morning lady and gentlemen. Do you have a permit to play in this location?'

'Umm,' muttered Esteban. 'Do we need one?'

'Yes, you do,' said the guard, in a neutral tone.

'How do we get one?' asked Carolina.

'From the constable's office in the market place. They aren't open for permits today but they are the day after tomorrow. In the meantime, I have to ask you to move on, out of sight of the palace.'

'That's a blow,' said Antonio. 'We really need to be here.'

'Why is that?' said Esteban, stabbing his finger accusingly at Antonio and raising his eyebrows in barely concealed anger. It had struck him hard that Antonio had said the wrong thing in front of Carolina.

'If we want to impress the palace we need to perform in front of it. Right across the square and as close as possible. Don't worry. We'll get a permit,' said Antonio, hoping he had calmed the situation.

'Why get that worked up, Esteban. Antonio's right isn't he?'

Esteban had aroused Carolina's suspicions. It had perplexed her and she dwelt on it for the rest of the day.

'Why don't we move far enough away to be out of sight of the palace and start again? This way,' said Antonio taking control. The other two followed and within a few minutes they were playing, 'She stole my heart and threw it in the river,' a raucously funny ballad again by Vásquez.

While playing this piece Antonio could not help wondering when Pedro might appear. Would he spot them in the street or appear at night in the inn? Which inn could he be using? What would he think about Carolina and how would he react to her? Would he be alone or with others of his cohorts, some of those Antonio had seen sitting with him in Jac's tavern perhaps?

'Wake up, Antonio! Are you in some dream or something,' said Esteban, after they had finished the song and even after the modest applause had died away. 'What do you want us to perform next?'

'Let's chance "Isabel, Isabel". Carolina and I will start on our instruments and you and Carolina come in with the words.' The street audiences of Valladolid were just as amused as those in Ávila and Segovia to listen to the odd risqué number, punctuated by otherwise quiet, decorous renditions of other songs in their repertoire.

Antonio and Esteban were anxious to obtain a permit to play in the palace square, despite Carolina not really understanding why.

'We have to impress the palace, if we have a butterfly in hell's chance of playing in there, either to the king or queen or both! All it wants is some influential official to like us and make a recommendation,' said Esteban.

'We are earning good money just playing around the town and outside the square. What's so special about performing at the palace?'

'Come on Carolina. We can then say we've played there! It's quite an accolade!

'Oh, all right. But we don't want to pay much for the warrant.'

All three turned up at the constable's office on the morning of their fifth day in the city. The sergeant on duty didn't take to the odd looking group and asked them why he should give a permit to a group with two dwarfs in it.

'Who do you think you are? Complaining about me because I'm short?' flared Carolina, 'I bet a dwarf did your job, he'd let you in, even if you are tall and stupid!' Then she started to sob.

Esteban threw a dismayed look at Antonio. This woman whom Esteban didn't want with them anyway could have just destroyed their chances of getting a permit.

'I apologise for my friend,' said Esteban, as Antonio stooped to put a comforting arm around Carolina's shoulders. 'Tell me. Is there a rule which says dwarfs should not perform music on the opposite side of the palace square?'

'Not exactly,' said the constable. 'But I have the discretion to refuse permits if I think it best.'

'Now I'm getting impatient,' said Antonio. 'None of us is a criminal. We have spent five days in your town without any incident. Quite the opposite. We've earned good money here and your street audiences have enjoyed our work.'

'I have decided to issue with a permit for seven days only. Any complaints and I'll withdraw it. Understand? Come back in a week if you want it renewed. That will be two *reales*.'

'We accept that,' said Esteban, immediately after the man had spoken and before Carolina, who by then had quelled her tears, had chance to comment or even refuse.

Armed with the permit, they made their way to the square and chose a pitch next to the church of San Pablo, the clock of which struck ten, just as they arrived.

'That's useful,' said Antonio. 'We'll at least know what time to stop for lunch!' Esteban gave him a knowing look while Carolina completely missed its significance.

'Pity we're going to have to share with this lot,' said Esteban, looking away from San Pablo to his right where a motley group of beggars had placed their bowls and sat leaning against the wall chatting to each other.

'Wish the wind was blowing the other way. Don't they stink of piss! I wondered where the smell was coming from! How far is it to the river? Tell them to go and wash in it!' said Carolina.

'We must behave ourselves here,' said Esteban. 'That sergeant is dying for an excuse to cancel our permit and an unprovoked fight with a bunch of beggars would be more than enough.'

'All right! All right! I was only joking.'

The three of them provided hearty entertainment for people passing through the square, many of whom stopped to gaze in awe at this unusual troupe. Even some of the beggars came to see, as did some of the officials making their way from the palace to other court buildings in the town. The guards were positioned in pairs at each extreme end of the palace and at the central main entrance. Antonio and Esteban made careful mental notes of when they changed: every three hours, on the hour, from midday.

'What do you think about moving off to that tavern over there for a drink and something to eat?' said Esteban, one lunchtime.

'Not a good move to give up the pitch,' said Antonio. 'Someone else is sure to grab it as soon as we go.'

'I'm getting hungry, too,' said Carolina.

'Just a minute, I'll read the permit again,' said Antonio. Sure enough, the permit prohibited the consumption of food in the palace square by permit holders.

'What do we do then?' said Carolina.

'You and Esteban go and I'll stay here to watch over the pitch. Leave your guitar, Carolina. I'm not hungry but we can drink here so please bring me a pot of beer.'

The two went off, leaving Antonio sitting on the paving stones and leaning against the wall. He sat there contemplating his position as an agent and wondering again how they could achieve their aims. By then it was after the church clock had struck one and a number of officials had come out of the main gate of the palace, presumably to take lunch away from their workplace or simply to go for a relaxing walk. He shuffled his bottom on the uncomfortable stones and settled against the wall thinking he might fall asleep for a few minutes before the other two returned. Then he saw him. The well-dressed, clean shaven man, wearing the identical, flat-brimmed hat, was Pedro. But for the shirt and his light leather boots, he was dressed in the clothes he wore on their first encounter, in Jac's father's inn. But he was not alone. Walking with him were two other men both untidily cast, one taller but broad in the beam and shoulder, the other much more rounded but equally scruffy and having a distinctive mop of blond hair, flowing out from under a battered, brimmed hat. Antonio racked his brain but couldn't remember seeing them before. He looked at them through half closed eyes, without lifting his head. Thankfully, they didn't look his way as they continued walking across the square and stepped into a two-horse carriage waiting for them at the northeast corner. Antonio could see no reason for reporting this sighting to Esteban.

That night the three of them were dining together in their inn. They were conversing in a stilted, uncomfortable way as if something was troubling the three of them. Carolina thought that they seemed to be living from day-to-day with no future plans. They had been performing together for little more than two weeks and none of them had mentioned plans for the future. She worked up the courage to say as much.

'Well, you two. Where will we be in two weeks' time? Are we staying together? What do you think? You, Antonio?'

Antonio knew why she'd asked him first. She probably wanted to maintain their relationship.

'I'd love us to stay together as long as we can but who knows where we'll be in two weeks. We don't even know if our permit will be renewed. And very little else, come to that.'

'There is something you are avoiding telling me, Antonio, and I'm not happy with that.'

Three men suddenly appeared at their table, Pedro and his two scruffy cohorts.

'Who is she?' he said, pointing to Carolina.

She retorted back. 'Who are you? Whoever you are, you've got a nerve, being that rude to me.' Her anger managed to control her tears and her little figure remained seated so she looked quite vulnerable.

'This is a music group I've set up, so I have every right to know, especially if someone else has joined. Are you a member of the troupe?' said Pedro, sounding less aggressive, if not apologetic.

'Yes, if you want to know. I joined them in Ávila and have been with them since!' snapped Carolina, still smarting from his previous question.

Pedro soon saw the error he had made in being so blunt. He quickly realised, as had Esteban and Antonio, that there were distinct advantages in having Carolina in the troupe, especially if the two others hadn't told her about the true nature of their mission. Antonio and Esteban explained exactly the role that Carolina had been playing and that she had turned out to be an excellent guitar player and singer and that without doubt her joining them had contributed to their significant collection of cash from passers-by.

'I am sorry to have upset you, Carolina. That was bad of me but you took me by surprise,' he said. 'Please let me buy you all a drink. These are my two deputies, Jaime Fernandez and Flavio de Trujillo.' Antonio recognised these two rough looking characters as the two who had earlier been walking across the square with Pedro. Jaime was the taller one and Flavio, true to his name, the rounder, fair haired one with the hat.

Antonio and Esteban gave each other a perplexed look. Esteban had no idea that Pedro would appear in Valladolid and had never heard of any deputies. He knew other people worked for Pedro but had never before heard them referred to in such terms. He and Antonio each realised that, with Carolina present, this was not the time to question Pedro. So they stayed in the bar and drank and chatted until Carolina said an ambiguous, still offended, goodnight and took to her room.

'What's going on, Pedro? We didn't expect to see you until we returned to Madrid. We are only part way into our mission,' said Antonio, thinking that if he spoke first and sharply, he would be giving nothing away about knowing Pedro was already there in the town.

'I have had to change the plan. There have been more petitions to the king about ridding the country of us *Moriscos*. And according to backstreet rumour the king will be announcing his decision within a week. This didn't give you time to return to Madrid and for me to put a plan in place so, with the knowledge you have gained, we will be attacking the palace and capturing the king tomorrow.'

'Just a minute, not us surely. Even with your deputies here, there will only be five of us. What good will we be against the king's guard force?'

'Let me finish telling you about the plan.' He cast a wary eye around the drinking room. There were only a few men and one woman, left in the place and they were at the other end of the room. He still felt it necessary to lower his voice. 'I have assembled two teams of mercenary fighters, one of twenty five and another of sixty. We will attack the palace at the nearest change of guard to midnight. When do they change and how frequently?'

'Every three hours, on the hour, and we know there is a change at midday. So there should be one exactly on midnight. They change by the chimes on the San Pablo church, the one opposite the palace.'

'That's our decision then. We go in at midnight, tomorrow. The smaller group, each member of which will be armed with a knife and a matchlock pistol, will be headed by Jaime and will attack the front of the building. The second group, headed by Flavio, will go in at the back, which is likely to be the serving staff entrance. Sixty armed mercenaries will attack that part of the palace. No one will expect an attack at both front and back. Each man has been instructed to kill everyone he sees, guards included, until he reaches the king's apartments, wherever they are. They will kidnap the king and take him to a house I've rented off the Plaza Mayor. We then post a ransom note. We kill him if they don't agree to our terms.'

Antonio's heart raced. He had to go to the palace. That night.

His mind was in a state of agonised excitement. He had no intention of sleeping and just lay on his bed, fully dressed, thinking about how the palace would react to his warning. Who would be on duty? Who would he tell?

A church clock chimed one in the morning. The time had come. He had left a candle burning on his dressing table and by its flickering light loaded his snaplock. He took his dagger from the saddle pannier and put it in his sock sheath. He put on his jacket, took the candle and crept out of the room with the pistol concealed in his jacket. The stairs creaked as he crept slowly down them. He must not wake either of Pedro's thugs, Pedro or Esteban.

As he entered the drinking room he heard a voice he recognised.

'Who's that? Where are you going?'

He didn't expect anyone to be there at this time of the morning and still couldn't see who it could be. He thought it was the blond man, Flavio. 'It's me, Antonio Hidalgo. I heard my horse cry out from the stables and I'm going to check that she's all right. She's an old mare and sometimes gets disturbed, especially when it's an open stable and the night is cold.'

'I don't believe you,' said the voice. Whoever it was, appeared from a booth, carrying a lamp. Antonio confirmed it: the bulky, fair headed

Flavio stood before him, as if to block his path. 'You are going back to your room, now. We don't want you or anyone else creeping off to the palace. They'd pay you a fortune for what you know.'

'Just get out of my way. I'm going to my horse whether you like it or not. If you don't believe me you can come, too.'

'I'm not falling for that. Just go back to your room. Or you'll get this up to the hilt.'

A knife shone in the light of the man's lamp. Antonio was tempted to disarm him but realised he might have another weapon. He dare not use his pistol for fear of waking everyone in the inn. So he took his knife from his sheath and stuck it exactly where the man at the Alcázar armoury had told him. Flavio fell to the floor. The burning oil fell on Favio's clothes and set them alight. Antonio quickly dowsed them with his foot. He tested the man's breathing. He was dead in a small pool of his own blood. Antonio had no time to dwell on this, his third killing in as many weeks. He stepped over the body and went to the front door which he unlocked and left on the latch.

He made his way calmly but in almost total darkness to the palace which was lit by braziers on the walls. He looked behind him. No one had followed. He went up to one of two guards on the main entrance.

'I need to see the head of security, urgently!'

'At this time of the morning? You must be joking. Come back tomorrow, my lad!'

'Just a minute,' said the other. 'What do you want exactly?'

'I know of a plot to kidnap the king. Tonight. You need to thwart it.'

'Who are you?'

'I am Diaspora.'

'We must let him in, Marco. Now! The deputy is in his office. We may need to wake him!'

'You take him.'

The second guard ushered 'Diaspora' into the main hallway and along to the Head of Security's office. The deputy was asleep and snoring like a stuporous camel.

'Wake up, governor. We've got a problem. One of our special agents wants to see you. Says it's urgent.'

He snapped out of his slumbers. 'What is it?'

'A plot to kidnap the king. You know about it, I think?'

'Yes but only that there is a plot. Dreamt up by some *Morisco*. We don't know when it will be put into effect or what resources they'll be using.'

'I know exactly.' Antonio related the plan, precisely as Pedro had told him.

'We will have to move quickly. We didn't expect it this soon. We need to speak to the *Tercio* commander and the constabulary.'

'You'll have to rely on what I've told you. I need to be back in bed before a body is discovered in the inn. One of the kidnappers. I had to kill him or he'd have killed me!'

'Which inn?'

'The Queen's Head and Crown.'

'I know a way back through the stables. That way you won't be seen. If you can speak to the *Tercio* commander, you may be able to help with the tactics.'

'I'll stay.'

'Come this way.' Antonio couldn't follow the route they took. The deputy took them out of a side entrance to an adjoining building, through its pitch dark corridors, lit only by a lamp the deputy carried and then into another building that seemed to face onto a huge open area, possibly a parade ground.

'There is always someone senior on duty at the barracks. The alert state is high with this plot on the horizon. But I doubt that they've enough *tercios* to deal with it tonight.'

They knocked on a large door. Light was seeping underneath it and lighting the floor where they stood. 'Probably someone awake in there.'

'Come in,' said a gruff voice from within.

'Commander, this is one of our agents, Diaspora. He has information about the plot against the king. It will be executed tonight.'

'Not successfully, if I've got anything to do with it. Pleased to meet you, Diaspora. I know about your mission, of course. My name is Ambrosio Spínola, one of the king's military advisors and a general,' he said, slipping in the mention of his rank with undue modesty. 'If you'd like to relate to me what you know, we can start working out a strategy to deal with it.'

'First, let me say, I didn't expect to meet such a famous person, general. Congratulations on your victory at Ostende.'

'But that was over a year ago, my friend. And a frightening number were killed.'

Antonio repeated what Pedro had said at the inn.

'Eighty five of them? No!' said Spínola.

'Yes, twenty five at the back and sixty at the front. That's what they are saying.'

'We hadn't budgeted for that number. We haven't enough *tercios* here to deal with that many but let's think this through,' he said calmly, just as Antonio would expect of a senior military figure. The three of them sat until three in the morning, scheming and calculating how to scupper Pedro's plans.

The Head of Security's deputy took Antonio back into the inn, through the entrance near the stables. Antonio crept up to his room, undressed and fell into his bed. Despite this excitement driven night, he too fell into a deep sleep. He was woken by a banging on his door.

'Antonio. Come quickly. Flavio is dead. He's been stabbed.' The voice was quaking in fear and horror.

'Is that you, Esteban?'

'Yes, it's me!'

'I'm just getting dressed.'

Antonio stepped from the room into the arms of a frightened Esteban, whose arms didn't quite reach around his waist. 'Someone knows what's going on. I'm scared. It could be me next or you or Pedro. Or even Carolina, now she's one of us!'

'Has anyone called the crown constables?'

'Yes. There are two of them downstairs inspecting the body.'

'Is there a weapon, a dagger or knife?'

'They can't find anything. The poor man is lying in a pool of his own blood. I've seen him. His face is so twisted, it looks like he's seen the devil!'

'Where is Pedro?'

'Gone. God knows where. Can't be far away. He's got a job to do. The constables want to speak to him.'

'He must be a suspect. Maybe they had a late night row. Over payment, maybe. Who knows?'

'Where is Carolina?'

'I don't know, probably in her bed still.'

'I'll knock on her door. Best she doesn't go down and see the body. See you in a few minutes, in the kitchen?'

Antonio knocked on Carolina's door. His anxiety increased as even after knocking four times and waiting, Carolina did not respond. He realised that Pedro had upset her the night before but could see no reason for her to disappear. He stood wondering outside her door. As he did so, she appeared from downstairs.

'Antonio, have you heard? That man Flavio has been murdered. Brutally. He's lying in a pool of blood in the bar. The constabulary told me. I could not go in there with a body lying on the floor. Antonio, I'm terrified. I don't know what to do!' She then collapsed in tears, wrapping her arms around Antonio's waist.

'I'm so happy to see you. I was really worried when you didn't answer the door. Listen to me, Carolina. This is important. I can't tell you what is going on here but you must not worry. I do know what is happening. Stay with me and you will be safe. You will be tempted to ask questions but don't because I can't answer them.'

'Why not? I ask questions all the time.'

'Just do what I say, Carolina. Trust me!

'So what are we going to do now?'

'We go downstairs and go straight to the kitchen. We have breakfast and work out where we will set our pitch today. I have seen Esteban and he is fine. He'll meet us there. The man Pedro has gone somewhere and Esteban doesn't know where.'

All three, Carolina, Esteban and Antonio met in the kitchen for breakfast. They decided to return to their pitch in the square, next to the San Pablo church, and work there for the day. Pedro had not instructed them to do otherwise and had vanished so they felt that their only option was to perform somewhere in the town and where better than in the square.

They arrived there later than they had the day before, at about eleven o'clock. The beggars were just as voluble, even to the extent of coming up to them and chatting. They had never before seen a group with two dwarfs, one a singer and guitarist the other a drummer and singer, working under the instruction of a tall person who was the obvious leader. Eventually, the beggars left them and they began their day's performing. They started with 'Taking roses to my mother'. When they reached the second verse they were confronted by a strange sight. Groups of what appeared to be civil servants emerged from the main gates of the palace carrying bundles of papers. These functionaries scurried across the square and a group of them, talking urgently to their nearest colleagues, dashed out of each corner of the square, with a determination to deliver these papers as soon as they could. One of them, a short man wearing a light brown leather shirt and darker brown leather breeches approached the troupe.

'Have one of these,' he said, as he thrust a sheet of paper into the collection pot which the three had put on the paving stones in front of them. He then dashed into San Pablo church with the rest of his bundle.

'What was all that about?' said Carolina, looking up towards Antonio.

'Hand me the sheet,' he replied. She passed it to him.

'It is written by hand and says:

26 November, 1605,
By order, a curfew will be imposed this day on this town. Unless
specific permission has been given, the citizens of Valladolid
must be within their normal places of residence by 10 o'clock
tonight and remain there until sunrise tomorrow.
Signed, King Philip III and His Majesty's Court'

'Does that apply to us,' said Carolina.

'I would say so,' said Antonio.

'But we don't have a normal place of residence. We have no residence,' said Carolina. 'All we've got is a room at "The Queen's Head and Crown".'

'For the purpose of the edict, that is our residence and we have to be at the inn and within its doors by ten tonight.'

The colour drained from Esteban's face as he realised either that it was by some accident of chance that this curfew was to apply or that it was being imposed because the palace had somehow discovered that there would be an attack on it at midnight.

'What's the matter, Esteban? You look pale. Is there something wrong?' asked Carolina.

'Yes, I don't feel well. It must have been something I ate for breakfast. I need to get back to the inn. I'll see you later.'

Antonio realised that Esteban wanted to find Pedro and warn him that the palace must know about the attack. He wondered whether he would find him. Pedro had disappeared and none of the three had seen him since Flavio's body had been discovered in the drinking room. 'I wonder when he'll be back,' said Antonio, looking down at Carolina who looked puzzled and angry. 'There are some strange things going on here,' she said. 'I'm not happy.'

'Just stick with me. I said earlier that, if you do, you will have nothing to worry about. Everything will become clear very soon. Now, let's carry on playing, just the two of us.'

'All right, Antonio. I trust you and if you say I'll be safe, I will be,' she said, not with great confidence but more in the firm hope that he would protect her. 'Can I ask you a question?'

'Of course.'

'Can we sleep in your bed tonight? I'd feel safer there.'

The two of them had been playing until well into the afternoon before Esteban arrived back in the square. His white face and dour expression betrayed the state of his mind if not of his body.

'How are you feeling now,' said Carolina, 'after a rest?'

'Not good. I went back to my room and slept for a couple of hours. I woke up to a knocking on my door. It was the taller of Pedro's deputies, Jaime I think. He said he had been looking outside the inn for Pedro and when he came back into the drinking room the landlord told him that Pedro came back into the inn from where ever he went. He said that two crown constables interviewed him for a few minutes then arrested him for the murder of Señor Flavio. The landlord told him that they marched him off somewhere but didn't know where.

'I decided to try to find him so I found the constabulary and asked if someone had been arrested. They told me that a man called Hajib al-Asadi or Pedro, as he was also known, was being detained in the town jail. I went along to speak to him but they refused to let me in. They said he was under detention, charged with murder. Do you understand why I'm concerned, Antonio?'

Antonio didn't want to arouse Carolina's suspicions. 'Yes, I do. And I am, too. Where do we stand if Pedro is charged with Flavio's killing?'

'I just hope they release him. I cannot see why he would kill one of his deputies.'

'Not unless they had a major disagreement last night,' said Antonio. 'It would have to have been major and the result of a fight, maybe.'

The three of them settled down to finish an afternoon's playing in the square, Esteban pocketed the money that passers-by had placed in their pot and back they went to the inn.

Esteban could not relax and during dinner leapt up from his chair whenever anyone entered the room. 'What's the matter with you?' asked Carolina. 'Why can't you sit still? Antonio is happy to eat and talk amongst the three of us. Why can't you be?'

'I'm still anxious about Pedro. I cannot believe he killed Flavio. He'd have no reason to. They've arrested the wrong person.'

'Well, who else could have killed him?' asked Carolina. 'The other obvious suspects are you, me, Antonio and this man, Jaime.'

'You're not suggesting I killed him, are you? That's ridiculous!'

'No! I'm merely talking about possible culprits but... judging from your reaction...'

'I'm having no more of this destructive nonsense. I'm going to my room!' An enraged Esteban stood up from the dining table and left the remainder of his lamb chop and the two of them sitting there smiling at each other.

'He's not happy,' said Carolina. 'Why is he so anxious? I really don't understand what is going on here! Come on, Antonio! You can tell me!'

'I wish I could tell you,' he said. 'But you made a certain request earlier today. I think it was at breakfast.'

'I remember. What's that got to do with Esteban?'

'Nothing but in case it has, I think I should grant your request and invite you to share my bed. Just for the night!'

Antonio and Carolina were enjoying each other's company on Antonio's creaking bed. It was approaching midnight but neither was especially conscious of the time. 'You are such a considerate lover, Antonio. You are making sure that my pleasure is at least the equal of yours. I may even be taking more pleasure than you...,' she said. She quivered in ecstasy and her voice faded to silence.

At that moment they heard a shot fired. Then another... and another. Then a brief fusillade of shots rang out.

'My God, what's happening, Antonio? Did I dream that or was it gunfire?'

'It was gunfire, coming from the direction of the palace. Let's look out of the window.' He feigned surprise.

'You can't see it, can you, not from here?'

'You can see some of the front of it and part of the square, if you look between those buildings. One is San Pablo.'

They could see people moving in front of the palace. Some were lying on the ground. Others were coming towards the palace with muskets or harquebuses at their shoulders aiming at a group of people standing near the entrance.

'It looks as if the palace is being attacked by one lot of people and defended by another. I can't make out which is which. They have been shooting at each other, for certain.'

'I'm frightened, Antonio. Really scared!'

'No need to be. You are with me. You are safe, believe me. Whatever has happened, it sounds as if it's over. Let's settle down and try to get to sleep.'

The attack on the palace disturbed Carolina so much that despite cuddling up to Antonio she hardly slept at all. Antonio, on the other hand, trusted the strategy that the three men had worked out early during the morning before so slumbered moderately well.

He woke at daybreak to a loud knocking on a room door further along the landing. Carolina just stared as he slipped into his breeches and, naked from the waist up, looked out of the door. There he saw the diminutive figure of Esteban, his hands tied behind his back, being escorted from his room by two men who appeared to be constables. As they passed his door, Esteban yelled out. 'They've arrested me for conspiracy and treason. Why haven't they arrested you?'

'I've really no idea,' lied Antonio.

After breakfast that morning the two of them went for a walk, if only to settle the still nervous Carolina. The streets hummed with people talking excitedly about events of the previous night. Antonio held on to Carolina's hand. She needed him to help her overcome the shock of discovering that a man she worked with and trusted had been charged with being a traitor and complicit in an attempt, whatever its motive, on the person of the king. On their way back to the inn she asked him, remembering Esteban's questioning her about whether she was a *Morisca,* whether this was a *Morisco* attack on the king. Antonio said that he could see no other reason for it. She said she felt betrayed by Esteban and that his agreement to her joining the group was motivated by the need for anonymity which another short person could provide. She did not ask Antonio about his place in this plan. There were issues here she did not understand and probably never would.

As they entered the inn, the landlord called over to him. 'Señor Hidalgo, I have a letter for you. A messenger from the palace delivered it an hour ago.' He placed an envelope in Antonio's hand. 'Let's sit at a table, Carolina. This could be important. For each of us.'

Antonio broke the red wax seal and read the letter. It said:

27 November, 1605,
For the attention of Diaspora.
May I congratulate you on the success of your mission to thwart the Morisco *attack on the Royal Palace. Your role was of considerable importance. This was especially so when you informed the deputy Head of Security that the attack was imminent and of the number of attackers. I have been instructed to inform you that, as a matter of some urgency, you are required to return to Madrid where you will take further instruction from Algebra.*

You will be taken back by carriage, which will meet you at your hotel tomorrow at 9 o'clock in the morning. The horses will be changed frequently to expedite your journey. Your own horse will be returned at a slower pace. Please arrange a meeting with Algebra the instant you arrive.

Your colleague Carolina was, in her absence, tried in Ávila for the offence of theft. The charge against her was dismissed for lack of evidence.

You must destroy this letter today, by burning it.

Kindest personal regards and best wishes for a safe return,
Signed, The Corregidor of Valladolid.

Antonio felt a strong sense of pride at what he'd achieved. Then he chuckled. What a peremptory letter. What did: 'take further instruction' mean? What if he decided to return to working only as a musician? How were they going to return his aging mare and when? Could Carolina return, at least part of the way, with him? What if he arrived back at three o'clock in the morning? Would he see Algebra then? No, Algebra might have to wait a day or two.

'What are you grinning at?' she said as Antonio threw the letter into the fire.

'Sit tight and I'll tell you some interesting news. You have been found not guilty of theft from that shop.'

'How can you know that?'

'It said so in that letter.'

'I can hardly ask you to show me, now you've thrown it in the fire. How do I know that what you say is true?'

'Once again, you'll have to trust me!'

'Trust you?' she jibed.

'I'm afraid so!'

'Why did you burn the letter?'

'I had to. The writer of it told me to!'

'Couldn't you have shown me the bit that applied to me?'

'Sorry but no! What I haven't told you is I'm going to return to Madrid.'

'Does the letter say that?'

'What you have to understand, Carolina, is that there things I cannot tell you. My job has various elements which I cannot discuss.'

'Don't tell me. You are a spy and it was your job to stop the attack on the palace. Congratulations, Antonio. You probably succeeded!'

'I cannot comment on that. Do not jump to conclusions! If I was a spy, I couldn't tell you, could I? Well, if I did, I'd have to kill you! So I'm not going to say whether I am or I'm not. You can make your own mind up. What's more important, I am travelling back tomorrow. A carriage is picking me up outside the inn at nine o'clock in the morning.'

Carolina burst into tears. 'You can't leave me here, Antonio. I'll die!'

'Come with me, at least to Segovia. You could then go to Ávila. Now you know the result of the trial you might want to go back and start again there. Make up with your father who will be missing you badly.'

'So you don't want me to come back to Madrid with you?'

'Let me tell you, Carolina. This letter is telling me that I have an assignment waiting me in Madrid. It could mean that I have to travel to Barcelona, Salamanca, Cuenca, anywhere, even abroad. So, even if you came back to Madrid, I might have to leave you there, for however long, I wouldn't know.'

Carolina wiped her eyes. She realised that they could not continue as a duet music troupe and it took a little time for her to accept that. 'Does that mean we'll never see each other again?' she said, starting to sob again.

'No. I'll give you my address in Madrid and I'll take yours in Ávila. Either can then call on the other. Who knows when? But you are a strong and independent woman, Carolina. You can make your own living. You don't need me!'

'I'll have to think about that. I suppose I've got until Segovia to make up my mind,' she said, almost smiling. 'I may decide to come to Madrid whether you like it or not!'

The following morning they got up early, packed and were waiting in the main room downstairs when Antonio's carriage arrived. By then Antonio had been to the stables and bidden his horse farewell and a safe journey back to Madrid. He patted her on the nose. She gave him a look of betrayal. Carolina had never travelled in such a sumptuous vehicle. Nor had Antonio. They sat arm-in-arm on the back seat. They arrived in Segovia at nightfall and stayed in a tavern that the *corregidor*'s office in Valladolid had booked in advance. The following morning at breakfast, Carolina told him she had decided to return to Ávila. Tears ran down her face as she did so. Antonio helped her to load her things onto a wagon which would take her there. Antonio bent down to embrace this tiny yet large character of a woman before he waved her on her way. He climbed into his carriage which resumed its journey to Madrid.

CHAPTER 12
The king's absence

'What? They tried it last night? You must be wrong!'

'No, last night, Philip. Seriously. Damned audacious attack it was, too.'

'Tell me about it.'

'By the blood of Christ we were lucky, I can tell you. If it hadn't been for Algebra's man, Diaspora…remember?'

'Of course.'

'…we'd have been in deep trouble. He came to the deputy Head of Security's office yesterday at one in the morning. The Deputy took him to see Spínola. Diaspora told Spínola that the *Moriscos*, led by this group Diaspora had infiltrated, had brought forward their attack to midnight that night. At least that gave Spínola time to concoct a plan.'

'What about Margaret? She was there with the boy!'

'No. The first thing we did was to move the two of them to Benavente's. They went out the back way. The queen in disguise.'

'Good! Damn fools not realising I was up here hunting with you and the others! What actually happened then?'

The duke related the tale.

'Was anyone at the palace injured?'

'One of the guards was shot in the kneecap but apparently it was his own gun! Other than him, nobody but some of the women on the staff were badly shaken. Mainly by the sound of gunfire. But we'd told them what to expect and to stay upstairs and away from windows.'

'So what were their numbers and where are the attackers now?'

'Altogether there were eighty five. We killed fifteen, seriously injured about twenty and the rest are unharmed.'

'Pity!'

'The injured and the other survivors have all been charged with treason, possession of and discharging firearms and attacking the residence of the king. There wasn't room in the town jail so we've put them in the cells in the barracks. They're even less comfortable there! There are a lot for the courts to handle but the trials begin next week. We are fine for witnesses, mainly palace staff, *tercios* and the constables. The accused, if found guilty, will probably be sentenced to death. Their leader is in very serious trouble. He is charged with murdering his deputy the night before the attack. Stabbed him in the stomach. He denies it, of course.'

'Do they have the murder weapon?'

'No. Not that I'm aware.'

'Probably didn't do it then. Why kill your deputy? Anyone thought of that? Maybe, it was Diaspora! He could well have had an excellent motive. Trying to escape the deputy to come to the palace!'

'I think you're the only one to think of that Philip! We should keep that theory to ourselves!'

'Would have been self-defence anyway! Well, maybe! Diaspora deserves some form of recognition. I'd like to meet him and thank him. By giving Spínola time to plan, he probably saved the queen's life… and the boy's! Is there more?'

'I've no more to say on that topic, Philip, except to say that Diaspora is on his way back to Madrid. He's probably reached Segovia by now. I can get him back if you like, but with the best riders in the land, he'd be back in Madrid before they reached him.'

'Don't worry. Another time. My last point is that I want a show trial for the accused. I want the trial proclaimed in every hamlet, village, town and city in the land. Get every town crier in the land to report it. I don't want any other *Morisco* gang to make another attempt on me like that!'

'I'll fix that. The second item is that I'm arranging for Algebra and some of his *regidors* to meet you. You wanted some of the key people to put the case to you for transferring back to Madrid and I'm in the process of agreeing a date… towards the end of January. Might be in Ampudia.'

'Good. Make it as late as possible. And I'll need some convincing evidence before I agree to move.'

Part III

CHAPTER 13
A new challenge

Antonio stepped from the carriage which stopped right outside Doña Marta's. It was seven o'clock in the evening and just beginning to get dark. Antonio would meet Algebra as soon as he could in the morning. In the meantime he'd drop off his saddlebag, his violin and things and go to see Catalina.

He knocked on the door and waited. 'Antonio, it's you! I have missed you!' She planted a generous kiss on his lips. 'Thank you for the letter. You're back sooner than I expected! How did it go?'

'I'll tell you. At my place?'

'I'll get my coat!'

They lay naked in Antonio's bed after a boisterous reunion. Its violent intensity exceeded even Catalina's expectations. 'My God, Antonio, you haven't had it for that long, have you?'

'You'd be surprised! I've done it three or four times with a dwarf but that's all.'

'I'm going home, if that's what you've been up to.' She slipped her leg from under the blanket, and her foot onto the floor. 'A dwarf! You've really let me down!'

'No such thing. She is the most charming lady, a brilliant guitar player. She sings well, too, and can act!' Antonio called her bluff. 'But if that's what you want to do, I bid you goodnight,' he said, looking to the door. 'I can put up with a few sparks of jealousy but you are implying that I've done something abnormal like buggering a goat. A dwarf is a normal person. They have the personality, feelings, skills and are as human as the rest of us. In some ways more so. They would never harbour thoughts like that about tall people. She joined our little group and because she did probably reduced any suspicion that might have fallen on us.'

Catalina turned from being angry to looking sheepish. She lifted her foot from the floor, slid back into the bed and cuddled up to him. 'I'm sorry, Antonio. It was the shock. Of course dwarfs are as human as the rest of us. She is probably a very nice lady.'

'Don't worry, Catalina. Yes, she is. I wouldn't go with some tramp of a woman. She is far from that.'

Catalina had made herself sound unnecessarily prejudiced and realised as much. The easiest way out of the situation was to change the subject and she wanted to know more, anyway. 'Well, how did, you get on then?'

'Mission accomplished!'

'Surely, you can say more than that'

'Not much. But you've signed the oath so I can go further. I can't tell you what the point of the mission was or what part I played in it. Pedro's colleague, Esteban de Recalde, and I set out for Valladolid. We went via Ávila and Segovia so we could play in these towns and make some money.'

He told her about the meteorite, about Lupita de Pastrana, her father and how Carolina joined the group.

'This Lupita. Did you…umm?'

'No. Not at all. Nothing physical happened between us.'

'You're only saying that because of my reaction to your dwarf lady! You did her, too, didn't you, you rascal!'

'No, it's true! Trust me, I didn't touch her!'

'What else, Antonio?'

He mentioned the highwaymen and that he'd killed two of them. He explained how ashamed and disgusted he felt with himself for ending two human lives. He said he still felt a stabbing guilt. He should have shot to maim them, not to kill. He'd taken everything from them, their friends, their women and their possessions, all they had, in leaving them dead on the ground. He said how Esteban was accidentally shot and how between them, Carolina and he had saved Esteban's life.

'My God, Antonio. So you killed two and saved a life. You did well. Sounds like you did it all single handed. Those highwaymen were swine, attacking you and your two dwarf colleagues! You were more than justified in killing them. What happened in Valladolid?'

'Pedro turned up unexpectedly with two deputies, while we three were dining at the inn. Then they must have had an argument. Pedro was arrested for stabbing one of them to death. The constabulary took him and he's awaiting trial in Valladolid!'

'Holy Mother of the Lord! So you teamed up with a murderer then? I bet you didn't expect that!'

'Innocent until proved guilty, mind you. I'm sure we'll hear before long!'

'Shall we do it again... before I go?'

'Congratulations, Antonio. You were brilliant. The king is so impressed he wants to meet you at some time!'

'Thank you, Silva. It was an interesting baptism and I enjoyed most of it. I still lose sleep at having to kill three men,' he said, with his head bowed.

'Three! We are certain you killed one... but three?'

He told Silva about the attack on the road from Segovia to Valladolid and his persistent guilt over the killings.

'I had no idea about the highwaymen. You didn't mention it in your letter! But we thought you may have killed Pedro's deputy, Flavio de Trujillo. I believe that was the man's name.'

'I had to. He intended to stop me getting to the palace to tell them about the attack. So it was him or me. I stabbed him in the stomach.'

'Well done, Antonio.'

'Luckily I wasn't suspected of the killing. They charged Pedro with it and he's now awaiting trial, along with the rest of his gang of mercenaries. May ask you a question, Silva?'

'Please do.'

'He is charged with something I committed and I am unhappy about that. Is there some way we can ensure he is not found guilty?'

Silva de Torres chuckled. 'He's in such trouble for the attack on the palace, a charge of murdering one of his accomplices will hardly affect the outcome. He'll be hung or burnt at the stake anyway!'

'I still feel guilty about it.'

'Don't! If there is any doubt he won't be found guilty. What we mustn't do is introduce doubt where there may be none. What we don't want is suspicion to fall on one of his other so called accomplices, namely you! But I congratulate you, Antonio. You did a wonderful and courageous job! Are you ready for me to tell you about your next assignment?'

'Fire away! If I don't want it, I must resign from being an agent. Is that right?'

'Indeed. I am so concerned that you'll refuse, I cannot tell you what it is! So I am going to feed it to you, portion by portion,' he laughed. 'I think I've found you another partner, another musician. Well, I may have! He plays the flute and sings... Oh... and he plays the dulcian.'

Antonio's heart sank like a bucket in a well of water. 'Not Iago the Bad?' He couldn't believe what he was hearing. Of all three of the Wandering Chordsmen, Antonio liked him the least. In fact he hated his trouble stirring ways.

'I've not heard him called that. He is Iago Pizarro and he lives in an apartment in the Calle de la Pechuga, not far from you, I think.'

'It's off Calle de Toledo, just down from me. That's him all right. I've been to a few parties at his place, just after we set up the troupe. We called him that because he'd been to prison, for killing a man. You haven't made him an agent, have you?'

'No. Not yet but, depending how he works with you, I'll consider it.'

'Tell me, why did you think of him?'

'It's a long story so I'll keep it short. I was talking to my private secretary, a few days after you went to Valladolid. You've spoken to him several times. His name is Hector Brondate. I told him that you'd presented us with a little problem and I wanted his advice in solving it.'

'I caused you a problem?' said Antonio looking anxious and puzzled.

'A minor one, yes. I was determined to keep you as an agent but, because you resigned, rightly so, from the Wandering Chordsmen, we needed to find a working colleague for you when you returned. It so happens that Hector lives in the same apartments as this Iago and they met in the street outside the day before yesterday. Iago looked pretty miserable and told Hector that he'd been sacked from the troupe and was looking for another job or another partner. Hector put two and two together and told me. So I want you to approach this Iago and set up a new troupe with him.'

'But... I don't even like the man. I'd hardly want to work with him. Have you or Hector spoken to him?'

'No. I am keen for you to try working with him. The reason is simple. You are in effect a spy. This means you need cover. You are known as a musician and the best possible cover for you is to continue in that profession. So I want you to find an excuse to go to see him... or make contact in some other way, but that's what you should do. Within a day or two, preferably today, before he finds someone else.'

Antonio felt as if he had no choice but to contact Iago and propose to work for him. He'd think about how and when.

'What if he refuses? He probably doesn't like me either!'

'Let me know if that's what he does and we'll start again. Happy with that?'

'Yes, I'll do it!'

'Excellent!' He took two large strides around his desk, grabbed Antonio, who remained seated, by the hand and shook. 'Now for the next part of the subterfuge!'

Silva stepped back to the other side of the desk and sat back down. 'I said before that I would be feeding you the next assignment in fairly small doses. This is partly because I don't yet know what in precise terms it will be. Sometime in the not too distant future, I am going to see the king in Valladolid, with a number of the *regidors* here, to argue our case for returning his court to Madrid. I have to meet the *regidors* first so we can put a good case together. That's my instruction from the Duke of Lerma. He and I will be discussing your next mission. We have some, shall we say, fairly firm ideas about it but they are not yet entirely clear.

'However, in order for you to carry out that mission you need to meet another of our special agents. He'll probably tell you his actual name but his code name is Lusitano. He lives in the Calle de la Gorguera, in the fourth house on the right past the Convent of the Shod Carmelites. Do you know where I mean?'

'Yes, off the Calle de Pardo? The convent is on the corner?'

'Right. You've got it. I've arranged for you to meet him tonight, at six o'clock. His wife may even feed you! He'll tell you more.'

'Tonight?' Why can't you tell me?'

'Yes, tonight. I'd prefer to leave it to him! Knock on the door, tell whoever opens it that you have an appointment. If it's a man ask him his name. If it's a woman, ask to speak to the man of the house. He will say he is Lusitano and you must introduce yourself as Diaspora. Got that?'

Antonio could see no reason for all this secrecy. Did Silva know what this character Lusitano would be saying or doing? Had Silva briefed him? Or were there still some unknown factors that Silva and Lusitano had yet to finalise before the meeting. He still wasn't sure about being a spy. One assignment was enough. He'd already risked his life, what three or was it four times?

'Here, take this,' said Silva, handing him a leather purse. 'There's your bounty. You really did well, Antonio, and higher authorities than me think so, too!'

Antonio's mind spun as he walked back to the Calle de Toledo from Silva's simple office in the Alcázar palace. The cold, dry wind had cleared the air of the morning smells and it hung only with the sweet smell of fresh horse urine and droppings. He had not enjoyed working with Iago before and he dreaded having him as his sole working partner. He'd told Silva that he'd go to see him and he'd do that first thing in the afternoon, after a modest lunch. As for this Lusitano character, he seemed a total mystery, apart, that is, from having an apparently generous wife. Antonio speculated about what the meeting with this shady individual could be about. Could he be involved in some illegal activity, smuggling perhaps, or prostitution. Could he run some of the town *mancibías*? But surely Silva wouldn't have any connection with these establishments and wouldn't expect him to, either. Did he have some special skill that Silva thought he'd need as a spy, particularly for the new mission? Yes. That was it. He was a master spy of some kind. An expert at infiltration. But Antonio had already infiltrated a *Morisco* group. So what more could be learnt?

Antonio pushed open the door to The Silversmith tavern, stepped up to the bar and ordered himself a large beer. He stood there, downed it in two or three hefty gulps and ordered another. He noticed a peculiar smell in the place and at first couldn't work out what it could be. Then he realised it was gun smoke. Someone had discharged a pistol in there, not that long before he entered. He looked around the cavernous drinking area while thinking about ordering a beef or pork pie or a bread and dripping roll for his lunch. Then he spotted him. Iago was sitting at the back, looking sorry for himself, sipping at a shining glass of wine and poring over some documents which were spread over the table in front of him. Could this be a lucky coincidence or should Antonio pretend not to notice him and go around to the Calle de la Pechuga a little later, after giving Iago time to finish his drink and his reading. No he'd speak to him then and there.

'Iago, how are you? Why are you drinking alone? Where are the rest of the troupe?' as if in total ignorance.

'Haven't you heard? I've been fired?'

'What happened?'

'It's not a good story. We were playing at the Príncipe a couple of weeks after you left. We were accompanying a play by Lope, The Dancing Master, and when we were playing in the third act, an actress fainted. She fell to the floor in a heap. I went across the stage to help her.

I touched her chest to feel her heart beat. The audience shouted out that I was assaulting her but I wasn't. The theatre manager came across the stage and thumped me in the chest and told me to leave. Carlos and Josep sided with the manager and, although they couldn't see what happened, they sacked me. Honestly, Antonio, I didn't try to touch her breasts. I was looking for a heartbeat. I thought she may have died.'

Antonio didn't know what to think. He could not judge Iago. He knew full well about his crimes and their punishment but whether he'd assaulted this actress or not he really couldn't say. So he decided to give him the benefit of the doubt. To do otherwise would not be the best way to start a new working relationship.

'I can't believe you'd have assaulted anyone, let alone an unconscious actress. Have you been charged with anything?'

'No. That was one of the conditions. If I left, there and then, I wouldn't have to face a court.'

'So you're looking for work?'

'I've been doing some street playing in the markets but I haven't done well. Any ideas? I suppose you're still working solo, aren't you? Shall we work together? How do you feel about that?'

'Yes and no. I ended up in a duet, then a trio, then a quartet then back to a trio. That fell apart in Valladolid and now I'm back on my own. So yes, we could earn a good crust working together. Why not?'

'Valladolid? Really?'

'I'll tell you about that some other time!'

'Start tomorrow?'

'Not tomorrow but the day after. Say, nine o'clock in the Plaza Mayor. You bring your dulcian and I'll have my violin. We can take it from there! Another thing, can I smell gun smoke in here?'

'Yes about an hour ago two men were arguing about a whore. I didn't hear the argument but one of them shouted something like, 'I wouldn't want her after you'd had your way with her, you *Morisco* scum.' The other man took a gun from inside his jacket, fired it at the ceiling and ran out. Everyone was so shocked that no one chased the gunman and he must have escaped.'

'Amazing! I often wonder what's becoming of this town. If people can't settle an argument without firing a gun, something is seriously wrong. Still, what I think won't change anything… See you the day after tomorrow then.'

Antonio walked from the Calle de Toledo to the house in the Calle de la Gorguera. He didn't know that part of the town that well but recognised the Shod Carmelite Convent of Santa Ana on the corner as soon as he saw it. He turned up the street, passed the convent where several novices were playing a ball game in the street, threw a stray ball back at one of them and counted the houses past the convent to the right. He stopped outside of the fourth which backed straight onto the road. Its outer wall leant forward as if to shelter anyone walking by. He thought he could see the silhouette of a woman looking out of an upper window. He looked up for a second or two and went to knock on the door. The absence of a knocker forced him to bang his fist on the bare wood. He stood back a *vara* and waited. A minute later the door opened and a friendly face greeted him.

'Señor, welcome to our home. May I ask you name?' The smiling man looked each way up and down the street, as if to indicate that Antonio should stay silent until they knew that the street was clear.

'Diaspora.'

'I am Lusitano. Come in quickly.'

It was beginning to get dark by then and the house was barely lit by the odd candle and oil lamp. His eyes adjusted to the poor light and he followed the man down the hall and into a drawing room lit mainly by a wood fire in a large, open hearth. A pot of stew hung precariously from a hook over the fire. It smelled like a pork and lentil broth of some kind, flavoured with a herb which Antonio couldn't identify. Despite being poorly lit, the house exuded a comfortable, homely feel, probably because of the flickering flames which licked the sides of the stew pot. Two wooden, double seat sofas sat, one each side of the fire, facing each other. The ends of them were so close to the fire that their arms must have been hot, almost to the point of smouldering.

'Have a seat,' said Lusitano, holding out an arm towards the sofa to the right of the fire. Antonio sat but his host remained standing his back to the source of heat.

Antonio placed himself as far from the fire as he reasonably could. 'Thank you.'

'So we are in the same profession,' said Lusitano, smiling broadly.

'Are you a musician, too? What do you play?'

'No! I'm a spy. Same as you!'

'Of course,' said Antonio, realising how stupid he had been but still not feeling much like a spy. 'I've been sent here with very little information, other than your code name and your address, of course. I'm sure you'll be telling me more. Any idea why Algebra sent me here? I'm not sure whether he was playing some sort of game or whether he had some good reason for leaving it to you to explain.'

'I've been doing this for a long time,' said Lusitano, stepping with his hands behind his back to and fro in front of the hearth. He paused for a moment before his next statement. 'There is an aphorism in our business which says, do not give information until it is needed. That's because it can be abused. I'm not suggesting for a moment that you would abuse anything Algebra told you. Maybe it's that little rule he had in mind. There is another which says, information should be given only once, preferably by its source. I suppose you didn't need to know about me before we met; and I am probably the better person to inform you.'

Lusitano possessed a substantial frame and stood a full six *pies* tall. He was much older than Antonio, probably in his early forties. He wore his hair long, almost to his waist, and tied behind his neck. It was hard to see the colour of his hair or clothing but his shirt was cream or white and tucked into his breeches. Even in this light, his skin seemed quite dark.

'Tell me, Lusitano, if you can and are willing, why am I here? Why has Algebra sent me to you and no other?'

'Before I do, permit me to ask you, would you like to dine with us? My wife cooks this wonderful pork dish which I'm sure you can smell. She would love you to stay for a meal. There is much we need to learn about each other.'

Antonio wondered what they so urgently needed to acquaint themselves with. Surely, it couldn't take the whole evening. 'Yes. Thank you for inviting me. I'd be delighted to dine with you.'

'That settles it then,' he said smiling infectiously. He then left the room, presumably to tell his wife that they would have an additional diner that night. In no more than a minute he returned and resumed his discourse. 'Algebra has sent you here for one specific reason. He won't have told you that I am a merchant. A trader. I export many different types of goods and products. All to different countries around the Mediterranean. My main importer is the Maghreb.'

'I still don't understand. Does he want you to give me some form of employment?'

'No. He wants me to show you how to trade.'

'I'm none the wiser now. Did he tell you why I needed your instruction?'

'No. That's as far as he went. I have to teach you all the detail, as if you are actually becoming a merchant.'

'When do I start? Is there a timetable? And when would I finish?'

Antonio was becoming frustrated at the fact of this almost total stranger knowing more about his future activities than he did.

'He insists that you fit this teaching in with your normal job. He doesn't want anyone else to know you are having it. Now let's go through for dinner.'

Lusitano escorted Antonio into a dining room at the rear of the house. The room concealed most of its features in the half darkness. Only two candles, placed one at each end of the table, illuminated it. So Antonio, even though his eyes scanned it, could barely see its size or any of its content or shape. The two of them sat on opposite sides of the table. Lusitano poured Antonio a cup of red wine. His wife appeared from the drawing room where she had filled two large plates from the cauldron over the fire. As she placed them on the table in front of the two men, Lusitano introduced her. Her eyes lit up in the candlelight as her husband said her name: Ishraq Alsulami. Antonio struggled to contain a gasp: a *Morisca*. Lusitano must also be a Moor. Perhaps he was of pure Spanish blood but had married a Moor. Surely, he couldn't be an agent and a Moor. She was much shorter than her husband but equally welcoming. Her dark dress extended down to her ankles and she wore a dark, probably purple veil. After placing the plates on the table, she went into the kitchen for some bread and some green beans.

'Ishraq will not be dining with us. She will eat in the kitchen and join us later. You have a lot to learn, my friend. In order to be a successful exporting merchant you have first to learn how to spot a product you can make money on. And that can be difficult.'

'I see,' said Antonio, not wanting to be plunged into the depths of learning at their first encounter. So he thought he'd change the subject. 'Tell me, Lusitano, what is you real name?'

He came straight out with it. 'Tariq Alabdari. You may be surprised to hear...I'm a *Morisco*!'

'I am surprised. How did you become a special agent without having pure Spanish blood?'

'Your colleagues are clever people. The further up the hierarchy they are the cleverer they seem to be. It was the brainchild of Philip II to have some of us serving him as spies. The price is that we spy on our own people. But Ishraq and I are true *Moriscos*. We don't go at the dead of

140

night to some secret mosque to pray to Allah. We go to Christian churches and pray to your God, his son and the Virgin Mary. Don't ask me how difficult it was to change from Islam to being Christians. Poor Ishraq became so unhappy she almost committed suicide. Then when we were at our lowest, at the depths of our misery, we met the priest at San Marco, our parish church. He told us that, while we and the Christians had different prophets, you have Jesus and we have Mohammed, we both worship the same god. That sufficed and we both became Christians. We were baptised within six months. We lost many of our unconverted *Morisco* friends who regard us as traitors and infidels.'

'What happens to you, then, if as they are saying, the *Moriscos* are expelled?'

'We stay. We have an agreement with the king that secures our future here, in Spain. If anything happens to one of us the other stays. It's as simple as that!'

'Do you have any offspring?'

'Yes. A daughter.'

'Would she stay, too?'

'You have hit on a sensitive nerve there, my friend. The answer to your question causes Ishraq and me much anguish. It is that the protection we have doesn't extend to her.'

'Does she live in Madrid?'

'Yes, in the Calle de la Cruz, just up the road and to the left. So not far away. She is a nurse at the General Hospital. If we stayed and she had to go, it would destroy us. We might even throw it all in here and go with her. But don't let's dwell on that. My view is that these expulsions will never take place. There is too much at stake.'

Having almost driven the man to tears, Antonio changed his line of questioning. 'How long have you been an agent?'

'Since '92. So about thirteen years, I suppose. I can't say I've enjoyed every moment, but it's not for pleasure,' said Tariq.

'It's still all new to me and I have to admit to enjoying the tension, the risk and the excitement,' he said, chuckling so as to bring a little light-heartedness into the conversation. 'I suppose Algebra told you about my mission to Valladolid.'

'Yes. I believe congratulations are in order. And you impressed the king!'

'It went well, I think but I'm none too happy about having the blood of three men on my hands. My consolation is that if I didn't kill them, for certain they'd have killed me.'

Antonio gave Lusitano an account of the incident on the road to Segovia and explained how Carolina joined them. He hoped that the more he revealed about his mission, the more Lusitano might reveal about his.

'You did well. There's no doubt at all,' said Lusitano, smiling.

'What about your missions? Are you free to tell me about any of them?'

'Umm… difficult question. But I can tell you in general terms. They mainly use me to spy on the *Moriscos*. You won't find that surprising. I have to pretend to be one and they fully accept me, mainly because of my Moorish name. You will know that there are tens of thousands in Granada and I've been there several times, mainly to find out what plotting and planning they are doing. I've also been sent to Valencia where they are relied upon to work the land.

'But some of my most challenging assignments have been abroad. They've sent me to Italy twice and to France. One of my worst experiences was over their wish to send me to Constantinople. It was in the reign of Sultan Murad III. Philip II thought he could do anything after we won at Lepanto. Anyway, they wanted me to go to Constantinople to see if I could find out about future plans the sultan might have to expand west along the coast of the Maghreb. It seemed much too far to expect me to travel there and too risky to my life. It would have taken months by land and sea and pirates are rife in those waters. Fortunately, my wife had fallen pregnant only three months or so before so I used this to tell them I'd rather not go.

'I realised that I had put my position as an agent at risk but I decided that I'd take a chance. Luckily for me, they found a willing *Morisco*. Apparently, they settled on a huge bounty. So he went. Unluckily, while on his way back, and while crossing the Aegean Sea, there was a bad storm and the galley he travelled on capsized. He was never seen again. We all did our best to comfort his distraught widow but two weeks after she heard of his presumed death she stabbed herself through the heart.' Lusitano became quite emotional while telling this story.

'I can understand your distress,' said Antonio, looking away from Lucitano. 'But I am reassured to hear that it is possible to turn down an assignment.'

142

'Take care, Antonio. I didn't exactly turn it down. I just told them I'd prefer not to go… and I gave my reasons. My luck was in and they accepted what I said.'

Just as Tariq finished speaking, his wife appeared to clear their dishes from the table. She smiled gratefully when Antonio told her how much he'd enjoyed her cooking. They each said they would take up her offer to bring them some oranges and grapes which, still smiling, she went back to the kitchen to fetch.

'Is there anything else you'd like to ask me?' said Tariq, peeling an orange and stopping to speak before putting a couple of pieces in his mouth. 'If you can't think of anything right now, you will have plenty of opportunity over the coming weeks.'

'Just one question. Do you trust Silva?'

'Umm… my friend. I have no reason not to trust him. And I've been dealing with him for almost five years now… since the king transferred responsibility for us Madrid agents to him from the Head of the Council for State Security. When they deserted us and went to Valladolid. My advice is to trust him until you believe you can't.'

Tariq had fascinated the young Antonio who agreed to see him the following day at ten o'clock in the morning, not at his house in the Calle de la Gorguera but outside a property in the El Rastro, the commercial district of the town. He had enjoyed the meal and the company and, after bidding him and his wife good night, set off from the house to his apartment in Doña Marta's house.

By the time he left Tariq's house it must have been ten o'clock at night. It was dark and cloudy. It took several minutes for his eyes to adjust to the uncompromising blackness. The only light available came from the windows of houses which overlooked the street, the odd stray flicker of a candle or an oil lamp, meant only to illuminate the inside of the house, not the street outside. Antonio had brought his dagger with him, in case he encountered any problems in the enveloping darkness of his return to Doña Marta's.

He walked to the right at the bottom end of the Calle de la Gorguera onto Calle Pardo opposite the Convent of Santa Ana. He knew the route quite well and could make out the familiar if barely distinguishable buildings. As he progressed through the Plazuela del Ángel he could hear an uneven clicking noise which seemed to be coming towards him. He located his dagger in its calf scabbard. The noise became louder as it came nearer to him and he approached it. 'Good evening,' said a disembodied voice.

He immediately realised that a blind man was walking right by him on the street, tapping a stick on the buildings so as to find his way. Antonio's heart slowed back down. 'Good evening to you, señor,' he said in mild relief.

He crossed Calle Atocha and started to pick his way along the Calle Barrio Nuevo towards Calle de Concepción, to join the Calle de Toledo. It was almost total darkness and he felt like that blind man as his eyes ceased their ability to discern even the largest objects. As he rounded the slight bend, a gentle light from an elevated window showed him that he was walking almost in the middle of the road. All he could hear was his own footsteps. He felt solitary and vulnerable but was comforted by the knowledge that he could quickly access his dagger. Then he heard it, a sound in an alleyway to the right. He stopped to listen and heard it repeat the same anguished message. A female voice was groaning, almost its last desperate breaths. 'Help me! Help me!' it said, its strength reduced to a whisper.

'I'm here and coming, now!' said Antonio.

Antonio made his way up the dark alleyway. He bent over to feel his way and to ensure he did not tread on the source of the frightened voice. He dreaded to think what state she would be in. He flinched as he touched her body. The woman was lying on the ground clutching her stomach. 'You are safe now. I'm here with you.'

'Thank God!' she cried and began to whimper. 'I've been attacked.'

'I know you, don't I?' said Antonio.

'And I think I know you.'

'It's you, Francisca de Polanco. Whatever's happened?'

'Antonio,' she said, and began to cry weakly as if even crying was sapping her strength. 'I was walking back home from my friend's house in the Calle de la Merced when some men attacked me…' Her voice faded as she passed out.

'Wake up, Francisca. Please wake up!' He took her by the shoulder and shook her gently. He shook her again and she came back round.

'I'm going to carry you home,' said Antonio. 'I'll pick you up and sling you over my shoulder. Try to keep talking. It'll take about ten to fifteen minutes to reach your house.'

Francisca carried rather more weight than her sister so Antonio struggled to lift her onto his shoulders but manage he did and they set off in the darkness.

'I'll try to avoid bumping into anything, but it's so dark here, I can hardly see at all. Are you all right up there?' He wanted to keep her talking.

'Yes but I feel as if I could pass out again,'

'Just keep talking, Francisca. About anything. Whom did you visit today?'

'My friend Inés. She works in the market and buys my purses. I had a meal with her and her husband. They are a nice couple.'

'Did you see who attacked you?'

'No, but there were at least two of them, probably three. They kicked me in the stomach before they went. I screamed out otherwise I'm sure they would have raped me.' She started sobbing again.

'We're in the Plazuela de la Leña now. There's the last embers of a torch on the wall of that building. Oh and another over there! That's better.'

'I think there was a pageant played here tonight. Must have been left from that.'

'At least I won't be knocking you into the walls now!'

'I think I'm feeling better now, Antonio. If you put me down I can walk from here.'

Antonio slid her to the ground. What welcomed relief. Within a few more minutes they were walking past the side of the San Felipe Convent and crossing the road in front of the Polanco's house in the Calle Mayor.

Francisca unlocked the front door of her parents' house. Señora Díaz ran down the hall sobbing and into her daughter's arms. 'Where have you been Francisca? We expected you three hours ago. Are you hurt? You look terrible!'

The señora took her daughter by the arm, led her into the drawing room and sat her in a chair.

'Tell me what has happened.' At that moment, Catalina entered the drawing room and didn't know whether to smile or grimace at the sight of Antonio, sitting on the sofa and tenderly holding her sister's hand. She stayed silent as if to await an explanation.

'They attacked me, Mama. Three street robbers and shoved me up an alley off the Barrio Nuevo. They stole my purse. I thought they were going to rape me. One of them threw me on the ground. Something disturbed them. One of them kicked me four times in the stomach. Then they ran off. I think I must have passed out. I shouted every time I heard someone near. No one came. It got darker and darker and I felt I was passing out again. Then I thought I'd shout out one more time before I did. So I just managed to call out. A nice man came to help me. It was Antonio! Just in time!'

Francisca's smiling mother went over to Antonio and planted a kiss on his cheek and thanked him. Catalina shed any jealous doubts and joined in the celebration. 'Well done, Antonio. You could have saved a life!' She decided not to say it would make up for one of those he took.

'You should report the incident to the constables' office, tomorrow. In the Puerta de Guadalajara. You never know, they may have a number of similar cases to investigate. Francisca's evidence could be crucial.'

'But I didn't even see them.'

'Yes but you were attacked between nine and eleven o'clock and that could be important information.'

Antonio said his goodbyes and walked the rest of the way to his rooms. He wondered, as he laid in bed, what tomorrow and his time with Tariq would bring.

CHAPTER 14
The merchant of Madrid

Antonio arrived at the agreed time outside of the building at the southern end of El Rastro. An odd smell pervaded the morning air. He sniffed a few times before he recognised it: blood. He could not be standing more than fifty *varas* from the town slaughter-house. They started killing cows and sheep there early in the morning and he could smell the sanguine already let. He knocked and tried the door of this unprepossessing building, which opened on its squeaking hinges into a cavernous room that must have extended into at least two of the adjacent buildings.

Antonio walked in. He could not believe his eyes. As far as he could see, the floor of the room was lined with rows of shelves which extended up to the ceiling. They reached from the front wall to the back. They were stacked with all manner of goods: pots and pans, shovels, hammers and pick axes; rolls of fabric in many colours and patterns; clothing: dresses in a range of sizes and hues, breeches in leather, suede, canvas and cotton; shirts mainly white but also in cream, brown and black; boots and shoes for men and women, mainly leather but also canvas and pig skin, handbags, shopping bags, purses; furniture: tables, sofas, mirrors, wardrobes, all stacked or standing like sentries on the floor; and wines: casks of wine, barrels of wine, large glass pitchers of wine, skins of wine, bottles of wine, all labelled by type and volume.

As Antonio looked dumfounded at this Aladdin's cave of goods and products, Tariq appeared from behind one of the racks of shelves. 'Antonio, good morning. I'm sorry I wasn't at the door to greet you! This is my warehouse. I hope you like it.'

'I cannot believe it, Tariq. There must be thousands of *ducats* worth here. What will you do with it?'

'Come to the back, into my office, and I'll explain it all to you.'

They walked to the back of the warehouse. They passed a number of Tariq's staff, moving the goods onto or off the shelves, onto or off carts they pushed from place to place in the warehouse. Antonio was surprised at the lack of windows. Tariq's men had lit oil lamps, not just attached to the walls but suspended from the shelves. The whole place glowed in light.

'Come in,' said Tariq, beckoning Antonio towards a chair opposite a small desk. The office displayed an easy modesty: there were no signs of the extravagance that Antonio would associate with a successful businessman, if indeed the display of the vast spectrum and volume of goods which Tariq stored here indicated the level of his success. 'Have a seat.'

'So, what are you going to tell me, Tariq?'

'I've thought about this and I'm going to give you three major lessons. I've told Algebra what I propose and he agrees. Today we are going to discuss buying. The second is about selling and distribution. Then, thirdly, I'm going to tell you about exports, the key to everything I do. Everything you see here is sold abroad, from the birch stick yard brooms to the kegs of Malaga beer and barrels of tempranillo from the Duero valley. Nothing here is perishable, except some of the more durable fruits and vegetables. Perishables don't travel well.'

'Is that the first lesson?' teased Antonio.

'Very amusing! I hope that doesn't mean you're bored!'

'Not at all. Just puzzled. I still don't see where all this is leading.'

'I'd tell you if I knew! Now we talk about buying. The basis is price and volume but you also need to think about storage and turn around. So you can see immediately that you can't look at buying alone.'

'So where do we go from here?'

'Let me take you back out into the warehouse.' Tariq led the way to the far side where a number of wooden barrels were stacked from the floor almost up to the rafters. Antonio followed meekly, still wondering what this could possibly be about.

'What do you think is in those barrels?'

'Beer, wine or fruit juice?'

'No. Olive oil. From the olive groves east of Seville. How much do you pay for a quarter of an *azumbre* of it? You probably don't know.'

'About four or five *maravedís*?'

'Usually about that. Well, I bought that lot for one and a quarter, that's four an *azumbre*, a quarter of what you paid. So if I can sell it for twelve an *azumbre*, I've tripled my money! And that gives the retailer a profit of four! Good, isn't it? There are about ten thousand *azumbres* there so that lot's worth a profit of eighty thousand *maravedís*. More than two hundred *ducats*. A lot of money, my friend!' Tariq rubbed his hands and smiled gleefully at Antonio.

'I think I can see a problem with that,' said Antonio. 'That assumes that your buyer, whoever and wherever he is, collects it from here. If you have to deliver it, there is a transportation cost.'

'Brilliant, Antonio. You are not bored after all. You are thinking about what I'm saying. And can you think of other costs?'

'Well...I suppose it costs money to store it here. These men of yours have to be paid. Who pays for transporting it from the olive groves?'

'I can see I'm going to make a good merchant of you, my friend. You've learnt more than most people know already and you've only been here two minutes! Any other points you want to make? Any questions?'

'Just one point really, those barrels of olive oil are very bulky and heavy. If you are going to make a lot of money, say from one wagon load of goods, don't you want to buy goods with greater value for the *libra*?'

Tariq's laugh sounded like an elephant blowing down its trunk. 'I'll be handing over my job to you next week! Come over here. I want to show you something really special which may impress you.' Tariq took Antonio back to his office. 'Sit back down again,' he said, indicating the same chair as before. He then took a key from a pocket in his breeches and walked towards a cupboard mounted on the wall. He opened the cupboard with the key. Inside was another cupboard, a metal safe, protruding from which were a dozen levers. Tariq took a piece of paper from the same pocket and referred to what was written on it to carefully position the levers on the front of the safe. After he had clicked them into their various different positions, he pulled a handle by the door of the safe which then swung open. He then took the oil lamp placed at the front of his desk and called Antonio over to look inside.

'See those pieces of jewellery. They have been made by a friend of mine in the Platería. I export them. Between us we make a fortune. There are diamond brooches, gold rings, a set of earrings and a necklace made of gold and decorated with diamonds and emeralds. There are rubies, amethysts, opals and tourmaline. All the kinds of gems you can think of. You can imagine that wherever you are selling them, they take up so little space, that taking jewellery is free! The risk of course is theft. And by the way, Antonio my friend, I want you to promise me that you won't tell a soul that these gems are here.'

'I promise. They are safe as far as I'm concerned! But only if you give me one of those sapphire tiaras for my lady!'

'That will be a pleasure, my friend. You give me two hundred *ducats* and you can have one for nothing.' They both laughed.

By the time they'd finished the day's lesson, Tariq had explained the intricacies of buying goods from a whole range of producers from olive farmers, wine growers, sheep farmers for their wool, fabric makers, potters, makers of pots and pans, furniture, clothing, including shoes and boots, gunsmiths to clock makers, makers of shovels, picks and axes, wood turners, coopers, wheelwrights, gunsmiths and even from musical instrument makers. The list could have been endless but Tariq knew when to stop.

He impressed Antonio most with the knowledge and confidence he seemed to have in his individual suppliers. He knew them by name and character to the extent that they could rely on him; and him on them. He ended by mentioning something that quite surprised Antonio: it was that he was one of only very few exporting merchants in Madrid. The city was a net importer, even in the dire state of its current trading.

'That's all for today, my friend. I can't expect you to take in more. Let's go back to my house and my wife will feed us!'

Antonio reluctantly took up the offer. He didn't want to misuse Tariq or Ishraq's hospitality. But on the other hand, this was a further opportunity to learn more about this interesting man and his wife; and a meal that Antonio didn't have to prepare for himself was something not to be missed.

They arrived at Tariq's house about half an hour later, having cut through some of the poorer back streets of the city. The walk served as a grim reminder of the raging poverty and starvation that existed in this once wealthy place. The lack of food made these people vulnerable to disease. Hundreds had suffered an agonising death inflicted by the ravaging plague. Five years before, when the town had enjoyed the advantages of the Royal Court's presence, there were far fewer signs of poverty and starvation. The fabric of the roads had been allowed to deteriorate. Loosened cobbles had not been replaced. Stones, some quite large, littered the ground. Even the horses' water troughs were no longer filled, except by a well-meaning *madrileño*. Things had changed so much for the worse since the move to Valladolid but no one seemed to care much, despite Algebra's promised meeting with the king which would probably come to nothing. The state of many he saw saddened Antonio but made him appreciate his own good fortune.

'What are you thinking?' asked Tariq, as they walked up the Calle de la Gorguera to Tariq's house.

'Oh! Just reflecting on how lucky I am compared with all those poor souls trying to feed themselves from what they can scrounge or do for a few *maravedíes* on the streets. Those women don't work there in daylight do they?'

'Yes, I've seen them. You just have to look away,' he said, turning the key to the front door.

'Papa! It's so good to see you. I'm dining with you and Mamá tonight!'

'Reva, I didn't expect to see you! What a lovely surprise. This is my new colleague, Antonio Hidalgo. Antonio, my daughter, Reva.'

Antonio marvelled at this beautiful woman standing before him. Her calm, friendly smile charmed him as did her glorious body. She stood with her head back in the proud pose of some ancient goddess, looking over her subjects. Her eyes glittered in the daylight which emphasised the smooth, untarnished skin on her face. She wore a yellow silk dress which reached from her narrow shoulders to her ankles. Antonio stood motionless and stared at her in wonder.

'I'm charmed to meet you, Señor Hidalgo. So you are working with my father? I hope he is treating you well. Has he shown you his emporium in El Rastro. He's so proud of it, yet you can't go there to buy anything!'

'I'm equally charmed, Señorita Reva. Yes, your father is treating me well. I've learnt so much about the business today, my brain is full to overflowing. I hope I won't forget too easily or I'll be no use at all. I still can't believe he has so many things for export.'

'Some of it has been there for years. It's too old for anyone to buy!'

'Don't believe her, Antonio. She is teasing you!' he laughed.

'It all looked very sellable to me!' said Antonio.

So this was the daughter whom Tariq and Reva would lose if the *Moriscos* were expelled. He couldn't believe her teasing when something as serious and terrible formed the basis of current rumour. He recalled that Tariq dismissed the possibility when it came up in discussion the night before. Perhaps they had chosen to live their lives on the basis of this optimistic assumption.

Antonio sat in the same seat on the sofa as he had the previous night. The fire had since died and apparently no one had replenished it but the room still possessed that comforting warmth. Within a few minutes, all four of them, Antonio, Tariq, Ashraq and Reva were sitting in the room and chatting. 'So why did you choose to work with my father?' said Reva. Antonio paused hoping that Tariq would rescue him.

'No. I chose Antonio. A very influential friend of mine introduced me to him. Well, not quite introduced me,' he said, realising his wife was in the house when he first met Antonio. 'He came with excellent credentials and I'm giving him some training. We haven't decided what he might do yet.'

Antonio decided to make Reva the subject of questioning, rather than himself. 'So what do you do at the General Hospital?' he said, smiling and looking in her direction.

'I'm a nurse and I look after patients after they've had operations. It's a difficult job because they are often in agony when they come back to the ward. The main part of the job is to give them comfort and apply tourniquets to stop the blood from flowing.'

'I can imagine you have some interesting, if harrowing tales to tell.'

'Yes, you are right. Many. The survival rate is quite good. More than half the patients who have amputations survive. We had one a few days ago. A man who lost a leg in a farm accident. Someone at the farm had the wit to apply a tourniquet before they put him in a wagon to bring him here. The surgeon had to saw the leg at the thigh and I'm sure he felt every stroke of the instrument, despite being drunk on brandy. He is now recovered but he was one of the lucky ones.'

'Maybe you know my girlfriend, Catalina de Polanco. She works there, too.'

'Catalina? Yes, of course. She's so energetic. She works on admissions and has some trouble with some patients. Some people want to just stay there. Especially the vagabonds and tramps. They pretend they're ill but Catalina's job is to see if they are. If not she has to send them away. She often has to get the constabulary in to help her. There are some things I can't tell you about Catalina but you probably know anyway.'

Antonio didn't know quite what she meant. He wondered whether it was anything to do with Catalina's love of aggressive love making. He wondered if he might seek some elucidation.

'Yes, she loves her men. She's insatiable. I'm probably not the only one. But I don't ask her difficult questions.'

'You may not be far wrong, Señor Hidalgo. She is popular with a lot of people.'

Antonio thought he'd leave that line of discussion and make an exit. Despite Reva's ambiguous reply, Antonio thought no less of Catalina. He could hardly complain when he had so many women acquaintances. While they had been conversing, Ishraq Alsulami had served a sumptuous chicken broth, leavened with home-made wheat bread. A glass or two of Tariq's wine helped it down.

'Well, Tariq, many thanks to you for the instruction today, and to you for the meal, Ishraq. I really ought to head back home now. When should I appear for the next lesson?'

'I'm going to be away. Doing some buying for a few days. Come in four days' time, on Friday, if you are free?'

'Perfect,' said Antonio, hoping that the next meeting might be sooner but saw the break as an opportunity to start working with Iago. 'Same time, same place?'

'Definitely!'

Early the following morning, there was a loud knock on Antonio's door. He wondered if he should be expecting a call. He had just sat down for a modest breakfast. Could this be any connection with his killing of Pedro's deputy? Had Pedro's brethren somehow caught up with him? Antonio would take no chances and loaded his snaplock. He then gingerly went to the door and quickly opened it and pointed his gun at anyone standing there. A man in a battered tricorne hat stood there.

'No need for that, señor! Are you Señor Antonio Hidalgo?'

'I am the same.'

'Well, put that gun away, señor. I've got your horse right here. You left it in Valladolid and the *corregidor* instructed me to bring it back to you.'

Antonio grinned in relief and thanked the man. He walked out to where the man had tied the horse up. The old mare looked at him as if to say she didn't approve of being deserted in that way. 'It's so good to see you back here, old girl. Let's go around to the stables and I'll give you some food and a drink.'

'Thank you for bringing her to me, señor. Would you like to come in for a drink or something to eat before you go?'

'No, Señor Hidalgo. I'll be on my way. Goodbye.' The man from Valladolid turned and went.

As he had promised, Antonio arrived at the northern side of the Plaza Mayor that morning as the clock on the San Ginés church struck nine o'clock. Iago the Bad had failed to arrive and had therefore disappointed Antonio who set his violin case on the street in front of him and started to play alone. For some reason unbeknown to Antonio, the *plaza* thronged with an unusually large number of people. He decided he would start playing anyway so started with a tune by Vázquez that he knew so

153

well he could easily play it and be looking around for Iago, and generally look at the activities of this extraordinary crowd, at the same time. There were a number of men building some sort of platform at the eastern end. He wondered whether it could be a stage and that there would soon be a play performed, a Juan del Encima or a Lope de Vega. The staging seemed plenty large enough. Then, after about half an hour of making this construction, during which Antonio had repeated the Vázquez at least four times, the same group of constructors unloaded about twenty or so chairs from a wagon that arrived in front of the stage. They put them in orderly lines on the stage and left it, completely unattended. Many of those already present in the *plaza* moved to positions in front of the stage to become part of an audience of a show which had yet to commence.

As the constructors disappeared out of the square, Iago appeared at Antonio's feet. 'I'm sorry I'm late. There's a huge demonstration heading for the plaza from the Calle Mayor. I got caught up with it while I was doing some shopping in the Plazuela de Selenque. There are hundreds of them. They look angry and aggressive. I've no idea what it's about.'

'We'll see soon enough. Looks as if there's going to be some speeches delivered from that stage,' said Antonio, pointing towards the seating.

'What shall we do?' said Iago.

'There are a lot of people already here. Look at the crowd in front of that stage.'

'Must be some demonstration. I wonder what it will be for... or against.'

'I'll pack my violin. Shall we watch from here?'

At that time, the crowd in front of the stage must have been six to ten deep and were chatting expectantly to each other. Apart from the odd case of a man teasing a woman or the other way around, generally taken in good humour, they were behaving well. Antonio and Iago stood and watched for about fifteen minutes before the parade from the Calle Mayor poured into the plaza from the Calle Nuevo. The participants were displaying banners and flags but neither Antonio nor Iago could discern a purpose behind the rally. The flag bearers, mainly ordinary looking men of no obvious allegiance, had scattered themselves throughout the mass of people. Iago said he thought the flags represented different trades or professions but he could not be sure. A few women had joined the throng and had remained in groups, possibly for their own protection. A woman on her own in this crowd could expect trouble and be seen as inviting it.

154

Within another ten minutes or so, the whole parade had settled in front of the assembled stage and was waiting for something to happen. Some people sat on the cobbles and others stood but most were facing the new construction. Then at almost exactly as the church clock struck ten, a line of individuals climbed onto the stage from the rear. Six of them wore the attire of priests and one that of a bishop. They all looked deadly serious and sat in the chairs provided. Then the bishop stood to address the crowd.

'Welcome those of pure Spanish blood,' he shouted as loud as he possibly could. The hubbub of the crowd ceased. His opening words had captured them. 'We are gathered here in the sight of God to share our views on the *Moriscos*. Those who are polluting our blood and our country. They give nothing and take everything. Despite the time they've had since their defeat at their last stronghold in Granada and their agreement to become Christians, hardly any have done so. They continue to worship a pagan god. This artificial deity they call Allah. They read from their rule book, the devil's work itself. What they call the Quran. They intermarry, interbreed. Incest is their daily practice. They gather in these secret mosques to plot against us Christians. And as for jobs, they take less pay than us and drive us Christians out of work. While hoarding their money and sending it to their brethren in Barbary. It's time we took some measures to rid our country of them. Send them back there. Rid ourselves of them for once and for all.'

A huge roar erupted from the crowd. Cheering broke out. The bishop's views had struck a chord with the people of Madrid, or at least with this audience. It surprised Antonio that feelings were so strong. His immediate thoughts were for *Moriscos* in the city. If this crowd were a measure of wider feelings about the *Moriscos*, those of them who lived in Madrid could be in imminent danger. The thought of Reva being attacked by this mob jolted Antonio into wishing to protect her. Not that she needed it. She lived in a supportive family who cherished her.

Over the next twenty minutes the views of this bishop were amplified and repeated by other clerics and lay people who came forward, one by one, to express themselves. A tall, thin, hand wringing priest said that those in other towns in Spain felt the same as the people of Madrid. He directed these people to visit Valencia or Granada to see for themselves. After each stopped speaking, the crowd applauded, shouted out and whistled. Then, after the last groundless, rhetorical utterance, given by a man dressed as a *tercio*, the audience broke up and started to drift out of the *plaza*.

'Let's set up now and play to them,' said Antonio. 'We could score well from this lot. They're so excited! They could feel generous, too. Know any anti-*Morisco* songs?'

'Can't say I do, but something just tuneful and jolly would be good! I know a few pro-*Morisco* songs like 'Woe is me Alhama' but we'd be strung up for playing that!'

'How about, 'The Shepherd Corillo', the Narváez version. Know that one?'

'Of course,' said Iago. 'I'll sing and you play.'

'I prithee keep my swine for me,
Carillo, wilt thou? Tell.
First, let me have a kiss of thee
And I will keep them well.
If to my charge or them to keep,
That doest commend they kine or sheep,
For thee I do suffice:
Because in this I have been bred,
But for so much as I have fed,
By viewing thee, mine eyes;
Command not me to keep thy beast:
Because myself, I can keep least.
How can I keep, I prithee tell,
Thy kine, myself that cannot well
Defend, not please thy kind,
As long as I have served thee?
But if thou wilt give unto me
A kiss to please my mind:
I sake no more for all my paine,
And I will keep them very faine.'

Those who stopped to listen to Iago's singing delighted in the words of this little ballad. A man and his wife stopped and remarked on the contrast between the teasing sentiments of the song and the violent proposals meted out by the clerics at the demonstration. Antonio said it was a pure accident of choice that they had come up with these pretty verses. Others who had attended the anti-*Morisco* rally tossed some of their loose change into Antonio's violin case, as they stood and listened to this plaintive number or as they left the square. Even one of the priests who spoke dropped in a four *maravedí* piece and Antonio thanked him.

'What did you think of that, Iago?'

'Not sure what to make of it. There's a lot of anger about the *Moriscos* but I can't say I share it. They don't seem to be doing much harm to anybody and certainly none to me.'

'I agree, Iago. I don't know much about them. The fact is they've done me no harm and as for that ranting bishop, you'd have thought a man of the cloth would know better. Live and let live, I say. I hear they've got a thousand gods in the East. So why object if some of our brethren worship a different one to most of us. It's interesting that we share the same opinions. Maybe we artists, singers, actors and musicians have a more liberal view.'

The two of them played and sang for the rest of the day. Their collection dropped dramatically in the afternoon but by then there were far fewer people in the *plaza*. And the influence that made people in the group behind follow the actions of the group in front had evaporated with the demonstrators.

Friday morning soon came round. Antonio woke early in anticipation of his next lesson as a merchant. He remained puzzled about the reason he was being given all this specialised attention. He had to trust Silva who surely could not be playing with him. There had to be serious purpose behind Tariq's training. Antonio, however, failed to divine what it could be. Several possibilities occurred to him: a mission to Valencia or Granada where the *Morisco* populations were high; a wider mission, to some of the larger cities in Spain from Salamanca to Barcelona and Seville to Pamplona which he didn't want; and what he dreaded more, a mission to Turkey, of the kind that Tariq had turned down. All would become clear, perhaps sooner than he might expect.

'Good to see you back,' said Tariq as he answered the warehouse door to Antonio. 'I had a horrible feeling you wouldn't come. I'm not sure what prompted that.'

'I certainly don't,' said Antonio, frowning at Tariq's remark. He wondered what could have prompted it, taking account Tariq's compliments about how quickly and keenly he was taking in what Tariq had told him. He wondered if it was something to do with Antonio's possible uncertainty about being a spy which he hoped he had not revealed. 'Anyway, here I am for the next in your series of instruction!'

'Let's go into my office.'

Antonio followed, still feeling sore but even more determined to see this course of instruction through to the end, however long it took and however many stages.

'You'll remember that the second lesson is to be on sales and distribution?'

'I remember well. They're obviously connected.'

'Good start!'

'There are some basic principles to selling which I'll explain now. Sit down. The first is a satisfied customer. Once you've sold you don't want the customer complaining. This is obviously connected with buying. You must buy quality and reliability. Otherwise you'll have them groaning. Avoid that for two reasons. A satisfied customer is a repeat customer; a dissatisfied customer is an expense you can do without. For a start, you'll have to replace the faulty goods, my friend, and that wipes out your profits. And if you want him to buy from you again you'll have to seduce him in some way. And I wouldn't rule out using a woman. But don't tell my wife I said that! But the problem can be avoided by buying only high quality products. My suppliers all know how particular I am and that they'll lose me if they sell me low quality goods, whatever their product may be. Is that all clear? Any questions?'

Antonio thought he'd rib Tariq and seek revenge for Tariq's opening remark. 'So how many customers have crossed you off their supplier list? Quite a few? Presumably, you learnt all this through the pain of experience.'

'Very amusing!' Tariq feigned a laugh but smarted inside. 'Yes and no. I lost an Italian customer for a large consignment of olive oil. The oil was bad. So I had to resupply him at great expense. Never heard from him again. The only other one I've lost was in the Maghreb. This was over a consignment of supposedly high quality fabric. I sold it in large rolls. It turned out that only the first few *varas* were high quality and the rest cheap cotton, stained the same colour. I was still there when he came to tell me about it. He had this cutlass and I thought he was going to kill me. I gave him his money back and more. Luckily for me he accepted and that was the last I saw of him. I was mightily relieved, I can tell you, my friend!'

Antonio laughed. 'So I was right: you've learnt from experience!' At that point he thought he'd teased Tariq enough, even though he'd taken it well. 'So what's the second of your basic principles?'

'Price the goods as high as you'd dare. You can always drop. But always have it in mind never to go below the price that gives the profit you want. At that point you may have to find another buyer!'

'But if you are selling abroad don't you fix the price in advance? Otherwise, you're at the mercy of the buyer. And you've gone to all that trouble to ship the goods to their country.'

'I was saving exports until last but you've got there already. Selling abroad is risky. You need a good profit margin. I have a customer in Barcelona. I take him wines from Malaga which I buy on the way. We always agree a price on the previous visit but it's not always possible to do that. But again, I give him a high price and we bargain over a few beers and settle on something he can work with to make a profit and I do likewise. Works well.'

'Barcelona's not abroad.'

'No, but the same principles apply. I have to ship the wine there so it's similar to exporting.'

'I'm not sure I could do the bartering. The customer would probably win on that one.'

'Yes, you could. You'd be surprised. You just stay cool and make sure they don't push you below your limit. The point is you are defending against their attack. So they have to take the initiative to make you cut your price. The best of my stories, but don't tell my wife or daughter, is when in '98 I sold about a thousand earthenware pots in the Maghreb. I shipped them to Anfa. They had to go inland a hundred or so *millas* so I had to hire four wagons. When I reached the customer, who had a shop with a market stall in this small town, his wife was working on the stall. She was horrified when I turned up with these wagons and drivers. Her husband had gone to Fez on business and I was a day or two early. I didn't want to overprice the pots so I started at what I thought was a bit on the high side of what I would accept and she said she'd buy them all for that. I asked her if she was sure. Anyway, she was adamant that she wouldn't bargain with me. So I knocked another ten percent off and told her about my excessive generosity. "You've just given me about five hundred *maravedís*, much more than a *ducat* and I didn't even ask you!' she said. 'How can I reward you?" She was a pretty thing, veil and all, and I looked her up and down. "Come inside," she said, probably realising what I had in mind. "Just a minute," I said. "I'll just send my drivers over to the bar for a drink." I gave them some change and, as soon as I got back, she put a closed sign on the market and the store. I followed her in. The next thing was we were both naked and all over each other on a sofa in her lounge. What bliss! It all lasted a good half hour and just after we had put our clothes back on her husband walked in. Then bold as brass, his wife went right up to him and planted a kiss on his lips. "You're just in time to see Tariq. I've just given him a bit of sustenance before he goes on his way!" Sustenance! I ask you, my friend? So I shook hands with each of them and went!'

'What a story. No, I won't tell your wife or daughter but only if you give me five hundred *maravedis*, the money you gave her for her body!'

'Blackmail is not on my agenda! I'd deny telling you so it would be your word against mine!'

'I don't believe you, anyway! They say that men above a certain age exaggerate their sexual prowess. And you are above that age!'

'Believe what you like, my friend! The fact is it's true!'

'I am only teasing you, Tariq! And what is the third principle of selling?'

'How do you know there is one?'

'It stands to reason!' Antonio chided.

'The third is simple. It is to make sure you can always deliver. All it means is that as a seller you must maintain your stock. You never know when that unexpected order will come in and you have to be ready to meet it! That's why my warehouse is nearly always full. The fourth and final one is: "first in first out".'

'What's that supposed to mean?'

'Whatever product you are selling, sell the oldest items in your stock first. I always say: the sooner you sell your pans, the later they lose their shine. There's a lot to that, my friend!'

'Hmm…I think I follow.'

'Let's break off for some lunch and I'll tell you about exports. Not that there's much I can add to what I've said. I've more or less covered it on the way to where we are now!'

A few beers and a rabbit pie with onions later, Tariq was explaining some of his philosophy about exports. Antonio listened, his head in his hands with concentration.

'Now we come to a subject in which I modestly call myself a specialist. The key to success is to know your customer. But that applies to all selling, as I've already explained. Equally important is distribution and this is where costs are so important. Inevitably, your means of transport is the galley. You must find out about their use. I don't own any and I don't want to. A friend of mine in Tangier bought a small fleet because he'd save on hire costs if he owned them. What he didn't understand was that to make ownership worthwhile, the galley has to be at sea all the time, except of course for maintenance. He had a lot of customers but not enough to keep his four vessels occupied. So he ended up bankrupt and gaoled for it.

'I use several ports, Malaga, Cartagena, Cádiz and even Marseilles. I know the fleet owners in these places and they know me. I know how much they charge, for full and partly full holds so I can factor in their charges into the minimum price I can accept for the goods I'm exporting.'

'Do you accompany the goods you export?'

'Good question. Nearly always. I supervise deliveries but that trend is changing and for some of the goods I export from France, I leave that to my agent in Marseilles.'

'Your business is bigger than I thought. Bigger than this warehouse.'

'You are right, my friend!'

'Tell me as a newcomer, Tariq, how do you find your customers?'

'Another smart question… There are three basic ways. You can buy them. You approach another exporter and ask him to sell. I don't advocate that. Second, you go abroad and find people who buy…the importers… and you convince them that they should be doing business with you. Believe me it's hard. But if you are persuasive, reasonable and clearly honest with them, they'll use you, more often than not. But the supreme way is by another importer's recommendation. It's best because there is no expense on your part and no work either! But you must be able to deliver. That's the key!'

Tariq told him more about the ports he said he'd exported from, the galley owners, how many galleys they owned, what products they preferred to export, where they sailed to, how long it took them to arrive at the foreign destination and most importantly how much they charged. The range of prices surprised Antonio who could not resist a further question.

'Simple. It all depends on how long it takes to reach the foreign port and how much he pays the crew. And how much effort is involved in loading your cargo!'

'Why did I ask such a stupid question? I could have worked that out!'

'You are showing signs of having enough for now. Anyway, I think I've reached the end of the course! Want to come back for a meal?'

'I hope you don't mind, Tariq, but I've promised my lady friend, Catalina, that I'll dine with her tonight. She's cooking a meal at my place! Thank you, anyway.'

On the way there, Antonio pondered what he had learned from Tariq and why. A musician training to be a merchant as part of being a spy. What was Silva de Torres really intending? The man surely had something important up his sleeve, otherwise he wouldn't put this new recruit through all this. Or could it be a test of some kind? He settled in the knowledge that he would find out eventually and that de Torres was paying him a *ducat* a day. He couldn't earn that as a musician, even playing solo to the king!

'What? You a merchant? But you're a musician!'

'I know. I can't explain it.'

'You mean you've no idea why?'

'Right. I told you about Silva didn't I?'

'Yes.'

'Well, he sent me for it.'

'I still don't understand.'

'I'll tell you as much as I know. Remember you signed that oath?'

'Yes!'

'Well, when I saw him after I came back from Valladolid, he gave me an address to go to.'

'Where?'

'To a house in the Calle de la Gorguera. One on the right past the Santa Ana convent.'

'I know. Those which slope out to the road.'

'Those are the ones. Anyway, I went there and this *Morisco* called Tariq let me in and showed me inside. Over a meal, his wife prepared, he told me that Silva had instructed him to train me as a merchant. I asked him why and he said he had no idea either.'

'Is that where you were coming back from when you found Francisca lying in that alleyway?'

'Exactly.'

'I wondered where you'd been but we were all so concerned about poor Francisca. If it hadn't been for you, Antonio, she could have been dead by now.' She started to weep and Antonio put a comforting hand on her shoulder.

'Now, now, Catalina. All's well that ends well. Did you report it to the constables?'

'Yes. Apparently, that was the second attack in that alley in a week. The constabulary have no idea who it was but will tell us if they suspect anyone. Francisca may be asked to appear as a witness.' Catalina calmed herself.

'How is she now? I am assuming she's all right.'

'She's had a couple of nasty dreams but apart from that she's fine. She's a strong lass. By the way, that merchant, does he have a daughter called Reva?'

'Yes, lives in the Calle de la Cruz, not far from them. I met her the night after he gave me the first lesson.'

'I know her. She's a nurse at the hospital. Where I work. She does operations and I do receptions. I often have to take patients through to her so I know her well.'

'I was going to tell you that I mentioned to her that my lady friend worked at the General Hospital. And, yes, she said she knew you, too!' Antonio could see nothing to be gained by saying that Reva had told him that Catalina had some interesting friendships there.

'I still can't see you as a merchant or a merchant come spy. Have you no idea where you'll be going or why?'

'I could be sent to Italy, to the Netherlands or even to Turkey but I cannot see a purpose behind a mission to any of them.'

'Nor me, but I know less about these things than you!'

'So what are you going to do for this meal?'

'I was up at the Selenque market this morning and bought a couple of tasty looking boar steaks and some artichokes. So get the hearth fire going. Oh, and you can pour me a glass of wine!'

Antonio went to his kitchen and bought back a piece of old cloth, some sulphur and some flints. With practiced skill he carefully placed a small pile of sulphur on the cloth and struck a knife across the flints. On the third attempt, the sulphur lit and within a few more seconds the cloth was burning away to itself. He piled some wood on his little conflagration and left it to burn through.

'I'll get some wine now.' He soon returned, carrying two glasses of a tasty looking white wine. 'How about that?'

By then, Catalina was sitting provocatively on Antonio's sofa, displaying quite as much as she intended. She put a hand through her red locks and smiled at him. 'What do you think, Antonio? Now or after dinner? How about in front of the fire, so we can keep an eye on it?'

A passionate fifteen minutes later, they heard a loud knocking on Antonio's front door. 'Quick! Slip your breeches back on!'

Antonio almost ran to the door to answer it before the person who knocked had gone.

'You are Diaspora, I think?' said a short, older, untidy looking man, who was leaning precariously on a walking stick.

'The same.'

'Note from Algebra.' He handed a sealed envelope to Antonio and in doing so almost fell.

'Thank you. Are you all right?'

'Yeah. Me leg's playing me up today. But I'm fine.' The man turned and limped away.

Antonio dashed back into his drawing room. 'I'm not sure I should show you this,' he chuckled. 'It's from my boss, Silva.'

'Open it up! It could be telling us what your next assignment is!'

'Us? I like that!' Antonio used the knife which he had used to strike the flint to open the envelope and eased out the neatly written page.

To Diaspora,
Please make yourself available for a meeting in my office on Monday next, at nine o'clock, a.m.
Signed, Algebra

Antonio paused for a moment. He was sure he hadn't mentioned the code names to Catalina. He had to assume he hadn't and if he had he shouldn't have. 'It doesn't go as far as we hoped. I've got to see Silva at nine o'clock on Monday morning.' He threw the letter into the leaping flames.

'Promise me you'll come straight around to tell me. It's my day off.'

'I promise. And I'll tell you as much as I can.'

CHAPTER 15
The return

Antonio could hardly sleep that Sunday night. His excitement at the thought of a new mission completely overcame him. He wondered where he would be sent. Would it be by land and sea or just by land? He had a feeling it would be to France. After all, the French were constantly fighting the Habsburgs and had sided with the Ottoman sultans. Maybe the king was concerned about some alliance forming between them and he would be sent there to find out. Or would he be going by land and sea to Constantinople. Were the Turks thinking of restoring Moorish supremacy to the peninsula? He hardly slept at all.

He walked to Silva's office in the Alcázar Palace and arrived on the stroke of nine.

'Good to see you, Antonio,' smiled Algebra, as private secretary Brondate showed Antonio in.

'Equally good to see you, Silva. To what do I owe the pleasure?' said Antonio, with a quizzical look in his eye.

'Firstly, how did your project with Lusitano go?'

'Not another delaying tactic,' Antonio thought, but also that he should play along.

'I liked him. He was informative, amusing and clearly a highly competent, experienced exporting merchant. He is also a good teacher and I learnt a lot from him. And he told me some good stories.'

'Good. You are probably thinking that your next assignment is to do with being an exporting merchant. Well, it isn't. I'm not going to delay telling you because we are both busy people. I'm sending you back to Guadalajara.'

Antonio blinked twice. So he wouldn't be going abroad, to France or Italy or anywhere else. At least not then. He hadn't expected to have to return to Guadalajara.

'Let me explain. I want you out of the way. Out of Madrid. I don't want any of Pedro's gang tracking you down. You may think that they didn't suspect you of thwarting them but I'm not so sure. Now the criminal trials are underway, we think his men are looking for a scapegoat who could be you. I value you too much to lose you. I could send you to Toledo or Cuenca. But the last place they'd expect to see you is in Guadalajara. That's the reason I want you to go. So it's a mission but not a mission!' He paused.

'…Oh and something else I'd like you to do is to ask your colleague, Iago, to go with you,' he chuckled.

'What's amusing you?' Antonio laughed back but didn't know why.

'It would be interesting to have a spy working with a non-spy musician who doesn't know you're a spy.'

'Isn't that what you had with me and Esteban?'

'Yes, but that was different. You were an infiltrator then. This time you are a straightforward musician.'

Antonio wasn't so sure about this idea. He didn't want to deceive Iago, nor did he want to put him in danger. 'Why shouldn't I go alone? What's the risk? I'm the one trained in the use of firearms, not Iago.'

'I'm sure you could manage going solo but to be a travelling duet would be better. How are you getting on with him?'

'Better than I thought I would and he'd be a good companion. But I'd be worried about putting him at risk. He probably wouldn't want to go, anyway.'

'I understand all of that but I don't think you are right. He might even appreciate a change. How much are you earning a day, when you play as a duet?'

'Not a great deal. I suppose about half a *real* each. Yes, about twenty *maravedís*. The day of the demonstration we did very well. About three *reales* each then. Why do you ask?'

'If he says he doesn't want to go, I want you to offer him an inducement of up to, say, a *real* a day.'

'That's about enough to pay for his lodgings. I won't be able to afford all that.'

'You will, because I'll be paying!'

Antonio felt that Silva was pushing him in a direction he didn't want to go. And he genuinely felt that Iago could be in danger if he accompanied him, especially if he was recognised by one of Pedro's cohorts.

'You really want him to go then?'

'Yes, but if he says no to your offer we accept and you travel as a solo player. What do you think? Your lady friend there will be pleased to see you,' he grinned.

'Obviously, I'll go. I wouldn't dream of refusing. But there is a problem we need to address.'

'What's that?'

'I'm sure you will remember that it was Jac who told me about the conversation she'd overheard Pedro having with his colleagues about kidnapping and holding the king to ransom. I told her I'd write to tell her the result of my telling the Corregidor of Guadalajara but never did. She is bound to ask what happened and whether the plot was thwarted. How do you want me to respond to such a question?'

'You must on no account tell her you are a spy. Tell her that what she said helped destroy the plot against the king. Play it down as much as you can.'

'I'll encourage Iago to come. When do you want us to go?'

'If you are on your way by the end of the week, with or without Iago, that will be fine. Go for two weeks. I'll have something else for you then, taking you away from Madrid. But I can't yet say what. Any questions?'

'Apart from still being puzzled, none.'

They shook hands and Antonio made his way to Iago's in the Calle de la Pechuga. He knocked on the door and waited. He knocked again after a minute or so but there was no sign of Iago so he turned and went. As he rounded the corner onto the Calle de Toledo he could see someone standing outside his door. He paused and looked again. It looked like a man he didn't recognise. A white stallion was tied to the rail outside. He wasn't sure whether to continue to the apartments or cross the road and make for the Puerta Cerrada. His curiosity overcame him. But he decided that if he didn't like the look of the character, standing there, he'd walk straight on towards the Plaza Mayor.

As he approached the house, the figure turned towards him and spoke.

'Antonio, it's you. I've been waiting here since nine o'clock!' The figure was a woman, dressed as a man: Lupita de Pastrana. 'I'm looking for work. But I thought I'd take up your invitation to call in and see you. You look surprised.'

'I am, totally. I just didn't expect to see you. Do come in!'

Antonio let them both in and showed Lupita into the lounge where the night before he had made love to Catalina. 'Have a seat on the sofa. Tell me your story. So you're looking for work?'

A stream of thoughts poured into Antonio's head. He saw her as a complication. What would Catalina think of this woman turning up here? Lupita and he had never been lovers and he didn't want her as a lover. He couldn't work out why. Perhaps her masculine clothes discouraged him. He couldn't let her stay at his apartment. Maybe he just needed to be rid of her. On the other hand, she could accompany him to Guadalajara, if Iago declined to go. Or could all three of them go? He wondered what Silva would think. He chuckled inwardly.

'Why are you smiling now? You looked as if you'd seen a ghost a minute ago?'

'No. I'm genuinely pleased to see you and I'm dying to hear why you are here and looking for a job. How's your mother?'

'My mother is part of the reason I'm here. She is fully recovered now and back doing all the jobs a wife and housekeeper does. Father was fine when he was looking after her. He had plenty to do and what with the cooking, washing, changing the linen, going up to the market, everything was fine. But as my mother got back on her feet and took over the reins, he became bored and miserable. You saw what a temper he has when he reacted so badly to you and Esteban coming into our house. Well, he started arguing with me, at every opportunity. There was nothing I could do. When he told me to go back to Madrid I decided I would come. I fully intended to anyway but thought I'd let mother really become strong before I did. Maybe I just outstayed my welcome,' she said, looking downwards.

'Not the best story, Lupita. So you have no work at present?'

'No. But I'm going to the Príncipe later and see if they need a singer.'

'Where are you staying? Presumably, at the house share in the Mentidero?'

'Yes. I'm not going to put on you, Antonio. You needn't worry!'

Antonio wondered about telling her that he was going to Guadalajara later that week and therefore that there may be an opportunity for her to join him, and possibly Iago whom of course she didn't know. Then an interesting thought occurred to him. Maybe she'd be a good friend for Iago. Yes, he'd tell her and that they'd be going for about two weeks.

'What a good idea, Antonio. I'd love that! Is that an offer?'

'Not until tomorrow morning. I have to discuss the idea with Iago first. I'll know soon after nine in the morning if we can take you on. We should meet at about ten o'clock tomorrow, if that suits you. Whereabouts do you live in the Mentidero?'

'The tenth house up on the left.'

'I'll see you there tomorrow, as soon after ten as I can make it! Here, have a drink of orange juice. You must be parched.'

'Mostly I need a...'

'There's one in my bedroom, around to the left.'

Antonio gave her a drink, she swallowed it quickly and then, at the door, they kissed each other goodbye. She climbed up onto her beautiful white stallion and trotted off. He still couldn't believe she had appeared unprompted. He felt a streak of excitement as she left. The trip to Guadalajara could be a different kind of adventure.

He locked up and walked around to Iago's house and knocked again. This time the door opened. Iago's eyebrows lifted and his jaw dropped a little at seeing a smiling Antonio standing there. He invited Antonio in and offered him a drink. Antonio couldn't anticipate Iago's reaction at asking him to go to Guadalajara.

'What's wrong with working here? The money is quite good and we have some regular stoppers.'

'I just fancy a change. You're wrong about the money. There's more in Guadalajara. Wait and see.'

'I'm not sure, Antonio. I'd be paying to stay here and for cheap lodgings there. I can't afford both.'

'What do you pay for your lodgings here?'

'Ten a day.'

'I'll pay you twice that to come with me. How about that?'

Iago's face twisted into a number of expressions. Antonio had to stop himself from giggling at these unexpected contortions.

'Call it twenty five and you're on!'

Antonio stepped over to Iago and shook his hand. 'Excellent, Iago. We'll do well. I'm sure of that! I have one more idea and you can still turn me down, if you don't approve!'

'Go on.'

Antonio explained how he met Lupita, that she was a brilliant singer, she was here in Madrid and looking for work. He said he was thinking of offering her a job in the troupe. 'What do you think, Iago? You'll love her. She's so nice.'

Iago's response surprised Antonio. Before he agreed, he wanted to see Lupita and, if he liked her, he'd agree. If not he'd turn down the idea. 'My view is that you aren't in charge of our troupe, whatever you think. We are equal partners so I should have an equal say in her engagement.' Antonio agreed and thought that he'd asked for that. He had still to negotiate with Silva but couldn't possibly let Iago know.

'What if I drop in to see you tomorrow, as close to 9.45 as I can? We can both go to the Mentidero where she lives and can both see her.' If

Silva didn't like the idea, Antonio could always change his mind about having her in the group. So he couldn't be caught out, either way.

Antonio remembered that he'd promised Catalina that he'd tell her about the new assignment, as soon as he could. He dashed around to see her from Iago's house. He had to think about whether to mention Lupita and what to say about her. He decided that Catalina would have no say in deciding whether Lupita should join the troupe so the best thing was not to mention her then but think again after she'd joined the group, if indeed Silva first and secondly Iago agreed that she should. There was no point in looking for trouble, especially in advance of there being any.

Antonio turned up just before nine o'clock the following morning to see Silva. He explained everything and asked what he thought of Lupita going. He wasn't particularly receptive, even though he remembered that Antonio had mentioned her in the letter he had sent from Ávila.

'A woman. You're jesting! What could she offer, especially now you've signed up Iago. Well done for roping him for twenty five a day!'

'More cover, Silva. And she's a good singer. She would give our group that much more professionalism. Even less likely that I'd be caught out as a spy. And she'd make more than her share of the income!'

'You are really wedded to this idea, aren't you? Is there a motive I cannot see? Could she be your next conquest?'

Antonio laughed. But he had a hidden motive, if it could be called that. If Lupita came, she could be a distraction for Iago. He wouldn't confess that to Silva. There are certain things in life you don't tell your boss, however good your relationship is with him. 'You flatter me. How many lady friends do you think I've got? And how many more do you think I can cope with?'

'We are both aware of Jac. You confessed your relationship with her, the first time we met. Listen, I'm going to let you go ahead with the three of you. However, if this woman compromises you, you could be in trouble. Do you understand that?'

'You've made it clear enough. It won't happen. So you can sleep soundly in your bed. I know where my loyalties lie.'

'I'm reassured, Diaspora.'

Antonio could not divine what Silva meant by 'be in trouble' but felt confident that the issue wouldn't arise. The last thing Lupita would want would be to cause problems, especially for Antonio.

Antonio had to run most of the way from the Alcázar Palace to be at Iago's by 9.45. Iago asked him in. 'Have we the time, Iago? I told Lupita that I'd see her at as soon after ten as I could make it.'

'I think we should discuss the Guadalajara idea further before making a decision. Where would we lodge? Where would we play? How long would be stay there?' His whole mood seemed strange and Antonio couldn't work out why.

'I thought we'd decided yesterday that we'd go. What's changed?'

Iago looked away and spoke hesitantly, unlike the confident, sometimes arrogant individual that Antonio felt he knew well. 'I'm not as sure as I was yesterday. I'm thinking that I'd rather stay here and work on my own. I still don't see the point in going there. We can earn just as much here. We know people at our pitches, especially in the Plaza Mayor and at the Plaza del Palacio.'

Antonio couldn't believe what Iago was saying. 'I've thought a lot about it and I've decided to go. I can't be angry with you and I don't want to fall out with you. I think I'll go anyway to see Lupita and ask her to come with me. Would you object to that, Iago? Would you like to come? The complication is that if she joins me and stays with me, we may have her in our group. When I come back shall we join up again to work together?'

They were soon tying up their horses outside of the house in the Mentidero and waiting outside. Lupita answered the door and invited them in. Antonio introduced Iago. He wanted to be as subtle as possible in explaining their presence. 'Iago is the other member of our group, Lupita. We are equal partners and while Iago won't be coming to Guadalajara with us, as we may all three join up when we come back, it seemed important that we three all met to, well, see how we got on.'

Lupita seemed nervous and unsure, even in asking them if they wanted a drink. It seemed an age before she returned from the kitchen with two overflowing jugs of apple juice. 'I'm still not sure what this is about,' she said as she put them on the table. 'When we spoke yesterday, you said you'd tell me today whether or not I could go with you.'

'Sorry, Lupita,' said Antonio, stepping in quickly before Iago had a chance. 'You and I are going to Guadalajara. That decision is taken. Do you still want to come with me?'

She came over to Antonio and kissed him on the cheek. 'I am so pleased! Of course I'll come.' She smiled all over her face. Antonio looked delighted.

'I've come with Iago because he wants to meet you. We could all be partners when we come back from Guadalajara. Happy with that Iago?'

'I'd like to know more about Lupita's skills. What she does. You are a singer I believe.' With that, Lupita's voice filled the house as she sang, 'Roses for my mother'. Iago looked stunned. Antonio grinned.

'You are a brilliant singer and I'd love you to join our group,' said Iago.

'There you are,' said Antonio. 'You're in!'

'Now I'm really excited, Antonio. When do we go to Guadalajara?'

'How about the day after tomorrow? I'll be outside on my horse at nine o'clock in the morning.'

Antonio would have to tell Catalina about going to Guadalajara with Lupita. He'd tell her that night. He should tell Silva, too.

Antonio decided to ride to the palace and see if he could have an urgent meeting with Silva who, as Antonio walked into his office, was arranging his papers in readiness to meet his other *regidor* colleagues to discuss the case for moving the king's court back to Madrid. 'I'm surprised to see you, Antonio. You look anxious as if something bad has happened. What's wrong?'

'Nothing, Silva. Nothing at all. I just wanted to tell something so that you could rethink your position, if you wished. Iago has decided that he doesn't want to go to Guadalajara. I've tried to persuade him otherwise but I can't budge him. He'd far prefer to stay here and play as a soloist.'

'Is there anything else? Anything on this Lupita woman, a bigger risk in my estimation?'

'She has agreed to come with me. She's looking forward to us playing together.'

'In bed and out?'

'That's totally unfair, Silva!' said Antonio, raising his voice. 'I have no intention of sharing a bed with her. If necessary it will be separate inns rather than share a bed.'

'So the relationship would be strictly professional then?'

'Yes. By the way, she's a *Morisca*.'

'Why didn't you tell me that before? It gives her a different dimension.'

'I should have but it didn't occur to me.'

Silva stood up from his desk and walked over to the window. He paused there for a few moments and looked out before turning back to face Antonio who was sitting in front of the desk. 'Yes, she can go. The fact that she's a *Morisca* could help if you are at risk. You will be able to introduce her as such and that will reduce any possible suspicion Pedro's men, if they are any there, may have over you. Good luck!' Silva smiled for the first time in the encounter. Antonio stood. The two men shook hands and Antonio left.

He had ridden to the palace and on the way back worked out a plan to discuss the 'mission' with Catalina. To give himself time to think he walked. 'You can walk, too, old gal,' he said, gently patting his aging mare on the side of her face. He would mention Lupita to Catalina and tell her everything he knew about her, including that she was a *Morisca*. That he'd already decided. He'd say he'd have nothing but a professional relationship with her. He'd offer to cook the evening meal for the two of them.

'Have you bought something special? Have you got something in?'

'I'm not telling you. It will be a nice surprise!'

They walked arm in arm to Antonio's, just as they did when he came back from his earlier trip to Guadalajara. He decided to speak to her over the meal. The last thing he wanted was for her to go before he'd prepared it. They both went into the kitchen and he showed her the succulent pork chops he'd bought. They went into the drawing room before he started the cooking and sat on the sofa. Should he tell her about Lupita then or leave it until later? Perhaps she wouldn't feel too bad about Lupita after a few glasses of wine.

'This could be our last chance because you will be packing tomorrow night and I'm working tomorrow!'

'Are you sure you want to?'

'Why not? Something on your mind?'

Antonio didn't want to take advantage of her. He didn't want to make love pretending that everything was fine, only to discover that she wasn't happy about Lupita. 'There is something I want to tell you about. I hope you feel you can trust me and accept the situation. If not, I'm not sure where we go from here...'

'Tell me, Antonio. I want to know. Now! Who is she?'

'Let me start from the beginning. I told you when we met after I returned from Valladolid, that we met a woman dressed as a man, on the way to Ávila. She approached…'

'Out with it, Antonio. Have you been screwing the woman? Why mention her now?'

'No, I haven't been screwing her. Aren't you going to let me finish?'

'Go on,' she said, frowning and crossing her arms on her chest.

'This woman, whose name, as I told you before, is Lupita de Pastrana, asked Esteban and me if she could join us because she didn't want to travel alone.'

'You told me all that nonsense. She's a singer come actress or something. She turned up at your front door. You asked her in and within two minutes…'

'Not true. Just listen!' Antonio's impatience grew at the same rate as Catalina's disbelief. 'Yes, she did turn up at my front door, two days ago.'

'I'm not sure I can take much more of this, Antonio. You tell me you fucked a dwarf half a dozen times and not this one. Then this one knocks on your door… why did you give her your address? Stupid thing to do. I'm supposed to be your God damned girlfriend.' She then started to sob.

Antonio went to put his arm around her. 'Get off me, you pig screwing liar.'

He didn't know how to respond to this savage insult. He paused for a moment. Had this got out of hand? Could there be any way back? Should he worry? Reva had told him, albeit in ambiguous words, about Catalina's relationships at the hospital so, if she left him, he would be losing an unfaithful lover. He too had been openly unfaithful to her but somehow, rightly or wrongly, as things were in Spain at that time, despite the church, most people accepted unfaithfulness in a man more than in a woman. He would make one more attempt at consoling her.

'No need for an insult as rich as that,' he said, smarting at the thought of it but putting on a smile. 'My relationship with the woman is and will continue to be purely professional.'

She snapped out of her tears. 'Continue to be? So she is going to Guadalajara with you? True or not true?'

'I've spoken to Silva…'

'I don't care a shit whether you've spoken to Silva or not! Is she going with you to Guadalajara?'

'Yes.'

'Then I'm off. That's the end of it.' She got up from the sofa, went out of the front door and slammed it behind her. Young though he was, he could cope with setbacks and this didn't rate that high. He'd enjoyed the woman's company and they had been good for each other. But if she couldn't trust him to have a purely professional relationship with a woman, there could be no purpose in continuing. He felt incapable of hating the woman or even disliking her. He just felt let down, deflated and rejected. He had hoped she'd be more reasonable but that was not to be. He decided to be strong and just let her go, if that's what she wanted.

The night before he and Lupita would start their little journey to Guadalajara, Antonio again tossed and turned in his creaking bed as he attempted to sleep. A journey to come, for whatever reason, affected him in that way. He imagined that his horse would sleep undisturbed.

'We're on our way, old gal,' he said as he put his saddlebag over her back. She snorted as if looking forward to a run. He had packed his gun and dagger and, of course, brought his trusty violin. He still felt bruised as he trotted the old mare along the Calle Mayor towards the Mentidero. He still couldn't understand why Catalina had refused to listen to his story through to the end. He eventually reached the conclusion that she had more to lose than he had. He would put her to the back of his mind and concentrate on the mission in hand. He could not imagine that Jac would have a problem renewing their intimacy, especially as he and Lupita slept in different rooms. He chuckled to himself as he contemplated the look on Jac's face as she learned about Lupita.

'Good to see you, Antonio. I've been looking forward to this so much, I haven't slept a wink. I paced the landing all night!' said Lupita as she gave Antonio a welcoming kiss at the door of the house she shared.

'I didn't sleep much, either but I never do before a longish trip.'

'I'm all ready to go. My saddlebag is packed and I've enough clothes for a week. Then it'll be a visit to a wash house or get the inn to clean them! And I've brought along a surprise for you. I'll show you what it is later!'

Antonio wondered what this 'surprise' could be. Something she had cooked for sustenance on the way, a drink or something? Time would tell. He had more to think about for now.

CHAPTER 16
Revelations

They were soon passing through the Puerta de Alcalá and riding at a trot. He had explained to her that his horse wasn't as young or as mobile as she once was, unlike her beautiful mount, so the trip would have to take a couple of days whereas one would be the norm. 'You are the man and should have the stronger horse.'

'Yes, but you usually dress as a man,' he laughed.

'No need while travelling with you, young fellow!' She looked attractively feminine in a yellow blouse over a white camisole, which revealed its pretty, cream lace straps. Her light brown, tightly fitting leather riding breeches and matching boots amplified her striking image. What a striking contrast to the dour looking individual, dressed in masculine clothing, he and Esteban met after the meteorite landed near the road to Ávila. Maybe he could take a fancy to her.

After a few refreshment stops on the way, they pressed on to Alcalá de Henares and stayed at the inn Antonio had used over two months before. By the time they arrived, they had both donned their leather jackets to keep out the cold of the evening. 'Quite a nice place to stop,' said Lupita, as they climbed down from their horses.

'Room for two?' said the landlady as they approached her desk in the drinking room.

Antonio would show his colours first. 'No, señora, two separate rooms, please.' Lupita looked at him with an ambiguous look which he interpreted as relief. He needed to speak to her about the mission in such terms that she could not possibly interpret his words as meaning he was spying so he decided he'd talk to her over dinner.

'There is something I want to explain to you, Lupita, before we reach Guadalajara. If we can, we'll be staying at an inn I know well. I have an interesting relationship with the landlady's daughter. More bluntly, we are lovers. I think you'll like her.'

'I have no strong views on that. Our relationship is professional but we are, I think, friends as well.'

'You're right,' he said. 'We are good friends and colleagues.'

'We all have little secrets! And you aren't the only one!'

Antonio wondered what hers might be but steered away from asking.

'So what happened in Valladolid? Where is Esteban? I know Carolina came back to Ávila. It was all a bit mysterious. The *corregidor* got her a pardon or something. No one knew exactly what happened but she is free as a bird now! And she's playing in a new troupe!'

Antonio thought hard before answering that question. He couldn't tell her exactly what happened so he'd have to invent a story. 'Esteban and I fell out. We had a row about whether we should stay in Valladolid or come back to Madrid. I wanted to come back and he wanted to stay. I told him we'd do better in Madrid because of the theatres. We could become part of a theatre troupe and do much better than just playing on the streets. We couldn't agree so we split up. Carolina came back with me but, when we reached Segovia, decided that she wanted to return home to Ávila. I wanted to go on to Madrid and, as far as she and I were concerned, that was fine. I'm really glad she's doing well in Ávila! I felt quite concerned for her as I watched her leave.'

'I'm sorry you broke with Esteban. You seemed to get on well, but he was quite fiery! Now for my surprise. I've brought you something. You'll never guess what it is!'

'Go on!'

'I didn't tell you, I play the flute and here it is!' She pulled her bag from under the table, took out the flute and played a few notes. Others in the room looked in amazement. Some even applauded.

'What an addition. We are a real troupe now. What freedom that gives us!'

'I knew you'd be pleased, Antonio. Thank you!'

They made an early start the following day and arrived at Jac's inn well in time for dinner. Antonio was surprised at how few customers there were in the normally busy drinking room. At least he would be able to talk to both Lupita and Jac without being overheard.

Jac couldn't believe that Antonio had arrived back there so soon. 'I'm so pleased to see you, Antonio. Who's the lady?'

'She's a colleague. We are working together and have come here to earn some cash. We are both street musicians now. We wanted a change from working in Madrid.'

'That's a comedown. You used to work in a theatre group. What's changed?'

'Tell me first, how is your father? He was improving well when I left.'

'He is so much better now. It's mother who is not so well. Mainly through overwork when he was ill. Even she is better today. I'm trying to do more so she can do less. Anyway, what happened to your job with the theatre band?'

It's a long story, Jac, but I'll give you the short version.' Antonio told her that he had broken with the Wandering Chordsmen and worked as a duet with Esteban. She couldn't remember him until he explained that he was the dwarf he saw being thrown up to the ceiling the last time he came to the inn.

'Let me sort out some dinner for you two. I've some beautiful lamb chops if you're interested or some pork fillets.' They chose the lamb if only because Jac recommended it so highly. Antonio and Lupita talked for several hours after dinner, mainly about how much Antonio knew about the town, where they would pitch to play, what they would play and how much they could expect for a day's work. Lupita felt tired after all of this talking, as she put it, and decided to go to her room.

Jac saw this as an opportunity to challenge Antonio about Lupita. She had finished the bulk of her work and brought a couple of beers over to his table, one for each of them.

'Well, Antonio. What's she to you then? Lovers or what?' she said, smiling only an apparent smile. She had no intention of sharing her body with him if Lupita and he were a couple.

'Our relationship is purely professional. Of course we are friends but that is because we work together. And we have separate rooms in your inn! We haven't played a note together since we were in Ávila a month ago. But she came to look for work in Madrid and here we are!'

'In Ávila? You played with her there?'

Antonio told her as much as he could about going with Esteban to Valladolid and meeting Lupita on the road.

'I can't believe she was dressed as a man. And fancy being almost hit by some great stone from the sky! What a shock! It's such a pleasure to see you back here. How long do you think you'll be here?'

'I don't really know, Jac. We are really here as street musicians. Maybe ten days. Are there any of Pedro's men who still visit your inn?', he said, not sure whether he wanted to know to protect himself or whether he could return to Silva with something he'd discovered about them.

'I'm sure there are some regular drinkers here who are part of that group. It's odd that there are none here tonight. If they are in tomorrow, I'll introduce you.'

Antonio smiled. Silva would surely be delighted if he could find out more. 'Have you finished for tonight, Jac?'

She knew full well what he had in mind. 'Why do you ask?'

'I just wondered if I could help you with anything.'

'Like getting me out of my clothes?'

'Something like that!'

'Let me get you another drink and you can follow me up,' she said, smiling and in a whisper.

Half an hour later, they were relaxing in Jac's bed having just made love. 'You are a good lover, Antonio. I always enjoy you!'

'The feeling is mutual, Jac. Have you a few more minutes before I go to my own bed?'

'You just want to cuddle up!'

First thing in the morning, Antonio and Lupita breakfasted and rode to the town square where Antonio and the Wandering Chordsmen had acted in Peribañez, just over two months before. They pitched there and played, on and off, all day. Autumn had dawned weeks before so they could perform in greater comfort than the troupe of actors and players could in the blazing heat of summer. Lupita surprised and amazed Antonio by her playing of the flute. She made it sing. With him accompanying her on the violin, she could bring tears to the eyes of some of the hardest looking characters who stopped to listen. After they had finished their first day's work, they had between them collected a creditable four *reales* and a few *maravedís*.

'I think I've had enough for today, Antonio. Let's ride back to the inn.' It was nearly six o'clock in the evening. Antonio willingly agreed and they went.

The two of them spent four days playing in this rich location. They would start at about nine in the morning and continue until six o'clock chimed on the church clock. In the meantime, Jac had failed to identify to Antonio any of Pedro's former colleagues.

'I wonder if they are using a different tavern. Is it possible that they know you are here and are avoiding you? Do they suspect you in some way or for some reason?' asked Jac, as frustrated as Antonio at having made no progress in spotting any of Pedro's men.

'I'd say it's impossible for them to know I'm here. Why would they want to avoid me? They can hardly know I reported what you told me to the *corregidor*. If they knew, I'd probably be dead by now!'

Lupita showed no sign of impatience or frustration and enjoyed herself playing in the *plaza* pitch. She even applauded in return those of the passers-by who applauded her singing or the efforts of both her and Antonio as instrumentalists.

On the fifth night, as Antonio and Lupita were about to finish enjoying a dinner prepared by Jac's mother, Jac approached their table. 'They are here, Antonio. The men you are interested in. They are in a booth towards the back. You can't miss them. They are each wearing wide brimmed hats, just like the one Pedro used to wear. There are three of them. I'll leave them to you now! I'll be here in the bar or in the kitchen.'

'Who are these people?' said Lupita.

'Some men who know Esteban. It would be good to find out where he is now and what he's doing. Stay and we can both talk to them, if you wish.'

'I thought you fell out with him. So why the interest?'

'Just harmless curiosity,' he said coolly.

'I'm tired so if you don't mind, I think I'll go to bed. Goodnight.' Lupita left him sitting alone at the table. He sat there for five minutes before he stood up and went over to the men.

'Good evening, señores. Do you mind if I join you for a drink. Anyone for another beer or a glass of red maybe?'

'Who are you?' said the man who looked to be in charge, a blotchy faced individual who appeared to have had quite enough to drink.

'My name is Antonio Hidalgo. I'm a travelling musician. There are two of us here, my colleague, Lupita de Pastrana and me. She's gone to her room and I just thought I'd join you men for a friendly chat.'

'Can't see much wrong with that,' said another of them, an older looking individual with a greying braid tied at the back. 'Especially if he wants to buy us a drink.' The three broke into laughter. Antonio went up to Jac and ordered the drinks they wanted. He chose another beer for himself and between him and Jac, they carried the drinks to the booth.

'You may as well sit with us. Plenty of room,' said the apparent leader.

'Thanks. I've said what I do. What about you gentlemen?'

'We three have very different jobs. I'm a wheelwright,' said the leader. 'Old Benito here is a brewer,' he said, turning to the man with the greying braid.

'And I'm a butcher,' said the third, a shorter, thickset man, with a large curled up moustache who blatantly decided to introduced himself and not just leave it to the apparent head of the group. 'And my name is Nicolas.'

'Hope I remember your names,' said Antonio. 'I've forgotten yours already, señor,' he said, turning to the apparent leader, a substantially large man with a large head whom Antonio thought he'd have trouble with in a fight.

'I didn't tell you mine!' said the man. 'It's Gabriel...after the angel.'

'Yes he nearly was the angel. His mother wanted to call him, Ángel,' said the one called Nicolas.

'Rubbish!' retorted Gabriel.

'So what brings you together?' asked Antonio, fairly confident that he already knew.

'We will get to that,' said Gabriel, taking a swig from his mug of beer. 'You brew this stuff don't you, Benito?' he said, interrupting himself.

'It's a good beer, clean and pure...not 'stuff' as you put it!' was the joking response.

'Yes, we'll tell you,' resumed Gabriel. 'It's a bit tricky and we don't tell everyone. But we will get there, to be sure. Let's chat around a few other things first. Starting with politics. What do you think of the *Morisco* problem?'

'It's easy to say where I stand. I'm a non-practicing Christian, what many call an unbeliever. So I can't see a religious argument against the *Moriscos*. No. I can't even see why they were expected to convert. I believe in live and let live. Worship any god you like, I say. And someone told me once that Allah is the same god as the Christians worship. So I can't understand the arguments against them. So I'm in favour of leaving the *Moriscos* to live as they please and worship as they please. In fact, my colleague, Lupita, is a *Morisca* and we get on well.'

'A very mature view, for a young man,' said Nicolas.

'I agree,' said Benito.

'Is what you are saying true or are you making it up?' said Gabriel. The others just looked at each other in amazement at this unexpected remark. Antonio winced inwardly. 'Have you any proof that you are a *Morisco* sympathiser?'

'Hmm…that's a difficult question for me,' said Antonio, then taking a draught of his beer. 'Put it this way. I can give you that evidence but only if you, too, are *Morisco* sympathisers.'

Gabriel stepped in quickly. 'And you would want some evidence as well, I suppose.'

'It's a case of mutual protection. We need to be confident before giving our evidence that the other side won't go to the authorities and report any illegal or questionable activity,' said Antonio, setting out concisely what he expected. 'Then there is the matter of who gives theirs first!'

'Well, it may surprise you to know that we are *Moriscos*,' said Gabriel. 'So by definition we are sympathisers! Do I need to put more cards on the table?'

'What if I play the next card in this game?'

'Go ahead,' said the butcher, Nicolas, almost undermining Gabriel.

'Right. Does the name Pedro or Hajib al-Asadi, mean anything to you?'

It soon became clear that the three knew Pedro and Esteban and knew that they were both incarcerated in a prison in Valladolid. Pedro had been charged with murdering a deputy but they refused to say why Esteban had been detained. They each bade each other goodnight and suggested that they meet the following day.

Lupita delighted in her time in Guadalajara. She revelled at the closeness of the audience, being able to see the reaction to her singing and flute playing. It differed so much from the remoteness of the audiences in the Príncipe or in other theatres. She enjoyed the fact that Antonio was only her friend and had, it seemed, no intention of wanting to be her lover. A little over thirty, she had no desire to be part of a relationship. She was wedded to her music and that was all she really wanted. Neither did she want riches. Her parents had quite sufficient wealth, mainly invested in her father's properties in Ávila and Salamanca, so if she earned sufficient to pay for food and lodging for her and her young white stallion, she was more than content. She could always ask her parents for financial help, if she needed it.

That day the two of them worked hard at their pitch in the *plaza* but he couldn't shake from his mind the expected encounter that evening with Gabriel, Benito and Nicolas. Would he learn more about any scheming in which this odd combination was engaged? Would he have to reveal more about his own role in the attempt on the king to reap the reward of treasonable revelations?

Once again, after dinner with Antonio, Lupita departed for her bed and left him to speak to the three *Moriscos* who were already ensconced in a drinking room booth, laughing and chatting amongst themselves. Antonio ambled over.

'Oh, you've come back,' said Gabriel.

'Thought one of you might buy me a drink.'

'Why should we when you failed to give us the full story?'

'What do you mean?'

'Nicolas and Benito made some enquiries about you.'

'Really?'

'You may remember the name, Jaime Fernandez.'

'Just let me think a moment. Umm…' Antonio hesitated. To admit he knew him would confirm to them that he was in Valladolid the night before the raid on the palace. He met him then for the first time and they must know that. What could be the risk to him if he made the admission they were seeking? If they realised that he had played a destructive role they might kill him. But if his true role was known to Pedro's henchman, why hadn't they sought him out in Madrid and killed him there. They wouldn't have waited for him to come, by chance, to Guadalajara. Silva was right on that count. The solution became obvious. They had discovered that he had gone to Valladolid as a member of Pedro's team. Assuming that they did not realise he was acting as an agent, his role could only be constructive. This being so they might ask him to join another group in a new plot to capture the king or a different plot.

'Yes, I remember the name well. I met Jaime Fernandez while Esteban and I were working for Pedro in Valladolid.'

'So you are the Antonio Hidalgo who went with Esteban. You picked up a dwarf woman and another woman who left you in Ávila. Is that right?' said Bendito.

'Why didn't you tell us before?' asked Gabriel.

'I didn't know you well enough. We were all playing with shadows last night and I decided to let you know I knew Pedro and how I met him. But I didn't know enough about you three to trust you with the more sensitive information, namely that I worked for Pedro in that mission in which he and Esteban were arrested.'

'Why didn't they arrest you?' asked Nicolas.

'When I realised they were arresting Esteban, I cleared my things out of my room and went into the dwarf lady, Carolina's. I hid in her wardrobe. They went into my room but I was hiding in hers. So I escaped. Carolina and I headed out of Valladolid as quickly as we could. We kept looking over our shoulders but no one came after us. Three days later I was back in Madrid.'

'You and the dwarf lady were the only ones to get away. You were lucky, believe me,' said Gabriel. 'The rest are all on trial for treason, possession of firearms, endangering the king and God knows what else. Well done for fooling them.'

'Well, are we going to ask him?' said Nicolas.

'Give me a chance. I'm still taking in what he's just said. At first I didn't believe him but he seems to be telling the truth.' He stood up and looked around the area of the booth but could see nobody else in the adjacent booths or tables. 'Listen, Antonio, and listen carefully. That attack on the palace failed. The next one won't. Do you want to join us a trusted member of the group which will plan it? Your experience of the last time will be invaluable. You can even go with your partner and act as a music troupe. If you agree we can give you exceptional terms. You could make some good money. You would start as soon as you could, tomorrow even.'

'Thank you, Gabriel. That is an exceptional offer. I would be delighted to take it up.'

Gabriel frowned. 'What do you mean, would be?'

'I would but I'm not available. Lupita and I have a meeting at the Príncipe theatre in Madrid next week about appearing in a play. We are both keen to do that. So I won't be taking up your offer. Sorry, my friend. I wish you luck.'

'I'm disappointed but that won't stop me buying you a drink. Get him a drink, Benito. I can't say we were relying on you because we only discovered by accident you were here. I must tell you one more thing. I'm sure we can trust you to tell no one about our developing plans. If we discover that you've told anybody else, we will kill you. Need I say more?'

'No. Why would I tell anyone?' said Antonio, shrugging his shoulders.

'For a reward. But your ultimate reward would be death,' said Gabriel, showing no emotion.

'You needn't worry about me. I was part of a failed mission before and I hope it is successful this time. Let's drink to that,' said Antonio, raising the pot of beer that Benito had bought him. The three of them raised their glasses.

Antonio made the first move to go. He wondered how convincing he had been with his story of escaping from Valladolid without being arrested. Whether he had or not, the three of them appeared to have fallen for it. His first priority became, from that instant, to inform Silva that a new plot against the king was being conceived there and, of course, to return to Madrid. He had to tell Lupita that they needed to travel back. He decided that he didn't want to disappear too quickly. That would serve only to raise Gabriel and his friends' suspicions. So they would, if Lupita agreed, stay for another two days in Guadalajara and then return, and leave early in the morning.

Lupita couldn't understand why he was so keen to return. 'But we are working so well here and together. I like it here; and playing with you, Antonio. Couldn't we just stay another week? Go on!'

Antonio didn't want to disappoint her so worked out a compromise, more than slightly weighed towards his own wishes and something that he felt Silva would find acceptable. He would write to him that night and they'd stay just for another four days. Lupita agreed.

'I'm so sorry you are going back, Antonio. When do you think you'll return?' said Jac, as they were lying a little breathlessly in his bed. 'I've seen so much less of you this time. I've just had to spend more time helping my mother.'

'I wish I knew when I'll be back but I don't.'

'Did you find out what you wanted from those three men?' she said, pulling the bedclothes over herself and turning to face him.

'Yes, and I'm grateful to you for pointing them out,' he said with a strong note of seriousness in his voice.

'Can you tell me more?' she smiled.

'Yes, but then I'd have to shoot you. Seriously, it's better that we don't discuss what they said. So I'm not going to tell you!'

'You bastard!' she chided and laughed.

That night, Antonio drafted a short note for Algebra. In case it was intercepted by those who had an interest in its content he wrote it, not in code but in an abstract which Algebra would understand but hopefully others would fail to. He merely said:

15 December 1605
Algebra,
The next play is being rehearsed.
I'll be at the castle theatre in six days.
Diaspora.

He would surely understand that. The following morning while he and Lupita were riding to their pitch at the *plaza*, he called into the *corregidor's* office with the letter asked the private secretary to seal it and arrange for its delivery to Algebra. He left the innocent Lupita outside, patiently astride her white stallion.

Four days later, they said their goodbyes to Jac and her parents and loaded their horses for the return journey to Madrid. 'We're on our way back home, old gal. Don't worry, we'll not be rushing you.' His trusty horse looked at him as if to say, I'm happy with that. She swished her tail, knowingly. They turned to wave to Jac and were on their way.

Antonio decided to turn up at Silva's office as soon as he could after nine o'clock in the morning. Hector Brondate welcomed him.

'Good morning, Señor Hidalgo. I'm afraid the *regidor* is at a meeting with the Head of The Armoury. Is there any way in which I may be able to assist?'

Antonio's head was exploding with the information he had garnered in Guadalajara and really didn't want to impart it to the private secretary, however good the man's intentions. 'I'm back from Guadalajara with some sensitive information. I am perfectly content to await his return. When, may I ask, is that likely to be?'

'He should be back by midday. Can I give you an appointment for say one o'clock?'

Antonio just about kept his frustration in check but it must have shown in the glaring of his eyes. 'Yes. That will have to do. Thank you. I'll be here at about five to.'

Astride his trusty horse and walking her back towards his apartment in Doña Marta's house, an interesting thought occurred to him. He'd go to see Catalina. She may have calmed down by now and be pleased to see him again. He'd risk an adverse reaction so, patting his horse's neck and pulling the reins slightly, he signalled her to trot to the house in the Calle Mayor. He tied up the horse and knocked on the door. Francisca opened it and immediately planted a generous kiss on Antonio's mouth. 'I'm so pleased to see you, Antonio. I've thought about you a lot these last few weeks. Do come in.'

Antonio was astonished and could not understand the significance of this kiss. He put a hand to his lips in disbelief. He couldn't imagine what had provoked it, or her remark about thinking of him. Francisca usually ignored him or at best dismissed him with a peremptory hello. 'Thank you, Francisca. I'd be delighted.' He glanced back at his horse as if to tell her that something strange and as yet unexplained was happening to him and followed her in. They sat on one of the sofas before she spoke again.

'Please don't ask about Catalina. I'll tell you about her later. But I think I'm in love with you, Antonio. I really do!'

'But…but…we've well… we've hardly spoken over the two years I've been coming to see Catalina. What's changed?' He was still in shock at what had happened on the doorstep. He was too shocked to show any sign of appreciating or wishing to reciprocate her feelings. It seemed that she wanted to take over where Catalina had left off. He wasn't sure he wanted that.

'I've always liked you, Antonio. And when you finished with Catalina, I saw this as my chance. I've been thinking about you ever since you went to Guadalajara.'

She slid up close to him on the sofa and put her arm around his neck. Her whole demeanour stunned him, almost into silence.

'You really flatter me, Francisca. I'm sorry that I'm so stuck for words. You've taken me by surprise. I just don't know to say. I'll have to think about it. Is that all right? By the way she finished with me, not the other way around!'

'I am a patient person, Antonio. Sometimes it takes time for love to blossom. I can wait. Can I ask you a question?'

He was relieved at her answer. She differed so much from the fiery Catalina who, in Francisca's shoes, would have shown him the door by now. Vagueness and uncertainty were not in Catalina's vocabulary. 'Yes, of course.'

'Do you have a current lady friend? I'd like to know that. And who is this Lupita that Catalina spoke of?'

'I do not have a lady friend at the moment. I know quite a number of women and I've bedded more than a few, including Catalina, but you knew that. Lupita is a colleague. She is a brilliant singer and flautist. We are a duet who play on the streets. You'll probably see us in the Selenque market or in the Plaza Mayor. But I promise you our relationship is purely professional. She's not interested in a relationship. She's in love with her music.'

'I'm happy with that, Antonio. I can understand you having the odd lady friend away from Madrid. But if you want a relationship with me, I would expect to be your one serious lady friend. My father would expect that, too. So would mother.'

Antonio didn't quite understand what 'the odd lady friend away from Madrid' meant, whether it followed that he could have intimate relations with them and still enjoy a relationship with Francisca. He didn't see the point in asking, especially not then. 'Give me time, Francisca and I will let you know.'

She still had her arm around him so he turned towards her and planted a kiss on her cheek. 'There you are, a sign of good faith.'

By the time he had told her about their trip to Guadalajara and she had told him the news about Catalina - she had gone to live with a nurse friend to the east of the town near the General Hospital - it was time for him to return to the palace to meet the *regidor*.

'I don't know what to make of Francisca's offer, old gal,' he muttered as he walked her back. 'She's a lovely homely lady and would make a good mother and wife. But I'm not sure I'm ready for home comforts yet. I'm still a young man.' The horse shook its head and sputtered.

Brondate greeted Antonio as he opened the door into the *regidor*'s outer office. 'He's still not back, señor. But I'm expecting him at any time and he is expecting you. Take a seat,' he said pointing to a plain wooden chair in a corner.

'Don't mind if I do. Have you seen Iago lately?'

'Yes, he's been doing some solo playing in the squares and in some taverns. I don't think he has anything else.'

'He said he'd join me and my colleague Lupita. I'll ask him.'

With that the *regidor* appeared and greeted Antonio with a vigorous handshake and a smile. 'You and your coded messages! "The next play is being rehearsed"! And, by the way, welcome back to the castle theatre!'

All three laughed at the *regidor*'s joke. 'Not a bad code for a beginner. Not many would have cracked that one. I had a job to myself!' he chuckled. 'But seriously, Antonio, your message has been passed to the Council for State Security and they are taking it extremely seriously. I cannot tell you what action they are planning to take but much depends on what you tell me now. Well done in taking the initiative when you weren't on a mission at all! Naturally, I want the full story. Come into my office. You, too, Hector. Take a note of this.'

Antonio gave Silva a detailed report of his meetings with Gabriel, Benito and Nicolas. He told him exactly what they had said.

'You mean you didn't get their patronymics or locatives?'

'No. Too difficult. Would have raised their suspicions. What I did find was that they are respectively, a wheelwright, a brewer and a butcher.'

'How do you know they were not fooling you?'

'Why would they when they were offering me a well-paid job helping them with their planning?'

'Don't ask me. I'm asking you!'

'I've come back here with some sensitive information. I took the initiative to find it… at considerable risk I might add.' said Antonio, beginning to lose patience with Silva. 'That is what I'm reporting to you. I did my best and I've checked what I was told for consistency. There is no doubt that they are beginning to plan another attack. It's now up to you to decide how to use the information I've given you, including my physical descriptions of these three men. Whoever returns to identify and arrest them could do worse than enlist the help of Jac.'

'Hm… I'm not sure about all this. The key information I need but you haven't obtained is their patronymics. I'm not sure what we can do with just their first names.'

'Here's an idea for you. Ask Jac in a letter for their second names. She'd be too willing to help! You could offer her a reward!'

'I can't do that. Ask someone who's not one of us to do our job! And I'm less sure about a reward.'

Antonio strained to contain his anger. 'Just you listen to me, Silva,' he said, not quite shouting. 'Nothing I did was conditional on extracting surnames, addresses or anything else from these people. If you don't reward her, I will. And what damn good are the surnames anyway? A name doesn't put a face on someone. My descriptions and knowing their occupations will be much more useful. Maybe I should have stayed there longer. If I did I would have found out more about them. I've certainly learnt from this experience.' He'd certainly learned more about working for Silva.

'I'm sorry, Antonio. I keep forgetting that you are still new to this shady business. After your amazing success in Valladolid, I think of you as highly experienced when you are not. There are many ways in which you are right.' He turned to Hector. 'You'll have to be careful minuting this. I don't want to appear unnecessarily difficult. And the Council will have to manage without these men's addresses and surnames.'

At least friendship appeared to be restored.

'Did you get Antonio's detailed descriptions of them, Hector?'

'I think so,' murmured the feeble sounding functionary.

Antonio couldn't resist asking the critical question. 'So what's the next assignment, Silva. Unless I am being dismissed because of this one!'

'Don't be absurd! Your next one will be abroad. You will be travelling on the high seas. I cannot say to where at this moment. Nor when I will know. The Council will tell me when they want me to send you. It depends on The Duke of Lerma's position, as I told you before.'

'Oh... they all know it's me who will be going then?' said Antonio, with renewed confidence and enthusiasm. At last his training with Lusitano would be put to some use.

'Yes. We spent a lot of money educating you. Too much to have to start again! Whatever mess you made of your free time in Guadalajara,' he chided or so Antonio thought.

'Should I start working again as a street performer?'

'Yes. That would be a sensible idea. I will contact you again when I have more to tell you. Let me give you this.' He handed Antonio a small purse which contained his latest payment.

CHAPTER 17
A major decision

For a Valladolid January, the one of 1606 was comparatively mild. The five men had assembled in the great hall of the fifteenth century castle in Ampudia, a small hamlet about five *leguas* to the north of Valladolid. The Duke of Lerma had taken the king and queen to Ampudia to celebrate the granting of collegial status to its church, which the duke had transformed with the aid of a large donation from Pope Clement VIII. True to his word, the duke had arranged for Silva de Torres and two less senior Madrid *regidors* to be present at this crucial and, as far as the duke was concerned, conclusive gathering. He had decided that the move would take place and he just needed to push the king towards agreement. The meeting had finished and the *regidors* had been escorted from the castle.

'Well, Philip, what did you make of all that?'

'Madrid is collapsing if they are to be believed. I'm not so sure.'

'But Silva de Torres is one of our most trusted men. You've delegated to him the powers to control our special agents. There is no other *regidor* we trust to that degree. You know that.'

'True, I'm sure.'

'And he was amply supported by his colleagues.'

'Do we have to decide now? Can't we delay it? We've been here for all but five years and I enjoy it here. All the hunting on your estates. You'd miss it, too.'

The Duke of Lerma let out an ambiguous utterance. It sounded like something between a 'tut' and a 'wheeze'. Perhaps he was half way through a sigh and changed his mind. 'With respect, Philip, you've missed the point. It's not what we want. It's what the people of Madrid want. We can come here whenever we wish. And I'm sure we will. And don't lose sight of all the hunting grounds near Madrid. You will remember that you asked to see these people because you seriously doubted what I was telling you. Now you've had it from them. I can decide if you don't want to do so. You've given me enough power.'

'I've decided. We've both decided. We'll go back to Madrid. The whole Court,' the king smiled vacantly, as if he'd uttered these words with great reluctance.

'Congratulations, Majesty. Everyone will respect you for that,' said the duke, not meaning it in the slightest. 'I'll begin the process. There will be various negotiations to conduct and appointments to make.'

'What negotiations?'

'Madrid want to pay you for going back there. Well, they don't want to pay but you know what I mean!'

The king smiled, almost to the point of salivation. 'How much have they in mind?'

'Something like a hundred thousand *ducats.*'

'By the blood of Christ. Never!'

'Exactly. We can try for more. I was thinking of a twentieth of their rents for five or ten years maybe but we mustn't push them too far. Handing out a few promotions might prove highly effective and not too expensive. De Torres could be elevated to *corregidor*, maybe...'

'He's the Algebra character, isn't he?' said the king, twirling his moustache with his right forefinger.

'Yes. More about him later. But we'll need to elevate a few more. More than just de Torres. Maybe a few local officials here. This town will suffer terribly when half of its population move to Madrid. It will be devastated. Might reduce the stench of the place though. Fewer assholes so less shit dumped into the Pisguera. The place could smell quite sweet after a month or so. So we'll need some of our people to take control. We certainly don't want any trouble here spilling over to Madrid.'

'I know what you are saying,' said the king, sounding puzzled and vulnerable. Lerma had him in the palm of his hand so could manipulate him like a glove puppet. 'What about Sarmiento de Acuña. He's a good *corregidor*. We could give him something of greater status while keeping him here to run the show while we're back in Madrid. Especially if it's going to be as bad as you say.'

'I'll think about that. We'll need someone to manage the move back. That's not your job or mine. Maybe Algebra could do it, especially if we gave him a leg up.'

'I like that, Francisco,' chuckled the king. 'What were you going to tell me about him? You're keeping that under your hat.' The king grinned in anticipation, as if expecting something salacious or at least defamatory.

'Yes, I think we've done with the move. Apart from finishing the negotiations and promotions. But I'll work on those and come back to you. Yes, he sent that *tio* Hidalgo to Guadalajara, the one who thwarted the attack on the palace. He sent him for his own protection... or so he says. From what he came back with, we suspect the same group is starting up again. Planning another attack. They want to kidnap you, just like the last lot.'

'You make it sound like they're planning to kidnap a donkey, not your illustrious monarch,' snorted the king, as he slapped his fist on the table.

'Profound apologies, Majesty.' The duke winced. 'I didn't mean it to come out as so matter of fact. I suppose it's that I feel so confident in stopping them.'

'Did he find out who they are?'

'Yes, their names, occupations and descriptions. Only thing he missed were the surnames. Not a problem. We'll stop them before they leave Guadalajara.'

'How do we know these people told Hidalgo the truth? Could have been just toying with him. Bravado! Wanted to appear like tough thugs. Is there any other, independent evidence? From someone other than this Hidalgo character. A woman overheard the last lot. Is she in this somewhere? Am I talking rubbish, Francisco?'

'Indeed not, Philip. We don't have independent evidence. But we can't risk waiting for it. We feel confident that Hidalgo - Diaspora - was not fooled. He seems to know what he's doing,' said Lerma, pouring well-meant praise on Antonio.

'So what are we going to do to stop them?' The king said, eyes wide open and raising his hands to head height. He still felt for James I and the plot to kill him.

'We are working with Alonso Guzman, in Guadalajara. He has put a team together to identify them and arrest them for treason.'

'They'd better get on with it. Just make sure they succeed,' said the king. 'And keep me informed. I want a daily report.'

Part IV

CHAPTER 18
Where next?

After the somewhat moody meeting with Silva, Antonio decided he'd head for Lupita's house and take a chance on whether she'd be in. It was almost a *milla* from the Alcázar Palace so he'd walk alongside his horse and reflect upon what Silva had said. Antonio still felt bruised at Silva's condemnation of his work in Guadalajara. What had he expected? He had discovered this information while acting purely on his own initiative. Antonio decided that he should not be too distressed by the interview. Various pressures, probably originating in Valladolid, were exercising Silva, both as *regidor* and as trusted delegatee of powers to engage the king's special agents. These could effortlessly transform any saint into a sinner. The meeting with Silva had, however, ended well and Antonio took comfort, if not pride, in it.

Lupita opened the door of the house she shared, almost at the instant he knocked. 'Have you been waiting for me in the hall?' he jested.

'I just happened to be here! So no! I didn't expect to see you today,' she said, looking puzzled and a little confused.

'I've come with some news!' He told Lupita that he would soon be sent on a new mission. He didn't know where that would be but he would certainly tell her before he went. And the likelihood was that he'd be gone for a good few months.

'What the hell am I supposed to do when you're gone? Working with you is the only job I've got. My only source of income. There's nothing doing at the Príncipe and none of my friends have any ideas for work.' The reaction of this normally placid woman shocked Antonio. So she had been trying for alternatives. He wondered why, especially when they seemed to be working together so well. Maybe she thought her talents deserved better than being exercised only on the streets.

'I'm sorry, Lupita, but don't forget Iago. He should join us now we're back. He welcomed you into our troupe, remember? And he's been working solo while we've been away.'

'I've become so used to working with you, I almost forgot!' Antonio was relieved. He couldn't face another problem involving a woman. The one with Catalina had to be sufficient, at least for then.

Iago smiled with delight. He immediately agreed to meet with them the following day in the *plaza* in front of the palace. He could be an awkward and temperamental individual but somehow he had quite taken to Lupita when they first met at her house in the Mentidero.

While walking back to his rooms in Doña Marta's house, he had another thought: Francisca. He'd tell her the news about going abroad. He thought it only fair to a woman who had expressed her love for him, even if he was not yet ready to reciprocate. 'Come on, old gal, time to stable you. I'll be back soon.' The horse seemed happy after its day walking the streets of Madrid and flicked her head accordingly.

Antonio walked back up the Calle de Toledo towards the Calle Mayor. Francisca's mother welcomed him into the house, while Francisca stood behind her. 'Hello, Antonio. Come in! You were only here this morning.'

'I was. Only I have something to tell Francisca.' The señora dissolved away and left the two of them in the hall.

'What is it, Antonio? Not bad news! Come into the drawing room,' said Francisca, after planting an affectionate kiss on his cheek.

'I thought I should let you know, I shall probably be going abroad sooner or later. I don't know where and I don't know when. I can't tell you more. I wish I could but I can't. Nor can I say how long I'll be going for. I'm sure I'll be able to tell you more when I know more myself. I hope you don't mind me telling you this. I thought it only fair. Especially after what you told me this morning.'

Francisca hugged him and remained silent for a few moments. 'Antonio, I'm truly grateful for that. I like to avoid unnecessary surprises so I won't be surprised when it happens. Would you like to stop for a drink?'

'Thanks but I'd better go. Our little group is playing in the Plaza Mayor tomorrow. I need to work on the programme!'

The three of them met in the *plaza*, set up their pitch and played. They followed Antonio's freshly prepared notes, based on the various songs and tunes which he, Lupita, Carolina and Esteban had performed in Ávila. He daren't include 'Woe is me, Alhama': none of them would appreciate a riot as vicious as the one in Ávila. But he did include some new songs which he knew quite well and felt confident that Lupita and Iago would soon pick them up, if they didn't know them already.

They played well together and with moderate success in all weathers. That year Madrid suffered a miserable start to its winter months so they did their best to add a little cheer, usually rewarded by generous passers-by. It seemed a contradiction in many ways. People who suffered incredible deprivation in this failing city willingly threw the odd *maravedí* coin or two *maravedí* piece into the little bowl they had placed in front of them. It seemed that the poorer the person the more generous they would be. Children delighted in the splash the coin made, if it had been raining and the bowl was all but full of water. The work also had its bad side. Several times their bowl was launched into the air by some ill-tempered brute. Often they were the subject of verbal abuse. On one occasion, a passing vagabond undid his fly and urinated into their pot. None of them expected that.

They would almost always end up in a local tavern, sometimes The Silversmith, where they would count their daily takings before either Antonio or Iago would escort Lupita to her place in the Mentidero. Antonio usually arrived home exhausted after these long days of constantly playing his trusty and valued violin.

One night, after they had been performing on the streets for nigh on six weeks, Antonio was about to enter the house alone when he felt a hand on his shoulder. He flinched. He was totally unarmed and could only use his fists to escape from any trouble. He looked around and gave a sigh of relief.

'I think this is for you, señor.' The knarled stranger, the same messenger as before, placed a sealed envelope into his hand and vanished. Antonio almost fell over in his efforts to enter the house. News from Silva! He'd be going abroad! He dashed up to an oil lamp in the hall way and opened the envelope. A note fell out. He picked it up and read it:

29 January 1606
Diaspora,
Urgent. Please meet me at 8 o'clock tomorrow morning, in my office.
Algebra

Antonio hardly slept that night. He just lay there contemplating the certain journey ahead of him. Where would he be going? First he had a feeling it could be to France. The French appeared to be siding with the

196

Moriscos and maybe he would be sent to Paris to discover whether they had plans to assist the *Moriscos* in their endeavours to attack the king or to make their position in Spain more secure. But France would simply be an overland journey and hadn't Silva talked about a journey by sea? Maybe Italy would be his destination. Did the Council for State Security need to know something critical about the disposition of the armies in the Italian states? While they were our allies, the feeling came across strongly that they could not always be trusted to support the interests of Spain. Or maybe he would be sent to… At that point his speculation dissolved into sleep, so sound that he struggled to wake in time to arrive at the Alcázar Palace for an 8 o'clock meeting. However, breathlessly and not without some anxiety, he did.

'Come in, Antonio. I have some important news for you. About your next assignment. Let me explain.'

Antonio wondered what this could mean. Would he be going abroad or not? Silva must have spent a significant amount with Lusitano on training him as a merchant. Surely he would be going on a trade mission.

'You will not be aware, just yet, that the king has decided to return his court to Madrid.'

'My goodness, Silva. When can we celebrate? What excellent news for our city!' Antonio realised straightaway that the consequences of this transfer would be colossal. A huge number of civil servants would descend on the city. Many would be handsomely paid and their cash would soon be circulating in the shops and markets. There would be more money for everybody to spend. Trade in every sector would increase. Property prices would rise and make it more worthwhile to build. Demand for goods would rise. Even street musicians like him, Iago and Lupita couldn't fail to benefit. But how could it affect his next mission and what would it be?

'This has important implications for you. The king and his government will begin moving within the next few weeks. Lerma is concerned that the *Moriscos*, or others, might see this as an opportunity to attack the many convoys of people and their belongings as they go from Valladolid to Madrid. We will be moving some twenty thousand staff and the king and his retinue. It is an enormous logistical exercise and I am in charge of organising it. On promotion, would you believe, to *corregidor*!'

Antonio interrupted Silva's flow. 'Hearty congratulations, Silva. That is brilliant news, for you, too! So where do I fit in?'

'Just be patient will you!' said Silva, feeling just slightly irritated that Antonio had chosen not to let him finish but, even so, smiling at the hearty recognition of his advancement. 'You will go to Segovia and listen out for any plots that might be hatching there to attack these convoys. This will mean delaying any trip we were planning for you to go abroad. Before you interrupt me again,' he laughed, 'I can confirm that you will probably, in due course, be going abroad on a key mission but that I cannot, at this time tell you what its aims will be.'

So only probably, not certainly, despite Lusitano's training. Antonio realised that he had erred in breaking the flow of Silva's discourse and realised that he should apologise.

'Apology accepted, Antonio. But thank you for your congratulations. I can understand your professional anxieties but you have nothing to worry about in terms of working as an agent. You will have to be patient about the foreign mission. My advice is to forget about it for now and concentrate on this one. There are several ways in which it will be different. Firstly, I don't want you performing as a street musician. Take your violin by all means. It will give you useful cover if you decide to play it in a tavern one night! Secondly, you will pretend to be a merchant. A wool merchant in fact, buying for export. You already know about being a merchant and I have an interesting idea which will help you. You can ask me what it is!'

'You are going to give me a thousand *ducats* to spend?'

'Not quite. You will not actually be entering any contractual arrangements, No. It is that Lucitano will accompany you!'

'Excellent! I like him. He will be good company!'

'Good. But he will leave you in Segovia and go to Valladolid, keeping an ear to the ground there.'

'Can I try an idea on you, Silva?'

'Go ahead.'

'When we were in Segovia last time, what, about three months ago, our music troupe stayed in an inn which Esteban recommended. I think I may have told you about it. I confessed to not being a *Morisco* in this *Morisco* stronghold and had it not been for the intervention of the landlady, Ángelita, I could have been kicked to death.'

'Where is this leading? Interrupting you this time!'

'This inn would be the ideal place to start because *Moriscos* meet there. If I went back as a musician, rather than as wool merchant, that would be consistent with my previous role. If a wool merchant they would suspect that something was wrong so I couldn't go there.'

'Brilliant, Antonio. You've convinced me. Musician you are, even a street musician. You might even want to meet up with someone to make a duet.'

'I'll see what I can do when I arrive there!' Antonio had quickly overcome his disappointment at not yet going on the foreign mission and was beginning to warm to the idea of this one, especially as he would be accompanied by Lucitano, at least until they reached Segovia. He could well be alone from then.

'We seemed to have settled on the idea then, Antonio. There is something else I must tell you. Communication is going to be the key to this assignment. I need to know what is going on as soon as possible after you find out. You should therefore, as usual, go to the *regidor*'s office with a letter to Algebra.'

'Some questions, Silva. Firstly, will there be anyone else, as it were, on the lookout, in Segovia? How soon do you want me in Segovia and when should I leave Madrid?'

'No, you will be our only agent in Segovia. I want you there as soon as possible and you leave with Lucitano in three days' time, if not before. I know your horse is a little old and therefore slow. So I want you to take one from the palace stables. I will arrange for yours to be looked after while you are away. Any more questions?'

'Presumably, Lucitano has been briefed?'

'Fully. He is expecting you to meet him to agree a time to leave. Can I leave all that to you?'

'Of course.'

'Good luck, Antonio. As I said, stay in touch. If you have any problems the *corregidor*'s office can help you. Or you can contact me. A response from here will, naturally, be a lot slower!'

With a manly handshake and smiling at each other, they bade each other farewell.

Antonio returned to the *plaza* to meet Iago and Lupita. He thought he should let the other two know as soon as he could that he would be leaving them for a time. Iago vented his fury. He fully expected that Antonio would work with the three of them as a trio, at least for three or four months. Maybe until one of them had found a job in a theatre or at least more lucrative work than being street musicians. He strongly objected to this sudden change of plan.

'So why exactly are you going to Segovia?' he said, looking accusingly at Antonio, as if he was going there for some illegal or at least unsavoury purpose.

Antonio decided not to lie. 'I am going is for personal reasons I cannot discuss. I'm sorry but that is how it is.'

'I think we should sack him,' said Iago. 'Don't you?' He looked at Lupita fully expecting her agreement.

'No. If Antonio has reasons to go there and he doesn't want to discuss them, that's up to him. We should simply accept that and wish him well. You'll be welcomed back with open arms!' she smiled. Lupita had saved the day, at least as far as Antonio was concerned. Iago didn't want to disagree with her as well. That would put him in the precarious position he didn't want to be in. So then they started to play together as if nothing had been said.

Antonio had to tell Francisca. So the night before his departure, he arrived at the front door of her parents' house in the Calle Mayor, to be greeted by her mother. 'Hello, Antonio. I'll get Francisca,' she chuckled, ushering him into the drawing room. 'Take a seat.'

Francisca was perplexed at seeing him. 'Whatever's happened? You've made a decision. You don't want me.' Then she started to sob. Poor Antonio failed to understand. Although he had not declared his love for her, the two had remained friends and had met several times in those six weeks or so. He had even spent Christmas day with her family, if slightly awkwardly with Catalina also there.

'Don't do that, Francisca,' he said, putting an arm around her shoulder. 'No such thing. I'm still very fond of you and have made no decisions at all. I just wanted to tell you that there has been a change of plan and I'm being sent to Segovia before I go abroad. In fact I'm off tomorrow and I'll be gone for a few weeks. I'm not sure quite how long.'

'Oh, Antonio, I'm so relieved. I was thinking the worst. I'm sorry. Why the change of plan? They are messing you around.'

'As I've said, there is business I am involved in that I cannot discuss. Save to say that my work there is not illegal. And I'll be playing as a street musician there, possibly in a duet. I'm not sure yet. I'll definitely come to see you when I get back and before I go abroad. Maybe we can go out again. I've only seen you here, apart from when I rescued you that awful night you were attacked.'

'Don't remind me. Please!'

They sat together on the sofa for half an hour and enjoyed a cup of grape juice each before Antonio kissed her gently on the cheek and left to pack his saddlebags for the journey to Segovia.

Lucitano met Antonio for an early breakfast. By then the Madrid winter had established itself and the early mornings were cold so a hearty meal of fried eggs, bread and goats' cheese, washed down with a mug of freshly brewed beer, made an excellent start to their day.

'So how long will it take us to get there?' asked Lucitano, placing his knife and fork on an empty plate.

'Don't know for sure. I've borrowed a young stallion from the palace. He's tied up in my stable. Lot quicker than my old beast. Two days, maximum but we'll have to stretch the horses.'

'The sooner we start the better then.'

Antonio couldn't believe that it was well over two months since he had met Lucitano, his charming wife and his delightful daughter. They were very relaxed with each other, despite Lucitano being at least twenty years his senior. Antonio went around to the stables to load his saddlebag and trusted violin onto the palace stallion. After he had done so, he went up to his own horse and patted her neck. 'I'll be away for a week or two so enjoy the rest, old gal. A man from the *corregidor*'s will be looking after you.' The horse looked at him disdainfully and snorted.

They were ready to go. Hardly a word was exchanged as they rode through the streets which were almost empty. The smell of night soil pervaded the air but it was not too strong in the cold of the early morning. There were a few beggars slumbering in doorways amid their untidy piles of worldly goods or wandering the streets half awake and half drunk. A few heavy wagons were creaking their way towards the markets.

They passed through the Puerta de San Joaquin, the gate to the north, and were well on the road. They drove their horses hard and by just after midday had reached the village of Galapagar, about six *leguas* or so from Madrid. 'Let's go in there, my friend,' said Tariq, pointing to a roadside inn with a large water trough outside. They tied up the horses, left them chomping at the cold water and went inside.

'Hello, my loves! What can I get you?' said the cheery, buxom landlady, with a black patch over her left eye and wearing a long brown dress.

'Couple of large beers will do us. Agreed my friend?'

'Perfect. I'm dry,' said Antonio.

As she poured the beers from a jug so large that she could barely lift it, the smiling landlady asked them where they were heading. 'To Segovia. On business,' said Tariq, just a little pointedly as if not welcoming being questioned, even though they were the only ones in the drinking room.

'That's a coincidence,' she said. 'My brother-in-law owns a shop there and his wife may be able to put you up. She runs it as a small lodging house. There are only three rooms to let but she might well be able to take you in. And she's not expensive.'

'What do you think, Tariq?'

'Give us the details and we can have a think about it.'

'The shop is in the Calle Centro and my brother-in-law is Sebastian Alonso González del Águilla. It's a musical instrument shop. He makes them. You can't miss it. His wife's name is Marta.'

They downed the dregs of their beer, thanked the landlady for her suggestion and left. Again they rode hard and reached the little town of Guadarrama just before nightfall. They stayed in a horrible little tavern, unfortunately the only one with vacant rooms. They dreaded the thought of eating there so left at daybreak and breakfasted at a wayside eating house two *leguas* from the town. A few hours later, horses began to struggle as they carried their riders up the slopes of the Sierra de Guadarrama and seemed relieved to be riding the descent towards Segovia.

'Is that the town I can see over there?' asked Tariq.

'Yes, for certain. I remember this view as I looked back down from here, only a couple of months ago.'

After about a further four *leguas*, mainly down the gentle slopes, they reached the city gates of Segovia. 'What say we have a quick look for the musical instrument shop?' said Tariq.

'Why not? If it looks comfortable and inexpensive, we'll take it. There is another place I want to visit eventually but it would be good to have somewhere else for now. The other place I have in mind is a *Morisco* meeting place and I'd rather not commit myself to staying there until I've been there as a user of the bar!'

'I think I can understand that,' said Tariq.

They soon identified a musical instrument shop in the Calle Centro and, having tethered the mounts, walked straight in. The place seemed empty so Tariq called out for service. A short, thin young man appeared from behind a display of violins. His head was topped by a narrow brimmed hat and his narrow front was covered by a new apron that just about reached the floor.

'Can I help you, señores?'

'I believe you have rooms for rent?' said Antonio.

'I don't really know. My wife deals with the lodgings. Stay there and I'll get her. Right?'

Within a few seconds, a dishevelled woman, whose clothes looked as if they had been rescued from a pile of garments long discarded by others, appeared in front of them. 'You want rooms then? We have two at a *real* a night and another *real* for dinner and breakfast. Have them if you will.'

Antonio wasn't impressed either at the woman's appearance or at her indifference. 'Can we see them first?'

'Follow me.'

She took a lit candle from the shop counter and shuffled out of the rear of the shop into a hall, illuminated by an oil lamp on the wall. She pushed open the door of a bedroom and asked them in. The room was not large but even by the light of the solitary candle they could see that it was spotless. The fresh, clean bed linen glowed with a healthy crispness. Saying nothing, she led them into the second room which beamed with an equally friendly welcome.

'What's there to eat?' asked Tariq.

'Got some nice pork chops I can grill and some fresh local vegetables. A mug of beer and a bottle of wine for two's included.'

'What do you think?' asked Tariq, right in front of her.

'Looks fine to me,' said Antonio. 'What about stabling?'

'Four *maravedis* a horse, a night' she said, in her disinterested tone.

'We'll have it then. Don't you think, Antonio?'

'Yes, I'd like an option to stay another couple of nights, not sure how many yet. That all right?'

'Fine,' she said.

Within an hour they had cleaned the day's ride from their aching bodies and were sitting at a table in the landlady's compact dining room awaiting the arrival of their pork chops. 'Well, here we are, my friend, about to embark on our mission. What are your intentions? How do you propose to start?'

'That's a tricky question, Tariq. And walls have ears, as you say. I'm not sure it will help you if I tell you; any more than you telling me yours will help me.'

'But, surely, we can exchange some ideas.'

'I suppose so.' Antonio was none too anxious to encourage this line of conversation so decided to say the first thing that came into his head. 'Tomorrow morning, I'm going to speak to the shop owner, this Sebastian Alonso character. I may even buy a new violin from him! I can certainly afford one! I might ask him if he knows of any musicians I could work with for a few weeks. As to the other side of what we are here for, I haven't any clear thoughts, but to say I must visit that *Morisco* tavern. The landlady was called Ángelita. I might ask her if I can play there for a time, in the drinking room. What about you Tariq? What are you going to do?'

'I'm going to head for Valladolid first thing in the morning. I can't see the point of staying any longer. Can you?'

'Not really. You may as well be on your way as staying here.'

'I agree. I'll go after we've enjoyed our breakfast. Going by these pork chops, it should be good!'

Tariq and Antonio met at the breakfast table. 'Tell me, Antonio, how do you think this *Morisco* situation will end? It can't be in anyone's interests to expel them. Can it be resolved? What do you think?'

'I know I'm only a young man, but I do have some thoughts. I tended to let the whole problem wash over me until I became a special agent. When I was a kid I thought that the best way to resolve a problem was by discussing it. That's what my father told me and the reason I got on with him so well was that if anything difficult cropped up we would discuss it. And problems there were, especially over managing the farm. And you can extend that to bigger issues like this one. The key to peace is dialogue. But the problem here is dialogue with whom? The *Moriscos* have no identifiable leader. All right, they have that fellow up in Granada but no one King Philip or The Duke of Lerma could meet as their representative. So the decision will be taken on the basis of what the government thinks at the time they make it. Aided, maybe, or hindered, by the views of the archbishops, the Archbishop of Valencia in particular. So we are here in a defensive mode. Our job is to defend the king against any *Moriscos* or anyone else who chooses to attack him and his court. And, of course, the key to that is information. And dialogue will be needed for that!'

'That's very sensible, my friend, if I may say. You are becoming a good spy. I am enjoying working with you. It's a pity I have to go to Valladolid'

'You must be well respected for Algebra to send you there. Surely, the local agents would be a better proposition?'

'Quite the opposite. Their faces are too familiar to the enemy!'

The two friends and colleagues wished each other luck. Tariq left Antonio sitting at the breakfast table, contemplating his plan for the day while finishing his drink. As he put his cup on the table he heard a rustling noise. Sebastian Alonso was coming into the room, his apron dragging slightly on the stone floor. He smiled nervously at Antonio, not knowing quite what to say. He was about the same age as Antonio, maybe a year or so younger. Antonio spoke first.

'Good morning, señor. So you are a musical instrument maker.'

'Yes, my father taught me. I've been making stringed instruments for about four years. I sell them and I buy them to sell.'

'I am a violinist. I'd be interested to see your instruments. Would you like to show me?'

The young man's face burst into a smile. 'Delighted to, señor. You may even be interested in buying one. The ones I make are a very good price. Got yours with you?'

'Matter of fact, I have.'

'I could take it for a reduction, if you wished.'

'Let's see what you've got to offer, first. I am very fond of my violin and I won't part with it easily!'

'Follow me, señor. So how long have you been playing? And have you come to Segovia to play? If so, you couldn't have chosen a better place. This is a musical city. People here love to listen to music and street players are very popular. There are other instrument shops here as well as mine. I suppose I shouldn't have told you that: you may decide to go somewhere else!'

The instrument maker was sounding a little less inhibited by then and this little exchange quite tickled Antonio. 'How do you know I'm a street player?'

'Didn't you say?' said the man, looking quite embarrassed.

'Don't think so but might have!' said Antonio, not the least bit concerned.

They entered the shop from the lodging house hallway. Antonio's eyes opened wide as he saw the number and range of instruments. There must have been a hundred. An elegant glass case displayed half a dozen beautiful violins. The polish on each gleamed in the low sunlight, beaming through the street window. On a stand against the wall stood a number of guitars, each strung and waiting for someone to strum a few chords. Antonio picked one up and brushed his fingers lightly across the strings.

'Did you make these? The tone is excellent. And the instrument is so comfortable to hold.'

'Sadly, no. They were made by a friend of mine who also has a shop here. We sell each other's instruments, so we compete and yet we don't! Right?'

'May I try one of these violins? That one. Have you a bow?'

'Of course. Here it is.' He unlocked the case and carefully withdrew the violin which Antonio had selected.

He placed it in Antonio's hand along with a bow. Antonio played the opening bars of 'You have killed me, maiden fair'. He was utterly intoxicated by the sound produced by this exquisite instrument. He played a different tune and then another. 'I cannot believe the sound produced by this masterpiece of a violin. You made it yourself?'

'Of course, señor. To a design invented by my father, based on an early Italian prescription.'

'You will want a small fortune for it, I'm sure!'

'You may be surprised, señor.'

'How much?'

'Five *ducats* and five *reales*.'

'Not too bad. What would you cut it by for mine?' Antonio sounded serious.

'Get it, señor, and I'll willingly tell you. No obligation either side!' Sebastian Alonso sounded quite excited, as if he was about to secure a deal.

Antonio returned with his violin in its battered case. He took it out and showed the instrument maker. 'Hmm. Not a bad specimen, apart from the case. I can give you one five for it.'

'Call it two and I'll give you three five?'

Antonio sounded just little doubtful and Sebastian Alonso detected that. 'Three eight and the deal is struck.'

'Done!' pronounced Antonio. 'To include a case!'

'It's yours!'

Both men were happy. Antonio surprised himself that he had parted with his old violin which had seemed like an old friend. But the new one was such a delight he could not resist.

While Sebastian Alonso wrapped the violin, nestled in its new case, in the finest of papers, he asked Antonio, 'So where will you be playing it first? I may even come to witness the historic event!'

'There are some good pitches in this town. Probably by the cathedral. But my first priority is to find a partner. I'm not bothered whether it is a man or a woman, but I need one. Someone to accompany me. Ideally, someone who can sing.'

'Hmm. I have an idea but I'm not sure whether I should tell you about it.' said the instrument maker, looking down to his shoes, almost in shame.

'Tell me! Not a performing bear, I'm sure!'

'No, no, no! A performing dwarf, actually. A family friend of ours is a dwarf. She is a guitarist, singer and actress. She lives in Ávila and had a brief time in a troupe there. For some reason, she didn't like them and she is coming to Segovia looking for work. In fact, she will be here within a week. I can introduce you, if you wish. But only if you are interested. Right?'

'Don't tell me. Her name is Carolina de Torres Madruga. She has gypsy blood!'

'How can you possibly know, señor?'

'I met her in Ávila about three months back and we played together in Valladolid. I'd be delighted to work with her again! It would thrill me no end!'

'I am amazed, señor. You could knock me down with a goose feather. She is coming to stay so you could be meeting her quite soon, but I'm not sure exactly when. Just one question, señor. Will she feel the same about you?'

'I can assure you that she will!' Antonio smiled in utter astonishment. What an amazing triple coincidence, she would be here the same time as he would; she would be staying in the same lodging house at the same time as he would; and she was looking for a partner with whom to work, at the same time as he was.

CHAPTER 19
The jeweller's

Antonio spent the rest of the day walking around the city. His sole aim was to seek out suspicious activity but he was uncertain where to look. He would not visit Ángelita's until he had secured a deal with Carolina. In the meantime, he would play his new violin on the streets of Segovia, generally keep an eye on what was happening there, and work out his tactics in finding what he wanted, if indeed it could be found.

The week went by and still there was no sign of Carolina. Antonio began to doubt that she would be coming to Segovia and wondered whether she had found another playing partner in Ávila. He even began to doubt that this was the Carolina he knew so well.

On the Sunday, he asked the musical instrument maker what had happened to her. He reassured Antonio that he had no reason to doubt that she was coming and that she would certainly be there in a day or so. Antonio felt he was simply wasting time, even though he had earnt almost two *ducats* playing at different pitches on the streets of Segovia. So he decided, the day he spoke to Sebastian Alonso González del Águilla, to seek out questionable activity by visiting three or four hostelries in the Plaza Huertos market. He'd start the following morning.

He tried several different taverns but could only see individual drinkers, most of whom were far too inebriated, even by mid-morning, to sustain a conversation. He pushed open the door to the third which looked quite salubrious from the outside. As he walked in his tender nose was assaulted by the most disgusting smell. He was tempted to put a kerchief over his nose but decided to bear it unprotected. Several groups of men were drinking and conversing in the bar area, and in the adjacent booths. He was not surprised that he didn't recognise a soul. A serving wench at the bar offered him a drink. He decided on a large beer and a cup of wine. He took his drinks to a table where a number of rough looking characters were arguing about something. From the bar he couldn't make out what. 'Mind if I join you?' said Antonio.

'Can't see why not,' said a swarthy looking character with a wide, round brimmed hat, a hooked nose and very few teeth. 'You from around here?'

'No. Madrid.'

A second of this motley gathering, equally weathered and wearing a dirty braid tied by an equally dirty white ribbon, spoke. 'Suppose you're looking for work? Not many honest jobs here!'

Antonio took a gamble. His aim was to penetrate these groups. To discover exactly what was happening in this town and what threats there might be to the king. 'Maybe I'll look for something dishonest then! I can turn my hand to most things! But mainly I'm a street musician.'

Then the third man spoke, a squat individual with an unkempt beard and an excessive paunch. 'Let's give him a try.' The man looked around the bar then lowered his voice. 'We need a distraction in the market place here, on Thursday. You can play some lively tunes while we do our dirty work. What about that, lads?'

The one with the braided hair spoke first. 'You've given the game away, Rodrigo. Now he knows anyway! You've cocked it for all of us now!'

'Don't be so quick to condemn,' said Antonio. 'I just may want to help you. I'd want an advance payment, mind you. And I'd want to know what you're up to.'

'Can't see what we can lose,' said the one with the round hat and few teeth. 'Let's give him a *real* or two for his help.'

'What say you, Pascual?' said Rodrigo, turning to the one with the dirty braid.

'I agree, if Geraldo agrees. I can't see what we can lose either. Better make it clear when we want him there and where exactly he should be.'

'What is this dirty work, exactly and why are you doing it? I'm not going to go near it if anybody's going to be maimed or killed,' said Antonio in serious vein.

'It's a robbery with a firearm. We intend to rob a jeweller's,' said Geraldo, with a slight whistle to his voice which Antonio imagined was caused by the gaps in his teeth.

'And why? Unless you tell me, I won't play!'

'Shall we tell him, boys?' said Geraldo.

'Why not,' said Pascual and Rodrigo virtually in unison.

Geraldo continued. 'We are, shall we say, sympathetic to the *Moriscos*. We will sell the jewels and put the money to their cause.'

Antonio could not believe his luck. A few minutes before, he was wondering how to progress in his mission and, aided by a few chancy words, had engaged himself with a gang of crooks.

'Where and when exactly?'

'Right outside of this tavern, just across the square. Eleven by the cathedral clock. Start some lively, noisy music then, exactly then.'

'I may have a woman accompanying me. All right? And I'll accept three *reales* now.' Antonio set the price.

Geraldo handed him some change. 'That's about three. If you don't show, I'll want it back, with good compensation!'

'You've overpaid me,' said Antonio, handing back a few *maravedís*. 'See you Thursday.'

Antonio stood and left the tavern. Somehow he'd need to reduce to a minimum his chance of being caught in this piece of trickery, especially if it all went wrong. Indeed, he could arrange for it to go wrong if he spoke to one of the local constabulary. He hardly knew anyone here and felt the constables might not be trusted so he decided then to let the robbery go ahead, unimpeded by the law.

He spent the rest of the day familiarising himself with some of the other taverns in this town but, conscious of the time, and after calling into three or four of these unsavoury drinking houses, decided to return to the lodgings before nightfall.

He was greeted by Sebastian Alonso González. 'I have good news for you, Señor Hidalgo! I've had a letter from Carolina, delivered by a rider. She'll be here at about six tonight. I'll reserve a table for the two of you!'

'I can't believe it's you!' said Carolina, rushing up to him as he entered. She stretched her tiny arms around his thighs and buried her face in his chest. 'Miracles do happen; and what a coincidence that you're here. Sebastian Alonso told me this morning! I almost came looking for you!'

Antonio pulled out a chair from the table and let her climb up and sit in his lap. They sat in an embrace. 'I was amazed when he spoke about this little person guitar player and singer. From Ávila, who'd just left a troupe? It had to be you and it was!' He kissed her on the cheek and they laughed together. 'Tell me because I'm still mystified. How do you know this Sebastian Alonso González del Águilla?'

'It's a straightforward story. He is as well known in Ávila as here. My father came to Segovia to buy a guitar for me... for my thirteenth birthday. I came too, with my mother, and he liked us. I don't know if it would have been different if we'd all have been tall people. We'll never know. But we've been friends ever since. I dropped in for a few nights after we parted here all those months ago! And don't you remember? I mentioned this place when we were here with Esteban, but he was set on staying at that woman Ángelita's inn. '

'No. I don't even remember you mentioning it. So what you've just said is a simple story of a family connection?'

'Nothing more. We all get on well. So why are you here, Antonio? I don't have to trust you again, do I, because you are doing something you can't tell me about? As in Valladolid?'

'You are right, once again, Carolina. You'll have to trust me again, I fear! The business I am in cannot be discussed. It's confidential. All I can tell you is what I do is legal. Does that satisfy you, if not your curiosity?'

'I've always trusted you, Antonio. You've protected me up to now and I've no reason to think otherwise!'

'There is something I want to ask you, dear Carolina, and you may not be surprised at what it might be!'

'Yes, we can share a bed! Why not tonight? You are an excellent lover and I want you!'

'Not that, Carolina. Not yet and maybe not here! But later, for sure! I wanted to ask you if you would form a duet with me. To play here in Segovia. It would be a temporary arrangement, unless you wanted to come to Madrid when I go back, in a couple of weeks. I'm not yet sure.'

'Nothing would please me more, Antonio,' she said, turning towards him and stroking his face. 'Nothing! Even if we only played together for a single day!'

Antonio needed to work out whether to tell her about the planned encounter with the thieves. His mind oscillated with uncertainty. On the one hand, if he told her, she would be implicated. On the other, if he did not tell her, he would prejudice his own honesty and her belief in him. Then he began to doubt his decision not to inform the local constables what was about to happen in the market square. Could this decision alone challenge his honesty or was it part of his job in penetrating the sub-culture of this town? Was he being unreasonable in believing, despite the absence of evidence, that the constabulary could not be brought into his confidence? Was he about to make a huge mistake that could destroy his career as a special agent?

'You suddenly look worried, Antonio. What's troubling you? Something I've said?'

'I am thinking about what I should do tomorrow!'

Then he remembered what Silva had told him before he went to Segovia: to go to the *corregidor* if he had a problem. So that's what he would do.

'So have you decided?' she said, still sitting on his knee.

'Yes, I have.'

'What then?' she laughed.

He explained that he knew about a crime to be committed on the Thursday. He told her how he had agreed to assist those who were to commit it but also said that he was to report the crime to the *corregidor* of Segovia. He said she would be involved if they were playing together at the time. 'But you told me that you were involved in nothing illegal! So how can I trust you now?' she said, not knowing whether to laugh or cry. 'You are about to be involved in a robbery!'

'Ah,' said Antonio. 'If I tell the *corregidor*, I'm reporting a potential crime. I'd leave it to him to tell me whether we should continue helping them. If we played as a decoy the constabulary could catch them in the act. So we would have assisted in solving a crime.'

'I think I follow and I'm willing to cooperate but only if you go to the *corregidor*.'

'I'll go first thing in the morning.'

Straight after breakfast, and leaving Carolina finishing hers, Antonio made his way to the town hall where he found the *corregidor*'s office. As usual with such places, it was patrolled by a junior official. Antonio asked to see the man himself. 'Can't help, señor. He's at a meeting at the palace in Valladolid. He won't be back for three days. Maybe I can assist.'

'Does the name "Algebra" mean anything to you?'

'Indeed it does,' he said, reassuring Antonio with his immediate reply.

'So if I say, I am Diaspora, will that name be familiar to you?'

'Just a minute, señor.' The official took a key from his pocket and let himself into the *corregidor*'s room. He seemed an age searching for a file or document Antonio could hear drawers being opened and closed and papers being shuffled through. Eventually, the bright sounding young man returned.

'May ask you a few questions, señor?' the man said, with surprising authority.

'Of course. Go ahead.'

'Tell me you full name, your address and where your parents live.' Antonio replied.

212

'Show me the tattoo on your shoulder.' Antonio undid his shirt and dropped it so the man could see.

'Fine. Yes, Señor Hidalgo. I am satisfied that you are who you claim to be. How can I assist?'

Antonio told him about the crime that was about to be committed. He said he hoped the authorities in Segovia would intervene and arrest these people as they were committing the offence.

'Leave it with me, señor. I'll tell what you've said to the constabulary. I can report it with the authority of the *corregidor*. It will be a matter for the constabulary to decide whether to proceed in this case. Please tell me where you are living and I'll ask them to inform you of their intentions. Are you happy with that?'

Antonio thought for a moment. 'No. I would expect you to advise the constabulary much more strongly to intervene. This is a serious matter, not just a robbery but a case of a crime being committed to provide support for the *Moriscos*. Possibly to attack the king. You know as well as I do that he will soon be passing through here on his way back to Madrid. So you should give the constabulary no choice but to arrest these three men and any others they engage.'

'I support your view, Señor Hidalgo but, as you will be aware, the fact remains that the *corregidor* has no control over the constabulary. Only the king has that power. However, I will insist that they arrest these people. The point I shall make is that if they don't and the king is attacked while travelling near here, they might well be culpable. Will that suffice, señor?'

'Perfectly. At present I am staying at the lodging house of Sebastian Alonso González del Águilla and his wife. I imagine I'll be there for a day or two more. So I will go ahead and lay on some loud music for these people. Do we agree?'

'Yes, señor. I shall give your current address to the constabulary and I'm sure they will contact you, should they wish you to do something different.'

'Is Carolina still here?' said Antonio, almost bumping into Sebastian Alonso, as he walked into his house.

'Yes, I think she's chatting to my wife in the kitchen. I'll get her if you wish.'

'Don't worry. I'll go straight through.'

Carolina gave him a puzzled look as he entered the kitchen. It was if she had been talking to Marta about something she didn't want him to know about. Antonio dismissed it as 'women's talk' and decided to say something before either of the two women had a chance.

'We ought to be getting on our way, Carolina. We need to start earning a living. Especially, if we want to continue staying in a town as expensive as Segovia!' He laughed as he turned to an unsuspecting Marta.

'I'm not so sure, Antonio. I've been thinking. There is something I want to discuss with you before we go. Excuse us please, Marta.'

'No problem. You go, if you must.'

Antonio followed her back into the dining area. 'What is it, Carolina? I thought you were happy to come with me to play in the market place.'

'I'm worried, Antonio. What if those robbers you spoke to decide to shoot their way out of being arrested? We could be killed. I'm worried for you as well as me!'

'Let's think about it, Carolina. Yes, there is a danger. They did mention weapons and are carrying them just as a threat. I spoke to the *corregidor*'s office - the man himself wasn't in - and they will strongly encourage the constables to arrest them. Shots may be exchanged. Mainly between the robbers and the constables. But they won't be the only ones with a gun. I'll have my snaplock pistol and that will protect us! And we'll be on the other side to the jeweller's. But you must not come if you're in doubt. Stay here. They don't know about you. And if they did, it wouldn't worry them. All they want is a distraction and it's my job to do that. I've already been paid three *reales*!'

'You reassure me, Antonio. I'll do it. I am excited to see the action. And you must make love to me, tonight!'

Antonio smiled in anticipation.

Thursday soon came and two of them gathered their music and instruments together, Antonio his new violin and a small drum, and set off for the market square. As they reached it, they could not resist looking around to see if anything odd was happening. The place seemed totally normal. Women were wandering from stall to stall, spending their little money on essentials of food and minor, hardly affordable luxuries, maybe the odd present for a husband or lover or a child for an imminent birthday. The few men in the square seemed more interested in finding their way

214

into the drinking houses. After all, it was after ten o'clock and these places thrived in the middle of the morning.

They set up their pitch just outside the tavern, Carolina nervously placed their collection bowl on the ground and they started to play. They began with 'Roses for my mother,' and then something a little naughtier with 'If you are going to bathe, Juanilla, tell me where'. A small group of spectators gathered as the launched into 'Albuquerque, Albuquerque', probably prompted by the thought of something more risqué.

By then it was about a quarter to eleven by the church clock and the two of them were beginning to feel a little tense. They decided on a short break, mainly to discuss what they should have talked about before, namely how they would make the commotion the robbers had demanded.

'I have a tambourine, Antonio. I brought it specially. It makes a lot of noise!'

'I have my drum, of course. Between us we can be really loud.'

'Here's an idea,' said Carolina. 'We can make a huge distraction by using both instruments to call the people here to dance!'

'At this time of the morning?'

'Why not? Segovians love to dance. Any excuse is good for them!'

Antonio looked straight at her, at first bemused and then, after a moment, with a wide smile. 'I like it. It doesn't matter if they don't dance. We'll have caused sufficient distraction!'

In the minutes approaching eleven o'clock they played a few more tunes but did not sing. One was a ballad and as the hand of the clock was on two minutes to, struck up a dance tune, a daring *chacona*. The cathedral clock started to strike eleven: one... two... three... They counted aloud. Then, on the eleventh chime, Antonio started to bang his drum, loud and hard, and Carolina to rattle the tambourine. They shouted out at the top of their voices. 'Anyone want to dance? There's no time like the present! Come on! Over here!'

Antonio glanced towards the jeweller's shop. The main feature that distinguished it from other shops was the sign 'Jewellers'. No elaborate display graced the window. It looked unkempt and rarely frequented, which was no surprise to them in such times of deprivation. The three robbers were coming around a corner and were about to enter the shop. Geraldo, in his wide hat, took the lead. The other two, Pascual and the plump Rodrigo, sloped along behind him. Antonio could see no sign of a weapon. They opened the door and went in.

Carolina and Antonio then played a *zarabanda* and quite to their surprise, two couples, a man and a woman and two young women came over and began to dance in front of them. Then another couple; and another. What jollity. The happy participants were laughing and jesting as they turned each other around to the throb of the music which Antonio and Carolina were making. Shopping in the market had all but ceased. The square became a party scene.

'Did you see those men go into the shop?' asked Carolina. 'I'm getting a bit scared.'

'Try not to worry…'

Then a shot rang out from the jeweller's. Just then the door burst open and Rodrigo, the squat, fat one, fell out onto the square, clutching his stomach as if he'd been hit. He attempted to get up but fell back onto the street. Then the other two emerged, their hands above their heads. They'd been arrested by the constables who had been waiting in the shop. There were five of them, all wearing tricorne hats and apparently led by one in a long, blue jacket with brass buttons.

The dancers stopped at the sound of the gunshot. Carolina looked terrified. They all looked towards the shop. The moment they saw the robbers, beaten and dejected, members of the crowd started to cheer and applaud the constables.

The apparent leader made his way over towards Antonio and Carolina.

The buttons on his tunic glistened as he spoke. 'It's all over now. We've arrested three robbers. No one was injured except one of them and we're taking him for treatment.' Then looking at no one in particular, said, 'Thanks to whoever gave us the tip off.' He then turned away and went. Members of the crowd looked at each other, then at Carolina and Antonio but nobody spoke.

'Well, anyone want to carry on dancing?' said Antonio, smiling broadly. The couple, who started the dancing earlier, began again, then the two women and within moments about a dozen couples were twisting around and turning to the boisterous music the players made. Antonio was mightily relieved that the grateful constable had not spoken directly to him. It could have been dangerous to have been noted by someone in the crowd as the individual who had informed the constabulary of the impending robbery.

After about fifteen minutes of sustained celebration and jollity, to a range of jigs and other dance tunes that Antonio and Carolina had spontaneously produced, the revellers had had enough and seemed to want to finish their purchases in the market. 'What about a break for some lunch? There are plenty of inns around here,' said Antonio.

'I agree. I'm so pleased you decided to tell the *corregidor*, Antonio. You could have been in bad trouble if you were seen to be part of it. You could be strung up in a prison cell, right now!'

'And instead I'm looking at a beautiful woman, right across the table from me! But you are right. The best decision was to report the robbery before it happened. I'm pleased that the constable didn't thank me directly. You never know. Some of the robbers' contacts could have been among the dancers and they could have made my life very difficult.'

'I don't understand why he did that. Maybe he just wanted to give you an indirect acknowledgement or let everyone there know that there are citizens of these towns who are prepared to help the law.'

'Either way, I'd have felt more comfortable if he'd said nothing. Anyway, we should continue our good work, playing the streets of Segovia. We will soon become part of the street scenery and people will be generous in their giving, I'm sure.'

So they continued playing on the streets. The two of them looked an odd sight with Carolina, her guitar almost dragging on the ground, singing at the top of her voice, while Antonio, so much taller, moved excitedly as he played his violin. He thought much about what more he could do to find threats to the king in this quite peaceful town. They continued their routine for another week and spent their lunches and evenings in taverns, listening and looking out for threats. Nothing seemed to be happening and Antonio was thinking of returning to Madrid after a morning's play in the freezing, winter streets of the town.

'Let's go to a tavern in the square for some food and a drink,' said Antonio.

'I'd rather go back to Sebastian Alonso's house. It'll be warmer in there and we'll be back there earlier. What do you think?'

'I agree, Carolina. I'm sure Marta will be happy to make us some lunch.'

The two of them packed up their instruments, collected up their money bowl and within a few minutes were back in Sebastian Alonso and Marta's house. Marta soon prepared a meal of soup, some stewed beef and beans, bread and some beer and the two of them were again chatting about what to do next.

'I'm beginning to get frustrated here, Carolina. Nothing I can use to inform my bosses is happening. I'd feel better if we were on our way back to Madrid.'

'I'd feel more comfortable making love to you... right now!'

'Now?'

'Why not? Marta has just gone out, Sebastian Alonso is in his shop and my room is right at the back of the house so we'll not be disturbed. We can make love to our hearts' content! Does this tempt you?' she said, dropping the shoulder of her dress, smiling and revealing a pink nipple atop a perfect breast.

'Love in the afternoon, eh?'

They each swallowed the last of their beer, took their empty cups and dishes into Marta's kitchen and walked hand-in-hand down the narrow hall. 'Chase me up the stairs!' said Carolina.

'No. Too much noise!'

Carolina shut her bedroom door behind the two of them. As if they had not a moment to spare, they each stripped off their clothes and threw them in a heap on the floor. 'Lie on the bed, Antonio. I'll climb on top.'

'God this is good!' said Antonio, as he assisted her naked little body in its movements.

'Let's try something different,' she said.

'I'm at your command,' he said, laughing in readiness but unsure for what.

'Pick me up and hold me against the wall!'

She rolled off him and he lifted her by her naked buttocks so she was facing him. 'I love those pretty breasts', he said.

He walked her towards the wall by the wardrobe and held her to it as he slowly began again. 'Now let me drop down on you a bit, so I can feel my weight on your body. That's lovely. I could stay like this for hours! But we won't! Put me back onto the bed and cuddle up to my rear then start again.'

'Before I do, I want to kiss you. Really kiss you. So lie on your side facing me and we'll kiss.' He wrapped his arms around her tiny body and gently parted her lips with his tongue. Then her tongue penetrated his mouth in reply. He put his hand through her hair. Their tongues intermingled and they could taste the flavours in each other's mouths. Then she turned over and he did as she had previously instructed, wondering who of them was enjoying this beautiful, rhythmic activity the most.

'You are a great lover, Antonio. You can make it last as long as you want!'

As she finished this charming utterance there was a persistent knock on the door. 'Who's there?' shouted Carolina, still lying on the bed with a motionless Antonio still embracing her.

'It's me, Sebastian Alonso. I'm trying to find Señor Hidalgo. I have a letter for him from the *corregidor's* office! Could you give it to him?'

'I'm not dressed now… so can't answer the door! Could you put it under please?'

They heard the sound of paper against wood as the instrument maker slid the letter into the room. 'Thank you!' shouted Carolina.

'Keep going, Antonio. The letter can wait can't it?'

'Tell me when you've had enough, lady!'

Not a minute later, Carolina let out a muffled cry and shuddered. 'My goodness, Antonio. What a climax to finish with. The unexpected interruption made it even better. That's not the first time we've been caught by a knock on a door!'

With that, Antonio concluded, too. 'Yes, I remember that! The thought of the young instrument maker outside with me still making love to you inside. It added to my excitement, too!'

They lay on the bed in conjugal satisfaction and wordless silence, just for a few minutes. Antonio spoke first. 'Thank you, Carolina. You've made me very happy. That was truly lovely. I hope I didn't hurt you in any way.'

'Not at all. You are a gentle as well as expert lover!'

Antonio retrieved the letter and opened it. His eyes almost leapt from their sockets as he read it silently to himself while Carolina looked on in puzzlement:

23 February, 1606
Diaspora,
We have evidence from Lucitano which suggests that an attack is to be made against the person of the king. It will take place on 2 March as he passes through Segovia. You, with the corregidor, *must prevent it. Start at the inn of your friend Ángelita. You may learn more there. Good luck.*
Algebra

'Hm. Interesting,' said Antonio.

'Anything I can comment on?' asked Carolina.

'Another assignment.'

'Oh no! You haven't got to leave me, have you?' said Carolina. Still naked on the bed, she looked up at him with a frown.

'No. But we move into Ángelita's inn. Tomorrow!' Antonio had been given just one week to save the king. He had to act quickly.

'Sebastian Alonso, we have to move. It's Antonio's job.' Such was the plaintive explanation which Carolina gave for the two of them leaving.

'Where will you go?' said Sebastian Alonso, not unreasonably.

'We are going to the inn run by a landlady called "Ángelita".'

'I know it and I warn you: don't. It's a *Morisco* tavern. Neither you nor Antonio are *Moriscos*. You might be safe as a small person with *gitano* blood. I'm not even sure about that. But he could be murdered in his sleep!' He drew his hand across his throat as if it was a knife.

'We've stayed there before and apart from a minor incident, they treated us well. We are musicians you understand and no one wants to cause us entertainers any trouble!'

'I hope you are right, Carolina. I'd hate anything to happen to either of you.'

They bid their fond and grateful farewells to Sebastian Alonso and Marta and made their way to Ángelita's inn.

'So why are you back in Segovia?' she asked, with a friendly smile as she led them up the stairs. 'You're lucky that I've got rooms at such short notice!'

'We are grateful even if fortune favours us,' said Antonio. 'We've come here to play our music and to earn our living. The best thing for me is that I am back working with Carolina here.'

'Where is your other colleague, Esteban? He used to come here alone and quite often but I haven't seen him for… nearly two months now.'

'He was arrested in Valladolid. Helping the cause, I believe,' said Antonio, surprising himself at his own openness but seeing an advantage in associating himself with the plight of the *Moriscos*. Ángelita's smile vanished as she digested the news. She said nothing but from her pained, almost tearful, look, Antonio could see that there was more to the relationship between her and Esteban than he was meant to know. She knew, of course, that they all went to Valladolid together and presumably why they went. So Antonio was surprised that she hadn't heard about Esteban's arrest.

'You are more than welcomed to stay,' she said, regaining her composure. 'You are good customers.' Neither was sure what she meant by that but Antonio saw that moment as a good opportunity to ask a favour.

'We were wondering if you'd like us to perform in your drinking room,' said Antonio. 'We'd love to work for your customers again, even without the doughty Esteban.'

'You can do that,' she said, smiling gratefully, as if few music troupes wanted to work there. 'Start today if you wish.'

Carolina went up to Ángelita and put her arms around her. 'Bend down so I can kiss you,' she said, while they were still on the landing. 'We are delighted and are sure your clientele will enjoy our music. They may even want to join in!'

Ángelita left them in their separate rooms but it wasn't long before Carolina was lying on Antonio's bed, laughing about their success in gaining work at the tavern. 'That was so easy. We must have played well last time. And I think your aims may be satisfied by our staying here. Whatever your aims are, of course! I wouldn't know, would I?' She chuckled at Antonio and at her own cheekiness.

She had touched a nerve but Antonio refused to be provoked. 'You'll have to trust me. I've said before that I can't divulge my work or who my bosses are.'

'I completely accept that, Antonio, but there is no harm in a little teasing surely!'

'Two can play at those games,' he said as he climbed right on top of her, took his weight on his elbows and started to move as if to make love to her.

'Yes, but that's not my favourite position,' she chided in return. 'I prefer to see some daylight!'

The two of them decided to survey the town that afternoon, to look for a good pitch for the following day. They headed for the cathedral square, not more than a few hundred *varas* from Ángelita's tavern in the Plaza San Martín. They agreed to just look around and have a relaxed look at the town rather than to do any performing. They couldn't resist going there via the Plaza Huertos, the scene of the excitement of Thursday before. The *plaza* looked quite different. The crowds had gone.

The market stalls had been dismantled. Just a few expectant beggars sat by their bowls on the approach to the church of San Agustín.

The following day they set up there and played all day long but walked back to Ángelita's almost empty handed. And Antonio was no nearer to engaging in the problem Silva wanted solved. They played in the square for another couple of days, still without much success. Then one morning, as they were walking across the square to set up their pitch, they were faced with a less than welcomed surprise. A beggar was heading purposefully towards them, from the direction of San Agustín.

'See him?' said Antonio. 'He's coming straight for us. I wonder what he wants.'

'Well see soon enough.'

The beggar was one of the shabbier of the breed. His trousers were tied around his waist by a length of well-worn string. His shirt hung loose and open, like a flapping sail, exposing much of his dirty chest. He wore a battered cap and no shoes. He walked with a shuffle, even though he seemed a young man. He stopped as he reached them and smiled.

'Were you the musicians who played in the Huertos Square, what, just over a week ago, when the raid on the jewellers took place?'

Carolina left it to Antonio to reply. 'Yes. As a matter of fact we were.'

'Pity it all went wrong isn't it?' the man said, as he breathed a strong smell of beer at them.

Antonio had to think carefully before answering. He assumed, rightly as it turned out, that Carolina would remain silent. If he disagreed with the beggar he would be admitting that he was opposed to the robbers and that he was the possible and even likely informer. Their fate was, until that moment, still unknown. If he agreed, he would be admitting to apparent complicity which might well suit the situation. 'Yes, it's a great shame. Those poor men were fighting a just cause. We were distraught at the way it all finished.'

'Then why did you resume the dancing? It was like you were celebrating their capture!'

'We didn't want the constabulary to suspect us! Do you think we are stupid? So we had to play a game!'

'Who do you think informed?'

'No idea. Whoever it was knew to the exact moment when the robbery would happen. We were just the decoys! Causing commotion. If

I knew where they were, I'd give them their money back! They paid me well!'

'They're in the town gaol, chained up to a wall. I've seen them.'

Antonio still wasn't sure where this chance meeting was heading and nor was Carolina who kept quiet during these exploratory exchanges. The fact remained that, unless something really subtle was happening here, the beggar was a *Morisco* sympathiser and he was probing Antonio and Carolina about where their sympathies lay. His main objective was to see if they had betrayed the robbers to the authorities or whether they too were genuine supporters.

'That's bad. We were lucky that the constables didn't suspect us.'

'I'm not sure that they didn't,' he said in a sarcastic tone.

'Are you accusing us of betrayal?' asked Carolina, looking up and staring into the man's unsuspecting eyes. Her sudden intervention made Antonio smile gleefully.

'I didn't say that,' said the beggar. 'Only, things are happening in this town and those of us with an interest need to know how what others think.'

'Don't let's clash swords,' said Antonio. 'Neither of us is a *Morisco* but we have strong *Morisco* sympathies and if that isn't clear enough, then I suggest we go our separate ways.'

'You've convinced me,' said the beggar. 'There can be no doubt about your position. Tell me, where are you staying?'

'We are at Ángelita's tavern in the Plaza San Martín.'

'There is a meeting there at seven, tomorrow night. You may wish to attend. Geraldo and his accomplices would have attended and I suggest you go, instead. I may be there myself, but not dressed or smelling like this!' This would give Antonio only two days to act before the attack on the king.

'What's it about?' said Carolina, making Antonio believe she was as much an agent as him.

'I can't give much away here, save to say that it is about defending the *Morisco* cause. In fact is about attacking. Attacking those who oppose us!'

'We'll be there,' said Antonio. 'Even if we are only the musical accompaniment!'

'See you there,' said the beggar who turned and walked back along the approach to San Agustín.

The two of them continued walking across the square. 'What did you make of that?' asked Antonio.

'Tricky question. Could be a trap. If they suspect you of betraying the robbers, Geraldo and his cohorts, we could both be finished. If they took you and killed you off, they'd hardly let me to walk out and catch the first wagon back to Ávila. They'd suspect me of being your accomplice. They wouldn't understand how I could be totally innocent, as I am, of course. Why do I associate myself with the likes of you, Antonio? It's tantamount to attempted suicide!'

'You just don't appreciate how lucky you are! They don't suspect us. You can rely on that. Just as well that constable who came over to us after the robbers were arrested wasn't too specific! Let's face it. We've no choice but to go along to that meeting, that is, unless it's held in some private room at Ángelita's.'

'So it could be lambs to the slaughter, Antonio?'

'No. Not at all. I'll have my gun in my violin case!'

It wasn't many more steps before the two of them arrived in the cathedral square. They could see several potential spots to set up their pitch and did so, just outside the cathedral. They played all day, but for a brief break for lunch and, tired and cold, walked back to Ángelita's.

'I've just had a thought, Carolina. This meeting. We should ask Ángelita about it. We needn't give anything away. We can tell her we've been helping Geraldo and his colleagues. Tell her a beggar told us about it and invited us along. See what she says.'

They found Ángelita as soon as they arrived back. 'Come into my office,' she said. 'I don't want to discuss it in the public area.'

They followed her in. There was barely room for the two of them to stand as she sat at a well ordered desk with small sheets of paper, evidently bills, arranged in neat piles. 'This is where you can find me if I'm not in the kitchen or serving in the drinking area. Just shut the door please, Señor Hidalgo.'

The two of them looked at her expectantly, not knowing quite what she would reveal. 'I'm not sure to what extent you know this, but my tavern is a gathering place for *Moriscos* in Segovia. They meet here regularly and there are some nearly every day. They are planning a meeting to discuss... I'm not sure how to put this... you are Muslim sympathisers aren't you? Just go over a few things for me...'

'Yes, we are,' said Antonio. 'We came here with the aim of making a living but also to support the cause. And why we were working with

Esteban de Recalde last time we stayed here. That's also why we helped Geraldo Perez and his accomplices in the jewellery shop robbery which went wrong.'

'Yes, I know about it. They were to sell the jewels and put the money to the cause.'

'So you can see we are strong supporters,' said Carolina.

'You've convinced me, so I'll tell you about it. These people loathe the king and his court. They see him as the symbol of Muslim repression. I expect you know that his court is to move back to Madrid. In not many days in fact, in three. He will be coming through here. It will be a royal visit. The meeting is about what the *Moriscos* will doing to greet him, shall we say? And there will be a lot of them. By all means go to the meeting. But don't be surprised if you end up by agreeing to play a part in some demonstration or worse.'

'Tell me,' said Antonio. 'Do you know who the beggar is who intercepted us and told us about the meeting?'

'You never know what's going on in this town. Yes, he would have appeared as a beggar, bowl and all. But there was more to that man than a beggar. The *Moriscos* have people in the town looking and spying on what is going on here. It's the same everywhere. Believe me. I can't think of anything else, so do you mind leaving me now. I have to work on the accounts.'

They thanked Ángelita and headed for Antonio's room. They couldn't wait to get inside and shut the door behind them. They each climbed onto Antonio's bed and spoke while facing the ceiling 'I can't believe our luck, Carolina. A chance meeting in the Plaza Huertos with a man who is probably a *Morisco* spy and we are invited to what appears to be a decisive meeting about what they plan to do when the king passes through.'

'I have a feeling your bosses, whoever they are and I wouldn't dream of suggesting, may find this information quite crucial.'

'You know I can't confirm or deny that young lady,' he chuckled. 'But I have a major concern.'

'Go on. Talking about it might just help you to resolve it.'

'We are still vulnerable you know. Vulnerable to the whims of the Segovia constabulary. The constable who came over to thank the crowd for helping, although looking at no one in particular, knew about us. He knew that we'd done the dirty on Geraldo and his gang. So, say one of the constabulary is a *Morisco*, and knows about our role, then he could let the leaders here know and then we'd be in real trouble. I'm not sure how far we go with this meeting. I'm concerned for your neck as well as mine.'

Carolina turned her diminutive body towards him and cuddled into him. 'I have an idea, Antonio.'

'I'd love to, but not now. I'm thinking. Trying to think a safe way out of this for both of us.'

'The damned cheek of you, Antonio! So am I! My idea is on how we can help ourselves, not how I can get your cock inside me!'

'I'm sorry, Carolina. I really am. It was just the way you turned into me. I was wrong to read more into that.'

'I've a good mind not to tell you, now!'

'I am truly sorry, Carolina!'

'No. I'm not serious! My idea is this. You go now to the *corregidor*'s office and tell them about your fears. What you need is for the *corregidor* to put some kind of injunction on the constabulary, preventing any of them from mentioning you and your role in the robbery to anybody.'

'You are brilliant, Carolina! That should do it. What do you think of getting some of his men to infiltrate the meeting? I'd suggest they should be armed and ready to use them if either of us was in danger, otherwise they'd just be here.'

'That's a good idea, too, Antonio. It can't be later than about four o'clock. Why not go there now?'

Antonio again presented himself to the punctilious and helpful official he had seen before.

'Welcome back Señor Hidalgo. May I congratulate you on the success of your mission to thwart the robbery at the Plaza Huertos jewellers. Well done! The robbers are now in gaol, awaiting trial!'

Antonio related the story of the meeting with the beggar, what the man had told him about the gathering of *Moriscos* which would take place the following night at their inn. He explained his fear of an indiscreet or deliberate revelation by a constable and the possible need for protection.

'Difficult. I cannot decide on either of these requests. All I can do is to put them to the constabulary.'

'I understand that fully. However, if the request is made with the authority of the *corregidor* the constabulary will find it difficult to refuse.'

226

'Of course, Señor Hidalgo. And I will make the request with his authority.'

'May I make one further request?'

'Indeed you may, Señor?'

'By the time of the meeting tomorrow, I would like to know the constables' decision. Could you arrange that please?'

'Certainly, Señor Hidalgo. I will call in at your lodgings or leave a note.'

Antonio explained, thanked him and returned to Ángelita's tavern, feeling a little more secure.

'Well done, Antonio. I feel better myself now. I'm sure everything will be fine.'

They decided to take up Ángelita's offer and play as a duet that evening in the drinking room. They agreed that it would be good for them, and for the attitude of Ángelita's customers towards them, if they were seen in the tavern before the meeting the following night. At least their faces would be familiar and they would be associated with the *Morisco* cause. The evening started quietly, despite the number of drinkers there that night. It was as if something more significant could be happening the following night. The bar hummed with expectant conversation: groups of men in every corner and booth were deep in controlled, whispered and private discussion, maybe rehearsing arguments or points to be made the following night. Try as they did, neither Antonio nor Carolina could hear what was being discussed. They could divine the odd word, phrase maybe but could not get to the nub of any particular exchange.

They played and sang to this audience. Then at about ten o'clock, the peace was shattered by the door smashing open and shouting from outside. A horse crashed through the doors, its eyes piecing and its nostrils snorting, its rider, wielding a gun and ducking to miss the door head. Then more shouting and a gun being fired at the ceiling. Men crammed into the back of their booth or ran to the corners fearing for their lives. Carolina and Antonio joined them. Another horse and rider broke in. He fired at the ceiling. The first rider shouted out.

'Get back from when you came from, you God damned Muslim bastards. Fuck off back to the Maghreb. Take your mother whore women with you! Burn in the fires of hell.'

Some of the *Moriscos* in the tavern attempted to grab a leg of the shouting rider and snatch him from his horse but he was too fast, as was his companion. Each of the riders turned and within a few seconds had disappeared back outside into the cover of darkness. They were gone. Silence. Then loud discussion. 'Who the hell are they?' 'It's a wonder no one was killed!' 'We've got to find them and wipe them out!' 'Someone get the constabulary!' 'Don't bother!'

'I'm terrified, Antonio. That was so frightening. I nearly wet myself,' said Carolina.

'I think it's safe now. Let's get back to the middle of the floor and start playing again. It'll help calm things down!'

They gathered their instruments and began to play, 'If you are going to bathe, Juanilla, tell me where'. A huge round of cheering and applause enveloped them.

Someone shouted out. 'Good work, you two. You are the heroes of the night!'

'Buy them a beer!' shouted another.

They took their fill of the welcomed drinks and decided to retire to bed.

'Let's go to my room,' said Antonio. They entered and Carolina climbed onto the bed. 'We can't stay here, Antonio. It's too dangerous. If it's not the *Moriscos* who could threaten us, it's the native Spaniards.'

'I don't agree, Carolina. We'll be fine. We have to attend the meeting tomorrow night. It could be vital.'

'But what if the horsemen return? We were all lucky that no one was hurt tonight but it could be a different story tomorrow.'

'It will be a different story tomorrow. What will happen is this. The *Moriscos* won't want their meeting penetrated. Not at any cost. So they will guard the doors. There will be armed guards on patrol. That's what I'd do if I were them. And we'll probably be protected by the constabulary.'

'All right. But I'll stay upstairs. I'm frightened.'

'Let's decide tomorrow. A day in the cathedral square will help us sort our minds out.'

'I'd like to sleep now, Antonio. Do you mind? I'm going to my own room now.'

'I'll see you into it.' Antonio understood that Carolina had been severely shocked by the events of that evening and wanted only to sleep.

He held her hand and took her the few steps to hers, kissed her on the cheek and watched as she closed the door behind her.

CHAPTER 20
The meeting

Antonio knocked on Carolina's door and suggested they walked down the stairs to breakfast together. 'I didn't want you walking around here alone,' he said, as they approached the breakfast table. 'Do you still want to go up to the square to play today?'

'Yes. I'd rather do that than stay here thinking about tonight,' she said.

It was a cold winter morning, even colder than the previous few days, so they wore their heavy coats. As a precaution, Antonio carried his pistol in his violin case. He told Carolina it was to make her feel secure. He could see from the expression on her face, supplemented by her unwillingness to talk, that she was still in shock at the outrage the horsemen had perpetrated the night before. And the men had escaped with their freedom. Once the two of them had started to play, Carolina became more settled. By the time the cathedral clock struck midday, she had put the night's events to the back of her mind and spoke cheerily again.

'We've done quite well this morning. But we've only sung the staid material. Let's try something a little more risqué!'

Antonio's relief showed on his face. He smiled a genuine smile as opposed to the one he had synthesised for her until then. 'Go on! What about "The shepherd's song"?'

'We'll do it. You play a verse on the violin. Then I'll sing it and play along, too.' Her full sized guitar, which she played so delightfully, made her diminutive form look even smaller and made Antonio feel even more protective towards her.

It was at that moment, that the thought of Francisca found its way into his mind. Carolina liked him a lot. He liked her. But despite the mutual attraction and their uninhibited lovemaking, he could not see the relationship developing further. He struggled to think why. Her size did not enter the equation. Nor did her background as a *Gitana*. Maybe the fact that she was a colleague, a fellow musician, influenced him the most. That must be it… or maybe not. Perhaps Francisca would become his wife. He could see the attraction of a woman who was attracted towards him as a potential spouse.

Oddly and coincidentally, Carolina was thinking about him at the same time. Her feelings were stronger. She felt she was beginning to fall in love with this considerate and protective individual. She loved his mysteriousness. That he wouldn't tell her more about his mission, his employer, even what he was doing here, heightened the desire and attraction. The fact that he was tall did not worry her. Nor that he was younger.

Within a minute or two of their launching into 'The shepherd's song', a modest crowd had formed. Once a few listeners had thrown some money into the pot many more followed. The pot overflowed onto the road and coins rolled across the stones. A round of applause erupted as they sang the final chorus. 'Time for a beer and some bread and cheese,' said Antonio. 'And maybe some olives!'

'You seem much better now, Carolina, dare I say?' he said, as they sat in the nearby tavern.

'Yes, I am. Having you by my side helps,' she said, swallowing a green olive before speaking. 'Not much but certainly a little.' They each laughed. Neither wanted to betray his or her thoughts about the other.

They resumed play at their pitch by the cathedral. Suddenly, Antonio spoke.

'Don't look up. It's the beggar again. The one who spoke yesterday.' Antonio felt uneasy about talking to this interfering stranger, still dressed in tatters and showing more of his chest than Antonio wished to see.

The beggar stopped and spoke. 'What wonderful music! Do you know the song "To Amirillis"? It's one of my favourites.'

'Yes, I know it,' said Carolina. 'Is that the one which goes?' and she sang and strummed the accompaniment on her guitar:

'Though Amirillis dance in green,
Just like a fairy queen,
And sing full clear
With smiling cheer…'

'Play it right through. Go on!'

Carolina looked at Antonio. Her eyes said that she wished she hadn't confessed to the beggar that she knew it.

'Sorry. It's not in our repertoire,' said Antonio. 'Otherwise we would.'

'That's ridiculous. The lady knows it well!'

Carolina rescued him. 'I only know the first verse well. I struggle with the others.'

'That's not the impression you gave a minute ago. And you, if you want to be dictated to by him…' the beggar said, nodding his filthy head in Antonio's direction, 'I suppose that's up to you.'

Carolina would not be provoked and said nothing. Antonio defended by asking him a question. 'Exactly why have you stopped here? Not just to listen to our playing, I'm sure.'

The beggar took the bait. 'You are right, young señor. I wondered if you were to attend that meeting tonight or whether you had decided against.'

'As we said yesterday, we have decided to attend. We were there last night. A rather unpleasant incident occurred.'

'Yes, I heard about it. The place was raided by two non-supporters on horseback. Caused a certain amount of havoc, it seems.'

'It was terrifying,' said Carolina. 'I thought they were going to kill us.'

'No chance,' said the beggar or whatever he was. 'They were just trying to scare everyone.'

'They succeeded, by the blood of Christ,' said Antonio.

The beggar laughed. 'People like that don't win. They merely pave the way for others to defeat them.'

Antonio thought that those were hardly the words of a beggar. A spy for the *Moriscos*, perhaps.

'Take great care tonight, if you don't want to be in trouble,' said the man. He bid them farewell, turned and went on his way.

'Was that supposed to scare us?' said Antonio.

If Carolina looked settled before, she certainly wasn't then. 'This meeting is definitely scaring me. What if the horsemen break in again? What if they kill someone next time? It could be you. It could be me. Or both of us… and some others, I'm terrified, Antonio.' She put her arms around him and buried her head in his chest.

'You are not going to attend, Carolina. You'll stay in your room. I'll go because I have to. And I'll be armed!'

'I have to be with you. To play.'

'No. I can see a way out. You'll feign illness. I'll make excuses for you. You'll be fine in your room.'

'I'll be worried about you!'

'Then you will worry. I know how to look after myself. Trust me. I've had the best training Madrid can give!' The thought of the laughing major flashed across his mind.

The two of them played into the fading light and returned to Ángelita's inn. The cold and the awkward conversation with the man dressed as a beggar had made them feel as tired as a pair of work horses at dusk. 'I'm for an early night,' said Carolina.

'I could sleep, too, but I have to attend that meeting. And I need to be as sharp as a razor.'

'Let's just have a quiet snooze. You'll be brighter after a nap.'

The two of them made their way to Carolina's room, cuddled up to each other, fully clothed, and fell asleep. They were awoken by the neighing sound of a horse outside the inn.

'Time I went downstairs to this meeting. I wonder what time it is,' said Antonio.

'I'm sure it's past eight. I vaguely remember hearing the cathedral clock chiming... about half an hour ago. Good luck down there, Antonio. I'll be thinking of you.'

Antonio flicked some water over his face from a bowl on a stand in the corner of the room. He dried his face in a fresh towel. 'I'll go now. Lock the door behind me.'

'Take your gun,' said Carolina, looking pale and anxious.

Antonio kissed her on the cheek and went.

He quickly slipped into his room, primed his snaplock, hid it in a white cloth and placed it gently in the case beneath the newly purchased instrument. He glanced in the dressing table mirror before making his way down the stairs and into the drinking area. He unlatched the door to face a rowdy crowd of men, almost all of whom held a jug of Segovian ale. 'Here's one of the musicians!' called out one of them. He was an untidily dressed individual wearing a beard and a wide brimmed hat that looked as if someone had recently trodden on it and left it permanently distorted.

'Where's his partner, the midget lady?' shouted another. It rankled him to hear Carolina addressed as a 'midget' but at least he referred to her as a lady.

'She's not feeling well. So I'm your soloist for tonight. I can't sound like Carolina but I can knock out a good song and play my violin at the same time!'

'Then get on with it,' demanded another, his instruction being greeted by the laughter of many more.

233

Fearing trouble if he did not respond as told, Antonio took his violin from its case and struck up the tune of 'To Amirillis'. This was no random choice. He hoped the tune would smoke out the man dressed as a beggar, if he were there, and sure enough...

'Thought you said you didn't know it!' shouted a disembodied voice from somewhere near the middle of the crowd, most of whom were on their feet. The source gradually made his way to the front, pushing his way past about a dozen or so others as he did so. Antonio hardly recognised him. The beggar had said as much. Gone were the pantaloons tied with string, the chest exposing open shirt, the battered hat and bare feet. Now he was dressed in a new, brown tricorne, a long black coat over black leather boots and a white shirt, decorated by a smart, black silk tie. He'd trimmed his ragged beard to a neat point and shaped his moustache to a rakish, symmetrical upward curve on each side of his face. Antonio could smell the musky perfume on his subtle umber wig which almost matched his darker, brown hair.

'No. It's just the words we don't know. We know the tune well!' smiled Antonio, wondering what the man's reaction would be and still unsure as to what his exact position could be in this confusion of masculine sweat and untidiness. His demeanour and countenance gave him an air of superiority over these other apparently inferior individuals.

'I'm so glad you could attend tonight,' said the man. 'We may have a challenging position for you and your colleague.' Antonio felt a sense of repulsion, a need to reject any such proposal. The last thing he needed was another assignment in Segovia. Quite the reverse: he wanted an end to this and make an early return to Madrid.

'Interesting,' he said calmly as if only slightly curious but maintaining a look of coolness that could not actually be taken as a refusal. 'May I ask what that might be?'

'You'll learn soon enough,' said the stranger, clearly knowing more than most about what was about to transpire at this meeting. 'I hope your lady companion soon recovers. Please give her my compliments.' He then disappeared back into the crowd, still holding his jug of beer.

Antonio decided he would play, 'Roses for my mother', an unprovocative, calming refrain which would help him blend into the background. He played the tune and sang the best he could while doing so. By then others had joined this gathering which he reckoned numbered at least eighty. Many had crammed their way into the booths and virtually all the chairs at the drinking tables were straining under the weight of their occupants, in some cases, two of them to a seat. Antonio began to wonder when the meeting itself would begin. Then he heard Ángelita cry out. 'Come to the bar now if you want a top up!' Turning his head in her direction, he noticed half a dozen, behatted serving wenches, in well used, cream coloured dresses, their cleavages teasingly exposed, each prepared to pour more beer from a large jug of ale. Chaos ensued as many of the men took up the offer. Ale sloshed from half full jugs as one man crashed into another to reach the bar. Many swore in frustration and came close to exchanging blows. Eventually, jugs refilled, they settled back to their animated discussions.

'Order! Order!' A gruff voice bawled out. 'Make way for Miguel Osuna.'

The excited chatter gradually subsided and gave way to the sound of a pair boot steps on the plain wooden floor as the said Señor Osuna made his way through the crowd. A couple of the gathered assembly gave him a leg up onto a table near the back wall. He stood proud and erect, his thumbs and forefingers gripping the lapels on his long black coat. Antonio almost dropped his bow. Miguel Osuna was the 'beggar' now transformed into a gentleman, not only well dressed, but of significantly elevated status and ready to address this motley congregation. Antonio realised that he and Carolina were in fact right: this man merely pretended to be a mendicant and was now probably playing his true role as spy.

'Gentlemen,' said Osuna, in a strong, raised voice, speaking as if he were addressing a gathering in the open air. 'Firstly, may I thank you all for attending this crucial meeting. Second, there are some here who may not know why we are assembled in this place. I will be short on the background before I give way to our plans. You are all *Morisco* sympathisers. You are not all *Moriscos* but that is another matter. The key point is that you are all people that I trust and so do our leaders. We are in danger, as a race and as a people. There is talk of our expulsion from Spain to God knows where, probably to the Maghreb. The forces of Catholicism are against us. So are the forces of envy and greed. Many native Spaniards would love to be as industrious as we are and as successful in business and in serving those for whom we labour.

'But we know no other realm. No other land. This is our land, our country and it has been since the beginning of the conquest led by our hero Tariq Ibn Ziyad in 711. So we will not be thrown away, sent to some barbaric, uncivilised place which is foreign to us and can only be foreign. So we are going to stay. Here in our Spain! That is our birthright!'

The place erupted with cheering and applause.

'Order… order.' The same disembodied voice.

'So what we are going to do is fight for our rights!'

Another loud round of applause and shouting. This time the assembly broke into a chant, 'Miguel… Miguel… Miguel!'

The same voice. 'Order… I say. Order.'

'Thirdly, we will use weapons but they will be honed by cunning. So, this is our plan… You all know that the king will be travelling through here in a few days' time. He has left Valladolid already. He will make one stop on the way and pass through this town on the 2nd, the day after tomorrow. But we will be waiting for him. There will be by then several hundred of us, from all around here. We are going to kidnap the king and hold him up for ransom…'

Another round of applause and shouting. Some threw their hats into the air.

'But the ransom will not be for any sum of money. It will be for a guarantee. The guarantee that we stay in Spain. We will remain here, whatever the Archbishops and their cronies say! If that guarantee is not given we will remove the king's fingers, one by one. One every two days and send them to that scheming ogre the so called Duke of Lerma. He will recognise them, the king's fingers. If we run out of fingers we will start on his toes and if we run out of toes we'll cut off his ears. Then, if we take off his second who knows what we'll take off next!'

An outburst of uproarious laughter.

'We will show the king no mercy until our demands are met. And, fourthly, here are some practical details. We will take the king as he enters the Huertos Plaza. According to our intelligence, he will enter the Plaza from the Calle San Agustín. He and his company will cross the Plaza to the opposite corner and make their way towards to the Palacio de los Condes de Alpuente, in the Calle Juan Bravo where they will stay the night. He will have a large retinue of hangers-on but he will be heavily guarded by the Madrid *Tercio*. They will be armed with staves or harquebuses. We estimate that there will be about a hundred *tercios* so we will outnumber them two to one!'

Another huge cheer went up.

'Calm down, gentlemen! We haven't bagged him yet! … Our attack will be against the king and only the king. We will have to attack those who defend him but our sole aim will be to capture him. We will have a hundred men waiting and disguised, just ambling and chatting in each of the two *calles* that cross the top of the Plaza. I plan that the signal to emerge from the *calles* will be given by our musician here who will, if he and his colleague agree, play a loud drum roll just as the king appears from the Calle San Agustín.'

His eye turned to Antonio who stared back at him, kept calm and suppressed any sign of emotion. The man could have no idea of what Antonio's true role could be. Whatever further detail emerged, he now knew the key facts. He had to report them to the *corregidor*, as soon as he could, that night. His mind suddenly worked faster. How would he escape this meeting? Could he? Would he just have to wait until the end? Would the *corregidor*'s office be open? Surely someone would be on duty. If not he would have to alert the constabulary. Were there any of them here? Surely not. All who entered had been checked at the main door. Would he tell Carolina that he was going? He would have to remain in this room until he knew the detailed tactics they would use in their attempt against the king. He had no choice but to stay, even if he could go.

'Once we have caught him, we will take him blindfolded to a safe house, not far from here, just off the road to Ávila,' continued Osuna. 'We are not an army and we cannot act like an army. But once we have agreed our strategy and tactics, we will keep to them. Any man who fails or runs away will be executed, by my own hand. I want five of you to volunteer to take the king to the safe house. None of the five will fight. They will be armed but on horseback, waiting in the *plaza* with a spare horse, a rope to tie up the king and the blindfold. They will be given the exact location of the house, once they have the king in their possession.'

Antonio cringed at the thought of these brutes having the king in their 'possession'. How much longer would this meeting last? A dozen or so hands went up.

Osuna turned to a lackey standing beneath him. 'Take down the names of five of them. Pick them at random.' The lackey moved into the crowd.

'Now we reveal more of our plan. The worst way to attack is for all of us to descend on the king at once. Such would be chaos and lead to more of your blood on the streets than any of us would want to shed. No. We will attack in tranches of a dozen men from each flank, that is, from each *calle* at the head of the Plaza. So we will use the famous pincer tactic employed so successfully at Battle of Mohács by Süleyman the Magnificent. Once you hear the drum roll. You will line up in the street in rows of a dozen men. You will be guided into these formations by my local commanders. There will be four in each flank. Stand up men so we can see you. On the tables if need be.'

Eight men, scattered in various parts of the room, stood, climbed on the tables and waved their arms aloft. Nothing distinguished these from the rest of the untidy mob save for their black tricorne hats. 'The commanders will wear those hats on the day! You will only attack the king's guards. On no account must you injure or kill the king. He is our prize and we must retrieve him intact! The king will be riding a horse or be passenger in one of the royal carriages. We doubt that he will be travelling with the queen but we don't know for sure and won't until the day. You must try to avoid injuring any bystanders. That cannot be good for our cause. But that may be the price of victory! Lastly, make sure you matchlocks are at the ready! And carry a knife, just in case. Are there any questions?'

A man with a full, untidy beard stood on one of the tables at the back. 'How much are we to be paid for this?' he said.

'Good question!' someone shouted.

'We all want to know,' bawled another.

'You aren't expecting payment are you? This is about honour. The honour of our people!' The gathered throng became agitated. Neighbour spoke to neighbour, urgently checking the views of those nearest them. Osuna remained silent. Then another individual climbed up onto a table nearer the front and spoke.

'You will have to pay us. Honour or not. We are putting our lives at risk. Serious risk and we want some compensation. If only a single *ducat*.'

'You must know that our funds are limited. Our latest attempt at boosting them by robbing the jewellers in the Huertos failed. I think I have a solution. I will pay each of you five *reales* but only if your mission is successful. Does anyone disagree?'

Not a hand raised itself and no one spoke.

'I will take that as agreement. Any other questions? If not, pick up your matchlocks.'

'I have a question,' shouted a man standing against the back wall. 'Why not charge a ransom on the king as well as a guarantee of our remaining in Spain? That way, you can pay us the *ducat* we want, maybe even more.'

'I thought I'd dealt with that,' said Osuna. 'We are not charging a ransom. That would reduce us to the level of common kidnappers and I'm not prepared to do that. It is a question of honour and I'm not about to sacrifice ours.'

The meeting closed on this negative note and the men gradually ambled towards the door where the each picked up a matchlock pistol from the table along with a powder horn, flints and fuses. They could not be better prepared for their mission or at least that was the view of Señor Osuna.

Antonio could go that night to the *corregidor* or to the Office of the Constabulary. He feared either option. There were about a hundred men at this meeting and despite the darkness in the streets, someone would be sure to recognise him if he were to leave the inn. If he did seek out the forces of the law what could they do? Nothing. No action could be taken, not that close to midnight. His only safe option was to go to bed and leave reporting to the *corregidor* until the morning. He would go early. But there was one piece of business that needed urgent transaction with Osuna. So he sought him out in the exiting, disorganised crowd.

'Senor Osuna. We need to speak. I am extremely flattered that you want me and my musician partner, Carolina, to sound a drum roll when the king is about to enter the Plaza Huertos. But we have a problem. I'm afraid that we will have left Segovia by then. We are heading back to our respective homes. In my case I have a meeting with a theatre group in Madrid. I'm not sure what Carolina's commitment may be but she needs to return to Ávila. I hope you will understand our situation.'

'You have put me in an incredibly difficult position. I was relying on your presence to do that. I am to say the least disappointed. I'll have to find someone else.'

'You should have no trouble. Anyone can sound a drum roll, once they have a drum. There's nothing to it.'

'The fact remains that you have made things awkward for me.'

'I'm sorry to say this, Señor Osuna, but you have created the problem yourself. If you had asked me before the meeting whether we were available, you would have discovered that we were not. It was wrong of you to assume that we would be able to comply with your wishes. That you announced publicly that you would ask us implied that we would be able to do it. You were wrong on that count. Your mistake, not ours.'

'I remain disappointed.'

'All I can do señor, is to wish you good night and, of course, success with your mission. You have thought it through well and I can't see it failing,' Antonio lied.

Antonio returned to his room. He sensed something was wrong but had no idea what. He tried the key in the door but it was already unlocked. He opened the door quietly and carefully and entered. The room didn't feel right and was dark as an underground cellar. There was someone there. He could smell an individual, someone who had been or was afraid. He picked up a lit candle in a holder from a table on the landing and entered. He could immediately see what had happened. Poor Carolina had been frightened by something and had come into his room. She slept soundly on the bed covers. What he didn't understand was why the room was unlocked. He could swear that he left it not only closed but fully locked. All would become clear in the morning. He slid onto the bed beside her and drifted into sleep.

Antonio woke before Carolina and got dressed. As he was washing she awoke, climbed off the bed and went over to hug his half naked torso. 'I am so pleased to see you, Antonio. I was so scared last night!'

'What happened?'

'As I was falling asleep, I heard the door knob turn. Someone was trying to enter my room. I hear a voice on the landing mutter something. I couldn't make out what the voice said but it was a man, for certain. He sounded to be in his forties.'

'Did you recognise him?

'No.'

'What do you think he wanted?'

'I've no idea. Maybe he wanted to rape me in my bed. I don't know. So I thought I'd wait until I was sure he'd gone and try to get into your room. I took the key from mine and luckily it fitted your door so here I am. I'm sorry, Antonio. I've trespassed in your room and caused you to worry.'

'Don't worry, Carolina. You are safe. That's all that matters. But did you leave my door unlocked when you came in?'

'Definitely not. I took the key out of the door on the outside and transferred it to the inside, locked the door and removed my key which is here on the dressing table. Actually it isn't! I'm scared Antonio, someone is trying to cause us trouble.'

She put her arms around him and broke into a quiet sob. 'I'm sorry, Antonio. I am a problem for you and you are good to me, Antonio. So good.'

'I'll get dressed. Then you get dressed and we'll go down for breakfast.'

'How did the meeting go?'

'I'll tell you, while we are eating.'

'Let's sit in this booth. I don't want to be overheard.' Antonio checked that there was nobody in the adjacent booths. Ángelita appeared to offer them some food. 'You chose us something, Ángelita, but the most important thing is some cold beer.'

Antonio recounted what happened the night before. 'Two things are important. I must go back to the *corregidor*'s office and we must leave here. I told Osuna that we couldn't play any part in the kidnap... because we were leaving Segovia. So we have no option.'

'You must go to the *corregidor*, as soon as you can. May I come? I feel vulnerable here.'

'You come, too, Carolina, but wait in the outer office while I tell him about their plans.'

'There is something else, Antonio. I don't want to return to Ávila. I want to come to Madrid with you.'

'What? Come with me to Madrid?' His thoughts turned to Francisca. What would she think of him returning with another woman? The fact that she was a small person was not relevant. The fact of her womanhood could be all that mattered to another woman, especially one who wanted Antonio as a husband. 'That could be difficult,' he said.

'Why is that? I think I am falling in love with you, Antonio. I want to live with you forever.' She climbed off her chair and went around the table to hug him.

'I am too young to commit myself to a future life with anyone. I would be a liability.' He wondered whether he should tell her about Francisca. He didn't want to hurt her feelings but neither could he enthuse about her coming to Madrid with him.

'Carolina, I must be frank with you. We enjoy a wonderful relationship. We work so well together as professionals and we have those wonderful, uninhibited sessions of love when we both feel the need. But I am sorry to say, I am not in love with you.'

She started to sob again. 'It's because I'm a dwarf. I know you men.'

'Please, Carolina. It's not that at all. I am only twenty one and I am just settling down to this work I cannot describe to you and in my job as an itinerant musician. I am not ready to commit myself, to you or to anyone else. I'm sorry.'

'Anyone else? Do you mean there may be someone else? You have been making love to me and cheating on another!' She screamed the last condemning sentence.

'Not so loud, Carolina. Do you want the whole place to know about our argument? Let me tell you some facts.' He went on to explain the fiery relationship he once had with Catalina and why it had broken. He told her that Francisca de Polanco, Catalina's sister, had fallen in love with him and that he had put that relationship on hold by telling Francisca that he was not ready to settle into a marriage.

'Maybe I should have told you about all this before but I thought we were just enjoying each other's company, in the physical sense as well, of course, and I had no idea until now that you liked me so much.' He avoided the use of the word 'love'.

'I don't know what to say. We made love several times before when we were together in Valladolid and it just seemed natural to carry on where we had left off before. But if it's so difficult for me to come back to Madrid with you, I may just go there on my own and find work there.'

'I have an idea. You know that Lupita de Pastrana is working in Madrid in a small music group with my colleague Iago. We called him Iago the Bad! He plays the dulcian and he's brilliant at it. Well, you could come back with me and join that group. I may be working with them myself for a time, before my next assignment in the job I cannot tell you about.'

'Where would I stay if I couldn't live with you?'

'You could stay in my house, at least until we find you something.'

'What would Francisca say?'

'Leave her to me!'

'You know, I really think you are wonderful, Antonio, even if you are not in love with me! But it's time we went to the *corregidor*. And, if you'd like to, we can have one of our tasty love sessions tonight!'

'Please don't distract me! I need to be sharp when I speak to the *corregidor*!'

Antonio explained to the assistant that he needed to see the man urgently, if he had returned. 'Yes, he's in his office. I'll ask him if he will see you, Señor Hidalgo. In brief, what is the subject for discussion?'

'The kidnap of the king. By two hundred *Moriscos*,' he said, with the total absence of emotion.

'Are you serious?'

Antonio just looked straight into his eye. 'I'll tell him straight away,' the assistant said. He dashed into the *corregidor*'s office without even knocking the door.

'You stay here,' Antonio said to Carolina, again with no emotion. 'I'll be out soon.'

The appearance and general countenance of the *corregidor* surprised Antonio. It was as if he had modeled his facial features on some beggar or vagabond. Perhaps it was some form of disguise. His full growth of beard almost totally hid any facial features he possessed, apart from his nose which leant disturbingly to the left, as if it had been broken many years before but hadn't grown back into its correct orientation. His hair, fairly neatly brushed but unwashed, rested on his shoulders. His clothes, his jacket in particular, possessed a threadbare quality, as if he had been wearing it well into what should have been its retirement to the poor box. He certainly did not look like a royal appointee to a significant local office. Yet he had a special presence that Antonio could identify with his post.

'I am pleased to meet you, Señor Hidalgo. I understand that you have a codename. Is that so?'

'Diaspora.'

'Fine. I understand you have some information about a threat against the king.'

'Yes, indeed I do.'

'Tell me.'

Antonio related Osuna's plan in detail, almost as he had announced it.

The *corregidor* peered down towards the papers on his desk and took a deep, nasal breath before looking up to speak. 'First, thank you for your report and, in particular, the detail in which you have delivered it.' He then paused for a few moments and started again. 'The fact is we already knew much of what you have told me.'

'What?' exclaimed Antonio, glaring wildly at the *corregidor*. Antonio's face reddened with rage. 'Do you mean to say, that I and my music assistant, Carolina de Torres Madruga, risked our lives to find out what you already know! And doubtless have already taken steps to thwart!'

The *corregidor* reacted coolly to Antonio's outburst. 'I'm sorry, Señor Hidalgo, but you undervalue your contribution. Your colleague Lusitano discovered only two days ago what these people were likely to perpetrate. He attended a similar meeting in Valladolid. So you have provided excellent confirmation of the events as planned. I commend you and your colleague for your daring in obtaining the information you did.'

'I apologise. I shouldn't have reacted in that way. I formed the wrong impression. I felt strongly for my colleague, not myself. I'm glad that Lusitano was able to give you something. What are the plans to deal with the threat against the king?' Antonio hesitated to refer to 'your plans' preferring something less personalised.

'I'm sorry, Señor Hidalgo. I cannot reveal that. Partly because our plans are not yet mature. You can be sure the king will be safe. Now we know the details of the plan of attack, we can deal with it.'

'Not yet mature,' thought Antonio. 'That means they haven't a plan yet. They need to get on with it.'

'Corregidor, I should go now, unless you have any further questions. We need to be on our way.'

'You go, Diaspora. Safe journey and thank you again.'

'Just one more thing. I promised Algebra that I would keep him informed,' said Antonio. He pulled an envelope from inside his jacket. It contained a letter he had written the night before to Silva. He had never written a longer missive. It described Osuna's plan in all its detail. It concluded by saying that he had just reported the relevant facts to the *corregidor* of Segovia.

Antonio and Carolina went back to the tavern and packed. Within minutes they had settled their account, bid farewell to Ángelita, saddled up and were on their way back to Madrid.

CHAPTER 21
The 2nd of March

'I am not amused,' said the king. 'Those bastards almost had me! I almost defecated! Especially when those Christ hating *Moriscos* started firing. Thank God I was in a carriage and not on a horse!'

'You were not at risk, Philip,' said the duke. 'We annihilated them.'

The king and the duke were sitting at the dining table in the great hall of the Palacio de los Condes de Alpuente, tucking into a course of venison, grapes and artichokes, all washed down with copious gulps of the local wine, a voluptuous valdepeñas. Each of the two diners recognised the grotesque, but unspoken, irony that this palace was a Moorish mansion, constructed in the earlier part of the previous century.

'What do you mean by that?'

'We killed or maimed nearly two hundred of them. *Morisco* mercenaries. Each carrying a matchlock pistol and a dagger.'

'And you say I was not at risk. Let alone the queen and the boy. Sounds like idle speculation to me.'

'Let me tell you in some detail, Philip. Yes, we suspected that you could be in danger on the journey to Madrid. But we took every measure in our powers to eliminate actual risk. You are aware that we sent two of your best agents into the *Morisco* enclaves, one to Valladolid. We detailed Lucitano to go there. And we directed Diaspora here to Segovia. They each came up with consistent information about a plan to attack you here. In the Plaza de Huertos.'

The duke reported the kidnapping plan in all its frightening detail.

'So what did you do to avoid the attack?'

'It could not be avoided only countered.'

The king felt he had the upper hand and continued his strident attack.

'Rubbish! Of course it could have been avoided. For one thing, if they planned a kidnap, you could have used a decoy in my place, even a puppet. And I could have travelled later or earlier than the published plan, even incognito. So I disagree.'

'With the deepest respect, Your Majesty,' continued the duke – he only ever used the term 'Your Majesty' in private discussion when he felt the king needed placating or when the king had the duke at the point of his sword, which he clearly did then. 'Your people have the God given right to see you in your travels. We are, in effect celebrating the rebirth of Madrid. That is why we are on this journey. There could be no scope for your passing through here in disguise or substituted. There would have been riots in the streets. Instead you received a tumultuous reception at the city gates.'

'Yes and a hail of gunshot once inside them!'

'Not so, Your Majesty. All went according to our plan?'

'Our plan?'

'Yes, a plan hastily conceived by myself, the Corregidor of Segovia, the Chief Constable and none other than a field marshal in the Madrid Tercio, one of Agustín Mejía's men. We armed every constable in the town and any we could pull in from the surrounding towns and villages. We engaged the whole of your Tercio guard which we marched here at such a speed to arrive at the Plaza Huertos a full thirty minutes before you, and we routed the *Morisco* attackers. We took them completely by surprise. The order was simple: "shoot to kill" so that is what we did. We haven't counted the dead just yet, but they amount to at least seventy and there are another hundred or so wounded who were treated where they fell or in the hospital of Segovia. Needless to say, Your Majesty, each man is under armed guard and under arrest and, once fit enough, will be taken to the local cells to await trial. So, to summarise, Your Majesty, you were not at any significant risk.'

The duke then felt he had won his case and paused for the king to speak.

'If you are so certain, I should concur, but reluctantly.'

'It appears that you have finished your venison, Philip.'

'Indeed I have. What delectable dish awaits us?'

'If I may, I would like to ask the guard outside to bring in a trophy.'

'Do so,' said the king, swigging noisily at the cup of the wine.

Moments later, through the elegant main doors to the hall, held open by two bewigged flunkies, the guard appeared carrying an oval meat platter in front of him. In the centre of the plate, facing the front and standing on what remained of its neck, stood a human head. Each of its eyes appeared to stare agonisingly forward as if still conscious of the fateful blow which separated it from the rest of its body. Its skin was a bluish grey.

'Who in the name of Christ was that?' asked the king.

'That is the head of the leader of the *Moriscos*, Miguel Osuna!'

The king stood and looked at it for a full minute, leaning forward, almost as if to smell it. 'All right. That's enough of your triumphalism. Have it taken away!'

The duke nodded towards the guard who clicked his heels, turned and took the object towards the sumptuous main double door. It opened seemingly of its own accord but pulled by the two flunkies who acted on the sound of the heel click.

A waiter appeared at the table with two plates of ham and asparagus. The two of them resumed their dinner and discussion. 'So what is the latest advice you can give me about the *Morisco* problem?' said the king.

'The archbishops still want rid of them. So do many of your populace. Your court is less sure. But there is a problem we need to deal with. Whether they are building warships to attack us.'

'What are you proposing on that front?'

'The issue is currently being discussed by the Councils of War and State. They will advise you in due course.'

'Pour me another glass of wine, Francisco. Please. Where did you get that one from?'

CHAPTER 22
Trouble in Madrid

Antonio and Carolina took a full three days to reach Madrid. They stopped for the second night at Galapagar and stayed at the inn where Sebastian Alonso González del Águilla's sister-in-law, made them more than welcome. 'Where is your colleague who stayed with you before?' asked the buxom, eye-patched landlady.

'I really don't know,' he lied.

'And who is your new company?'

'Permit me to introduce you to my treasured colleague and friend, Carolina de Torres Madruga. She's a musician and we play together for our living.'

'Would you like a room each?'

Carolina stepped in as smartly as the crack of a whip. 'We don't mind sharing, do we Antonio?'

He suddenly had no choice. How could he possibly disagree with the tiny lady, especially as she was giving a clear indication of a need for nocturnal activity?

'Umm... er... no. We'll share!'

'That's it then,' said the buxom woman. 'I have a lovely room for you, upstairs towards the back. Room twelve. Here's the key. Would you like a meal this evening? I have some lovely lamb chops!'

'In an hour?' said Carolina.

'Come down when you're ready.'

Just five minutes later, Antonio and Carolina were lying naked on the bed in room twelve.

'You naughty girl, Carolina! You really put me on a spot! How could I say we wanted a room each when you said we'd share? That would have caused you such embarrassment!'

'I've no regrets!' she said, cuddling up to him.

'I hope I don't disappoint you. That's all I can say!'

Then she slid on top of him and rubbed up against him as she held her face over his. 'Go on, Antonio, kiss me on the lips! Now!'

He pulled her head towards him and placed his arm around her shoulder. Then he kissed her, sliding his tongue between her lips and deep into her mouth. They kissed each other with the passion of re-united lovers which in a sense they were.

He lifted her up and turned her around so that her legs were placed each side of his head and her bottom sat on top of his chest. 'I could look at you there all day,' he said. 'You won't know how beautiful you are. But let me pull you closer and kiss you!'

'That's gorgeous, Antonio. You know exactly where to touch me to give me maximum pleasure! Who taught you these skills?'

'A good lover should never reveal his secrets!'

'But you aren't just good, you are brilliant! Come on, who told you what to do?'

'I'll have to stop to tell you. I'll be speaking straight at your prettiness!'

'Don't worry. She won't mind if you look up occasionally though!'

'It was a milkmaid on my father's farm near Pedraza. When I was about fifteen, I helped her in the cowshed with the milking. It was about seven in the morning. Just after we'd let the cows back out, she told me to follow her up a ladder into the hay loft. She told me to take all my clothes off and as I did, she removed hers. Then she gave me this most intimate tour of her body. She showed me to her secret place and took my finger in her hand. She guided it to those sensitive spots which I now know so well and love to touch on you. Then she showed me how to make love and we did it twice. She told me I'd make a good lover!'

'So that was your first time then. She took away your virginity!'

'Good God no! She was about the sixth or seventh woman I'd made love to.'

'Who were the others then?' laughed Carolina, not sure again whether to believe him.

'I used to do it with another of father's milkmaids, his stable maids and even with one of the girls who worked on his land. The other milkmaid took my virginity when I was about… twelve or thirteen, I suppose. She was so desperate…she'd have killed me, if I'd refused. I thought I'd killed her when she passed out. She moaned and collapsed in the hay loft. The same loft and at the same time of the morning! I panicked and fanned her with my trousers but she soon came round. I had to explain what happened! The lying bitch claimed I'd raped her! I ask you. A twelve year old raping a thirty year old milkmaid who could easily control a rampant bull! But she soon realised that it was her who'd virtually raped me!'

'No wonder you are such a good lover, Antonio!' she laughed. Then, in almost a weep, 'But you don't love me when I wished you did.'

'Don't worry,' he said as he lifted a hand to touch her face. 'We are great friends and colleagues and will remain so, whatever happens!'

'You sound as if you believe that.'

'I do. Let's get dressed and go to dinner.'

Antonio's first duty when he returned to Doña Marta's house with Carolina was to make peace with his ancient mare. She snorted as he entered the stable around the back of the house. Whomever Silva had appointed to take care of her had performed to good effect. She looked as well as she'd been in six months. She had obviously been exercised, quite often. Not only did she look healthy she was evidently pleased to see him, which she showed by vigorously flicking her tail and smacking her tongue on the roof of her mouth.

'You kept telling me what a worn out mare she is and yet she's in good fettle!' said Carolina, looking on.

'Someone has looked after her well.' The horse snorted in agreement.

'Nice rooms,' said Carolina. 'I'd love to stay here with you but I must find somewhere of my own.'

'Let's not worry too much about your moving out. You've hardly moved in yet! There are two bedrooms so we can have one each. We shouldn't sleep together … not every night!'

'I agree, Antonio! It will be good to have some privacy and I don't mean that in an unpleasant way!' she said, smiling. 'My main concern is about your friend Francisca. What will she think of me staying here? All sorts of things will be going through her mind, many of which will be accurate!'

'Leave her to me. I haven't thought much about that. We may have to keep the physical side of our relationship away from her. On the other hand, I don't want to lie. It's not good to lie to a prospective wife! Definitely not… not before you are married!'

'So how are you going to manage the situation?'

'I'll think about that. In the meantime, you put your things in the spare room. The biggest issue on my mind is to report to my boss. I need see him about what happened in Segovia and ask him about my next assignment. We should also let Lupita know you are here. She'll be stunned! We'll see if she recognises you! You'll also have to meet Iago. It's up to them to decide whether to engage you in the troupe.'

'Now I'm worried,' said the wide eyed Carolina. 'Is there any doubt?'

'In my mind, no. But our main worry is Iago who has never met you!'

Antonio wasted no time in reporting back to Silva. Hector Brondate warmly welcomed him but with his usual weak handshake. Antonio had to wait an hour until Silva returned from an audience with the king. It did not surprise Silva that the king objected strongly to some of the arrangements he had made for the king in the re-furbished Alcázar palace. He had told Silva that he wanted to be in closer proximity to his councils, especially the Councils of Castile, of War and of State Security. The price, as Silva had explained, would be greater remoteness for the court musicians, the other councils and the treasury. Nor was the king happy with the décor in his quarters which extended to most of the West Wing. Apparently, he didn't want regal opulence, merely something presentable to other members of his family and to the various senior officials and dignitaries he had to deal with.

These issues, presented to Silva in front of the Duke of Lerma, who had hardly uttered a word at the meeting, had put Silva seriously on the defensive. So he returned to his own quarters in not the best of moods. The lugubrious Brondate could see from his snarling demeanour, his grimacing lips and twisted eyebrows, that Silva would hardly delight in seeing Hidalgo. He had, however, no choice but to inform him of his presence.

'Too bad. I don't want to see him,' glared Silva.

Brondate wrung his hands. 'I'll tell him. Right now!'

'Stop! Stay here! Let me think, will you? Yes, I will see him. I can give him fifteen minutes. Definitely no more. Tell me when it's up,'

Antonio entered from the outer office, by-passed by Silva de Torres who had used his corridor entrance, a trick he often deployed to avoid unwanted visitors already lurking in the outer office.

'Go in, Señor Hidalgo. I advise you not to dwell on the less relevant detail. He can give you only fifteen minutes. He's asked me to stop the meeting after that.'

'Good morning, Antonio!' He came round his table and hugged Antonio, like the prodigal son. 'Thank you for the letter. Is there more to add? I must be quick. I have some serious issues to deal with today. Failure could lead to my execution!'

251

'No. The Segovia mission concluded satisfactorily, as far as I know. I'm here to find out about my next one.'

'Do you know how the mission concluded? Probably not.'

'No.'

'We virtually obliterated those who conspired to kidnap the king. Killed nearly half and arrested the rest for treason. The leader, Osuna, I think, was decapitated by sword in the Plaza Huertos. It took four blows.'

'I had no idea!'

'Your next mission will be to Morocco. I'm telling you that in total confidence. I've no idea when that will be. Within months, possibly weeks. I'm awaiting instruction from State Security.'

'With whom, if anyone, will I be travelling? How will I get there? Where in Morocco. It's a big country!'

'I can't tell you. What I am instructing you to do is to restart your work as a musician and wait for me to call. Go back to your troupe! Here is your bounty for the Segovia job. Well done. You did brilliantly! I'm afraid you'll have to go now. Farewell, Diaspora!' They shook hands. That damned name again.

Antonio put the little leather purse in an inner pocket in his jacket. He nodded towards Brondate as he left.

'I can't tell you, Carolina. I truly don't know! He wouldn't tell me,' he lied. 'I must rejoin the troupe and you will join it, too.'

'Surely, you have some idea. He couldn't have left you with no information about it.'

'Sorry, but that's where you're wrong. In my profession, you never give information away before it's needed. And I don't need to know… at least not yet!'

'You almost told me what your profession is then!'

'I think you may know already but I cannot tell you!'

'What am I going to do while you are away? Can I come with you?'

'An interesting question! But I can't keep you in suspense. It wouldn't be fair on you. We must work on the assumption that the answer is no. So unless you go back to Ávila, you'll need to be earning your living in Madrid.'

'That won't be a problem. I can earn a living anywhere!' she said, with just a hint of anger.

It took a full week for Carolina to settle into Madrid. She found it difficult to cope with the geography of this large town and with people staring at her: there were few dwarfs in the town and it seemed that the locals found her something of a curiosity. She told Antonio about this and he just told her to 'smile back' if she could bring herself to. She would then soon be regarded as 'normal' and those who stared might well accustom themselves to her regular and frequent presence on the streets and even be friendly in return.

Most of all, however, she wondered what the reaction would be to her joining Antonio's music troupe. She soon found out. Within a few more days, the two of them had arranged to meet with Iago and Lupita, both together, at the house Lupita shared with her friends in the Mentidero. Lupita recognised Carolina immediately and greeted her like a long lost sister.

'I can't believe it's you, Carolina. I've often thought of you but never did I think we'd meet again!'

The little lady hugged Lupita with a passion, wrapping her arms around her waist. 'I can't believe I am seeing you, either!' she said with tears running down her face.

Iago had never met Carolina before so understandably showed little emotion, other than a slightly wry and curious smile, when Antonio introduced her. Antonio could see that Iago did not warm to his diminutive friend. He had probably never spoken to a dwarf before. So Antonio wondered whether it would be prudent to mention then the idea of her working in the troupe or to leave it until another time, perhaps when Iago appeared to be in a more receptive frame of mind. His doubts were jolted by Lupita who suggested that all four of them adjourn to 'The Stage', a tavern the actors at the Príncipe often used, just off the Mentidero.

As they stepped through the door of the inn, betrayed only by the its name painted in small letters half way up the door, the combined stench of stale ale, urine and actors' sweat hit them.

'Must we go in here?' asked Lupita, looking if she was about to throw up.

'We could always try "The Pen and Ink Pot" on the other side of the street,' said Iago.

'Come, on. The beer's cheaper in here and we'll soon get used to the smell,' said Iago.

They each agreed to step in. The sight which confronted them stunned them into silence. Two women, apparently either actresses or *putas*, were brawling with each other on the filthy, sawdust strewn floor. They punched each other and shouted while attempting to rip each others' clothes. Antonio decided to intervene. He grabbed the arm of one of them who immediately kicked him in the leg.

'Careful, señorita! I'm only trying to help you!' said Antonio. 'Your clothes are so torn you are showing more than your modesty should allow.'

'She has shit on me so badly, I've got to win this one,' said the woman who, by then, was bleeding from her pretty but dirty face.

'What's she done that demands your violence?' asked Iago, coming to Antonio's aid.

'She stole an acting role from me by pretending she was me, the bitch. The theatre manager believes her even though he gave me the job and turned her down. Now she's in it, he doesn't want me! I'm furious!'

'Surely, you can resolve this without a fight,' said Antonio, as the women stopped throwing punches. 'Ask her for some form of compensation or threaten to take her to court.'

'Just you keep out of this, mate,' said the other woman.

'I think she's saving you from more injury,' said Antonio. 'At least you've stopped hitting each other now.'

Whether Antonio's words had affected them or whether they were too bruised to continue, the women stopped their fight and went their separate ways, each to opposite ends of the tavern. Antonio and the other three made their way to the bar where Antonio bought a round of beer. 'Here's to Antonio's return,' said Lupita, gently planting a delicate kiss on his cheek.

'I'll drink to that,' said Iago. 'I imagine you'll be working with us until your next assignment whatever that might be!' He sounded cynical about Antonio, as if Antonio was treating the troupe as his second job, which it was.

'No one has seen that as a problem so far,' said Antonio.

'That's because you haven't been here for close to three weeks. We've had a hard time while you've been out of action.'

Antonio saw this as an opportunity. 'I have an idea for you. If we take Carolina as a member, we'll be bigger and stronger so if I have to go again, or should I say when I have to go, you will be sure to do better.'

'Great idea,' said Lupita. 'I'd love to work with Carolina again.'

'It's a bad idea. A joke. We don't want a dwarf in our troupe. People will stop to look and go straight on. We'll lose money,' said Iago.

'You talking nonsense, Iago,' said Antonio, finding it difficult to control his fury. 'We've had good experiences with Carolina. She's a great guitar player and sings like an angel.'

'I agree with Antonio,' said Lupita, shocked by Iago's words and almost unable to speak.

'This is Madrid. Not some piddling little town like Ávila. People here won't put money in our pot for her playing. If she set up as a curiosity, they just might!'

Carolina could stand no more of these insults. She went up to Iago, pulled back her right arm and swung her clenched fist, as hard as she could, right into Iago's genitals. Eyes open wide, he fell to the floor in agony, clutching himself and shouting out. 'You bloody little bitch. That puts the end to it. I'll never work with you! You freak!'

Iago struggled to his feet and looked down meanly at Carolina. Fearful that he might strike her, Lupita and Antonio grabbed his arms and pulled him back. Most women in this situation, whether a little person or not would have started to sob but not Carolina. She stood upright with her hands planted firmly on her hips. After a few seconds composing herself she spoke.

'I feel so much better now. You got what you deserved, Iago the Bad. I now know why you are called that!' And knowing that with Antonio and Lupita on her side, she was in a strong position, said, 'Look, I don't want to be a part of making the decision. It's up to you three to decide whether or not you want me in the troupe. I leave it to you.' She then walked over to one of the women who had been scrapping and started to chat to her and her friends.

Antonio, still enraged with Iago, spoke. 'If you can't work with my colleague simply because she's a dwarf, then I can't work with you. It's as simple as that. And I'm shocked and disgusted by the way you spoke to her. You should never have called her those names, however hard she hit you!'

'I can't continue working with you for the same reason. I'm disgusted, too!' said Lupita, looking hard at Iago.

None of the three of them knew what to say next, even though the implications could not be clearer. Antonio waited a moment, hoping that Iago would simply resign but he didn't so he took the initiative, hoping that Lupita would follow.

'In which case, you are fired, Iago. With immediate effect!'

'I'm not so sure,' said Lupita, backing down. 'Maybe we should give him another chance. After all, he's a brilliant dulcian player and we'd miss that.'

Iago looked at Lupita with a grateful smile. Antonio wondered what sort of game she could be playing. He could only glare at her in frustration. Had Iago and she become lovers while he'd been away? Somehow he thought not. A physical relationship seemed outside her domain, at least to Antonio. Now what should he do?

'Now you are in a minority,' said Iago, grinning at Antonio. 'My view seems to have prevailed.'

Antonio took a gamble. 'In which case, I resign. Carolina and I can continue working together here and you two can go on alone. Good luck!'

Lupita immediately embraced him and almost in tears responded, 'No Antonio, you can't go. You are one of our team. You and I started it. I agree with you now. Iago must go!'

'You sure?' said Iago.

'I'm sorry, Iago, but yes. I'm certain.'

Iago turned on his heels and moved towards the door. 'I've had enough of your fooling around, Antonio. You never know whether you're coming or going. And you prefer women to men,' he said, staring around but looking at Lupita in particular. 'So I'm fed up with you, too.' He paced towards the exit and slammed the door behind him.

Carolina had been keeping an ear on what was happening between the three and, immediately Iago went, rushed over to Antonio and Lupita. In tears, she hugged them both. 'I'm so grateful to you two,' she said, almost choking. 'Why are people like that? He was so unkind!'

'Don't even bother to think about it. What he said says far more about him than about you, Carolina. You are one of us now! Welcome to our little troupe!' said Antonio.

'Yes, we'll work brilliantly together! I'm sure of that!' said Carolina.

'I utterly agree!' said Lupita

Antonio, Lupita and Carolina formed a highly effective team. Not only did they play well together, they maintained and even strengthened their previously formed friendship which, of course, began many months before on the road to Valladolid.

Several times, the troupe were attacked by street robbers who ran off with their day's hard earned takings. Antonio attributed their vulnerability to the fact that their membership comprised only one man and two women. They were less able therefore to defend themselves than a group made up solely of men. They often discussed these attacks and wondered whether, through some misguided act of revenge, Iago had tipped off some likely thieves. They had no way of determining the veracity of that suggestion which remained a matter of pure speculation. Certainly no evidence emerged to support it. Carolina and Lupita were each concerned about how they would survive without Antonio when the time came for him to depart on another of his mysterious missions. It was clear to each of the three of them that not only would Lupita and Carolina remain good and faithful friends but the two of them would form a competent duet and do well on the streets of Madrid, especially now that the king had returned with his court and the wealth of the city would rise up again. At least some in the city would have money to spare.

Antonio was confronted with more than Carolina's future. He decided to see Francisca within a day of his return. The last thing he wanted was for one of her friends or her mother to spot him in the street and her to learn about his arrival in the town from someone else. So, having reported to the overstressed Silva, he left Carolina at his rooms in Doña Marta's house and went to see Francisca. He knocked on the door of the family house.

'It's you, Antonio,' said an anxious looking Señora Díaz. 'Come in quickly. Francisca is in bed. She's very ill.'

'I'm so sorry. For how long?'

'Just over a day. She woke up yesterday morning and vomited as soon as she got out of bed. She is so hot and has these constant headaches. And she's aching all over. But worst of all she's got this rash on her arms,' said the señora. Then she broke down and uttered the fateful words, 'It's probably the plague.'

Antonio put an arm around her shoulder. 'Now, now. Maybe you are thinking the worst when it's nothing of the sort. It could be a number of things. Can I see her?'

Antonio's mind became the intersection of many thoughts. Francisca could die. That would be terrible. What would he do if she asked him to marry her as a last act of love? Should he tell her now about Carolina? If she was as weak as her mother was suggesting, any difficult news could finish her off. Should he tell her about the new mission that could be close and that he could be away for many months, even years? And what about the news on the reconstituted troupe, now him and two, not to say attractive, women?

'Yes, come in. By all means look into her room. I think she's asleep now.'

Antonio crossed the threshold and followed the señora to Francisca's bedroom door. Francisca looked far from well. Her closed eyes were swollen and her face glowed with an unhealthy redness. Her hair looked greyer than her usual colour. To Antonio, she seemed to be burning with a fever of some sort.

'I think we should leave her now. Let her rest,' said her mother.

Antonio sheepishly obeyed. In a way he was relieved not to have to speak to the poor, sick woman. He'd be searching for words and would make none sound like good news. If indeed it was the plague, he could catch it.

He and the señora adjourned to a drawing room and each sat on separate sofas.

'I am so worried about her,' said the señora. 'I cannot sleep at night and wake up in tears.' She almost cried again as she looked sadly at Antonio.

'What does the doctor think?' said Antonio.

'He's not sure. He says that all will be clear in two days. If it's the plague she will be delirious and her armpits will be swollen,' she said with tears running down her face. 'She'll be dead within another two.' The poor woman collapsed in tears and slid off the sofa onto the floor.

Antonio quickly closed the door so the señora's wailing would not wake Francisca. He strode back to her and helped her back up onto the sofa. 'I'm sorry, Antonio. I completely lost control. I cannot tell you how worried I am about her.'

'I am worried, too. I am fond of her, you know.'

'Yes but she says you don't love her and don't want to marry her. You don't return her love for you.'

'That is not the exact situation Señora Díaz. But it is not far from the truth. I told her I am still a young man. I am not yet ready to marry. I am a musician as you well know but I have, shall we say, other interests. These often take me away from Madrid. As you know, I have spent the last few weeks in Segovia.' He saw that as a possible opportunity to mention Carolina but decided that it would be better to tell Francisca herself, assuming he would speak to her again.

'Before that I was in Guadalajara. But I could be sent anywhere, anywhere in the king's realm. To Italy, to France, to Barcelona, the Netherlands or even to the Maghreb. So I am controlling my emotions and not committing myself to a poor woman who could lose me for months or years or even for ever. It wouldn't be fair. Maybe, I didn't make it clear enough to your lovely daughter but that is the exact situation.'

'But you had a relationship with her sister before she broke it off! So is it the situation, exactly, as you put it?' She looked at him with an untrusting coolness.

'You are asking me to explain sensitive issues. Yes, I did have a relationship with Catalina and I still admire her. But I respect Francisca even more. She is a different kind of woman and I wouldn't for my life want to hurt her. Need I add to that?'

She seemed to understand clearly what Antonio said. She smiled knowingly as if fully satisfied and not wanting further detail or explanation. He felt that at least to some degree he had, by this explanation, regained her confidence.

'If Francisca is still asleep, may I come back tomorrow to see her? I am as worried about her myself but from a different perspective.'

'Let's go to her room and see.'

They were confronted by a frightening sight. Poor Francisca had vomited on the floor and lay across the bed staring at the ceiling and speaking to someone or something that was nowhere to be seen. They could not make out what she was saying and merely looked sadly at each other. She gave no sign of recognising either her mother or Antonio.

'Maybe it would be better if you went, Antonio. She is delirious. Not a good sign,' said the señora, looking down at the floor and wiping her eye with the corner of her pinafore. 'I will clear up her mess.'

'I can see myself out, Señora Díaz. I truly hope she is better tomorrow.' He thought of using 'pray' rather than 'hope' but couldn't bring himself to do so, even though the señora might have preferred it. 'I shall certainly return tomorrow. At midday if that is all right.'

The poor woman could not speak but gave a single, little nod of her head.

Antonio felt hideous, almost sick, as he walked from the Polancos' back to Doña Marta's house. His mind reeled in confusion. He felt immensely sorry for Francisca. He felt guilty but not regretful at having such an intense physical relationship with Carolina. Most strongly, Francisca's condition saddened him and he wondered what the outcome would be. A tear ran down his face at the thought of the inevitability of the outcome. There could be little doubt: the only conclusion to the plague was death.

'Whatever's the matter?' said Carolina, who was sitting on a sofa as he walked into the lounge. She could see from his lack of humour and dour look that something had seriously upset him.

'It's Francisca. Looks as if she's got the plague. She's delirious and suffering badly.'

'Oh God! That's terrible. I'm so…so sorry,' she said. She stood up and went over to hug him, putting her arms around his waist. 'What can we do for her?' she said, in an expression of amazing selflessness.

'I don't know. I wish I did. Something tells me you should meet her. I still don't know what to tell her about you. The greatest sadness is that it may not be necessary,' he said, looking to the floor.

'Is there no hope? Could she speak? What do the doctors think?'

Antonio explained what had happened at the Polancos' and what Francisca's poor mother had reported.

'So it is not a final conclusion. It sounds bad but there is hope. Maybe we'll see tomorrow or the day after.'

'I suppose you are right, Carolina,' he said, still sounding dejected.

They sat together and discussed the situation. They agreed that it would not be right to tell Francisca, in her current state, about Carolina. It would be downright selfish and could even kill her. If Antonio was to be honest and straightforward with Francisca, he would have to tell her about Carolina, once she was better, hoping of course that that would be the outcome. In the meantime, Antonio would be the only one of them to visit her, if for no other reason than to avoid Carolina catching whatever illness had inflicted itself on Francisca.

Antonio dreaded midday. He tried not to think about Francisca but he simply could not dispel her from his mind. He even went to chat to his aging mare about her, aiming to clear his mind. Then the time came for him to walk the short distance to the Polancos'.

'I do hope she's better, Antonio. I really do,' said Carolina, standing on tiptoe to signal him to bend down to kiss her. Please come straight back to tell me. Whatever the news.'

'Straight back,' he said with not the trace of a smile.

'Sorry Antonio, but you can't come in. Not good news. The doctor is with her. She doesn't even recognise me.' Señora Díaz broke down and cried on his shoulder.

'I'm so sorry,' said Antonio, giving her a warm hug. 'Please mention me to her. That may just help, if only a little. I'm very fond of her, you know.'

She released herself from his embrace and stood back in the hall. 'But you don't love her, do you? I'll think about that.' She closed the door.

He stood there blankly staring at the door and then moved away. It wasn't his fault. And love was a difficult thing to say, let alone to give.

'She's worse, if anything,' said Antonio, his voice almost breaking with emotion.

Carolina hugged him. 'I feel as bad as you. It's awful when this happens to someone you feel for.' She hesitated to say 'love'. 'The tragedy is that many thousands in Spain have died of the plague, men women and children. No one knows what to do about it. It's terrible.'

Antonio looked at her blankly. 'I'll go again tomorrow. I can't sit here thinking about her any more. Let's go around to Lupita's and see if she wants to play one of our pitches for a few hours.'

Antonio explained the situation to a sympathetic Lupita who had heard about Francisca but had not met her. The three of them, not in the greatest of spirits, walked to a pitch near the Puerta del Sol. Antonio played with as much dedication as he could generate. After a surprisingly productive afternoon, they agreed to work the following morning, up to about eleven thirty, at a pitch in the bustling market in the Plazuela de Selenque.

Once again, Antonio was dreading his midday visit to Francisca's. He walked slowly towards the house. He feared not only the inevitability of the news on Francisca but the likely reaction of her mother who seemed to want him to be the whipping boy for her accumulated emotions. He paused outside of the house for a full half a minute. Then he stirred himself to knock on the door.

'Come in Antonio. It's wonderful news. Francisca is talking and laughing. She's still not well but the doctor said it was a bad case of the fever. It nearly killed her. But she is better now. Come through to her room.'

The cheery señora knocked on Francisca's door. 'Are you decent? Here's a visitor for you!'

'Antonio, I'm so pleased to see you. It's all right mother. You can go now. I'll tell Antonio when I've had enough of him. Then he'll go!' she said, smiling but looking thinner than Antonio remembered and redder in the face as if she still harboured the heat of the disease. 'I have been terribly ill. The doctor told mother that I almost died of a horrible fever. But I'm so much better now. I'm still feeling hot and I'm aching so I'm not completely better. Mother tells me that you have visited several times and that you have shown great concern for me. You are kind. I cannot thank you enough and yet I had no idea you were here!'

'I won't keep you long, Francisca. You still need to rest. But I'm delighted you are improving. I felt really bad yesterday when your mother came to the door in such a state. But I can smile again now. Not only are you better but she is, too!'

She sat up in bed as she spoke. She wore a heavy blue nightdress and a many coloured knitted shawl, draped over her shoulders. He went to plant a kiss on her cheek but she stopped him, telling him that he could still probably catch the fever and she wouldn't want that. They talked for a good quarter of an hour. He went as far as explaining the coincidence of meeting Carolina in Segovia and her joining him to form a duet. He told her he had only been back in Madrid for three days. He decided that he would not say then that Carolina had come back to Madrid with him, that she was staying at his rooms in Doña Marta's house or that the two of them had become lovers. What he would reveal about that relationship and when would be something to be decided. He left her sitting in bed and blew her a kiss as he went towards the bedroom door.

Weeks and months passed. Francisca relapsed into the fever and caused much anxiety. Eventually, she recovered, much to everyone's relief, including Antonio's who still harboured affection for her. Antonio and Carolina agreed that she should move out of his rooms at Doña Marta's house. Lupita and her friends at the Mentidero agreed to rent her a room at theirs. Carolina never really felt comfortable with living with other women, despite their friendliness and full acceptance of her. So she often returned to spend an evening or even a night with Antonio. Neither of them could see anything to be gained from telling Francisca that they had lived in Antonio's rooms or that they were still lovers. So they kept these simple facts to themselves. He, Carolina and Lupita established themselves as a strong and popular group of street musicians. Their favourite pitches were at the Puerta del Sol, the Plazuela de Selenque and the Plaza Mayor. They earned most at the Plaza de Palacio, mainly from dignitaries visiting the palace and senior, well paid officials, but street troupes were prohibited from playing there, in full view of the palace, so they frequently found themselves moved on by some officious flunky or by palace guards.

Antonio wondered many times when he would be given the new assignment. When his patience finally expired, and rather than call on the sometimes irascible Silva de Torres, he decided to visit Tariq Alabdari to ask him if he knew what was happening. Ishraq Alsulami, his charming wife, answered the door. At first, mainly because she had only partially opened the door, she didn't recognise Antonio. After all it had been over a year since she had previously seen him.

'Do I know you, señor? What do you want?' she said, her voice shaking perceptibly with a strong note of apprehension.

'Yes, you do know me. I am Antonio Hidalgo, a friend and colleague of your husband, Tariq. You took me in a year or so ago and he and I enjoyed the delightful dish you served us.'

She opened the door wider. 'Of course I remember you, Señor Hidalgo. Come in quickly. I am so afraid,' she said, her face contorted with emotion.

Antonio crossed the threshold and she rapidly closed the door behind him. 'I am afraid for Tariq. He left home on one of these so called missions, about a month ago. He said he'd only be gone two weeks and he's still not returned. I am worried sick and so is our daughter, Reva. Is there anything you can do to help us?' She then broke down in tears. Reva heard her crying and emerged from a drawing room.

'Yes, Señor Hidalgo. We don't know where he is or where he has gone. Please can you help?'

Antonio fully understood their plight and readily sympathised. Tariq's absence gave Antonio an immediate and welcomed excuse to go to the palace and see Silva.

'Yes, I think I can help. I'll make some enquiries and come back tomorrow.'

Reva hugged him and kissed him on the cheek. 'That would be wonderful, Señor Hidalgo, wouldn't it, Mama?'

The funereal Hector Brondate wrung his hands when he saw him. 'To what do we owe the pleasure, Señor Hidalgo?' he said.

'There are two issues I would like to discuss with Algebra,' he said coolly.

'May I ask what they might be?'

Antonio explained. Moments later he was sitting facing Silva on the opposite side of his desk.

'Perhaps I should have invited you in before,' Silva said, as if he had initiated the meeting. 'We are still not ready to send you but it will be weeks now, not months and thank you for your forbearance. I'm afraid I cannot tell you about your ultimate destination but you could be away for up to a year, perhaps longer. It's far from clear at this stage. So start your packing. You'll probably need a trunk and I can supply one if you wish. You'll need to be armed with your pistol and knife so make sure they are in good condition. Lusitano will accompany you. Once again, we'll take care of your horse and keep an eye on your rooms. As soon as I have a date for you, I'll let you know. Any questions for now?'

'I happened to speak to Lusitano's wife yesterday. She's extremely concerned about him. She hasn't heard about him or from him for a month now and she expected his return in two weeks. No more.'

'That's where we have a problem which is delaying your departure. We sent him to Portugal, as she said, a month ago. He is on a highly secret mission so I cannot tell you the details. But coincidentally, we heard indirectly from him today. We understand he will be leaving there for Madrid in two weeks' time. We were about to send a messenger to inform his wife but perhaps you could do that?'

'I'd be delighted to, Silva!'

Tariq's wife embraced Antonio as if he was her lover when he told her about his expected return. Unlike most *Moriscas* he had known, she kissed him full on the lips and hugged him tightly. On releasing him from this surprisingly intimate hold asked him if he wanted a meal but he needed to tell Carolina his news about the assignment to come.

Although he reminded Carolina that she knew he would be leaving for quite some time, she found it difficult to accept and control her emotions. She hated the idea of him being away for so long and worried about what could befall him over the period of a year or even more. Antonio reassured her as best he could but she remained worried and sceptical. At best, she would miss him as a lover naturally would. She promised him that she would remain in Madrid while he was away and continue in the duet with Lupita. In a sense, Antonio, while he admired and liked her immensely, saw her presence as a complication. It was Carolina's idea the she return to Madrid with him from Segovia and he had accepted that, if not, encouraging her. So to a good degree he had to take responsibility for her being in Madrid.

Francisca's reaction differed markedly. She accepted that Antonio could look after himself. She knew, he presumed from her sister Catalina, about the training he had been given by Major Rodrigo Gutierrez, head of the Alcázar Palace Armoury. While she did not know that he and Carolina were lovers, she felt that his absence might even have a positive effect on his ambiguous relationship with her, Francisca. Even so, she would miss him, the more so since she had fully recovered from the fever which almost killed her.

Part V

CHAPTER 23
Unexpected danger

Silva must have been feeling sentimental. He gave Tariq a week at home with his wife before calling him and Antonio in to meet him. Antonio had had enough of the interminable waiting. He enjoyed playing his violin and even singing with Carolina and Lupita but there, ever present in his mind, was the exciting prospect of a more distant journey. A mission to where?

'The Maghreb. Marrakesh. That's where you'll be going.'

'The two of us?' asked Antonio 'Good news. How will we get there? What is…?'

Silva cut him short. 'Let me speak, Antonio. Is it just me you interrupt when you get excited?'

Antonio apologised humbly.

'Yes, just the two of you. You will be travelling together. You'll each be armed of course and I am making each of you responsible for the other's safety. Do you understand that?'

'I'll guard him as if he is my own son!' said a smiling Tariq, who was just about old enough to be Antonio's father.

'I'll guard him as if he was my grandfather,' said Antonio, laughing.

'You obviously won't go about your business displaying weaponry but I'm sure you know what I mean. Now to the mission itself. You'll be leaving Madrid in three days' time and travel on horseback, using a military horse relay, to Cádiz. There you join a merchant galley which will hug the Atlantic coast and pass by the Straights of Gibraltar on its way to Anfa, which is the Maghreb port for Marrakesh. You won't know that Anfa is under the control of Philip the Third as part of our union with Portugal. No? He probably doesn't know either!'

All three laughed.

'So you will make a base there. That will be easy. The town is actually administered by the Portuguese who have a military fortress there. They call the place Casa Branca. But Spanish is widely spoken and you will negotiate a let on some rooms for a year. The terms are that the lease must be renewable, in case your mission takes longer. I don't want you staying in some Maghreb palace. So something modest and inconspicuous. But near the centre of the town so it's easy to get to and protected by the presence of people living nearby. In other words, nothing isolated and vulnerable. Any questions, so far?'

Tariq spoke first. 'How do we communicate with you from there?'

'Good question. Because it's under our control, we have the Portuguese equivalent of a *corregidor*. He has the codename "Mauretania". What audacity. Anyway, we have a link, via sea and land back to me. Once you have secured a base you must go to his office - you'll soon find it - with a message to me about where your base is located. As you know, it will find me, if you put only "Algebra" on the envelope. On no account tell him where you are living. He can find out for himself. He is Portuguese after all. But you must tell me exactly where it is, in case I need to send others to get you out of there.'

'Why haven't you found a base for us?' asked Antonio.

'Simple. This is a highly secret mission and to find lodgings for someone not living there would create suspicion. You finding somewhere will be the natural thing to do. And there is the cost. Doing something like that remotely would cost a king's ransom. We may yet have to pay that to recover you two!'

'Not amusing!' said Tariq, laughing anyway.

'So we are in Anfa. Then what?' said Antonio.

'I'm getting to that,' said Silva with the hint of rebuke. 'Here is where I explain your mission and give you the background.

'The background first. The king is concerned that the *Moriscos*, or more precisely, their allies in the Maghreb, in Morocco actually, may be building warships with the aim of attacking Spain… you know, as they did in 711 and later. The Duke of Lerma agrees that His Majesty has a point. After all, the relationship we have with the *Moriscos* now has not been worse since the Second Rebellion, what thirty five years ago?

'Your mission, overall, and I'm sorry about the delay, is to find out what is going on in their shipyards and what kind of craft they are building. You must also determine whether they have any plans to fight us on the seas. Any questions?'

'Seriously? In only a year? How many ports and shipyards have they got?' said Tariq.

'That's why the second part of my instruction is so important. The mission is not as open as it sounds. We've done much of the planning for you. Of course you will inspect the port of Anfa and its yards. But we want you to go right to the political centre of the Moroccan kingdom to complete this mission. The sultan is Zidan al-Nasir. He's only been in power since 1603, just after the death of his brother, Mulay al-Mansur. So he's still inexperienced. The country is in chaos. He's already lost some of the north and of the south; and there are threats on other areas, too. So we want to exploit his court at their weakest moment.

'We want you to penetrate the palace of El Badi which is close to the Kasbah. This should not be as difficult as it sounds. While Tariq has been on his recent mission, we've equipped the merchant ship you will be travelling in with some products fit for a king, even a sultan!'

Antonio and Tariq laughed at Silva's attempt at humour.

'You will approach the palace with the apparent aim of selling some of these wondrous materials and objects to the sultan and his court. You will befriend some of his officials... that will take time... and somehow trick them into telling you about their policy on the construction of warships and, in particular, whether any would be targeted at Spain. We have arranged for you to stay at a house near the Kasbah. The *corregidor* in Anfa will give you the address. It's near a safe house used by his officials when they visit Marrakesh and he'll give you a key to that, just in case. Any further questions?'

Tariq reacted to Silva assembling the merchandise. 'I have to say, I object to you putting a cargo together in my absence. If you've used my suppliers, I really strongly object.'

'We would have got you to purchase the goods but didn't have the time so we used suppliers of our choice. Whether they are yours as well, I don't know. But don't worry. You will be rewarded enough for this mission, many times over that which you would have lost.'

'I'm not so sure about this place near a safe house used by the *corregidor* of Anfa's people,' said Antonio. 'You didn't trust them to find a place in their own town so what makes you think they could be trusted to find us a place in Marrakesh?'

'Simple. The smaller risk was for you not to have to find somewhere in Marrakesh. You would automatically raise suspicions. You are infidels in their eyes.'

'How about getting back here?' said Tariq.

'Needless to say, we've put some thought into that. Your safe house will be the place you rent in Anfa. But if there are problems, you must head for the *corregidor*'s office. He has been briefed to provide you with shelter until we can get you back to Spain.'

'What do you mean, "if there are problems"?' said Antonio. 'That's pretty vague!'

'From here it's impossible to predict what could happen. So this is simply a precaution.'

'This doesn't seem well planned, to me,' said Tariq. 'First you use my merchants, then there are some vague arrangements to protect us in a friendly port. Not good!'

Silva began to show signs of exasperation and wished he'd spoken to each of them separately. He felt cornered and decided on a robust way out. 'Listen! We've gone to great lengths to ensure your safety, both in getting there and in coming back. This isn't some routine… admittedly important… mission to Segovia or to another place in Spain. It's to an alien country for something extremely sensitive. We cannot plan for every contingency and if you think you could do better, perhaps you'd like to suggest how.' He sat back in his chair and awaited their response.

'I suppose your best interests are served by getting us back in one piece. Otherwise you won't get the information the king so desperately wants. I support what you say, on reflection.'

Silva stepped in before Tariq had a chance to speak. 'A sensible view. Thank you, Antonio.'

'Yes, for the same reasons, I agree with Antonio,' said Tariq, not at all shaken by Silva's immediate approval of what Antonio had to say.

'Neither of you appear to have touched on the most difficult potential problem. That is getting you back from Marrakesh to Anfa. If the sultan's men discover your true purpose, you could be in deep trouble. In that case you will have to use great cunning to escape back to Anfa. I have appointed you to this mission because of your guile. I'm sure you'll be able to crack that particular nut… if it needs cracking.'

To Silva's relief, the two of them had, at least for then, exhausted their questions. Silva, the upper hand regained, instructed them to be ready to leave from in front of the palace in three days, on the Monday morning at 9 o'clock. He wanted no emotional goodbyes with friends or relatives. They should have been conducted in private before then.

Apart from finishing his packing, Antonio needed to tell the women in his life of his imminent departure. Lupita fully accepted the situation and wished him good fortune. She said she hoped to welcome back into the troupe on his return. Similarly, Francisca wished him the best of luck and a safe mission. She showed little emotion considering her reaction after her illness. This, however, did not worry Antonio because she had acted similarly when he first told her about the long assignment to come.

Carolina's reaction affected Antonio quite badly. Wisely, he decided to tell her over a meal at Doña Marta's house, the night after he and Tariq had met Silva. She became almost hysterical.

'Antonio, how can I live without you for so long? A year and maybe more! I'll die! I cannot see how I can survive. I know we are just lovers and colleagues and I understand that but I won't be able to cope without you. You are my protector! My guardian! And I shall be constantly worried about you.'

'I shall miss you, too, Carolina. We work and play well together. But I have to go and you have to survive without me. The mission I am being sent on is so important. I cannot refuse to go and the future of Spain may depend on it. I have told you about my colleague Tariq. He is coming with me and we will, I promise you, look after each other. Please be of good heart in letting me go. I don't want to be worrying constantly about how you are surviving without me. That could dangerously affect my dedication and concentration.'

Much to Antonio's relief, Carolina responded well to his plea. She saw immediately the problems that she could create if he was worrying about her. 'I am being selfish, Antonio,' she said, recovering well. 'You must go and I promise I will survive. Of course I will miss you. But I will be mature and sensible. I suppose, as a little person, I feel vulnerable in this town. But I don't want to return to Ávila. I'll continue playing with Lupita. My future is here!'

As she was leaving, they agreed to meet for a meal at Antonio's house, the night before his departure.

'I want to give you a night to remember,' said Carolina, as she stepped over the threshold and not knowing whether to laugh or cry.

'Brilliant! I hope I respond well. I'll enjoy it for sure!' said Antonio, as he leant down and put his arm around her narrow shoulder. He could see that she was still unsure about him going.

'This is delicious,' said Carolina, sitting at his table and taking her first taste of this dish. 'Where did you get the recipe from?' He had prepared a pork meal with a tomato and chive sauce.

'My mother. She used to make it quite often. My father really liked it!'

'Have you told them about the new mission?'

'God, no! I hadn't even thought of it,' he said realising how insensitive he had been towards them.

'You left on good terms with them didn't you?'

'Yes! Excellent. But they didn't want me to go.'

'Then you must tell them. Before you go, you must write them a letter. I'll see it gets to them, if I have to deliver it myself!'

The little lady gave her all in the love session she herself initiated. She teased him mercilessly as she removed her clothes, slowly, item by item. She undressed him and rubbed herself against him.

'You are an angel and a great lover, Carolina. I shall miss you terribly,' he said.

'So are you, Antonio. And I'll miss you.'

With her facing him, they pleased each other until they mutually erupted in a frenzy of farewell.

'Carolina, that was spectacular.' He sighed as he felt as if she was making a last play at love but knew she was not for him, great lover that she was. He wondered then what the future had in store for this energetic, excellent musician who wanted him for ever. Who knew where his mission would lead and whether he would see her, or any of his friends again?

'I've been told to do my farewells in private and not where we leave which will be outside the palace. So by all means stay the night and we can delay our separation until the morning.'

'And I can cook you breakfast before you go,' she said with tears running down her face.

Silva attended their departure. It appeared that his presence gave it an official seal of approval. Three riders joined Antonio and Tariq. Each looked young, in their early twenties. Their apparent leader introduced himself as Alfonso. Bernadino and Carlos introduced themselves, too. Antonio wondered at the alphabetical coincidence and guessed that these were not their real names.

'Have you ever ridden in a relay,' Alfonso asked. They each said no.

'Then you need to know how it works. Each of these stallions can gallop, on and off, for about an hour, maybe more… maybe less. That's about six *leguas*. It's a hundred and twenty *leguas* to Cádiz so we'll be changing horses about twenty times. We'll be there after two night stops, one in Valdepeñas and another after Córdoba. And we go through Sevilla. To protect ourselves from highway robbers we must stay together, not more than three lengths apart. We should each carry a charged pistol, tucked in the saddle leather and one of these whistles.' He handed them out. 'And when I say "stop", we all stop. We each watch out for each other and if any horse becomes lame or one of us has to stop, for whatever reason, he blows a whistle and we all pull up. Got that?'

Antonio and Tariq smiled and nodded. They were each looking forward to this ride. Silva waved as they departed. They trotted to the Puerta de Toledo and then broke into a gallop. Neither Antonio nor Tariq had ever ridden so fast. By the time they arrived at a roadside inn, just beyond Valdepeñas, the two special agents were sore and exhausted. Antonio reckoned they had changed mounts at least eight times.

'This is murder,' said Tariq, as he dismounted and handed his horse to one of the relay stable lads. He rubbed his thighs to loosen up the muscles.

'Thank God it's only for another day or so,' said Antonio, climbing down from his mount. 'Imagine doing this for a living!'

By the time they reached Cádiz, the whole journey, the dust on the road, the countless times they dismounted and remounted, the smell of the horses, Alfonso's shouting from the rear, the pains in their bodies, the agonising experience had become an unmemorable blur. At least they were in the hands of competent practitioners and, much to their relief, had arrived there safely. The two of them shook hands with the soldiers before they departed, having dropped the two agents at a particular tavern, apparently at Silva's insistence.

Cádiz was a dirty, albeit busy, town and the two of them took little pleasure in being there. During the afternoon they took a stroll around the port.

'See those wrecks over there,' said Tariq pointing to some burnt out galleons. 'The English and Dutch did that, attacked and captured the city… about ten years ago. All by command of their Queen Elizabeth the First. Walter Rayleigh was one of the naval commanders. Set alight to our fleet and a lot of the town, then left with their booty. The place is still recovering.'

'I think I've heard about that,' said Antonio, but sounding uncertain.

The only good thing about the town was that their tavern stocked a tasty beer which they consumed in abundance. That night, while sitting at a table and after they had eaten a mediocre meal of cold fish and onions, a well-built man with a beard and tightly plaited hair approached them.

'Are you two looking to travel to Anfa?' said the man.

Not enthusiastic about giving away information, Tariq replied. 'Who is asking?'

'My name is Gonzalo Ortiz de Montoya. I'm the first mate of the merchant ship, *Constelación de Orión*. The captain has sent me to meet you. We have been detailed to take you to Anfa, if you are the gentlemen I believe you are.'

'What makes you think it's us you're taking?' said Antonio.

'I do not have your names. But I do know that two men, under Tercio escort have been brought here to travel to Anfa. If you are not those men, I am sorry to have troubled you.' The man turned away as if to leave.

'We are those men,' said Antonio. 'When do we leave?'

'Thank you. I can understand your caution. The ship is not yet ready to sail. Some of the cargo has not arrived... including your luggage. We are expecting it all in the next day or so,' he said, with not a hint of urgency. If the mission could take over a year, the intrepid travellers were beginning to see why.

'Does that mean we have to stay in this hovel until the ship leaves?' said Tariq.

'Sorry but yes. Most others are worse. It'll be two nights at most.'

'We'll see!' said Antonio.

'I'll call again when it's time to go.'

Gonzalo proved to be right. He came back to the tavern early on the Friday morning. Antonio and Tariq were eating their breakfast at the table where he had interrupted them, two days before.

'We're just about ready to embark. I'll give you an hour. You can't miss the ship. She's the only one in full sail and she's straining her ropes to go!'

Carrying their saddlebags over their shoulders, they were soon ready to join the *Constelación de Orión* and walked leisurely to her moorings. The mighty ship stood proudly at the quayside and moved gently in the swell of the tide. The sails on all three of her masts flapped vigorously in the easterly breeze, like the wings on a flock of standing cormorants. The dockside hummed with activity. Men with barrels on their shoulders were carrying on board what the two presumed was water or beer. Some were unloading anonymous packets and parcels from a hand pushed wagon and handing them to others who carried them onto the ship. Crates of vegetables and fruit were waiting on the quay to be taken aboard. The whole operation was being overseen by a large, heavily bearded man with a blue, brass buttoned jacket and a red bandana, standing to one side at the top of the gangplank.

'Welcome aboard my beautiful ship, the towering *Constelación de Orión*, which reaches to the heavens, just like her namesake! You must be our two first class passengers. For Anfa, I believe, our singular port of call. I am Captain Hernan de Porras, master of this magnificent vessel. She's the largest merchant ship ever constructed in Cartagena. She displaces more than six hundred *toneladas*. Your luggage arrived at six o'clock this morning and I've had it transferred to your cabins. They are located in the bows of the ship and are the most comfortable, indeed luxurious, on the galley.'

Then he looked straight at Tariq. 'I know you, don't I?'

'I thought I recognised you, Captain Porras. I think you took me to Tangier once. That was a good few years ago! About seven or eight?'

'Yes, I recall you telling me about an extraordinarily fortunate conquest you succeeded in making there!' the captain chuckled into his beard. He put on the airs of some swaggering lawyer or equally pretentious professor.

'Yes, a shopkeeper's pretty little wife, while he was returning from Fez!'

'Not that story!' said Antonio. 'It was true then?'

'I wouldn't lie to you, would I?' said Tariq.

All three laughed as they reached the two cabins. Antonio had never seen a galley before, so didn't know what to expect. The captain pushed open a door to one of the cabins. Antonio recognised his trunk standing against the bottom of a surprisingly wide bed. He'd half expected to see a hammock slung between a pair of uprights. As he entered the luxurious quarters he could smell newly cut timber, as if the ship had been recently built. A wardrobe stood against one wall and a dressing table, complete with a mirror on a stand, leant against the other. The curtains and bedspread shone a bright, orangey red which closely matched the mats, neatly arranged on the polished timber floors.

'New ship?' said Antonio.

'Fairly. Constructed in the autumnal months of 05. So only two years of age. How can you ascertain such a notion?'

'The furnishings are new and it still smells of new wood.'

'Glorious, isn't she? I have to admit, I feel exalted by her. She has a self-assured dignity. An indestructibility.'

'I love her already,' said Tariq, stepping into his quarters which were furnished in an opal blue. Along with Antonio, he hoped the captain's remark about the vessel's invulnerability was true.

Captain Hernan de Porras left them to settle into their cabins but, before doing so, invited them to join him for dinner at eight by the ship's clock.

'The pompous idiot's a drunk,' said Tariq. 'No wonder he was "in no fit state" to meet us and sent his first mate instead. He must have been sleeping off a hangover!'

'Got to know him quite well, then, did you?' said Antonio.

'Too well! Got drunk with him a few times. Mainly on beer and rum. That's when all these stories come out!'

The mighty ship eased its way from the quayside at exactly midday. Antonio and Tariq stood overlooking the bows from the top deck as it did so. It seemed to be alive, like some giant sea monster, as it slowly pulled away from quayside, which gradually became smaller as the ship approached the distant harbour mouth. They could hear the gentle ripple of the waves against the hull as she cut her way through the tranquil waters and feel a gentle rocking motion as she moved slightly from side to side and her bow rose and fell. 'There's no going back now!' said Antonio, over the sound of the wind striking the sails.

The two of them spent the rest of the day exploring this wondrous ship. They soon became accustomed to the movement of the mighty leviathan as it made its way slowly south, staying within sight of the coast. Even so, they held on to the nearest rail or rope to steady themselves, especially in those first, nervy hours.

'I wonder if we can see what Silva bought for us to sell,' said Tariq, as they returned from one of their sorties around this fascinating vessel. 'Let's go down to the hold and look.'

They were astonished at what they saw. Silva had been right when he described his purchases as 'fit for a king, even a sultan'. The fabrics alone must have cost a fortune. The hundred or so rolls, standing vertically like a series of Doric columns, and secured by mauve ribbons to the inside of the hold, showed their regal colours, even in the subdued light. There were purples, golds, fabrics in bronze, some in burgundy, others in pink. There were barrels, presumably of liquid: honey; olive oil; sherry; fruit juices: orange, grape, apple and perhaps of beer; some of wine. There were cooking implements: forks, knives, pots and pans of different sizes, cauldrons, kettles. There were tools of various kinds, all in boxes: saws, chisels, hammers, mallets, sledgehammers and, among the objects which impressed them most, weapons: pistols, harquebuses, blunderbuses, staves, pikes, knives and daggers, some in knee holsters.

'My God, Antonio. Silva could have taken this lot from my warehouse. But he didn't. Not one do I recognise! I wonder where he bought them from.'

'Most from your suppliers, I imagine. Makes me feel good that these are the quality of products we are expected to sell in Marrakesh. However do we to get this lot to the city?'

'Camel train! It's the only way to carry them. And we'll probably have to return to Anfa because we won't get all this on a single team of camels!'

Antonio had only heard of camels: he'd certainly never seen one. He imagined they looked like horses. He'd soon find out.

Antonio and Tariq tidied themselves up before making their way to the ship's dining room which was amidships on the main deck. It was just on the hour and the captain was already sitting at his table. He looked up.

'Enter, gentlemen! Perambulate yourselves towards me,' he said in a genuine if awkward welcome. He stood to pull out two chairs. The two of them sat down, Antonio next to him and Tariq on the opposite side of the table.

'Thank you, Captain de Porras,' said Tariq.

'Formality is not exigent. You can refer to me as Hernan, which I imagine will be your indubitable preference.'

'Indeed it will,' said Antonio.

'Retrieve some beers, first mate,' the captain instructed loudly, but looking in no direction in particular. It was as if his number two was lurking somewhere between posterity and high heaven. Gonzalo Ortiz de Montoya leapt up from an adjacent table and gave the captain a venomous glare.

'At your ready, captain,' he said coldly but loud enough for his master to hear. 'Right away!'

Moments later, three large pots of beer appeared at the captain's table, brought by a manservant, not the first mate.

'Here's to the extraordinary success of your mission!' The two of them wondered what the captain knew. 'Let's hope you dispose of it all at the highest prices achievable!'

The looked at each other in relief as the captain swigged his way through what looked like more than half of the pot. 'Come on you two. Drink up! We are in for a glorious session tonight. I can easily instruct a man to articulate you to your beds!'

'I'm not used to heavy drinking,' said Antonio. 'I've only been drunk once in my life.'

'It's not an exceptionally strong beer. It's a creation of Cádiz. My brother owns the brewery so I obtain it for an excellent price. We can proceed to rum, once we've consumed sufficient. Another round, please, first mate,' he demanded, slurping the last few drops from his pot. Moments later, three more jugs of beer landed in front of them, each accompanied by a large, well-cooked lamb shank and a pile of brown bread.

'Here we have genuine sustenance which will aid in absorbing the beer. We'll be capable of consuming at least an *azumbre* each now!'

'May I ask a question?' said Tariq.

'Proceed!' said the captain.

'When do we arrive in Anfa?'

'Critically depends on what speed we can maintain and that depends crucially on the wind strength and direction. We are subject to a moderate northerly at present and are maintaining six knots. I'd say we'll be in port by the end of Monday. We are mooring in Gibraltar overnight and re-embark at daybreak. What is our position now, first mate?'

'I'll go to the crow's nest and find out.'

'Someone bring more ale!'

The fresh pots of beer arrived at the same time as the first mate. 'We're just pulling into Gibraltar, captain. Should be moored up within twenty minutes,' he said.

'I'll imbibe to that!' said the captain.

'Who's piloting the galley?' asked Antonio, 'obviously not you nor the first mate, and she can't moor herself!'

Tariq laughed.

'Good question,' said the captain. 'My third in command is outstandingly brilliant at the wheel. He's guiding her now and you won't feel a thing when she docks.'

Just another jug of beer later, Antonio and Tariq were staggering their way back to their cabins, giggling drunkenly as they did so.

Antonio awoke with a screaming headache. He'd never had such a bad one before but he'd never before consumed as much beer in one night. He eased himself out of bed but promptly fell back onto it. He tried to stand up again and held on to the bed head to help him. Now on his feet he could feel a strong swaying motion. Clinging to the furniture, he made his way to the cabin window. All became clear: the ship had left Gibraltar and was sailing in an almighty storm which was tossing it to and fro. Much of the lateral movement was caused by the moving ship, and the hangover the rest. His head felt slightly better now he was on his feet, if only just, and hanging onto the bed which was tightly secured to the deck. He wondered whether Tariq was awake and how he felt. Did Tariq have a hangover? After all, he had drunk as much as Antonio, if not more.

Antonio decided to make his way to Tariq's cabin which was only next door. As he opened his own cabin door, it slammed back into him and knocked him painfully onto the new but unwelcoming polished floor. With the door banging repeatedly into the wall, and the wind whistling in his ears, he used the doorpost to clamber to his feet. One of the orange mats crumpled and slid from under him. He wondered then about the wisdom of attempting to reach Tariq's cabin with the ship rocking that violently. He decided to try.

The swaying vessel almost threw him on to the deck again as he yanked his cabin door closed behind him. Suddenly he felt as if he wanted to be sick. He could not hold it back and spewed onto the deck floor. The taste of it disgusted him and made him wretch again. This time nothing came up. As he staggered into Tariq's door the ship took a sudden movement to one side. It attempted to right itself but remained listing to port. Antonio lost his balance as he groped his way towards Tariq's cabin on the sloping floor. His face grimaced in pained relief as his hand gripped the handle of Tariq's door. The ship took another lurch as if trying to wrench the handle from Antonio's hand. He held it tighter and shouted.

'Tariq, are you in there?'

There was no reply. Was he sleeping? Was he there?

'Tariq, for the love of God, answer me!'

'Yes, I'm in here. What do you want?'

'Don't you know we're in a hell of a storm?'

'Yes, of course I do. That's why I've tied myself to the bed.'

'We should go up on deck, to see if we can help up there.'

'Don't be stupid. The ship's crew will manage and we're a damn sight safer down here! Hang on tight and I'll let you in?'

Tariq took a minute or so to untie himself from his bed and make his way to the door which he opened with Antonio still holding the handle on the outside.

'God you smell bad. Have you spewed up?'

'Yes, and I feel better for it. My bad head's almost gone now.'

'Here. Rinse your mouth with some water from this and spit into the sink.'

The ship suddenly lurched again as Tariq passed a leather bottle to Antonio who just managed to grab it to stop it falling. As Antonio took a swig, the ship jolted again. There were some loud creaking noises from below. By some kind of miracle, the ship had righted itself, while still moving violently in the storm. The listing had gone.

'It's moving about the vertical now,' said Tariq. 'I thought it was going over. Then we'd have been in trouble!'

Antonio and Tariq sat in Tariq's cabin, holding on tight to anything they could. The ship continued to pitch and roll in the violent storm. As they clung on, not saying much to each other but feeling mighty sick, they wondered if they'd get off the *Constelación de Orión* alive. It seemed to get worse. Suddenly, they heard a distant crash of thunder, then another and another. It was getting closer by the minute. Then it sounded overhead. The loudest of thunder cracks assaulted their ears. The whole ship shook. Seconds later, the ship quaked again as something large crashed onto the floor above.

'By the blood of Christ, what was that?' said Antonio.

'Something has been struck by lightning and fallen to the deck. Let's get out of here! The ship could be on fire!'

Grasping anything to hold them steady, the two of them clawed their way along the lower deck, towards the steps. The insistent wind almost pushed them off their feet. It howled as they clambered up and onto the open upper deck. The pouring rain and wind lashed at them. Then a shout.

'Get back down, you stupid idiots. You'll be blown into the sea up here.' Antonio glanced over his shoulder. It was Gonzalo, stripped to his breeches and along with four other members of the crew, equally lacking in clothing, heaving at a thick, wet rope. He could see through billowing smoke that a mast had been ripped down. It was on fire and the men were doing their best to drag it over the side before it set the rest of the ship ablaze. They gave it some final heaves and it fell over the side.

'Get back down, I said!'

The two of them descended and eased their way back to Tariq's cabin, feeling helpless and chastened.

The storm subsided as suddenly as it had started. 'Seems like we're back on an even keel now. The rocking has all but stopped,' said Tariq. 'But there's damage and I wonder what that will mean for the voyage.'

'I don't know if we can still sail without that mast,' said Antonio. 'I don't know which one it was.'

'Nor me. We'll soon find out.'

With that a loud banging on the door startled them. 'It's me, the captain! Let me in! Oh! You are both present here. Good. So I can inform you both simultaneously. We only just survived that monstrous storm. We attempted to anchor and ride it out but we repeatedly lost the anchor point. So we directed our craft into the storm and returned, up the coast. We'd have been driven onto the rocks if we'd attempted to reach land. As you know… you should never have endeavoured to come on deck… we were struck by a lightning bolt. It splintered the foremast which caught fire. If it hadn't been for the prompt intervention of the crew… along with the pouring rain… the whole ship would have become a conflagration. The result is we will be postponing our voyage to Anfa and heading to Tangier for repair. It could delay us for a week…a fortnight if we're unfortunate. My advice is to descend to the hold and examine your part of the cargo. It's my considerable pleasure to invite you again to dinner tonight, at my table. I'll see you then, if not before.'

The two of them climbed into the hold to examine their part of the cargo. The movement of the ship and incoming seawater had all but completely destroyed it. The rolls of delicately coloured fabrics were lying in a brown soup of salt water. Most of the earthenware pots had been smashed. The movement had dented, if not crushed many of the pots and pans; the weapons were in pieces and sodden; barrels of oil, beer and wine had ruptured and their contents had ruined the carpets and fabrics. The two men looked at each other.

'Not much here we can sell,' said Antonio.

'Virtually nothing. Even the whole casks are stained.'

'We'll have to restock.'

'That's a good trading expression! My teaching has clearly helped you!'

'We can only treat this disaster with humour, Tariq. Especially as we have survived to see it!'

'Glad you see it that way, too! So what's the plan, Antonio?'

'We spend the next few days sorting through our cargo. We keep what we can sell. And destroy the rest. Throw it overboard. We work out what we need to replace and get a message to Silva to renew what's destroyed. Simple as that.'

'If we can do it today, we can send the message from Tangier.'

The two men laboured into the night to produce a list of items that had to be replaced. By the time they met Captain Hernan de Porras at the dinner table they looked exhausted.

'My God, you two! What has committed you to this level of fatigue?'

They described what they had done and their plan.

'Ridiculous! Where do you intend to merchant your goods?'

'Marrakesh,' said Antonio.

'You can purchase every item in Anfa. In their wonderfully colourful markets… and for a highly agreeable price. Barter for it! You'll pay considerably less for it than you would in Spain. And you won't be delaying your sojourn.'

'Can you see a flaw in the captain's idea?' said Antonio.

'I'll have to think about it but, offhand, no. It seems a brilliant idea to me.'

After dinner, the two met in Antonio's cabin. They had consumed less beer that night so could talk sensibly.

'I can see two problems,' said Tariq. 'We have a fair sum of money between us but not enough to replace all the damaged goods. And much of what we'd buy in Anfa could probably be bought in Marrakesh.'

'I don't agree. We visit the *corregidor* or the equivalent and ask him to finance us. And we know what Spanish fabrics, pots, pans, wine barrels and fabrics look like so we only buy those. The only problem I can see is getting the weapons. They give us credibility so we need to replace them and they won't be on sale in any marketplace.

Not much later that night, the crew of the storm battered and beaten *Constelación de Orión* moored her in Tangier. Within a week, a team of shipbuilders were replacing the broken foremast with a specially constructed new one, spars, cross beams and sails included. Two days further on, the galleon left the docks and eased her way back into the gentle swell of a passive Atlantic Ocean. With majestic dignity, she filled her sails, raised her bow and put herself on course for Anfa.

'What an incredible sight,' said Antonio, as the rejuvenated galleon eased her way towards the quay. 'I've never seen such a beautiful city.'

'Goes right back to before the Romans. Caesar Augustus turned it into a port and it's thrived ever since. He's the one Zaragoza is named after.'

'You are quite an historian, Tariq.'

'I only know what I've picked up visiting these places!'

The city glowed with colour, from the curved, gold topped temples to the fronts of the bars and shops on the harbour side, each washed in a different hue. Antonio had never before seen people dressed the way the people of Anfa dressed. Dozens of men in white kaftans, some carrying unusual looking objects, presumably purchased from the local markets, others walking purposefully, appeared to Antonio to be an unarmed, uniformed force of some kind. 'Why are these men all dressed the same?' he said.

'It's normal in these parts of the Maghreb. The heat can be unbearable here and white, flowing fabrics are the most comfortable. Wait until you see what the women wear.'

'I can see some from here. At least I believe they are women. Covered from head to toe.'

'You've seen them. Mainly in black. Don't ask me why!'

As they carried their saddlebags towards the gangplank, Captain Hernan de Porras appeared before them to wish them his best for their onward journey.

'Gentlemen, it has been a singular pleasure to indulge you as my passengers. You have survived one of the worst storms I have ever experienced, and I have traversed some terrible tempests, I can inform you. But now to some practical issues. My first mate, Gonzalo Ortiz de Montoya, wishes to know where you want to take delivery of the remains of your cargo. And of course, your trunks.'

Neither of the two travellers had an answer. After all, they were completely new to Anfa.

'I am sorry, Captain, but we are somewhat embarrassed by your question. All I can suggest is a small area in a dockside warehouse... at least until we have sorted something out ourselves,' said Tariq.

'I know just the place. Gonzalo will take you there and arrange something. Wait here. I'll fetch him. In the meantime, I shall bid you farewell and wish you a successful mission in Marrakesh.' They shook hands. The captain saluted them, clicked his heels and went back on board. Moments later the first mate appeared.

'I have been told to help you,' he said, smiling. He took them to some run-down looking premises, just off the quayside. He knocked on the door. A man with a tidy, black moustache dressed in a white kaftan and wearing a red fez with a black tassel appeared. Gonzalo spoke to the man in Arabic. The man nodded in agreement. Tariq thanked him.

'He's agreed to take our goods and trunks for what seems a reasonable price,' explained Tariq. 'So Gonzalo is going to arrange for them to be brought here. All we need to do is to find somewhere to stay, as Silva said, near to the centre of the city, and see the *corregidor*.'

'Before you go, Gonzalo, can I ask you a question?' said Antonio. 'I'm sure we can find a market where we can replace our damaged goods. But you seem to know your way around well. Can you tell us where we can buy replacement weapons?'

'Good question, my young friend. Go to the central square in the Medina. There is a street they call Straight Street, off the northern corner. There is a gunsmith up there, about the fifth or sixth shop on the left. Go and tell him Gonzalo Ortiz de Montoya sent you. He's sure to be able to help. I must get back to the ship now. Goodbye gentleman and good luck!'

The two of them were alone, for the first time since leaving Madrid. They felt strange, just with their saddlebags slung over their shoulders. But their saddlebags contained their guns and knives and this reduced their sense of vulnerability.

'We need somewhere to stay tonight,' said Tariq. 'Shall we find somewhere and then go to the gunsmiths or go there first?'

'Let's go to the gunsmiths. He may have some ideas of where we can stay.'

'And where we can find somewhere more permanent,' said Tariq.

'Excellent thought,' said Antonio.

They followed Gonzalo's imprecise instructions and, after taking a few wrong turns in the labyrinth of narrow streets of the Medina eventually found a street called Straight. 'What did he say, the fourth or fifth on the left?' said Antonio.

'That's right. There it is. The one with the picture of a pistol over the door.'

They stepped over the threshold of the store into a veritable armoury. It reminded Antonio of the one in the Alcázar Palace with the laughing major at its head. In the subdued light of the interior, they walked past the shelves of pikes, staves, harquebuses and arrays of pistols, each decorated in Arabic symbols and lettering. There were swords, helmets, breastplates and all manner of body and limb protection.

Suddenly a short plump man, in a white kaftan and a large, white turban appeared from behind a large screen and spoke. 'May I help you, gentlemen,' he said, in rapid Arabic.

Tariq replied, 'Yes, señor. We have been sent here by Gonzalo Ortiz de Montoya, first mate of the galleon, the *Constelación de Orión*.'

'Not him! I know him well!'

'The very same!' said Tariq.

'Friend of yours?'

'No. Merely an acquaintance. We travelled on the *Constelación* from Cadíz. Arrived here an hour ago.'

'So what do you want?'

Tariq told the man the story of how the ship was almost scuppered by the storm, that they were merchants on their way to Marrakesh, that their weapons for sale were destroyed in the storm and that they wanted to replace them.

He beamed a broad smile. 'I have everything you need!'

Within an hour they had agreed the list of weapons they would purchase on return to the shop, once they had somewhere to keep them.

'What do you mean, somewhere to keep them?'

'We are looking for a place in Anfa to operate from. Yes, our main market will be Marrakesh but we need a base here. In or near the Medina,' said Tariq.

'I have the solution. My brother Ahmed is a landlord here. He has twenty houses in and around the Medina. I know he has several to let. I'll close the shop and we'll go to see him.'

They couldn't believe their luck. Not only had they purchased the weapons they needed but it seemed they were about to find their base in Anfa. The three of them walked the maze-like complex of streets until they reached an opulent looking house overlooking a street so narrow that two loaded horses could only just pass each other within it. The gunsmith knocked on the door. They waited until a woman, completely covered in black, except for a slit through which her dark eyes peered, opened the door. She lifted her veil to speak.

'It's you, Mohammed. Come in. Ahmed is with a tenant, in the back. I doubt that he'll be long.'

The woman, they assumed to be Ahmed's wife or daughter, showed them in. The entrance hall smelled of spices and perfumes, a sure sign, thought Antonio, of a rich owner. She led the three of them through to a large drawing room, decorated in a way which seemed strange to Antonio, almost shocking. Carpets with strange curly patterns, like coloured writing, decorated the walls which were lined with large sofas, each covered in the same bright green fabric, which stood next to each other like a line of giant frogs. A canopy was suspended from ceiling wires over the seat of one of the sofas, the one in the centre of the far wall and also bright green.

'Sit down, please but not in that one,' she gestured to the one with the canopy. 'I'll bring you something to drink.'

All three sat and waited for a full half hour, sipping at small cups of a strong, quite refreshing drink which Antonio guessed was tea. Eventually, Ahmed, dressed in a similar kaftan to Mohammed, but with a purple turban, arrived and went to sit in the canopied sofa. There were no handshakes but on route to his chair, he stopped to kiss his brother on both cheeks.

'What can I do for these men?' he said, directing his question to Mohammed, as if the other two were not present.

'They came to my shop to make a number of purchases and want to rent a house in the Medina. I suggested you might be able to help them.'

Then glaring at Antonio and Tariq, said, 'Who are you people? You're not from this country. Why are you here?'

'We are merchants from Madrid,' said Tariq. 'We plan to be here for a good number of months, maybe a year or more and we want somewhere to rent and use as our base. Our market is mainly in Marrakesh so we will spend most of our time there or travelling to and fro. Our merchandise will arrive here from Cádiz.'

'Hmm,' muttered Ahmed, still with a penetrating stare. 'I'm not sure I can help you.'

His brother broke in angrily. 'Why not? There's that house in the Alt Baha. Ideal for them. They are good people. Recommended by my friend Gonzalo Ortiz de Montoya. Very respectable man. You know Gonzalo!'

At first Ahmed, sitting high on the sofa, appeared not to welcome Mohammed's intrusion. He pondered for what seemed an age to Antonio and Tariq. Antonio wondered why he acted in this way. Still, there were other landlords or property agents they could approach if he wanted to be so precious. Then he spoke.

'You didn't say they had Gonzalo's confidence. I must therefore help them. Yes, the house in the Alt Baha would be perfect. Would you like to see it?'

The four of them walked about four hundred *varas* through the intersecting array of narrow, busy streets in what Antonio thought was a vaguely westerly direction. They passed dozens of bustling shops with people entering and leaving them or merely looking at the colourful variety of goods on display. Eventually they reached a more residential area. Ahmed took out a key and opened the door of a moderately large, drab looking, flat-roofed house which opened directly onto the road and stood only a *vara* or so from its neighbours to each side. A horse and cart could barely squeeze between it at the properties on the opposite side. Ahmed opened the door and showed them in. The house contrasted starkly to the unashamed luxury of Ahmed's. Rough cut stone slabs, infilled with dirt or dried mud, lined the floors. Brown wattle covered the bare walls. Antonio thought it strange that there were lit oil lamps attached at intervals along the walls of the otherwise unwelcoming hall. Surely, no one could have known in advance that they were to visit the place.

'Come this way,' said Ahmed, leading the four of them through to the back of this deceptively large property. They passed several closed side doors before Ahmed pushed open the one at the end of the gloomy corridor. The room emitted beams of bright light which dazzled the two Spanish merchants. Antonio had to shield his eyes, at least for that moment of adjustment. As he did so, he noticed the seductive aroma of a delicate, ambrosial perfume spreading from the direction of the light.

'Go in,' said Ahmed. The source of the sweet, seductive fragrance became clear. A beautiful, slim woman, displaying her sultry face and wearing a peculiar light blue garment which combined ankle length breeches with a camisole top, was sitting cross-legged on a high backed chair, adjacent to a high table. Her hands moved quickly and precisely as she expertly embroidered a large piece of fabric, attached to a frame shaped like a small harp.

'This is Safia,' said Ahmed. 'She is the housekeeper. I own her and she is part of the deal. If you rent the house, you pay for her as well. She cleans, cooks, makes the beds, shops from the markets and so on. But don't touch her. I'll kill you if you do. She was almost raped by the previous tenant. I arranged for his execution and the dissection of his corpse. He is now buried in several places around Anfa.'

Antonio looked at Tariq who returned his glance.

'We need to see the whole property,' said Tariq.

'Go ahead and we'll stay here,' said Ahmed.

The two began to explore. 'What do you think, Antonio?'

'I like it in an odd sort of way. It has an anonymity about it that would suit our purpose. It's not somewhere I would like to live on a permanent basis but there are enough rooms to use as a warehouse and leave us space to stay. The beds don't look that comfortable but I've seen worse. I'm not sure about the housekeeper but she would at least guard the place when we were in Marrakesh. Let's negotiate a price.'

Ahmed bargained hard. It took a good ten minutes of arguing before they settled on a price of eight falus a week. 'Come into the kitchen with me and Mohammed.'

'These are your new tenants, Safia.' She smiled and bowed deeply to the two of them in turn. 'Get some drinks!'

She poured a strong looking concoction from a leather bottle. They each downed the fluid in a single gulp. It tasted like something a rat wouldn't swallow. It was as much as Antonio could do to hold it down. The men shook hands and Ahmed and his brother departed.

Antonio and Tariq quickly settled in to their strange abode. It seemed odd to them to have this seductive woman, whom they daren't touch, as a housekeeper. She soon earned her wages: nothing seemed too much trouble to her. They had her cooking for them washing clothes and drying them, making beds and everything that made life there comfortable and easy. She even found a hand cart which the three of them used to transport the merchandise, stored just of the quayside, to their new home. At Tariq's suggestion, the two men decided not to replace all their goods lost at sea. They could not possibly transport it all to Marrakesh, even on three average size camel trains, so they decided to replace enough to set themselves up in business there and return to Anfa for more after they had sold what they could of the first consignment. As Antonio pointed out, this would minimise their initial outlay and mean that they wouldn't have to approach the *corregidor* for financial help.

'So we won't have to visit him at all then,' said Antonio.

'Sorry, but you are wrong, Antonio. We need those addresses in Marrakesh. The one where we will be staying and the one they use for their staff there. And the key.'

'Of course! I'd forgotten that! Oh! And we have to send Silva a message with our address here!'

'Well done! I'd forgotten that!'

It took a week of visits and bargaining at the market to buy what they wanted, then another two days to find a camel train willing to take them. The train puller, an odd but fitting title, was a wizened Tuareg tribesman. He told them his name was Amanar which he said meant warrior of the desert. For all they knew, thought Antonio, they might need someone with that ability to see them to Marrakesh. The lines on Amanar's face were close and deep, as if he had been etched in a hundred sand storms. Tariq negotiated long and hard until Amanar threw his hand across his chest to show he would accept nothing lower. The two of them shook hands and the deal was struck. They'd bought their ticket to Marrakesh. The question of their return remained open.

CHAPTER 24
The road to Marrakesh

The night before their departure from Anfa, Antonio lay on the creaking bed, staring at the ceiling of his room in the house in the Alt Baha. He wondered how Carolina would be managing without him and whether she and Lupita were still working the streets of Madrid as a duet. He missed Carolina more than anyone else, including Francisca, who still badly wanted to marry him. He liked her but remained unsure of a future with the woman. He wondered whether Carolina had sent the promised letter to his parents in Pedraza and what they might think of his going to Morocco. He even had a thought for his aging mare, probably enjoying its new, if temporary, life in the palace stables. He had trouble believing that from Jac, the inn-keeper's daughter in Guadalajara, telling him about the *Morisco* plot to kidnap the king, now more than two years before, he had changed his career from being a wandering musician to being a spy, now on a mission so crucial that the future of Spain could depend on it. But at heart, he still felt that he was first a musician and even more pleased that, there in his trunk, well hidden, lurked his new violin, ready to give a tune at his own bow strokes and fingers on the strings.

In his room next door, Tariq's mind had turned itself back towards Madrid. He badly missed his wife, Ishraq Alsulami, and Reva, his beautiful if enigmatic daughter. He hoped that Silva would provide them with any protection they might need. They were, like Tariq, true Morisco converts, unlike many who had converted in name only and who continued, at great risk, to pray to Allah. Therefore many *Moriscos* regarded Tariq and his family as traitors who, if times became difficult, could be vulnerable to the remonstrance of their own people. They occupied one of his concerns: the other was the business he had left in the charge of his deputy, a man he felt, while competent, could not be wholly trusted.

First light saw the two of them making their way to the stables at the southern corner of Anfa from which the camel train would soon be departing. Antonio had never seen a camel at such close quarters before and stood at the gates, looking towards the twenty or so men who were loading these peculiar animals with the goods they were taking to Marrakesh.

'How are you supposed to ride an animal like that?' he said, smiling wryly to Tariq. 'It's not exactly designed to be ridden!'

'It's not difficult. Once you are on and get into the animal's rhythm, you'll be fine. Don't even think about galloping! It's walk all the way!'

'So how long to get there?'

'Hard to say. Depends on the weather and how many stops we make… to take on food and water. The desert is a cruel place. Without water it will kill you. It can drive you mad.'

'Mad?'

'Yes. Combination of thirst and heat. Hunger doesn't help. See those huge gourds they are loading on those camels now. They're full of water. They'll keep us going until the first water stop.'

'Where will that be?'

'Wish I knew. But Amanar will know and he'll get us there. Fear not.'

Antonio was impressed with Tariq's blind faith in the camel train puller whom they had hardly met. Antonio could understand Tariq's logic: if you are paying a man to take you across the desert you have to trust him. He'd been there before and survived. It's no different from putting your faith in a sea captain. So there's no reason to worry until something goes wrong.

Antonio counted thirty camels. He soon discovered that about half were loaded with the goods of other customers. Amanar's men had wrapped all of the objects placed in their care with a heavy cloth, presumably to protect them from the sun and sand. Casting an eye along the train, Antonio found it difficult to work out what some of these objects could be. Some were obviously barrels of some liquid or another: perhaps of wine, oil or some other exotic liquid. Who could say what most of the anonymous boxes contained? But one in particular looked like a coffin: surely they weren't carrying a body.

Antonio stared vacantly at the camel Amanar had brought him. From the extravagant hand waving invitation Amanar made and his generous smile, Antonio could see that this beast would be his mount, the animal which would carry him to Marrakesh. It soon became clear what Antonio should do. With the click of a finger, Amanar made the camel drop onto its haunches. He signalled Antonio to climb up. With Tariq looking on, Antonio placed a leg over the camel's back and sat on the red saddle, placed on the rear slope of the animal's hump. Amanar snapped his fingers again and the camel went to stand up. As it did so, it moved forward slightly. Antonio was unprepared and lurched backwards. In a natural reaction, he rapidly moved forward only to overcompensate and slid down the front of the hump, overbalanced and fell off, right at Tariq's feet.

Tariq had probably never laughed so loud in his life. Nor had Amanar. Each bellowed peals of mirth while Antonio clambered to his feet, brushing the sand and dust from his clothing. The camel flicked its luxuriant eyebrows but otherwise ignored Antonio's plight.

'That funny, was it?' scowled Antonio. 'You put one of these animals in front of me. Give me no instruction and expect me to ride the Christ damned thing! Who's surprised I fell off?'

'It wasn't for our entertainment, I can assure you,' said Tariq, wiping a tear of laughter from his eye. 'But entertain you certainly did!'

Antonio soon recovered and within moments had perched himself atop the camel's hump and, at the hands of a patient Amanar, confidently held the animal's reins. He made a number of turns, climbed on and off a few times and, having secured himself back on the camel's hump announced he was ready to depart.

The journey ahead of them would be long and arduous. Marrakesh nestled some fifty *leguas* away in the northern foothills of the Atlas Mountains. The weather at this time of the year could not be predicted. There was no road as such, no delineated track or path. The moving sands ensured its obscurity. So the train had to rely on the experience and sense of direction of the rugged faced Amanar and his team of ten men, a mixed crew, some apparently older than him but some much younger, two of whom could be his sons, to find their way to Marrakesh.

Suddenly, Amanar sounded a horn, waved his arm in the air and led them on their way.

'Can't we go any faster?' said Antonio to Tariq who, at that moment, rode alongside so could easily hear.

'A camel train can only move at the rate of the slowest camel. The loaders do their best to see that the beasts are properly loaded. They put more on the camels which are younger and haven't done the journey for a month or so,' said Tariq, rocking gently to his camel's rhythm. 'The ones that arrived in Anfa last week, won't have fully recovered so they'll have less to carry. It's a matter of good handling.'

'That doesn't answer my question!' said Antonio, not used to this crawling pace, not even when riding his ancient mare in the hot streets of Madrid. 'It'll take a week or more to get to Marrakesh at this rate.'

'That might be a good result!' said Tariq.

Neither Tariq nor Antonio could guess when the camel train would stop or when it would be moving or, once moving, when or where it would stop again. The train puller, Amanar, drove the caravan for five hours before stopping at an unmanned station near an outcrop of rock about ten *varas* high. Several dead trees stood alongside the outcrop, as if it had provided them with protection at the time they were growing. Amanar's camel halted ahead of the rest which in turn starting from the front, dropped to their haunches to allow their rider, if it had one, to dismount. Otherwise, to give their legs a rest, while still carrying their loads.

Amanar walked the length of the train to carry out an impromptu inspection. With the aid of a judiciously placed foot, he tightened up some of the ropes securing the loads. Others of the team assisted him while some had themselves taken the initiative to adjust the tethering. They stopped for a good two hours before starting up again. Antonio and Tariq refreshed themselves with a few drafts of water from a leather bottle and a shared pastry biscuit.

The camel train made steady if laboured progress across the uneven, unmarked terrain. Antonio expected the desert to be a vast expanse of sand so was surprised to find that so much of their path was solid rock, covered in a shroud of fine sand no more than a *pulgada* deep. The thin layer hardly slowed their progress. But in many other areas its depth made walking quite difficult, even for the camels.

Whatever level of confidence Tariq expressed in Amanar, Antonio felt uneasy about this exposed journey. At least a horse rider could dig his boots into his animal's side and spark the beast into a gallop, away and out of trouble. The burdened, fixed paced camel provided no such flexibility, capable only of plodding deliberately across the sand strewn wasteland. Antonio couldn't escape the fact of their vulnerability, in particular, to an ambush from attackers concealed by the rocky crags they frequently passed.

Night fell with a surprising suddenness but as it did, the train entered a canvas village of scattered tents. There must have been thirty or even more. It puzzled Antonio, still astride his nameless animal, that such a collection of shelters existed and even more so that Amanar was able to lead the train to this location, despite the lack of obvious landmarks. Antonio could see, as they entered the village, that it was being illuminated by the flickering light from braziers as some men already there were setting them alight. The tents appeared low and black, like giant bats resting on the sand.

'Sorry, my friend, but we're going to have to share one of these tents,' laughed Tariq.

'Just with each other?' said Antonio, sounding resigned to the situation.

'No. With the other ten in the camel train!'

'Not the camels?' jested Antonio.

'Don't be stupid! The camels sleep outside. The drivers! Amanar says there will be about ten of us in each tent. A couple of other camel trains are already here.'

As Antonio and Tariq entered the tent which Amanar had assigned to their group they detected the smell of spicy food coming from within. A few paces on and they could see that their tent had been erected in a group of five tents which enclosed a large flat area of dry sand from which the contents of a large cauldron were spuming clouds of vapour as it sat suspended over a huge fire.

'Looks like our dinner is cooking over there,' said Antonio.

'Smells like some sort of broth or stew,' said Tariq.

Within not many minutes, Amanar and his men, Tariq and Antonio were consuming the surprisingly tasty concoction, along with men from some of the other camel trains. Tariq chatted to the men and acted as interpreter for Antonio. He said that the men seemed concerned about the weather. Antonio shrugged his shoulders. The two of them spent the rest of the evening playing dice with the camel teams before they retired to their ground hugging beds among the others in the tent.

'I wish I could communicate with these people,' said Antonio. 'Would it be possible for you to teach me?'

'I don't see why not,' said Tariq. 'Many of the words are the same in Spanish and Arabic. You'll soon pick it up.'

Antonio slept well until he woke to the sound of a continuous, distant roar. It sounded like the deep, loud note of a bull about to charge at a *matador*. He had no idea then what caused it. It became louder and closer. Then louder still until it almost deafened him. He could see by the light of an oil lamp that most of the other men were also awake and that Tariq was stirring in his slumbers. Tariq climbed up and joined a group of the men who were talking anxiously.

'What is it? What's causing the noise?' said Antonio.

'What they were talking about last night. A sandstorm. It's a bad one.'

'Now what do we do?' said Antonio.

'What we're told. The safest place to be is here, in the tent.'

One of the other men approached Tariq and said something urgent to him. He waved his hands towards the perimeter of the tent. Others were unfurling ground sheets that were rolled inside the edges. They then moved some heavy stones from a large pile near the centre and placed them on the ground sheets to hold them in place. Some of the rocks were so large it took two to move them. Tariq returned to speak to Antonio.

'We have secured the tent as best we can. All we can do now is wait until this storm passes.'

'How long will we be here?'

'None of them know. It could have blown over by the morning or it could last for days. Their main concern is lack of water. It seems we've only got enough to see us through until tomorrow night. The next water hole is a good day's travel from here. They are rationing it from now, just in case. So no water will be available until tomorrow morning at breakfast and then only a half a cup. Amanar suggests we all go back to bed and do our best to sleep through this. In two minutes he's going to put out the oil lamp.'

Antonio couldn't sleep and, from the turning sounds he could hear from Tariq's bed, he couldn't either. He wondered how the camels could survive this tremendous beating of wind born sand. He couldn't hear a sound he could associate with them so imagined that they were sleeping through it. They looked as if they could survive almost anything. They had surely experienced these conditions many times before.

Daylight seeped in where much sand had found its way. Despite the tents appearing black from the outside, the amount of light that came through the fabric itself, by the time the sun had fully risen, made everything inside the tent visible. The men, all of whom had 'slept' fully clothed, were up and talking to each other. One was unwrapping what appeared to be bread or biscuits and some grapes for breakfast. Another laid out some cups on a short stool and half-filled them from a pitcher of water. The roar of the storm persisted.

Amanar came over to speak. 'We have no idea how long this storm will last. But we cannot move from here until it has subsided. In the meantime, we'll just have to entertain ourselves with card games or dice. By the way, don't bet with my men or you'll lose!'

'Why can't we move?' said Antonio.

'Can't you hear the storm and feel it trying to rip the tent from the ground? The sand will blind you. And it will tear into your face. It's solid, not like rain. And it'll be impossible to find our way in it. Apart from that, the camels won't budge while it's like this. Now they are sheltering behind the tents and the barriers, we won't be able to shift them.'

'What about our goods?'

'They are safe on the camels' backs. The men have covered the merchandise so it cannot be damaged by sand.'

The freak storm - for that is what it turned out to be - persisted. It raged throughout their second day and into the night. By the following morning, they were completely out of water, as were the men in the other tents. The storm raged on…and on.

'I'm really thirsty,' said Tariq.

'Me, too,' said Antonio. 'What are we going to do?'

'I'm thinking of going out to find water.'

'You'll die if you do that. Stay here. If I'm going to die of thirst, I'd rather do it here.'

'I think you are right, Antonio. It would be stupid to go out, however thirsty we become.'

They were too thirsty to sleep. The dry pains in their stomachs were killing them or so they thought. Antonio began to feel dazed. He felt as if his brain had dried out. Later that third night, with the storm still showing no sign of relenting, Antonio passed out. He could not guess when but at some point in the night he awoke as Amanar shook his shoulder so hard, he thought his back would break. Amanar held a pitcher to Antonio's mouth and signalled him to drink. Whatever it was that Amanar was giving him, it tasted disgusting. Antonio thought he would be sick. The disgusting fluid stank.

The following morning, Amanar woke Antonio, again by shaking him violently. Antonio went to stand up but couldn't; he drifted back into a thirst induced coma. He felt like death. He could see his past life flash before him. He imagined he was a child again, playing on the farm in Pedraza. Then making frenzied and passionate love to Catalina. He could see himself with Jac in Guadalajara. Then entering Silva's office in

Madrid. He felt the crash of the meteorite as it landed on the road to Ávila. Then firing the shots that killed the highwayman on the way to Segovia. Then, the last time he made love to Carolina. Her final goodbye. He was dying. Dying of thirst.

He dreamt he could feel himself being shaken again and a voice shouting loudly at him in Arabic. It was urgent. He woke. Maybe the storm had stopped. Maybe some cool, fresh water awaited him. He stared head of him. It was Amanar, pointing to Tariq. His white faced figure lay flat on a bed. His eyes stared into the void above him. Antonio had lived through it, still parched with thirst, and all but dying for some water; but clearly Tariq hadn't. Antonio managed to stand and drift over towards his friend and mentor. What would he do, now that Tariq had died? Antonio was alone with these Arabs; he couldn't speak their language; he was doomed. His heart began to race and pound against the wall of his chest. He didn't know what to do; how to react to this desperate situation. How could anyone have predicted that it would end like this? Was this the end? Maybe not. He would have to go alone to Marrakesh and achieve the mission's objective. Somehow, even if it killed him. There was no way he could turn back. He could not and would not admit he had failed because his friend had died of thirst. If he did, he would be branded as a coward, someone who knew not the meaning of honour. He had no option: he had to go on. God only knew how.

He leant over Tariq's body and attempted to kiss him. Antonio's tongue had dried to the point that it would hardly move in his mouth. He could hardly speak. He wanted to say farewell to his friend and helper but his mouth wouldn't let him.

Tariq suddenly moved and sat upright on the bed. 'What in the name of hell are you doing?' he said.

'Kissing my dead friend goodbye!'

'I thought I was dead but now I know I'm not!'

Right at that moment, as if dictated to by the rising Tariq, the storm suddenly began to subside and, within a few more minutes, calm was completely restored. Antonio's sadness turned to unbridled elation. The thrill of knowing that Tariq had survived and that the storm was over. But the thirst persisted where emotion took over.

Amanar spoke seriously to Tariq while Antonio awaited a translation.

'He is going to bring us some clean water. He had to put some by for a full day's ride to the waterhole.'

'What? He let us almost die of thirst and now he says he's had water all along.'

'That doesn't quite tell the story. The fact is he had to reserve enough to get us from here to the next stop. We now know we can make it. Even if we have no more today.'

With that, some of the drivers circulated with cups of water, one each for Tariq and Antonio. 'Sip it. Don't down it all at once!' said Tariq, passing on the message.

It tasted like nectar to each of them. What a relief.

'What I don't understand is: what was that disgusting liquid they made us drink, what two days ago?'

'Camel's piss. Didn't they tell you?'

'No!'

'They told me and I immediately vomited. I didn't recover until you came to kiss me. That was enough to wake the dead!'

'How did they get the stuff?'

'They tie pots on the animals' hindquarters. Need I say more?'

In four more days of uneventful travel, the camel train, driven by its wearying crew, pulled through the city gates to the north of Marrakesh.

'Exactly where do you want to be dropped and what about all your merchandise,' said Amanar to Tariq.

'We will be living in a house on the southern corner of a street called Derb Chtouka. Don't ask me where it is because I've no idea. We've never been to Marrakesh before.'

'And you want to make a living as a merchant. You are joking! I know the street well. On the south side of the city, within the walls. That house on the corner is quite a large property, I think. We'll break the train and I'll come with you to the Chtouka.'

Marrakesh impressed Antonio with its bustling activity and stoic beauty. There seemed to be more people there than could possibly inhabit the city. All but a few wore strikingly colourful clothing, unlike the uniform white of Anfa. They crossed a huge, bustling market square - the Jaama el-Fna - where almost anything imaginable could be bought.

'This is where we should set our stall,' said Antonio. 'Look at the sheer number of people here. We'll sell out in a couple of days!'

'You're an optimist!' said Tariq. 'We'd have to stand out from this lot! The choice is massive. There must be two hundred stalls here, if not more. But I like the idea of trading in this market. Amanar says the palace is quite nearby and we don't want to be too far from our quarry!'

The massive palace, perched on top of a modest hill seemed to oversee the city like an enormous, silent guard. He had never been to Granada before but the castle fitted well what Antonio imagined the Alhambra to be like with its Moorish ramparts and towers. They soon reached the house on the corner of Derb Chtouka.

'This is the one,' said Amanar, as they reached the southern end of the Kasbah. Amanar knew virtually every house in this beautiful city. 'You see, it's a big one. You might even be able to store your merchandise in there.' This street and surrounding roads were narrow and the men and their loaded camels virtually blocked it, much to the annoyance of passers-by who glared hard at them. The intrepid three dismounted and stood by the tall, aquamarine front door. Tariq pulled the chord of a bell which rang repeatedly inside the hall. Nothing happened.

'You know the house. Do you know the owner?' said Tariq.

'No,' said Amanar. 'Let me give it a knock with this.' He banged the door hard with the brass handle of his camel whip.

A small panel, at eye height, slid slowly open. A man's voice uttered some unfriendly sounding words. Antonio looked at Tariq who replied, quite abruptly. They had launched into a heated discussion. Then Amanar interrupted as if it was anything to do with him. The voice behind the door seemed angrier still at Amanar's intervention. Tariq moved his hands up and down in an attempt to calm the situation, assuming the man could see him. Suddenly, the voice uttered what sounded like the 'ahs' and 'ohs' of sudden realisation. Then further discussion with Tariq who then explained the situation to Antonio.

'He is expecting us. Thought we were arriving five days ago and had almost given up.'

The small panel slid back. A tall, clean shaven man, but for his smartly trimmed, black moustache, opened the tall, blue door. He wore a long, flowing turquoise kaftan, which almost covered his red leather shoes and which he had tied with a wide bright red sash around his trim waist. A turban also green but of a lighter shade adorned his head.

'So you are the gentleman who will be renting my house. I'm charmed to meet you. I am sorry for the initial confusion. I wrongly imagined something was amiss when I saw the three of you and those camels.'

They each shook hands, Amanar included. The gentleman introduced himself as Jabir al-Malaki, a property agent and resident of the city of Marrakesh.

'I think you may know that we are merchants and have brought a number of items to sell here from Anfa and Spain,' said Tariq. 'We wondered if it would be possible to store them in your house.'

'Of course. I was expecting that. Those who arranged for me to let the house to you informed me that you would have merchandise and that you would need to store it. I have a substantial warehouse across the courtyard at the back. I showed it to the man who came here on your behalf. He was impressed.'

Tariq, Antonio and Amanar unloaded the camels and took their products into the warehouse, through a door in the wall along the street side of the house. It took a full half an hour to complete the task, after which Amanar tied the camels together, ready to lead them away. Before bidding Antonio and Tariq farewell, he agreed to make his company available for further expeditions between Anfa and Marrakesh, as needed. He presented Tariq with a piece of paper giving the company's address.

'Make sure you keep that safe,' said Antonio, anxiously. 'He is our only ally in this town.'

'Which way do we go in?' said Antonio. 'Through the back door over there or do we go round the front?'

No sooner had he asked the question when the man in the turquoise kaftan appeared, arms crossed at the threshold of the back door. 'Come in this way, gentleman. You must be thirsty. Here, come and have a drink.'

Jabir al-Malaki poured the three of them a small cup of coffee from a metal jug standing over an oil stove.

'Try this,' he said. 'If it's too strong I can add some water.'

'Just right,' said Tariq, in a tone which indicated that he was unsure but too polite to say so.

Antonio lifted the cup into the air as if to show approval, if approval he meant.

'Sit down,' said Jabir al-Malaki, pointing to a large table in the centre of a well equipped kitchen. 'We need to discuss a few of the details. You must treat my house as if it's your own. It's plainly and simply furnished but I trust you will be comfortable. Your bedrooms are on the first floor. You can decide which you wish to occupy. I live in the house next door, in the Derb Chtouka. I share it with my sister. You'll meet her in due course.

'I hate to have to discuss payment but it's better if we do now. It will save any problems in the future. I agreed with your representative that the rent would be forty falus a month. I trust that is acceptable. That includes the free use of the warehousing facilities. I must depart now for other business in the city. If there is anything you want, please call on me or my sister.'

Antonio and Tariq couldn't wait to explore the house on their own. It was even larger than they thought, extending to a half floor of two rooms on the second level with an open patio overlooking the adjacent area.

'It's good that we are on a corner. Ideal for spies!' said Tariq.

'Really?'

'Yes, you can see any attacker coming from either direction. We must each have a bedroom overlooking one of the roads, the Derb Chtouka and whatever that road is called,' Tariq said looking out of a first floor bedroom window. 'We need to check the walls.'

'The walls?'

'Yes, we'll go around and check for any hollows where anyone could be concealed. We must check for hidden doors. We cannot afford to have anyone listening to the discussions we'll be having here. We'll be discussing tactics and our exact plans. Let's do that now. We must take special care with the wall we share with Jabir al-Malaki. He is a potential problem. I don't trust him.'

The two of them surveyed this extensive property. About ten minutes from starting, Antonio went to look for Tariq. 'Come and look at this!'

Tariq followed Antonio into a bedroom with a shared wall. 'Look at that panel at the side of the wardrobe. It's loose. It opens into a corridor along the wall to next door.'

'My God,' said Tariq. 'I was thinking of sleeping in this one, mainly because it overlooks the road.'

'Shall we go in?' asked Antonio, looking quite excited about what he had found.

'No, not yet. We must wait until Jabir al-Malaki and his sister are out of the house. But I agree. We need to see where this corridor leads.

In the meantime, we should select our rooms and do some exploring of this city… before nightfall.'

Antonio selected a room looking directly on to the Derb Chtouka while Tariq chose one on the adjacent side. It seems strange that the journey back to where you've come from always seems shorter that the journey to your destination. So Antonio and Tariq were quite surprised to find that the El Badi palace was so close to their house in the Derb Chtouka, less than eight hundred *varas* away. They couldn't believe their luck. On the other hand, the Jaama el-Fna market was at least as far north again.

They spent much of that day and the next surveying the area and working out their strategy for securing the information Silva, and indeed the king, wanted. It would not be easy. They were completely new to the city and no one would just let them into the El Badi palace. Quite the opposite: there were guards at every entrance and exit and regular patrols of guards all around the perimeter. They thought of breaking into the palace, either by climbing a wall or knocking out a couple of guards but soon realised that the problems such action would present were virtually insurmountable and that the risks too great. It looked forbidding and impenetrable. Somehow, and as Silva had said, they needed to gain sufficient confidence of someone working at the palace that this person would give them at least some relevant information. Presumably that 'someone' would be one of their customers.

They discussed where to sell their products. Would it be in the Jaama el-Fna or near the palace? Would they work under the cover of a shop or in the open market place? After their first few days in Marrakesh, the arguments became more heated and came to a head.

'You're talking nonsense, my friend! We cannot work in the open!' said Tariq. 'You're a musician and used to working in the open, but the quality products we have for sale cannot be either displayed or sold outside!'

'Why not? It would be much cheaper to rent a stall and sell items from there.'

'But what about storage? We don't want to have to bring everything back here after a day's work.'

'Why not. We could hire a wagon and driver.'

'Just listen to me Antonio. I don't want to be unkind but I am the merchant, not you. I don't care about the cost of renting a shop, provided it's in the right location. Silva gave us plenty to spend and we'll soon be earning plenty of cash to keep it going. Another thing. Customers prefer to buy from a permanent shop rather than a makeshift stall. Stall holders have the reputation of being fly-by-nights. They sell you rubbish. You get it home and realise its worth. You take it back and they're gone, never to be seen again! We definitely don't want that. We want to set up a reputable business, my friend. Nothing less. We want the palace to come to us: not us to them. When our reputation reaches them, they won't want to stay away,' he chuckled. He could sense that he had won Antonio, whom he regarded as a reasonable man, around to his way of thinking.

'All right! But only if we can find the shop we want. Otherwise…'

'We'll find one. I saw some vacant ones as we crossed the Jaama el-Fna. If not, we might even find one nearer the palace.'

'She's gone! I've just seen her turn towards the El Badi. They're both out now! What about some exploring?'

'Not so excited, my friend. We've only been here three days and you want to break into next door!'

'But we have to know where that corridor leads and what they could use it for. I'm surprised you don't believe it's urgent,' said Antonio, somewhat crestfallen.

'I suppose you are right. We may be able to use it ourselves. Go and light a candle. We'll do it now.'

They opened the wardrobe and eased the loose panel off the wall and into the back bedroom. 'What if I go first, Antonio? Give me the candle.'

Antonio followed Tariq. The narrower corridor constricted them to the extent that they had had to move sideways.

'Aha,' said Tariq. 'They are expecting us!'

'What do you mean?'

'There's a thin thread across the corridor. At knee height. See, it's tied to those eyelets!'

'Well done for noticing them!'

'A spy's job to look for such traps! So take care to climb over. I know it will be awkward.'

The corridor took them along the shared outer wall of the house. Then it stopped. Tariq, in the candlelight looked puzzled. 'It doesn't go anywhere. I don't understand.'

'Try tapping on the wall. Their wall,' said Antonio.

The wall sounded solid. Solid stone. But it seemed odd to them that the corridor should be blind, especially given the thread across it. There had to be something that they had missed.

'Try pushing the wall, at the end,' said Antonio. 'Surely there's a door somewhere!'

'I don't want to end up in the back yard!'

'Not that wall, the one into next door!'

Tariq pushed at the wall. Again nothing. 'I don't understand,' he said.

'Let me try,' said Antonio. Tariq squeezed himself into the end to give Antonio room. 'What's this?' said Antonio. 'It's a lever of some kind.'

Further up the wall, above head height, a metal lever, painted grey, the same colour as the wall, stood vertically in a recess. There was just sufficient room to insert a hand to grip it. 'Give it a pull. See what happens!'

Antonio pulled the lever and as he did so a section of the wall, the size and shape of a door, moved with a creaking noise inwards, on its hinges.

'Excellent, my friend! How did we miss that?'

'No idea. All I can think is that the candle light didn't show the gaps between the wall and the door. It's a very good fit!'

'You're right. Let's go in!'

With a degree of trepidation, the two of them passed through the doorway into a small room, a mere three or four *varas* square. By the light of the candle they could see a single, made-up-bed on the opposite, yellowish wall, a small mahogany, well used wardrobe, an old desk, another door, presumably into another room of Jabir al-Malaki's house and a knurled wheel, about a *pie* across, on a spindle about half way up the wall adjacent to the door they had opened. The most notable feature was the absence of a window.

'My God,' said Tariq, 'I didn't expect this. It's part of the house and from the age of the furniture, has been used for a good few years, my friend.'

'Used for what?'

'Probably spying on unsuspecting residents of this place. It means that we have to take our own precautions in detecting whether there is anyone using the corridor to spy on us.'

'Any idea what?'

'We could put our own trip wire across the corridor with something attached to the end to warn us. A small bell, for example.'

'We could use the corridor and the room to spy on Jabir al-Malaki or even his sister, if we needed to! And as a hiding place, if we thought we were being pursued,' said Antonio.

'The good thing is that we know the room is here and they don't know we know,' said Tariq. 'Let's go back before they come back into the house.'

'Just a minute,' said Antonio. 'Surely, we need to wind up that wheel to reset the door. Otherwise they'll know we've been here. And we won't be able to open it from the corridor side!'

'Great thinking, my friend!'

They made their way back into the corridor. Antonio pushed the grey lever back up into its recess. The heavy door closed, almost of its own volition. They chuckled at their success. Within a few minutes they were sitting in the expansive kitchen discussing their access to the mysterious corridor.

'Tomorrow we'll buy a small bell, some fine thread and some means of setting up our own little trip wire. Some hooks or something similar. We'll set the bell in the kitchen. That's the furthest point from the wardrobe with the entrance to the corridor. Then we'll see what happens!' said Tariq.

Full of enthusiasm for their new idea, Antonio and Tariq worked hard during the following day in finding a bell in the Jaama el-Fna and fixing it so that it would ring, if they were disturbed.

'That's fine,' said Antonio. 'That's that problem solved but we still need to work out how we are going to sell our wares. And where!'

The next few months proved to be among the most difficult of their stay in Marrakesh. As hard as they tried, no one wanted to rent them a shop. They could not work out why. The only conclusion they could reach was that they were foreigners and no one wanted to trust them to pay the fees. They discussed the problem at length until Antonio came up with an idea:

'We know we are going to be here for a time, at least six months so why not offer a property agent six months' rent in advance. No one else would do that and we've still got plenty of Silva's money to use.'

'We can but try,' said Tariq, with no great enthusiasm.

Two days later they were paying an agent a full six months deposit and had secured a well-appointed shop in the Plaza de Mellah, a market square right next to the El Badi palace. They couldn't have found a better place. They'd landed a tidy, double fronted store in the south eastern corner. They were just two of a number foreign market traders. Jews, Turks, Arabs and even a Portuguese occupied this small but open square. They were laughing: they would fit in like a hand in a glove!

So they began to trade. They decided to specialise in two quite unrelated lines of merchandise: soft furnishings, that is, carpets, curtains and bedding – purchased from a local company – and weaponry. They decided to be somewhat less than open about the armaments and stored them at the rear of the shop on the upper floor, partly because they were in no rush to sell them and because they provided protection, should they need it. They also had to display the other goods they'd brought from Anfa.

As Tariq had expected, they slowly and gradually built up a reputation for quality and reliability. But four more months passed and they seemed no nearer to achieving their main objective.

The day they had renewed the lease for another six months their conversation took a direction which Tariq did not expect.

'I don't know about you, Tariq, but I have an urgent need. While in Madrid I enjoyed a good life with my woman and I need a woman here. What should I do? I'm getting frustrated to the point of desperation.'

'Surely you don't want to form a relationship with one of these Muslim women. She'll expect you to marry her!'

'No. I want something purely physical but a woman with whom I could enjoy a regular encounter would be ideal.'

'They are fewer here than in Madrid and most of those kinds of activity are undertaken behind the shutters or in the worst kind of establishments where the women are all but beggars. I wouldn't touch them with an oar from a quinquerene. There are sure to be some higher class *burdels* here but I wouldn't know where to find one!'

'I'll find one, somehow!'

Antonio had always been an industrious individual and soon worked out how he would find a *burdel* in Marrakesh. While business was particularly slack or in his breaks he would wander around the city and simply look for one. A useful clue might be a nervous looking man emerging embarrassingly from such an establishment. It didn't take long to find precisely what he was looking for. Late one morning while walking through the Kasbah he spotted an elaborately dressed man emerging from a doorway. He looked quizzically at the man who saw him and hesitated before stepping into the street. As Antonio approached the house, the man smiled and paused, unsure as to whether to leave the door ajar for Antonio. Although Antonio was assiduously studying Arabic, he knew only a few phrases and immediately greeted and thanked the man before walking brazenly into the hallway of the house. Antonio glanced around. The walls were extravagantly papered and adorned with erotic paintings of veiled but half naked women. A reddish purple carpet, with a pile so deep he felt as if he was walking in mid-air, covered the floor. Oil lamps flickering on the walls gave the property an embracing glow. As he stepped further into the hall, a plump woman, wearing a translucent white veil, an almost transparent red skirt and an article of clothing that covered and contained her substantial breasts emerged from a door.

'marḥaban,' she said, hello.

Antonio replied with a 'good morning and then: 'miḥtāj musā`da law samaḥt' Can you help me? He was at the limit of his Arabic so just said what he wanted in Spanish. 'Have I come to the right place to make love to a woman?' he smiled.

She first looked at him in puzzlement then, to his utter amazement, replied in perfect Spanish. 'Yes, señor. We can cater for your manly needs here!' Then after a slight pause: 'For a price!'

She beckoned Antonio into the room she had emerged from and offered him a seat opposite a small desk.

'Welcome to our first class brothel,' she said, as she sat in a chair on the other side of the desk. 'Let me explain. This is not like one of your establishments in Madrid. Anything goes in Madrid and you can do just about anything you like there. Our women have to be respected, even in this profession. You may not see one naked; nor may you see her face. And you may not handle her intimate parts without her expressed approval.'

'What's left?' grinned Antonio.

'Virtually everything. Provided she is happy with only one candle in the room and the curtains drawn, she may work naked. And she can touch you and make love to you. If you are interested, one of the girls will be available on about five minutes for a fee of ten falus which you pay me.'

'Ten falus? That's a week's rent!'

'Take it or leave it, señor. That's the price and there is no bargaining here. We are not selling pots and pans in the market place.'

'I'll stay,' said Antonio, letting out in pretext a resigned sigh but inside burning with need.

'Ten falus then,' she said putting out her hand. Then she smiled. 'You will be well rewarded. I can assure you. Follow me.'

Antonio followed the woman further into the house to a stairway that took them to the second floor. The minimum of oil lamps lit their way, giving the impression of dark, delightful depravity. Antonio held the banister rail so as not to stumble on the carpeted treads. His expectation grew as did his excitement. 'I must control myself,' he thought. 'Otherwise this will be over before it starts.'

The landing shed little light as the woman lead him towards a door which she opened into an equally shady room. He could barely make out a double bed the headboard against the far wall. 'Go in and lay on the bed. Your woman will be here in minutes.'

'How do I communicate with her? I can't imagine she will speak Spanish.'

'She won't. Tell me what you want and I'll instruct her.'

'She should lie in the centre of the bed and I'll take her on top. I'll make myself ready but not before she arrives and undresses.'

'You want her naked then?'

'More or less!'

'Fine. No extra charge!'

Antonio lay on the bed and wondered what the *puta* would be like. Would she be a young woman or someone old enough to be his mother? Would she be plump, thin or nicely voluptuous and desirable? He must have laid there for ten minutes before the door opened and a woman appeared and stood in the doorway. In the vanishing light he could see only her silhouette. She wore a veil and a long, almost transparent dress. She greeted him with a friendly, Arabic hello and walked across to the bed. She then dropped her dress to the floor and climbed on to the bed and shuffled herself across next to him. He felt the warmth of her body and delighted in the smell of her extravagant perfume: rosewood, cedar and orange blossom. He felt her touch him, attempting to prepare him. She then murmured something incomprehensible which he took as an invitation to start. 'My God, this is good,' he thought to himself as he enjoyed her silkiness. It didn't last as long as he had hoped but the waves of satisfaction as it ended almost overcame him. He eased himself off her.

He couldn't help but thank her and did so several times. She then climbed off the bed and rang a small bell which he could hear but not see.

Seconds later the door opened and the madame whom he first met came in, carrying a lit candle before her. By then the *puta* had picked up her dress and, no longer veiled, covered the front of her body with it. As the madame approached, he could see the *puta's* face. He realised that he had seen the woman before this tender encounter. Was she a woman he had noticed in the market? Perhaps she was one of many to whom he had sold something in the shop. Was she one of the stallholders from whom he had bought a drink or some bread? He was certain he had seen her previously but couldn't place her.

He dressed himself and, escorted by the madame, descended the two flights of stairs back into the hall and out of the front door. She bid him a friendly farewell and invited him to return.

As he walked back to their house in the Derb Chtouka, it suddenly dawned on him. The obliging *puta* was Jabir al-Malaki's sister.

CHAPTER 25
A helping hand

'I don't believe you! His sister! A whore?' laughed Tariq. 'I did wonder where she went in the afternoons. Now we know! I wonder if we can turn this to our advantage, my friend. Did she recognise you?'

'I don't think she did. I saw her face by the light of a candle the madame was holding when she came to take me out. She was intent on covering herself and I don't think she saw mine.'

'I wonder if her brother knows what business she's in!'

'I don't know. But my bet is that he doesn't!'

'If not and it got out, that would bring shame on his whole family.'

'So we may be in an even more advantageous position over him. He thinks we don't know about the secret passageway into their house and he probably doesn't know his sister is a whore and certainly won't know that she's served one of us!'

'Not one of us! You!'

'I wonder if she has customers from the El Badi palace. She could be our way in!'

'You are a genius, Antonio. When do you want to have her again?'

'Maybe it's your turn!'

'I'm a married man and intend to stay faithful to Ishraq. She'll be faithful to me and expect to trust me. So she's your call, Antonio, my friend,' he said laughing.

'We need to think about how we handle this,' said Antonio. 'The whole thing could bite us if we don't get it right...and we shouldn't rely on her to get us into the palace.'

The two of them became firmly established merchants in Marrakesh. They dealt in quality goods; they did not price to make excessive profit so they became respected and trusted, just as they had hoped. They also built up a range of potentially useful contacts. The individual newly promoted to the post of Head of Security at the palace became one of their best customers. He spent a small fortune on carpeting and curtains for a house he had purchased near the Jaama el-Fna market. The sultan's Head of the Royal Bedchamber bought so much bedding for the rooms in one of the wings of the palace that they had to re-stock from their local supplier to meet her order. Eventually, the sultan's Head of the Palace Armoury discovered that they sold weapons and came in person to buy a range of pistols for the guards patrolling inside. Despite their contacts in the palace and the volume of sales they made to staff there, they were no nearer to entering the palace.

Then, one night, Antonio came up with a plan.

'Tariq, we've been here a year selling our goods to all and sundry and we're no nearer to getting into the palace than we were the minute we set up the shop. But I have been thinking. I haven't visited Jabir al-Malaki's sister at the whorehouse since I saw her for the second time. I'm sure she didn't recognise me then but, having seen her a few more times around here since, I'm absolutely certain it's her.

'I've been thinking about what you first mentioned. We make an attempt to get information from her about buying for the palace and who is responsible for it. This is how it would work. I go back and do business with her again. But this time, I tell her who I am and threaten to tell her brother about her working as a *puta*. It'll be a test of her reaction. I'll soon find out if he knows or not. If not, I'll blackmail her into revealing the goings on at the palace. What do you think?' By then, and with the indispensable help of Tariq, Antonio had all but mastered spoken Arabic so would have no difficulty communicating with the woman.

'Hmm. I'm not sure. If he does know, he might just throw us out of the house.'

'So what! We'd soon find somewhere else!'

'Really? With a built in warehouse like ours?'

'That is the risk. The reward could be huge. You can bet that many of her customers are officials or even family members at the palace. We haven't yet succeeded in getting in and she could be the key!'

'What's your name?' said Antonio as he lay there, having made love.

'Why should I tell you?' she asked, suddenly pulling her body away from him.

'Reasonable question isn't it? I just like to know the name of the lady I've just made love to! Otherwise it remains a purely mechanical act, meaning nothing but carnal satisfaction. It simply helps to personalise the joyful event,' he said, chuckling.

'No. I won't say. I simply refuse. You've no right to know.'

'I can sympathise with that. At least to some degree. But I know who you are.'

'What do you mean?'

'Just what I say. I know exactly who you are.'

She looked directly at him in the dim light of her room on the second floor. She was stunned into silence.

'I'll explain,' he said. 'When I first visited you, I saw you without that veil and immediately realised that you are the sister of our landlord, Jabir al-Malaki.'

'Don't tell him!' she shrieked. 'He'll kill me if he finds out. I'll do anything for you but please don't tell him.'

At that moment, there was a knock on the door. 'What's going on in there?'

'Come in!' said the *puta*. The madame entered, carrying her candle.

'Give me the candle,' said the *puta*. 'Let me look at you now. Yes, you are one of my neighbours, from Madrid, I think. It's a wonder we hadn't met at the Derb Chtouka.'

'What's going on?' said the madame. 'Why were you screaming out?'

'Just the surprise of recognising each other,' said the *puta*.

'Shall I escort him out?'

'No. I'll ring the bell when we are ready,' she said calmly, seeming to accept her predicament, at least to the extent of not wanting to worry the madame who left them in the dimness, taking her candle with her.

'What if I ask you for information in exchange for keeping my mouth shut? And perhaps the occasional paid liaison? Would you accept that as a deal?'

'Why do you want information? What do you want to know?' She ignored his reference to working with him again.

Antonio glowed inside at getting this far with the woman. He needed a little time to think about handling her questions. He and Tariq had not planned this far ahead. 'So are you going to tell me your name?'

'I still don't see why I should.'

'The reason is simple. I shall respect your wish and we will be speaking to each other quite often, if you are to help me with information. My name is Antonio. Antonio Hidalgo. It's a Spanish name.'

'My name is Fatima al-Malaki. You can call me Fatima.'

'Thank you. We are making progress already! Let me tell you this. I have no intention of hurting you. And I shall not take advantage of you and your profession. Quite the opposite, I'll treat you with the utmost respect. And, provided you keep to your side of our agreement, your brother need never know about your profession.'

'Fine, I'm relieved to hear that. You still haven't told me what you want.'

'You probably know that my friend Tariq and I run a shop near the palace. I want to know who your rich customers are, especially those who work at the palace, where they live and how to identify them. We don't want to rob them or hurt them. But we want them as our customers. So we are talking about sharing your clientele. We can send some of ours to you, if you wish!'

'Are you sure that is all you want?'

'What else could we want? We are a growing business. Not many months ago, we had nothing and we want to become bigger. Maybe to the extent of having a larger shop. Perhaps in the Jaama el-Fna.'

I'm not sure I follow you' said Fatima. 'You want to blackmail me, just for more customers in your store? It's like asking a ransom for a pot of coffee!'

'It's not as simple as it may seem. Making a strong business in this city means a great deal to us so we are prepared to take some risks, even though they may not all be financial. And we want to get to know some influential people who can help us promote our business. Would you like to start today, giving me the information I need?'

'No. I have another customer in ten minutes and need to start preparing myself,' she said.

'When can we meet again?'

'Tomorrow at noon. I will let you into another secret then. Something to our mutual advantage.'

'I'm impressed at the progress you made, my friend. This could be just what we wanted.' Tariq smiled.

'She talked about "another secret" she would let me into. I'm wondering what that could be about. She surely knows about the corridor into the upstairs wardrobe. I can see how we could use it to communicate with her.'

'We will have to be so careful now. You see, Antonio, we have put ourselves in the typical position of blackmailers: hated by the victim. She may have sounded friendly when you left but she could be enticing you into a trap. Just think. You've changed from being a willing, paying customer to being a threat to her freedom. If she could do away with you somehow, say by killing you, that threat would vanish. She may regard me as part of the threat so we are now both in danger. And that danger could be much more serious if she manages to work out our true motive and tells one of her customers who happens to be a high ranking military official what we are about. We need to think carefully about this and arm ourselves, if necessary.

'The key to this is what she means by "another secret".'

Antonio and Tariq thought hard before his noon encounter. They wondered if they could somehow turn his general request for information about her customers into something more specific about staff at the palace. Antonio arrived at the allotted time and duly paid the madame who escorted him back to Fatima's room, closed the door and left him there. He could see the outline of a female figure lying on the bed.

'Welcome back, Antonio, if I may call you by your first name.' He recognised her low pitched voice. Could she be holding a knife or something by which to strangle him? Killing him would solve one problem, albeit while creating another. While he had changed the relationship from a straightforward one between a *puta* and her customer to that of a blackmailer and his victim, he felt reasonably safe with her. Even so, he had no intention of touching her sexually, just in case any unpredictable and unprovoked violence punctuated their intimacy when he would be most vulnerable.

'How would you like to start?' she said. 'Shall I remove my clothes?'

'Can we delay the lovemaking? I'll give you a rest today! It's information I'm after. About your customers.'

'I'm telling you nothing!'

'What?'

'You heard. Nothing! I've told my brother everything and he forgives me. So does the rest of my family. So, if you don't want to make love, you may as well go. Shall I ring the bell?'

Antonio couldn't believe it. Surely, something he had said only the day before hadn't influenced her to take the kind of risk inherent in making such a revelation to her family. He knew that many young Muslim women had been murdered for less. If she had made such a confession, why had she returned to this place? Surely, not to keep the appointment with him. True forgiveness could only mean not coming back here to continue being a *puta*. If she had returned for some other reason, that could not imply being ready for him on this bed. She could only be lying.

'So, you'll have no objection to me speaking with your brother and mentioning your immediate past. I could even ask him straight, whether you had confessed to him,' he said, getting off the bed where he had been sitting while talking to her.

The woman Fatima started to sob. He put his arm around her shoulder. 'Get off. I don't want your comfort. All right. I lied! It was worth a try! What exactly do you want to know?'

'I want to know who the main buyers are at the palace, assuming some are your customers. Not only do I want to know who they are but I need to know when the next large procurement will take place and your help in getting us into the bidding. We don't care what the palace will be buying but we want to make a bid. I expect you to help,' he said, firmly but politely. He'd never before spoken so insistently to a woman, not even to Catalina before she deserted him.

'Impossible. I can give you one name but how do you expect me to find out what he is buying next?'

'You simply ask him. Then you recommend us as suppliers. It's easy! What's the name?'

'His name is Abdullah al-Nath. He usually visits on a Wednesday but he doesn't always ask for me.'

'You ask the madame if you can deal with him, the next time he calls.'

'What if she refuses?'

'Just say you like him and if you perform to his expectations, he may well recommend your brothel to other men at the palace.'

'All right then,' she said, 'I'll do that today.'

'You mentioned "another secret" you wanted to tell me about. What is it?'

She paused before replying. Then she shuffled around on the bed. At first, he thought she'd changed her mind. Then she spoke, quietly, as if she didn't want anyone else to hear but clearly and emphatically.

'I seem to have no choice but to see you again, at least until you have squeezed from me the information you want. I don't want to meet you here. There is a secret corridor in our house…' She went on to explain where it was and how to gain access to it.

'We already know about it. We discovered it by accident.'

'But there's a secret room at the end of it,' she said, surprised that they had found it.

'We know about that, too. The room with no windows,' he said coolly and without emotion.

'My God, you know about it all!' she said, almost in a state of shock. 'How did you find it?'

'It was surprisingly easy.'

'I'm amazed. But that doesn't affect what I'm going to suggest. If I have to see you, I'll meet you in that room. You don't object, do you?'

'Not at all,' chuckled Antonio. 'I might have suggested it myself! We only seem to meet in dark places so nothing will change! Let me explain something else to you.' Antonio told her about the fine twine that he and Tariq had attached to the bell which would ring in their kitchen if anyone came along the corridor.

'I'll come through and ring the bell if I have anything to tell you. My brother will suspect nothing because the room is off my bedroom. I dare not be more open and come to your front door. Someone would suspect something and I'd have difficulty in explaining it.'

Antonio and Tariq continued to labour in their shop, selling their goods to a variety of different people. Weeks went by with no news from Fatima al-Malaki. During that time they challenged each other about finding some other way of penetrating the palace but to no avail. They could see only layers of security protecting it. Their lack of progress was gnawing at them like the thirst they experienced in the desert. They discussed the possibility of Antonio returning to see the *puta*. They wondered if this Abdullah al-Nath she mentioned, Head of Procurement, had returned to the brothel and whether she had succeeded in persuading the madame that he should be her customer. Their doubts and general lack of progress pushed their thoughts towards being back home in Madrid. They might even have to consider abandoning the whole exercise. Then one night, while they were eating in the kitchen and feeling at their lowest, the little bell rang above them.

'It's her!' said an excited Antonio.

'Not so quick, my friend. Could be her brother.'

'I'll go and see.'

'Take a pistol. Mine is primed.'

With his heart pounding in his chest, Antonio climbed through the wardrobe and peered into the corridor. There was no one there but he could see light coming into it from the other end, through the open door into the al-Malakis' house. He stepped into the corridor and eased his way along. He stopped to think. If the woman Fatima had rung the bell, why hadn't she stayed in the corridor? He tapped the gun barrel on the door. A deep female voice spoke.

'Come in, Antonio. It's Fatima.'

He still felt unsure and hesitated for a moment. Then with the pistol pointing ahead of him rushed into the room and aimed it in turn towards every corner where someone could be hiding. She looked at him in bewilderment.

'What are you doing, Antonio?'

'Just checking that you are alone.'

'You don't think I'd trick you, do you?'

'No, but I had to be sure. You may have been forced here in some kind of trap. So I had to check!'

'I think I understand. I have some good news for you. Abdullah al-Nath saw me yesterday and told me about a piece of work that will be taking place at the palace. They are expecting some important visitors from Constantinople in two months' time and want to re-carpet and re-curtain five rooms there, a meeting room, a banquet room and three guest bedrooms. I told him all about you and your shop and its reputation in the city. So he is going to invite you to bid for the work. You will receive the papers next Monday!'

'That's good news, Fatima,' he said with a degree of coolness. 'You've done good work, assuming it all turns out well.' He hesitated to mention the possibility of her lying to him. She sounded genuine and pleased with herself.

'Does that mean my secret is safe with you?'

'Not just yet, but likely it will be,' he said, giving himself plenty of room for manoeuvre but granting her some relief at the same time.

'In which case, I feel nearly free again. Why don't we celebrate?'

'Celebrate?'

'Yes! Make love to me now! I won't charge you!'

Antonio would have loved to take up her offer but thought that if he were to lie half naked on her bed, he would feel vulnerable. He was still unsure whether she was trying to fool him. And he'd have to let go of his gun. So like a true professional he refused her offer.

'Thank you, Fatima. I'm grateful, but I must go back downstairs. There is a meal waiting for me.'

The following Monday came and went with no sign of an invitation from the palace. At least one of them had looked up when anyone came into the shop. Their usual policy was to leave their customers to wander around freely and approach one of them only when they wanted to ask a question or make a purchase. After closing the shop they looked at each other in dismay. Each of them felt cheated by the woman, Fatima. Tariq spoke first.

'I didn't think we could trust that hell damned woman!'

'It's early days,' said Antonio. 'Maybe they are just late with the invitation. Let's hope for the best.'

The following morning, while each of them was dealing with a different customer a man in a purple kaftan with a striking yellow turban came into the shop and shouted out.

'Is there a gentleman by the name of Tariq Alabdari or one called Antonio Hidalgo in this shop? Have I come to the right place?'

Antonio immediately excused himself from speaking to his lady customer.

'Yes, sir. I am Antonio Hidalgo.'

'Then I'm pleased to make your acquaintance. I am Abdullah al-Nath, Head of Procurement at the El Badi palace. Here is a tender document,' he said, handing Antonio a parchment scroll, tied with a bright blue ribbon and sealed with red wax which had been embossed with the sultan's coat of arms. 'If you wish to give us a quotation for the work described within, we must receive it at the main gate of the palace by nine o'clock in the morning of next Monday.'

Antonio and Tariq pored over the complex tender document well into the night. It described the work Abdullah al-Nath wanted in such detail that the two of them found it almost impossible to understand while it took the form of a twenty *pie* scroll. So they cut it up into lengths and pinned them to the kitchen table. The document provided carefully drawn diagrams and stated the dimensions of the seven rooms - no longer five - which required refurnishing. One was a meeting room, another an antechamber to the same room, one an adjacent library and four were bedrooms. It specified the type of carpet from the pile depth to the type of weave and colours in various pattern designs which were also provided. It specified the new curtains in equally minute detail, down to drawings of the pleats, the type of fabric and the pattern. The document even specified the order in which the rooms were to be furnished and the number of men required to carry out the work.

'We can't do this,' said Tariq.

'Why not?' said Antonio.

'We cannot satisfy their security requirements. See here,' he said, pointing to some words towards the end of the invitation to tender. 'It says, "The contract can be awarded only to an observer or observers of Islam."'

Antonio paused before he spoke. 'There must be a way around that. You're an observer of Islam aren't you?'

'No. I'm a true convert. You know that!' said Tariq, sternly.

'No such thing. You've just reconverted.'

'What! Go to a mosque five times a day? You are joking.'

'No. I'm serious. It says "awarded to an observer". You will be the observer, at least until we win the contract,' said Antonio, with a note of desperation in his voice. He could see this as a serious opportunity to penetrate the palace and one that may not readily be repeated.

'I'll find the mosque nearest to the shop,' said Tariq reluctantly.

They laboured night and day to complete the tender. Tariq's experience as a merchant proved invaluable. He recognised that they should not quote for any carpet, curtaining or fixtures that they could not supply within the stated timescale. This meant chasing potential supplies in the town and getting written quotations from them. They had one minor embarrassment when one of the potential suppliers turned out to be a bidder himself. It didn't take long for the man to realise that he might as well help the two Spaniards, in case he didn't get the job and they did so he would still sell some carpets.

They spent some time working out their pricing strategy. They had to win the bid, even if they made a substantial loss. They would surely be challenged by Abdullah al-Nath if he regarded their bid as unrealistically low. It meant little to them, however, as Silva would surely not criticise them for deliberately losing his money. He would regard gaining access to the palace as crucial and for which making a profit was irrelevant.

'If we were challenged by the palace, we could argue that we took a deliberate loss so we could advertise to our other customers that we are furnishers to the sultan. What better publicity is that?' said Antonio as, on the Sunday night, they were putting the finishing touches to their bid.

Antonio delivered it as Tariq attended morning prayers.

They fully expected to hear the result of the bidding process within two weeks, the usual amount of time to elapse before such decisions were announced. They heard nothing. Three weeks went by then another week and yet another. They were becoming impatient. The man who quoted them for some carpets and who had made a competing bid came to ask if they had heard only to learn that they hadn't heard either. So at least, as far as they could see, none of the bidders had been informed and they took some comfort in the fact.

Exactly five weeks and one day after Antonio had delivered their bid, that is, on the Tuesday, an official arrived at their shop with a letter from the palace. From the thickness of the envelope, it appeared to be a short, single page letter, much less substantial than the more detailed set of instructions that they could expect if they had won.

'Do you want to open it, or shall I?' said Tariq. 'It doesn't look like good news.'

'I'll open it, if you wish,' said Antonio, looking decidedly glum as he took it from Tariq. 'My God! It's not what you'd think! They want to meet us to ask some questions about our bid!'

'Give it back!' said Tariq, by then smiling from ear to ear. 'I must see it!'

'Extraordinary! So they want to see us at the palace tomorrow at noon. If you rough out a reply I'll take it there!'

They spent much of the day working out what questions the palace could have about their bid. Could it be about the pricing? Could it be about the availability of the carpets or curtains for which they were quoting? Could it be about the feasibility of the programme they had put together about completing the work? What about the staff they proposed to use? Did they want more detail about them?

'I think I know,' said Tariq, the ever resourceful spy. 'They want proof of who we are. Did I see some of the Alcázar notepaper in your room?'

'Yes. I brought some. I don't know why. I can't use it here.'

'Yes, we can. We are going to produce some forgeries tonight.'

'You mean you are! I can't write in Arabic!'

They produced two letters, one for each of them, which read:

To whom it may concern:
This is to certify that the holder of this letter is ....,

of ..... in the city of Madrid. He has been authorised by me to travel to the city of Marrakesh on business as a merchant in the sale of goods.
Signed,
Silva de Torres - Corregidor of Madrid,
this day, 27 November, 1607

'That should do the trick,' said Antonio. 'I'm just concerned that they look so fresh and new.'

'We'll put them in the sun for half an hour tomorrow morning.'

Feeling nervous and expectant, the two of them arrived at the palace main gates fifteen minutes early. A guard emerged from a tiny office to question them, through the metal pales of the pedestrian entrance.

'Do you have any form of identification?' Tariq took his forged letter from a scruffy envelope. The guard snatched it from his hand, glanced at it and gave it back.

'You got one?' he said, addressing Antonio. He waved his under the guard's nose.

'Head of Procurement's expecting you. My assistant here will take you.'

The guard opened the gate and let them in. They followed his assistant across a narrow courtyard, through an arch under a large ornate building then up to the top of a green and black tiled open staircase. They stopped as their eyes opened wide at the magnificent view of the palace's main courtyard below. They had never seen any structure as enchanting. The centre was adorned by two enormous identical, rectangular pools, some four to six *pies* deep and connected by a narrow walkway. Four huge sunken gardens, flanked the sides of each of the pools, which were set symmetrically between the gardens. Orange trees, planted in neat rows and columns decorated the gardens, along with flowers in reds, yellows, blues and white. Two turbaned workers were using large wooden beams to sweep what appeared to be leaves from the surface of the pool as about twenty gardeners were pruning the trees and picking selections of flowers. The whole area, some hundred or so *varas* square, was bathed in an air of peacefulness and serenity.

The guard's assistant opened the door into a long, brightly lit corridor. The sun poured in at head height through large, open windows. They walked through its beams as they kept a few paces behind the man.

He suddenly stopped in front of a yellow, heavily patterned door. He knocked.

'Come in,' was the welcoming call from within. All three entered. The assistant went up to Abdullah al-Nath who was sitting behind a desk in his elaborately tiled office and whispered something in his ear. Al Nath stood and went towards them. He was wearing a bright red kaftan and apparently the same yellow turban that he wore when they first met him. His feet were bare.

'It's good to see you again. Thank you for coming to see me,' said al-Nath, looking towards each in turn. Antonio looked surprised at this friendly greeting. He expected something sterner and questioning so wondered whether al-Nath was attempting to trick them in some way or hoping they might drop their guard. Tariq looked at al-Nath with equal suspicion which he amplified by his next words.

'Would you care for a coffee?'

Antonio and Tariq glanced at each other.

'We'd be delighted,' said Tariq, smiling. Al-Nath clicked his fingers and, moments later, a beautiful young girl, veiled and wearing a pink, loose fitting top and matching pantaloons tied just above her ankles, brought in a tray of steaming drinks, placed them on al-Nath's desk and promptly went. They each took a cup.

'That's better. I want you to be relaxed. I can understand a certain amount of anxiety but I am not here to trick you or confound you in any way. Each of us is a professional and I intend to treat you accordingly.'

'We would expect no less,' said Tariq, taking the lead. 'How may we help you?'

'First, I'd like to say what an excellent job you made of your tender reply. Without giving anything away, I can tell you it was by far the most detailed and comprehensive. There are just a few questions. I understand that you presented some identification documents at the gate this morning. May I see them please?'

They each handed him the forged letters. Tariq took his from its envelope but Antonio left his enclosed. Abdullah al-Nath walked back to his desk and sat in his chair. He took a magnifying glass from his desk, held it gently by its carved ivory handle and examined Tariq's letter. 'When did you write this?' he said.

'When did I write it?' said Tariq, raising his eyebrows. 'I didn't. A Moor on the staff of the Corregidor of Madrid wrote it, the week before we left. The Corregidor signed it.'

'I'm only playing with you,' said al-Nath. 'It's fine. The Arabic isn't quite right but its meaning is clear. I shan't even look at yours, Señor Hidalgo!'

Each breathed an inward sigh of relief and avoided looking at the other.

'Naturally, I have some other questions,' said al-Nath, gently placing his hands on the back of his yellow turban. 'Have you spoken to all these suppliers? How do you know they will deliver? And how can you be sure of the quality of their products?'

'Over to you, Antonio,' said Tariq.

'I did all of the negotiations,' said Antonio. 'They have given us strong assurances about quality and delivery and are willing to sign contracts with us that we've shown them in draft. Tariq wrote them all. My knowledge of written Arabic is somewhat limited.'

'You speak it well,' said al-Nath. 'Contracts are important. They are the documents of last resort. How have you chosen these people and do you have real confidence in them?'

'We chose them from our own suppliers so they are businesses we deal with regularly. We know from our experience with them that they deliver well on quality,' said Antonio, firmly and confidently.

'Hmm,' sighed al-Nath, in contemplation. 'Yes, I think I'm happy with that. So there are no suppliers you have not dealt with previously?'

'None,' said Antonio.

'As you know, I expect you to engage four men to complete the work. I don't want people contracted to work here I can't trust. Have you appointed your men?'

'Not yet,' said Tariq. 'But we don't see any problem in engaging some good people.'

'You will have to give their details to the Head of Security here so that he can establish their credentials.'

'I don't remember seeing that in the tender document,' said Antonio, making it sound like a routine point rather than a criticism.

'I have to admit, it was an omission on our part but I'm sure you will understand.'

'No problem,' said Tariq.

'I think you have answered all my questions,' said al-Nath, getting out of his chair and coming around the desk towards them. 'I can now inform you officially that you have been awarded the contract.'

Antonio and Tariq looked at each other with their eyes wide open. They were astonished that they had been told so peremptorily and so soon after they had met al-Nath.

'We are delighted,' said Tariq. 'And truly grateful.'

'I'll second that!' said Antonio.

'Normally, I would inform you by letter. But the work has become rather more urgent and I want you to start as soon as you can. We have some of Sultan Ahmed the First's officials from Constantinople visiting us in three weeks from tomorrow. We want the work completed by then.'

After a few more minor exchanges, al-Nath shook hands with them and they went.

'I still can't believe we won!' said Tariq, laughing all over his face, as they entered their house. 'Now we are really under pressure, my friend.'

'I can't either!' said Antonio, shaking hands with Tariq. 'We can congratulate each other. The contract has to take priority over sales at the shop! The key is to find the four workers, as soon as we can!'

Antonio looked after the shop while Tariq appointed the four. Each was a skilled craftsman in his own right while the fourth was prepared to act as the foreman and supervisor of the others. Tariq soon obtained their security clearances and all six, along with their contracted suppliers were ready to start working in the El Badi palace.

The day before they started, the two of them were enjoying a meal of lamb and rice while discussing their tactics, when they heard the familiar ringing of the tiny alarm bell. They each looked at the other in astonishment.

'Are you expecting a call?' said Tariq, looking wide eyed at Antonio.

'No such thing!' Antonio laughed at Tariq's ill-conceived joke.

'One of us better investigate and I vote it's you!'

'I'll go but not before I've primed my snaplock.'

Antonio went upstairs, pistol in hand and opened the wardrobe door. Then he lifted out the panel into the no longer secret passage. A subtle odour tickled his nostrils. He recognised the combination of delectable perfumes which Fatima al-Malaki wore on their first encounter in the dark bedroom at the *burdel*. Could she be there or was this some form of trick? He called out her name. No answer. He peered into the corridor. He could see light coming from the door into the al-Malaki's. He stepped in and walked along.

'Fatima, are you there?' he said, while standing by the opening.

'Yes, Antonio. Come in! I have something for you!'

He burst into the room wielding the pistol.

'Don't shoot! Don't shoot!'

'You are safe with me,' he said, coolly. 'I wanted to see if you had a welcoming committee. It's good to see you after so long. Why do you want to see me?'

'Abdullah al-Nath came to see me yesterday and told me that you had won the contract. Congratulations!'

'Surely, you didn't come up here solely to tell me that,' he said, suspecting more.

'No. I want to ask you something. I want you to release me from your blackmailing threat. You've got what you want and can have no reason to tell my brother, now that I've helped you so much in gaining the work at the palace,' she said. Her eyes were full of emotion. She knew her family could disown her or worse if they discovered that she worked as a *puta*.

'And what do you have for me?'

'If you agree, I will thrill you with the delights of my body. You can do anything you wish! As long as it doesn't hurt!' He could see her smiling in the candle light. This was only the second time he had seen her without a veil. She had the prettiest rounded face with large brown eyes and lustrous dark hair. He could feel her attraction like iron pulling a loadstone.

'I will release you, Fatima,' he said. 'I will never tell you brother and that is a promise. Allah strike me dead if I break it. But I'm a man of honour and I'm not saying that because you have offered to make love. You deserve it. We might never have won the contract had it not been for you. My only question is about helping us. My colleague Tariq and I may need help while we are here. I'm not sure how or when but if we get into trouble could you perhaps help us out?'

'You are so vague! How can you get into trouble? What are you thinking?' she laughed, as if not to take him seriously.

'We are Spaniards, not Moroccans and the relationship between Spain and the Moors is not good. We do feel vulnerable here. If suddenly we are the targets of some purge or persecution, we may need help. That is all I am asking, Fatima. No more or less,' he said, sounding as if he was genuinely fearful.

'I am not sure I'll be able to, Antonio, but I'll do my best to help, if necessary. Come nearer! Please make love to me,' she said, slipping her camisole over her head so that he could see the outline of her petite breasts in the candlelight. 'I don't want to stay here much longer because my brother is due home in about half an hour.'

'I shall make love to you now, Fatima, and I shall pay you. I haven't made love since our last encounter at the *burdel*. You have the prettiest breasts and your eyes are so attractive. I could love you all night.'

'Then do start. As I said, you can do anything you wish,' she said, removing her pantaloons while lying on the narrow single bed against the windowless room's wall. This woman seemed to thrive on playing the active role of a worldly *puta*, despite her appearance of religious compliance and respectability.

Antonio indulged himself in the pleasures of her body. After caressing her with his tongue and fondling her wetness, he readied himself to enter her.

'I am enjoying you,' he said, softly and remembering with pleasure some of his previous loves: Jac and her teasing; Catalina's almost painful attacks on his body; and the thrill of loving the ever resourceful Carolina. A few minutes more of ecstatic pleasure and he shuddered to a conclusion.

'Thank you!' he said, smiling joyfully.

'The pleasure is mine, Antonio. I enjoyed it, too. I am one of the few who can enjoy it. Many of my sisters have been cut and cannot. I cannot charge you after what we have discussed and agreed. But if you need me later, you may have to pay for other services!'

He couldn't understand why he did so, but he planted a spontaneous kiss on her cheek. He then picked up his snaplock, left her lying naked on the bed and returned via the wardrobe, replacing the loose panel behind him.

'Took your time!' said Tariq, as he stepped through the kitchen door.

'It was worth it!' said Antonio, grinning.

'Don't tell me. I thought I could hear a bed creaking!'

Antonio avoided responding to the implied question. 'Much more important. In return for removing the threat of blackmail, she agrees to help us if we land ourselves in trouble here.'

'Well done, Antonio. We might need something other than the safe house down the road!'

CHAPTER 26
At long last

'Watch out! Mind that ditch!' shouted the duke. The king's horse reared up and almost threw him in. The king shifted his weight in the saddle and eased off the reins and stirrups so the horse could recover its balance.

'Whoa there! Good girl! A missed ditch is worth a hundred *ducats*!' said the king. 'Thanks for the warning, Francisco. A lapse of concentration on my part!'

'Something on your mind, Majesty?' What with the royal guards, the Head Huntsman and his men and sundry others who had accepted the king's invitation, there were at least fifty other horse riders at the boar hunt in the Vela, a large open area a few *leguas* to the west of Madrid. So with all these others present, the duke could hardly speak to the king in more informal terms.

'You could say that,' said the king. 'Damn *Moriscos*. Still don't know what to do about the plague of them.'

There had to be a decision one way or another and the king had to make it, whether he liked it or not. Over the eight or nine years of his reign, the king had ordained many enquiries into the issue, only to be given as many different opinions. He had been solicited by many, most vociferously the Archbishop of Valencia, Juan de Ribera, and his fanatic adviser the Dominican friar, Jaime Bleda. They wanted the *Moriscos* expelled from Spain and sent to Morocco. The Archbishop had denounced them as 'pertinacious heretics and traitors to the Royal Crown'. Then, three months or so before this hunt, on 4 April, the Council of State, attended by The Duke of Lerma and other dignitaries including the powerful Juan Hurtado de Mendoza, the 6th Duke of Infantado, and the Count of Alba de Liste, made a crucial but unanimous recommendation to the king. It was that they, too, were in favour of expulsion. The *Moriscos* of Valencia should be the first and that they should go that autumn.

'Everybody wants an answer,' said the duke, looking across to the king who by then had resettled himself in the saddle and was riding at the front of his entourage back to the palace. The Head Huntsman and his assistants had strung a dead but still warm boar on a stake suspended between two of his men's horses.

'You just have to remind me, Francisco.' He emphasised the 'have to'. 'No sooner than the hunt has finished and I'm still elated at the catch! I feel I should completely ignore you!'

'Whatever you wish, Majesty. But it won't go away on its own!'

'All right. We'll get rid of them. I've decided. Here and now!'

'You can't decide just like that, sitting on horseback on the way back from the hunt!'

'I just have! You can like it or not!'

'I'll call secretary de Prada when we get back and we can formalise it then. All right?'

'Do that,' said the king, in a half-hearted attempt to assert his authority.

The duke could not believe that the king had made this momentous decision. He had pestered the king so many times since that April meeting of the Council of State. He'd set up meetings specifically to extract a decision from him. He'd entertained him lavishly at his own expense and asked him while he was semi-inebriated. He'd taken him to drinking sessions and music pageants. Still he couldn't make him decide. But there, just after almost falling into a mud filled, stinking ditch, and sitting astride his favourite hunter, he'd resolved it. Lerma dashed into the king's outer office. Andrés de Prada sat at his desk, looking half asleep.

'Wake up, fool! Go and get the Duke of Infantado. We are meeting the king in five minutes. He's in there,' he said, pointing to the door of the inner office.

'What's it about?'

'You'll find out soon enough. Get Infantado!'

Lerma, the Duke of Infantado and de Prada sat in an awkward arc around the king's desk, De Prada about a *pie* further away than the other two, in recognition of his inferior status.

'Where do you want me to start?' said the king, looking to Lerma for guidance.

'With your decision, Majesty. Everything follows from that.'

'What decision?' said the king, looking puzzled.

'You know! About the *Moriscos*!' bellowed Lerma. Then, 'Sorry, Majesty. I didn't mean to shout.'

'Blood of Christ. Yes. I made a decision, didn't I?'

'Would you like to enlighten us, Your Majesty?' said the Duke of Infantado, indifferently.

'I've decided that they should be expelled from Spain, starting with the ones in Valencia. That's what the Council of State recommended in April and I agree with the Council. They were unanimous. And anyway Margaret wants it.' The other three glanced at each other in glum astonishment at this mention of the queen.

'So we must at least outline a plan, now, don't you think, Majesty?' said the Duke of Lerma.

'Yes, we must agree something as soon as possible. The Council want to implement the decision in the autumn and that's not far off now,' said the king, as emphatic as he had been for months.

'We first need answers to some fundamental questions,' said the Duke of Infantado. Up to then, he had been ambivalent about expulsion but had suddenly adopted a more positive view, probably influenced by the fact of the king's decision. 'How many are there in Valencia and what about the rest of them in Castille, Aragon and elsewhere?'

'I've spoken to Ribera about this,' said de Prada. 'About a hundred and fifty thousand in Valencia and about the same in the rest of the kingdom, give or take.'

'Is our fleet big enough to transport them?' asked the king.

'Probably not. We'll need help from the merchant ships,' said Lerma.

'We need to fill some posts, make some appointments, urgently. There's a huge amount to do before we take the first shipment to Morocco,' said the Duke of Infantado.

'How about Pedro de Toledo? He's already in command of the Mediterranean fleet. He'd be ideal,' said Lerma.

'I'm not so sure,' said de Prada. 'I spoke to him a while ago. He's dead against expulsion. He thinks they should stay here. They've been born and bred here and given sensible orders and more opportunity to adopt Christianity. That's those who haven't converted when we all know that many have.'

'Do we care what he thinks?' said Lerma. 'He's paid to lead the navy, not to have opinions. Especially, if they don't accord with ours.' They all chuckled, even the king.

'He's in charge of the transportation by sea then,' said the king.

'And General Agustín Mejía in charge of the military?' said the Duke of Infantado.

'Excellent choice. He's got more forces under his command than any other general. Many more than Spínola...who'll be as envious as the devil!' said the king, smiling mischievously.

'Are we going to make more progress today?' said de Prada.

'No,' said the king. 'And I don't want anything about this to leak out. Francisco, you speak to de Toledo and Mejía but in total confidence. Don't forget, we've still not heard from Diaspora or Lusitano about the Moroccan's intentions. I don't want anything made public until we know whether our fears about them attacking us by sea are well founded or not. We may yet end up enlarging our fleet. But God only knows how we would pay for it! In the meantime, go and work out the details but keep me informed.'

Just occasionally, and this was such an occasion, the king would pull the issues together and impress with a point that no one else had thought of. They seriously needed to know what their intrepid spies had discovered.

CHAPTER 27
The palace

Antonio and Tariq had signed up their suppliers to deliver direct. Their newly engaged workers were ready to start. Either Antonio or Tariq would go to the palace and oversee the work. They would ensure that the Head of Procurement's specification was met. This meant checking that each carpet and each curtain was installed in its exact, designated location. They decided to do none of the physical work themselves. They would spend any time they had spare in familiarising themselves with the layout of the palace and various possible escape routes they may have to use, should their true intensions be discovered.

'I feel quite nervous,' said Antonio as they left the house in the Derb Chtouka and made their way to the El Badi. They had agreed to be there at 9 o'clock to meet their installation team and the suppliers of some of the carpets.

'Oddly, so do I, my friend. And I think I know why!'

'Yes, it's the importance of what we are doing. The future of Spain could well depend on the success of our mission and we still don't know whether or how we will find the information we want!'

As they approached the main gate, a group of seven men were waiting for them in the shade of the palace walls. A bulky, clean shaven individual, in a light brown, tightly wound turban and a kaftan in a much darker brown, came towards them.

'This is Murat,' said Tariq. 'He is the supervisor of the other three and will do much of the work himself. This is Antonio Hidalgo, my partner at the shop.'

'I'm delighted to meet you,' said Antonio as he and Murat shook hands. 'I've heard only good things about you and I'm sure we'll get on well.'

'Allow me to introduce my workers,' said Murat, turning towards three men who were standing expectantly together. One could hardly be called a man. He was a fresh faced lad of about fifteen with short, cropped hair and wearing a white shirt and light blue breeches.

'This young man is Ali. He will do the fetching and carrying. This is Hassan,' he said, turning towards a plump, tall individual who nodded towards them. 'And this is Mallik. He is a mute but is a tremendous worker. He can hear and understand you but won't reply.'

Mallik who was tall, thin and wearing a beard down to his waist smiled and bowed to each of them in turn.

The other three men gathered there were their suppliers. They were standing guard over hand carts loaded with glowing new fabrics and colourful, new carpeting. Tariq went up to them and spoke. The three followed him, dragging their laden carts towards the security guard at the palace entrance. The same characterless guard who met Tariq and Antonio at their earlier visit to Abdullah al-Nath, came out of his small hut.

'I think we're expecting you. I need to see your identification.'

Each of the men proffered a document, Antonio and Tariq their well creased forgeries.

'You'll need one of these.' The guard then gave each of them a wooden, numbered disc. 'Don't lose it. You must hand it in before you leave.'

Antonio looked at Tariq and Tariq looked at him. They each looked mildly surprised. The palace had not revealed this security measure to them before. It had to be some means of ensuring that the guards could check whether all who had entered the palace had left after transacting their business. They realised that this could create a problem for them but imagined there had to be some means to break it.

One of the guard's assistants led the group, with Tariq and Antonio at its head, into the palace. They walked into the building through the main door, across the courtyard and through the arch they had passed through before. The magnificence of the palace still amazed them. The polished marble, the delicately carved cornices, the tiled mosaics and the paintings of battle scenes on the walls drew their startled eyes in wonderment. The assistant led them out into the main courtyard along what Antonio worked out from the position of the sun must have been the northern wing.

'Have you been here before,' said the assistant.

'Only once, to see Señor Abdullah al-Nath, on an upper floor,' said Tariq.

'What do you think of our palace?'

'It's beautiful,' said Antonio. 'It must have cost a fortune to build; and an age, judging from the intricate tiling and detail.'

'It did, on both counts! It was started in '78 by the illustrious Moulay Ahmed al-Mansour, the current sultan's father, and finished in '94. It cost a fortune and we treasure it and always will!'

As they made their way to the bedroom suite, busy, turbaned palace officials, all men, passed by or walked towards them, staring at them curiously as they did so. The palace hummed with important state activity. They must have passed ten to a dozen beautifully carved, lofty doors, most of which were closed, before the assistant stopped and looked behind him. The whole group were following, the three suppliers still pulling their loaded hand carts as if they were tethered to them like oxen. Some of the group made slower progress such that Tariq and Antonio were well in front and Murat and his team were thirty or so *pies* behind.

'I understand you start with a suite of four guest bedrooms. They're in here,' he said, unlocking another ornate door. 'I leave you at this point. Don't forget to hand your wooden token in when you leave. If we don't get all the ones we've handed out, we do an armed search.' How different was the tone he used then from that he used to talk about the palace.

Antonio and Tariq led the team in. The rooms had each been recently redecorated. They resonated in a range of reds, yellows and gold. They could smell the drying oils of the paint but the floors had been abandoned in a state of filth and were scattered with rubbish.

'What a God forsaken mess,' said Antonio. 'We can't do a thing without clearing this lot.'

'Don't worry,' said Murat. 'Leave it to us. My team will soon clear up and I'm sure your suppliers won't mind us using their carts to take away the rubbish and dump it. It'll probably take most of the day, by the time we've cleaned the floors to make them fit for laying carpets. Why don't you two leave us to get on with it and come back tomorrow?'

Tariq and Antonio took the hint and left their team in the visitors' suite. They handed in their tokens and returned to their shop.

'We'll have to make sure the work runs late,' said Antonio. They'd closed the shop and were sitting in the back office by then drinking tea.

'I agree and for the same reason as you, I imagine,' said Tariq. 'We need to have access to the palace while the sultan's officials are meeting those of Ahmed the First.'

'Exactly!' said Antonio, 'but have you thought of a way around those wooden discs. There must be one.'

'I suppose you mean, if we stay the night in there, we need somehow to return our discs without handing them in!'

'I think I've solved that one,' said Antonio. 'The guards pick up the discs from a pile. They ignore the number, as far as I can see. So, when they hand each of us a disc, one of us causes a distraction, hands his disc to the other of us who replaces the two discs in the pile.

'What I haven't cracked is how we can get the two discs we need to get out, after we've spent the night in there.'

'Easy, my friend. There are two ways around that one. We could simply forge a couple of discs. We buy a saw, a piece of timber, the thickness of the discs, cut out some discs and scratch some numbers on them. We then make them look worn. If we do a good job, no one will tell the difference. In fact, we could hand in some forgeries on a day we come out and keep the originals for the night we want to stay!'

'I like that idea! But what do you think about this one. We all go in, as usual, and take our tokens. While we are in, we steal the tokens of two of the men, say Mallik's and Ali's. When they leave, they explain to the guards that somehow they've lost their tokens. The guards may be angry with them but they are sure to let them out. And they'll let them in again the next day, probably with a warning to take better care of their tokens!'

'How do we steal them, my friend?'

'I noticed today that they put them in their tool bags. We take them from there! We could make forgeries, just in case. And we don't need to steal both tokens on the same day!'

The following day, the carpet laying began. Antonio and Tariq saw no point in putting up the curtains before all the carpets had been accurately positioned in their respective bedrooms. The team worked hard to ensure that the carpets were exactly where they were designed to be. Hanging the curtains consumed the most time. While all had been made to fit the widows, some had been too tightly or unevenly gathered, or stitched with short hems and this meant making a degree of adjustment. It took the team four days to complete the bedrooms which left a week and a day to furnish the meeting room, its anteroom and the library.

'At this rate we'll definitely finish early,' said Tariq. 'We'll have to create a delay. The meeting with the Ottoman officials is in nine days' time, on the Wednesday after we're supposed to finish on the Monday. Any ideas?'

'Yes but it would mean losing money. We aren't going to be in profit anyway.'

'Go on!'

'We damage a carpet or a curtain, while putting it in place. Probably a curtain. If we stained or somehow tore a carpet, we'd have to have it re-woven. But I imagine it would be much easier to make a new curtain.'

'You must be right, my friend,' said Tariq, looking serious.

On the day their team began working on the bedrooms, the voluble guard's assistant escorted Antonio and Tariq to the other rooms. He took them from the guest bedrooms past one of the sunken gardens and one of the four smaller pools in the corners of the main courtyard, in which a number of semi-naked women were relaxing. They wondered where the longest curtains were to be hung. Now they could see. These twenty four *pie* drapes would be hung at the arched windows to the sides of the Audience Pavilion, the main room of which, just inside a huge entrance portico, was the meeting room. Its grandeur struck them like an exploding Chinese firecracker.

'I've never seen a room decorated like this,' said Antonio. 'It's magnificent!' The floors and walls were tiled in a patterned mosaic which showed water falls in leafy, wooded valleys. Gold leaf covered the stone columns which supported the ceiling and rooms above. The ceiling had been painted in patterns that, according to the assistant, represented the sultan's flag and coat of arms as well as pictures of crucial events and sayings from the Quran.

'God, this must have cost a king's fortune!' said Tariq.

'Yes, a sultan's actually, even more than we spent on his harem in the Khayzuran Pavilion, named after Sultan al-Mansour's favourite wife.'

The meeting room was all of forty *pies* square. The only sources of light were the main entrance portico with its door into the room and the two arched windows, one in each of the side walls. The guard then showed them the antechamber and the library, which contained hundreds of volumes, arranged on carved and gilded shelves. The tender invitation documents could not possibly have prepared them for the grandeur and beauty of these rooms.

As soon as the bedrooms were complete and in exact accordance with the tender, the team proceeded to start on the rooms in the Audience Pavilion, starting in the meeting room. The work went well and Murat proudly announced, after only eight days, that the work in these last three rooms was ready for final inspection. By then it was getting towards evening and Tariq and Antonio each needed a candle to check the installation.

Everything looked just perfect and Tariq wondered what they could do to delay the completion when Antonio shouted across the meeting room.

'Help! I've set a curtain alight in the ante-room!'

'You damned idiot!' shouted Tariq as if he meant it, while he and Murat dashed in to see flames rising up the side of the curtain just inside the door. 'Start beating it out!'

Murat grabbed a spare piece of fabric and used it to dampen the flames which by then were almost licking the rail at the top of the curtain. Antonio and Tariq joined in while sparks flew across the room as they succeeded in putting out this minor but crucial conflagration.

'What the hell did you do?' said Murat. 'We've only just hung that one?'

'There was a thread hanging down on that side and I was using my candle to singe it off. The next thing was the whole thing was going up in flames. I'm sorry,' said Antonio, sounding sincere.

'We have no choice but to get the supplier to make another curtain, at our expense, and re-hang it,' said Tariq.

'What do we do about the smell of smoke?' said Murat, glaring at Antonio.

'Open the window. There isn't much and it will soon blow away,' said Tariq. 'I think we should tell Al-Nath.'

No sooner had he uttered the name and the man himself appeared at the door.

'What's going on?' he said, frowning and raising his arms in the air.

'Everything is under control. We've had a minor accident, trimming off some oddments of thread and we've managed to singe one of the curtains,' said Tariq, doing his utmost to play the incident down. 'All it means is that we'll have to replace the curtain on this side with a matching one. Not a problem.'

'But I wanted you out by the end of Tuesday at the latest. I told you about a crucial meeting we have here on Wednesday,' he said, reddening with anger.

'Please don't worry,' said Antonio. 'Our suppliers will make another curtain which we will install tomorrow. Then we will be clear by tomorrow night.'

'In which case, I want only you two to bring in the curtain. There are serious issues about the security of the meeting with the officials from

Constantinople so the fewer there are of you the better.' Al-Nath pointed directly at Antonio and Tariq.

'Consider it done,' said Tariq. 'You need not concern yourself. We'll go to the supplier first thing in the morning and get him to make up an identical curtain. We'll be here by midday with any sort of luck.'

Al-Nath walked off, fuming like an over-excited dragon and left the three of them looking at each other.

'Oh dear!' said Murat. 'I suppose we deserved that!'

'No, Murat, I did. I caused the problem not you. I take the full blame. I'm only too sorry that you won't be needed to refit the curtain.'

'It won't be a problem. All you do is to hang it, hook by hook on the new rail. You'll find it very easy.'

'There's nothing more we can do now. Let's go,' said Antonio.

Their suppliers had already left the palace by the time Murat and his team and Antonio and Tariq emerged onto the road outside, having given in their security tokens. Antonio and Tariq bid the team farewell, promised to pay them as soon as their payment for the work came through and started to walk back to the house in the Derb Chtouka. Each realised the seriousness of their situation and that, come what may, at least one of them had to be in the room when the meeting between the officials from Constantinople and those of the palace took place.

'How will we manage this?' said Tariq.

'Simple but risky.' Antonio explained his plan in detail to Tariq. 'At least we've now got two security tokens!'

'I never heard a word about them, either from Mallik or Ali! Did you?' chuckled Tariq.

'Not a word!'

They spent much of the following day in negotiation with the curtain supplier He realised the pressure they were under to replace it. So he charged them as much as he dare for the new one and wouldn't part with it without full payment in cash. His assistant made the curtain while Tariq returned to the Derb Chtouka for the money. By the time they had paid for the curtain and returned with it to the palace, it was well into the afternoon.

They went straight to the faceless security guard on the gate who let them in and handed each a wooden security disc. Tariq feigned a trip on a step and pretended to fall on his face. 'What's going on?' said the guard.

'Clumsy me! I fell over on that step. I think I've twisted my ankle.'

'Let me give you a hand,' said Antonio, easing the wooden disc from Tariq's hand and, along with his own disc, placing it back in the untidy heap on the security officer's desk.

'That's better,' said Tariq, by then on his feet. 'I think I'm all right now.'

'Do you know where you've got to go?' asked the guard.

'Yes, to the main meeting room on the ground floor. The one we've been re-furbishing. We have to replace a damaged curtain.'

'I heard about your little fire,' laughed the guard. 'Just a second and I'll get you an escort.'

The escort unlocked the room, let them in and left them there. They soon replaced the curtain. 'Now what?' said Tariq.

'We stay here until the meeting.'

'We'll have to hide somewhere. What if Al-Nath appears to check the installation?'

'He'll only want to look at the new one we've just put up. Let's go and hide.'

The two of them sneaked into the library. 'How about under there,' said Tariq. They eased themselves under a table between two long rows of heavily loaded book shelves and let the tablecloth back down. It reached almost to the floor so made it difficult for anyone to see them.

'I feel like a child playing a game!' said Antonio.

'Have you any other ideas for getting in tomorrow? We are going to be here all night otherwise.'

'I wonder if we could come back and say we wanted to check the curtain we had to replace.'

'Too risky, my friend. We could but only if Al-Nath had given his authority. If we asked him if we could return tomorrow, he'd wonder why we couldn't carry out our tests today. No. We're going to have to sit it out tonight and take up our positions in the meeting room early in the morning.'

Twenty minutes later, while they were discussing the finer points of their plan, they looked at each other as a door closed in the adjacent ante-room. Then they heard voices, at least four of them, maybe more. They froze under the table. They couldn't make out what the voices were saying but it sounded to Tariq as if they were talking about flowers, arranging them or storing them. They heard the door through to the library open and footsteps coming towards them. Then loud voices. They feared the worst. Next they heard the sound of heavy objects being placed on the table above them. A man spoke.

'Put the rest over there.'

They recognised the voice as Abdullah al-Nath's. He was instructing some of his staff or others. He spoke again.

'I want you here tomorrow morning at 8.30, to place them on the main table in the meeting room. And put two on the small table where the sultan will deliver his address.'

A number of flunkies acknowledged his instruction. Then all four or five went from the library into the ante-room, closing the door behind them. Seconds later and after the sounds of footsteps had died out, the door, presumably to the main meeting room, closed. Then an awkward silence.

Antonio went to speak. Tariq placed a hand over Antonio's mouth to stop him. They said nothing for a quarter of an hour or so.

'It's safe now,' said Tariq. 'We were so lucky. Lucky not to be spotted and lucky to learn about what's happening in the morning.'

'So we have to be in our positions by shortly after 8 o'clock. How do we do that when we won't know the time?'

'By the call of the Imam!' said Tariq, pleased that he had thought of the answer before Antonio.

'Of course! Now you are a Muslim, you were sure to think of that!'

'At the 8 o'clock call for prayer, we leave here for the meeting room. That's when the excitement starts.'

'Dare we sleep?'

'Not both at the same time. You have a sleep first, Antonio. When you wake, I'll sleep. But only until 8 o'clock!'

Neither slept soundly but rest they did. They were prepared, they thought for any contingency. Each carried his snaplock pistol, tucked inside a bag, Antonio's with the contract and Tariq's with the tender invitation.

'Time to get moving,' said Tariq, waking Antonio who by then had spread himself from under the table to the surrounding floor of the library. Each could smell the flowers El-Nath had left there.

They each stood up and brushed their clothes down in a natural reaction to sleeping, if only spasmodically. They crept towards the library door. Antonio opened it gingerly. At least they hadn't been locked in.

There was no one in sight. They crossed the floor of the antechamber and stood by the door to the meeting room.

'What do you think?' whispered Antonio.

'Open it!'

They sneaked in. It looked as ready as it could be for the crucial meeting to take place, except for the placing of the flower vases.

'Where do we hide?' asked Tariq.

'Behind the curtains to the window by the library.'

'Why that one?'

'Easy means of escape. We can climb through the window and into the courtyard if necessary. And this side is nearer the palace main exit!'

'Good. You are becoming a useful spy, my friend!'

The tall, arched window was wide enough to allow the two of them to sit behind the open drapes, one each side. They took up their positions. They were confident that they could not be seen from inside the room. But they'd put themselves in a dangerously precarious position and knew it. If anyone as much as moved a curtain they'd be seen, if not caught.

'Are you all right over there,' said Tariq, just loudly enough for Antonio to hear.

'Fine,' he replied. 'We wait here now and just listen to what happens.'

Nothing happened for what seemed an age. It must have been at least an hour before the meeting room door banged open against its hinges. Then an urgent voice shouted an instruction: 'Quick. Get the flowers. They'll all be here in a matter of minutes. Then put the water jugs and cups on the tables, one at each position.'

It was the familiar voice of Al-Nath, now so excited that he could explode at the least provocation. They heard the scuffling of busy feet as his assistants brought in the water and flowers and noisily placed them on the meeting tables.

'Don't forget to put one on this table, the one the sultan will be seated at,' instructed Al-Nath. Then something the two men dreaded. 'I must check the curtains.' This could be the end of what the two had spent the previous six months and more building up. He worked his way around the room as Tariq and Antonio, without as much as whispering to each other, slid up the wall from their seated position and eased themselves as closely as they could to the wall. They heard Al-Nath walk around and inspect the curtains. He smoothed some down, presumably to even them and to see that they hung to their best advantage. Some he pulled back to ensure the maximum amount of light came in. He eventually reached the alcove in which the two of them were hiding. He was just about to open them wider when a person close to him spoke.

'Look what we found in the library,' the male voice said.

Al-Nath looked around. 'What is it?'

'It looks like a plan of these three rooms'

'Where did you find it?'

'Under the table in the library… where we placed the flowers last night. It wasn't there then.'

'How do you know? Did you look?'

'No but I'm sure it wasn't there.'

'Don't worry. We had contractors in here yesterday finishing off their work. I expect one of them dropped it. There's nothing we can do about it now. In one minute the sultan will be here and the officials for the meeting.'

Then the sound of footsteps as Al-Nath and his assistants left the room and closed the door behind them. Both Antonio and Tariq breathed again. Like true professionals, neither said a word, realising that they might not be alone, despite the silence.

About five minutes later, they heard the door open again and a large number of people come in from the main courtyard, about thirty they imagined and if the number of vacant chairs they had seen was any indication.

A different voice rang out. 'Gentlemen, please stand behind your chairs. You will see your place name on the table. The esteemed officials of sultan Ahmed the First will sit to the left of the main portico and ours will sit facing them.'

The two of them could hear the sound of people moving quickly around the room. That soon subsided and gave way to excited chatter between those standing next to each other. No one came near the curtains.

The main door opened again and the voice that gave the previous announcement spoke once more. 'Pray silence for Sultan Zidan al-Nasir.'

The sultan entered to a polite, if somewhat subdued, round of applause.

The announcer's voice again: 'Please be seated while the sultan makes his address.' The sultan then spoke. Antonio and Tariq nervously remained standing.

'Gentlemen, it is a great honour for us to be blessed by the presence here of a delegation from the government of the great Ahmed the First, supreme master of the Ottoman Empire.' Ahmed I was a young man of hardly fifteen years of age but Zidan al-Nasir avoided mention of his youthfulness. 'I would like to extend to you the warmest possible welcome. I wish you and my officials a highly successful meeting. I hope as a result we shall be trading with your country even more in the future and both our countries will benefit. Good day. May Allah be with you.'

A more enthusiastic round of applause filled the room. The door closed as the sultan left.

The meeting began. First, the leaders of each delegation introduced their members to those on the opposite side of the table. They named their colleagues and explained their functions. Each side contained a Treasury representative, an official from the Department of War, three from the Department of International Trade, and, much to the silent delight of Antonio and Tariq, one from the Department of Shipping.

The opposing treasury officials set about each other with unprovoked aggression. Neither seemed likeable characters. They waded into an argument about currency exchange rates. Each wanted to minimise the value of the other's money and neither wanted to acquiesce in front of his colleagues. The bad tempered argument raged on and threatened the success of the meeting. The destructive tone of their exchanges prompted the most senior official from Constantinople to intervene.

'That's not the way to conduct important business. This meeting is supposed to be conducted in a civilised way and I won't have you,' he emphasised, probably pointing to his disruptive colleague, 'taking that bullying stance.'

'I entirely agree,' yelled the leader of the Moroccan delegation. 'My man is equally to blame. Please continue but give each other proper professional respect.'

The tone changed. The two aggressors started to behave like old friends and eventually settled on a rate of exchange which each of the leaders approved. Then they discussed how any excess in cost balances should be handled and whether each country should have banking facilities in the other. These financial considerations took an hour to conclude.

The agenda then turned to the drawing up of a peace accord between the two countries and formalising the relations between them. The meeting agreed that a small committee would draft a treaty after this meeting and that it would be based on the Moroccan treaty with France.

341

Antonio and Tariq, standing silently, found the discussion tedious and unnecessarily prolonged. They had negligible interest in what had been discussed, at least up to that point, and felt tired after almost a night's absence of sleep. The discussion took a welcomed turn.

'We wondered whether Sultan Zidan al-Nasir wanted us to build him any warships?' said the man from the Ottoman Shipping Department. 'Now that your relations with Spain are so poor. To defend yourselves against the aggressor?'

'Really,' laughed the Moroccan counterpart. 'You have taken me by surprise. Our relations with Spain are... well... not bad. No not bad at all. They have some problems with the *Moriscos*, our erstwhile brothers, but they are internal problems and do not threaten our relations with Spain. Indeed we trade with them quite freely in a range of products from olive oil to carpets, even to textiles and raw cotton. So we have no need for warships, certainly no more than those in our current fleet.'

While they could not see each other's reaction, each was surprised. The tone of the discussion with Silva before they left seemed to predict imminent danger, such as almost to demand the renewed construction of Spanish warships. Still, this is what the meeting had delivered and was all they could report back. It felt like an anti-climax considering what they had invested in getting to this point. They were both elated that they now possessed this information. They had come to Morocco for no other reason than to find it. They waited patiently off-stage for the meeting's conclusion, the emptying of the room and their exit using the tokens they had stolen from Ali and Mallik.

Having dealt quite peremptorily with the question of building warships the discussion turned to more prosaic items of trade: food, especially wheat, maize and barley, and meat, mainly beef and lamb but also chicken, citrus fruit: oranges, tangerines and lemons; and other food such as cheeses of various kinds, almond nuts and dates, and melons of which Morocco had large excesses. About their natural resources of ores: iron ore, copper, tin and zinc; then gemstones, silver and gold, brooches, rings and pendants.

The conversation turned to fine fabrics such as carpets and curtaining. The Moroccan delegate talked exaggeratedly about the quality of their carpets. He stood up and waved his hand towards the floor.

'You can see what I mean here. Look! Get up and stand on it. Take off your shoes. Let your toes feel the quality of the pile! And look at those beautiful colours. We have the finest and rarest dyes!'

Then they could hear the official moving across the room, still talking.

'And look at this curtaining.' He was so close that Antonio could hear him breathing. 'My God!' shouted the man as he lifted the curtain to display it. 'There's a man here! Spying on us!'

A shot rang out. The man fell to the floor screaming and grabbing his bleeding leg. Tariq stood in front of the open curtain, holding a smoking pistol. The meeting degenerated into chaos. Men dived under the table. A courageous few came to aid the injured man. Others just stood there and shouted. The two of them dashed towards the main door. Antonio opened it and they ran.

CHAPTER 28
Shots in the palace

They were in trouble. The courtyard was so open. Several officials were going hither and thither within it.

'I'll cover you as you reload,' said Antonio. That took Tariq about ten seconds. It seemed an age. Then several men emerged from the main entrance to the Audience Pavilion. One of them, the sultan's treasury official, shouted out. 'Stop them! Stop them! They are spies!'

No one reacted. The two of them ran as fast as they could along the side of the huge rectangular pool.

'We're running on the wrong side! We should be over there,' shouted Tariq, pointing.

'We'll cross the pool halfway, along the narrow path.'

By then others from the meeting were chasing them and shouting.

'No don't go across there. A couple from Pavilion have gone that way and will catch us.'

They kept running along the pool edge to its end and turned towards the main entrance. The two men running after them had all but caught them. Tariq turned and aimed his gun at them. They froze to the spot and held up their arms. 'Don't shoot! Don't shoot!'

The two of them kept running until they reached the arch which led to the main entrance. A single guard stood on duty. He was wiping sweat from his brow as the two slowed down to approach him.

'Where you going in such a hurry?' The guard said. Then he realised. 'You came in yesterday and you must have stayed in. You're under arrest.'

By then other men, some from the meeting and other officials appeared only *pies* away. 'Get out of our way!' shouted Antonio, pointing his gun at the guard's head. Tariq smacked the guard in the face with the side of his gun. He fell. The two of them jumped over him and they were out.

They ran down the road into the Plaza de Mellah, wielding their guns above their heads. Shots rang out behind them as palace guards fired into the air. People in the square stopped in their tracks. A woman holding a large vessel of water on her head lost her balance and dropped it onto the stone paving. Its contents soaked her clothing and splashed onto others passing by. A horse reared up at the commotion and tipped out the contents of its cart. Apples, melons, lemon and oranges scattered across the square. Unable to resist the temptation, and despite their latent fear, small children rushed to the fruit, grabbed a few of what they liked the most and returned to take cover, behind a wagon, a parent or a market stall. A brave old man picked up an earthenware jug from a table and threw it at the fugitives. It smashed on the ground, some ten *pies* from them. Most in the square either cowered towards the ground or ducked behind some form of shelter. No one wanted to stop them.

'Those two are the shop owners! That shop in the corner!' shouted a man in a red fez. 'I bought a carpet from them!'

'Bigger fool you!' replied a plump, noisy woman.

They sped into an adjacent road and headed down the labyrinth of narrow streets for the Derb Chtouka, running all the way. By then they were clear of the chaos of the Plaza de Mellah, away from the confused guards and able niftily to conceal their weapons in their breeches. So as not to raise the suspicion of their neighbours, they approached their house at walking pace, unlocked the door and walked in. They locked and bolted the door behind them.

'They know where we live. We have to take cover,' said Tariq.

'We have to take our things from here and head to the Anfa *corregidor*'s safe house. We know where it is,' said Tariq.

'I've a better idea. We take our money and other essentials and head through the secret corridor to Fatima's. She'll look after us! We keep the safe house in reserve!'

'Let's do that, straightway,' said Tariq, with hardly a moment's thought.

They raced around filling a bag of clothes each. Antonio quickly packed his violin and while he did so, Tariq piled their money into a canvas bag. Then they dashed up the stairs, with Antonio carefully guiding an oil lamp, to the room with the wardrobe.

'You do this,' said Tariq. 'You know what you're doing.'

Antonio climbed into the wardrobe and located the small handles which they had to turn to open the secret door.

'How can we secure it from inside the corridor?' said Tariq.

'Whoever designed it had thought of that. We take the panel through, and pull it back into place with these handles on the back. We then turn the four small handles on our side to engage with the securing slots. See. Done!'

'What's that banging?' asked Antonio.

'I think we've made it just in time. Let's go through to next door.'

The banging persisted. Four men, including two guards from the palace, were hammering their way into the house. Soon they were in and running around frantically searching for their quarries. They re-grouped in the hall then between them decided on a more thorough search, in cupboards, behind curtains and any other place where the two could have hidden, including outside in the store area.

In the meantime, Antonio and Tariq had hit on a problem. They tried to open the door with the lever concealed high up the corridor wall but it moved against no resistance so the door wouldn't open. The wheel on the inside had not been rewound. They were stuck: in the no man's land between their house in the Derb Chtouka and their neighbour Fatima and her brother next door.

'Now what do we do?' whispered Tariq. 'We can't go back. I can hear the palace guards carrying out a search of our place.'

'So can I! You'd think they could do it with less noise. They'll wake the neighbours… What's that?'

They could suddenly hear voices. There were shouts and shouted replies. They lay down on the floor, in case any of the guards decided to take a random shot through the moveable panel. Then they heard a kick against the panel, then another. Their pursuers had clearly failed to see the small catch handles holding the panel in place. They cowered and feared the worse. 'How in God's name have I got myself into this mess,' thought Antonio. 'Why did I give up a career as a musician to put my life in this kind of danger?'

Then as suddenly as the bangs and kicks had started, they stopped. The guards retreated and closed the bedroom door behind them.

'My God, we're safe!' said Antonio.

'Maybe not. Who knows? They may well come back and have another go or have gone for some heavier gear to smash the wardrobe panel in. I tell you, my friend, it's as well it's a tight fit. They'd be through here by now if it hadn't been.'

'I guess we just sit here until Fatima comes into her room. Then we bang the wall!'

'How do we know when she's in there?'

'We don't. We'll just have to guess!'

'Then we bang the door.''

'She's sure to hear us.'

'I hope she does!'

346

Just as they had sat it out under the table in the library the night before, they began to relax in the secret corridor, by then feeling that the imminent danger had passed. Tariq fell asleep and began to snore, so Antonio let him rest. They had been there for about three quarters of an hour. It couldn't have been much past midday when they heard a sound coming from the direction of Fatima's room.

'Someone is winding up the wheel,' said Tariq. 'Surely it wouldn't be Fatima, this time of day?'

'No. Prepare for the worst. Let's load up in case we have a fight on our hands.'

They remained sitting and primed their snaplocks in near total darkness. The oil in the lamp had all but died to a blue, weak flicker. They felt anxious. This could be a trap. Not being able to break through into the secret passage, the guards had decided to go next door and challenge Jabir al-Malaki about some hidden space between his house and theirs. He'd been forced to tell them, probably at gunpoint, that Antonio and Tariq were about to break through. The guards would at best arrest them or, at worst, kill them in cold blood. The two fugitives talked about the options. Should they hand over their weapons and give themselves up? The certain result would be execution for espionage, a hideous death by hanging or burning at the stake. No. They'd shoot it out. They may need to reload a few times but they weren't going to surrender, not without a fight.

The wheel stopped moving. Their tension mounted. This was the moment they'd dreaded. They sat there waiting. And waited. Nothing happened.

'What do you think?' said Tariq.

'Let's take a chance. If the palace guards were there, they'd have opened the door by now. I don't think they know a thing about the secret corridor. So we pull the lever and hope for the best.'

'Let's do it!' said Tariq.

Antonio heaved at the lever on the wall. The door creaked open into a lit room. Antonio and Tariq stormed in, their guns at the ready.

'My God, Antonio. I'm not sure whether I expected to see you or not. I took a chance and rewound the wheel so, if you needed to, you could get in. And here you are! You and your friend are hunted men! Everyone in Marrakesh is looking for you. There's a reward on your heads: five hundred falus dead or alive! Now you've landed yourselves on me. Expecting my help are you?'

347

'Yes, Fatima. We are indeed,' said Antonio, with eyes partly closed. 'What if I handed you in?'

'That's an option. By the way, I am Tariq. I'm pleased to meet you!'

'But you know the price,' said Antonio. 'We'd let your brother and your family know about your whoring. They'd kill you before anyone killed us!'

'Wait a minute,' said Fatima. 'I never did say I wouldn't help! How can I? What do you expect me to do?'

'Very easy,' said Tariq. 'Take this piece of paper. See that. It's the address of a man called Amanar. He's a camel train driver. Go there and tell him we want him to take us to Anfa. On his next train.'

'What if he isn't there?'

'We'll worry about that if he isn't,' said Antonio.

'Come through. You can put those guns away. I'll get you some food and drink.'

With whatever degree of reluctance, and without explaining her actions to her brother, the following morning, Fatima found the camel train owner's house. He, his wife and his five children lived not far from the Derb Chtouka, a few roads to the east. She soon learnt that he was still on his way to Marrakesh from Anfa. She'd have to call again. Her disappointment showed as she walked slowly back to her house. How could she conceal these men for another three days? How could she feed and water them without her brother knowing? She sneaked up to her room and through it into the room where Antonio and Tariq were hiding. They looked at her expectantly.

'Not good news. Your friend the camel driver is on his way from Anfa. His wife thinks he'll be back in three days. She won't commit him to anything. It's as if she has nothing to do with his business. She asked me to go back and see him when he's there. How can I conceal you here for that long? Someone is sure to suspect something. My brother for one.'

'It shouldn't be too bad,' said Antonio. 'Not if we use you and our place next door. What we do is this. You supply us with food and water. We'll pay you for it. We sleep here but we go next door, via the secret corridor of course, and eat upstairs. We stay there during the day. We don't light lamps or candles or go near the windows. If anyone is keeping an eye on the house, they'd expect us to enter through the back door, not through a bedroom wardrobe! Let's face it, we've got away with using it and no one else knows about it. We won't be in your house when your brother is about and when we are he'll be asleep!'

'Well thought through, my friend. I'm glad I brought you with me! But what if her brother comes into the house next door? He may be forced to show palace guards in as they search for clues about us or take his next lot of lodgers on a guided tour!'

'Easy. If anyone comes in while we're there, we just remove the wardrobe panel and come back through. Make sure you rewind the wheel, this time, Fatima.'

They could be mistaken in putting their trust in Fatima. While they were in her house, next to her bedroom, she could be arrested for harbouring fugitives. But if they had decamped back to their place, she would be much less vulnerable, especially if the door from the secret corridor was closed. She may decide she'd had enough of their threats and report seeing them in their house, through a window, maybe. So at nightfall before their second night in her secret room, Antonio crept out through a ground floor, back window, climbed over the wall behind the storage area at the back of their house and located the so called 'safe house' which belonged to the Anfa *corregidor*. As he approached it, aided by the light of a waxing moon, he saw that the house was in complete darkness. Tariq had given him a key to a side door so he opened it. He stopped for a full minute before venturing in. As he did so he felt a hand grab his neck and another put the cold barrel of a pistol against his temple.

'Who the hell are you?' said an invisible voice, close to his throat. Antonio paused to think. Should he assume that this was one of the *corregidor*'s men or some thief or vagabond who had broken in to take refuge himself or rob the place. Then he realised that the voice was not that of a Moroccan native.

'My name is Antonio Hidalgo. I and my colleague are being hunted by guards from the El Badi palace.' Antonio was concerned for his life. One press of the trigger and he'd be dead. He continued, just as anxiously. 'My colleague and I are accused of spying, I imagine for the King of Spain.'

He was stunned at the reaction. At least four invisible men laughed and cheered. He couldn't believe what was happening. Candles glowed and oil lamps flickered as screens were taken from the lamps and the newly emerging light dispersed. He could see faces, not Moroccan faces, no turbans and no kaftans, just men dressed in breeches and shirts, just like any man from the Peninsula. Someone spoke.

'What an amazing happening! We've all heard of your audacious piece of spying… and we could reap the reward upon your head! But we won't of course! We are from Anfa. We are the *corregidor*'s men. Naturally, we can't tell you why we are here but you have fallen among allies and we'll get you back to Anfa!'

Another chipped in. 'How did you get the key?'

'From your man in Anfa. He told us before we left that we could use this place as a safe refuge, but only if we had to.'

And another had his say. 'How do we know you are telling the truth and that you aren't some stooge from Sultan Zidan al-Nasir, come to smoke us out?'

'Have a look at this. My proof of identity.'

The questioner opened the crumpled-up letter Antonio had taken from his pocket, took it to a nearby candle and read it out loud. 'To whom it may concern: This is to certify that Antonio Hidalgo…' He read almost all of it and finished by saying: 'And it's signed Silva de Torres, Corregidor of Madrid. It looks genuine to me,' he said, looking open eyed at the blatant forgery.

Antonio couldn't believe his luck but in a strange way he could. This had always been regarded as a safe house and sure enough that is what it had turned out to be. He told them that Tariq was back at the house, alone and vulnerable.

'No time like the present. Antonio, you and us three. We'll go now and rescue Tariq. The sooner he's here, the better. We'll arm ourselves and go.'

As they arrived at the house in the Derb Chtouka, three turbaned men were standing outside by the front door. Two were carrying guns and standing by while the third was wielding an axe at the door trying to break in.

'Let them have it!' said the man who had earlier held his gun to Antonio's head. By then they were no more than twenty *pies* away. Shots rang out. Antonio aimed his pistol at the head of the axeman and fired. He hit him in the face and he fell, his hands covering his gaping wound. Seconds later the man twitched to his death. Another ran off, clutching his shoulder while the third, with blood pouring from his stomach, slumped over the wall. Antonio and his protectors, none with the slightest wound, ran into the house through the broken door. Antonio shouted out, 'Tariq! It's me, Antonio! Come down quickly!'

They heard the sound of feet pounding the stairs as Tariq dashed down from his hiding place above.

'My God, am I glad to see you. That could have been real trouble. I think Fatima has squealed on us. I tried to open the door through from the corridor but the wheel hasn't been wound up. Nothing happened when I shouted and I feared the worst. Who are these people? They are my friends already,' he grinned.

Antonio replied, 'They are Portuguese, from the safe house. Let's get our things and go there.'

Within a few minutes the two fugitives and their four new helpers had shut themselves in the safe house and locked and bolted the door behind them. The four drew the blackout curtains at the downstairs windows so they could not be seen from the outside.

'João, go and sort out some beers,' said Hermínio,' a tall thin, individual with a beard who seemed to Antonio to be the leader of the group. 'You Spaniards would appreciate a beer, I imagine. It's illegal of course. We brew it here, round the back!'

'I'd love a beer after what we've been through in the last few days,' said Tariq.

'Me too,' chimed Antonio.

Moments later, João, who seemed hardly old enough to be an agent for the Corregidor of Anfa, brought through six sloshing mugs of beer on a wooden tray. He gently placed it on a large table in what was a dining or meeting room. João looked towards Hermínio in an attempt to seek approval.

'Help yourselves, men. You, too, João. Let me introduce you to my colleagues. This is Gonçalo, my deputy. We run a small mission here in Marrakesh. It's mainly to promote business between Anfa, which is Portuguese, and Marrakesh. But we perform other functions which you can guess at and we won't admit.'

Gonçalo shook hands vigorously, first with Tariq and then with Antonio.

'I'm delighted to meet you, gentlemen. I hope we can help you. By all accounts you are the most wanted men in Marrakesh. How many did you kill at the palace?' The short, stocky, long haired deputy laughed at his own question.

'Not sure,' said Antonio. 'No more than two, but we had to return some fire when we were fleeing across the palace square.'

Hermínio introduced the fourth of his team, a large, heavily built individual with a pronounced paunch and muscular arms. 'This is Otávio. He's our strong man. He's our major form of defence. He can punch a hole in a copper pan!' Otávio didn't utter a word but nodded his bald, ear-ringed head at each of them in turn. Hermínio didn't introduce João, presumably because João was too junior to involve him in such formalities.

'So, exactly what do you want from us?' said Hermínio. 'We can't keep you here indefinitely!'

'Very easy,' said Tariq. 'All we want is a safe escape from Marrakesh, back to Anfa. We can pay. We've made good money from our ventures here.'

'Otávio and Gonçalo are going back in a few days. They will take you and look after you. We know a good camel train driver and he's sure to want to help you out.'

'Not Amanar?' said Antonio.

'The very same!' said Hermínio, enjoying the coincidence.

'He's not due back from Anfa for a few days yet,' said Antonio. 'We tried to book the journey with him but failed.'

'You need to know his wife. She won't help just anybody who turns up at her door. But you needn't worry. Gonçalo has already arranged his and Otávio's return and he'll go to her tomorrow and sort something out for you. Gonçalo will have to explain that you are wanted here and there may be a premium charge on your fare back. Amanar may have to make special arrangements to conceal you, if only to get you clear of the city.'

Five days later, having given his camels a few days' rest, Amanar was prepared to take this odd foursome to Anfa. But Antonio and Tariq were still wanted men with a price on their heads. So the inventive Amanar came up with an idea. He would conceal them among other items his train would be taking to Anfa. He insisted that the two fugitives arrive at his house in the darkness of the night before, giving them no choice but to comply.

The following morning, his wife having given them a hearty breakfast of fried eggs, beans and bread, Amanar took them around to the rear of the house and showed them his loading area.

'You'll have to climb into these. One each! Then I nail the lids down. There's plenty of spaces for air to get in so you won't suffocate. It won't be the most comfortable trip but we'll get you out of them as soon as it's safe,' he chuckled. Before them lay two lead lined, wooden coffins.

'You are joking,' said Antonio with a pained look.

'I'm not getting in that,' said Tariq.

'In which case, gentleman, you'll have to find someone else to take you. God knows who because as soon as you turn up and start speaking with a Spanish accent, most camel train drivers I know would rather turn you in and collect the reward than take you to Anfa.'

'We'll do it,' said Antonio. 'We have no choice. And how much will you charge us?'

'Exactly what your heads are worth A thousand falus a piece?'

'I understand it's five hundred,' protested Tariq.

'It doubled yesterday.'

The two of them laid themselves out in the coffins. The lead, thin though it was, felt cold to the touch. But they could breathe easily and a certain amount of light came through the air vents under the lid. Amanar took a hammer and placed the point of a coarse nail on the edge of the coffin near Antonio's head. He banged it in. Antonio could sense the vibration and the deafening noise which seemed to crush him. He shouted out but the hammer bearer ignored him. Amanar used a dozen more nails to secure the lid. Antonio had never felt a greater sense of restriction in all his life. Amanar then started nailing Tariq's lid. As he finished he bellowed out an instruction.

'You'll be in there for no more than a couple of hours, if that. I don't want you making a sound. Dead bodies are silent and you must maintain that silence until we let you out.'

Aided by four of his colleagues, Amanar loaded the coffins onto separate camels. The two fugitives were pummelled and knocked on the coffin sides as they were manoeuvred into place. Then they stayed in these impossibly uncomfortable positions until Amanar gave the order for the camel train to leave. At least, once the camels were moving, there was some predicable rhythm to the movement and each man was able to brace himself, to some extent, to minimise being beaten or bruised by the bare coffin walls.

Otávio and Gonçalo did all they could to ease the fugitives' discomfort. Each walked alongside a coffin and surreptitiously spoke to the occupant, Otávio to Antonio and Gonçalo to Tariq. Otávio tapped on the side and told Antonio not to fall asleep. A woman walking on the opposite side of the road looked askance as Antonio laughed aloud.

Eventually the camel train reached the city gate. A turbaned guard holding a pistol above his head forced them to a half expected halt. His colleague stood at his side.

'Why are you stopping us?' asked Amanar.

'We have been instructed to search all those leaving the city. Five days ago, two spies killed a man at the palace and escaped. We've searched everybody leaving through the city gates ever since.'

'Feel free to check everybody on my train... and the luggage as well if you want.'

Both guards inspected the camel train, one starting at each end. The coffins were suspended about half way along. The guard who spoke reached them first.

'So what's in here?' he said, taking a kick at the coffin containing Antonio.

'The body of a woman. We are returning it to Anfa for burial. Here are the papers.' Amanar handed a scroll to the guard who unwound it as he read.

'Hmm. I'm not sure I like this. He held his gun as if to fire at the coffin.'

'Don't you as much as dare!'

'If there's a corpse in there it won't be any more dead if I shoot it.'

'But it will have a bullet hole in it and as you have read in those papers, she died of an illness, not by the gun. Her relatives will attack and blame me if her body is mutilated at all. So put the gun away. Take the lid off and inspect inside, if you are that keen, but shoot that body and I'll report you to the authorities as soon as I return.'

The man relented. 'I suppose that goes for the other one as well. Let me see the papers for that one... poor old sod, run over by a horse and cart.'

'Yes. A sad case,' said Amanar.

'Off you go.'

The silent guard opened the gate to allow the camel train through. The two fugitives breathed again. Within a quarter of an hour or so they were out of sight of the guard post. They continued for another half hour and pulled into a sheltered area away from the road.

'Get them off the camels and open up the coffins,' said Amanar. 'No one will see them from here.'

Four of Amanar's team, two on each casket, used metal levers to ease off the lids. They helped the fugitives to their feet. Each looked disorientated and grazed by their motion in the boxes.

'My God, I'll never do that again!' said Antonio.

'I feel sick,' said Tariq. 'That was the worst journey I've ever made.'

Amanar offered them water which they took with alacrity. For obvious reasons, he didn't want them too full of fluid before he nailed them in. He then took two creamy white kaftans from a saddlebag. 'Take off your Spanish clothes and step into these,' he said. 'We don't want you identified now you're out of the boxes.'

Without a word of complaint, and doing their best to protect their modesty, they clambered into the kaftans.

'Now we'll help you with these.'

Amanar and one of his assistants wound a yellow turban around each of their heads and made it secure. They looked at each other and grinned.

'Let's get on our way,' said Amanar.

Neither of them enjoyed the monotonous and exhausting journey across the desert to Anfa but at least they had left their dangerous, albeit successful, adventure in Marrakesh behind them. Amanar's camel train, some thirty camels long, took them right to the door of their rented house in the Alta Baha. Amanar surprised them with both a firm handshake and a strong masculine hug, a gesture not expected from a wind hardened Toureg tribesman. A cynic might suggest that he was anticipating the 2000 falus they were due to pay him.

Moments after they knocked on the front door, Safia, the pretty housekeeper, let them in with a welcoming smile and laughed as she pointed to their Arab dress. Antonio, so tired he could hardly stand, surprised her with a greeting in Arabic. They spent that night in deep sleep in their uncomfortable but welcoming beds. The following day and after some hours of enquiring, they discovered that the inimitable Captain Hernan de Porras and his *Constelación de Orión* were three days away from Anfa. What a welcomed discovery: it meant that they could relax for a few days and take stock.

The delicate aromas that emanated from the delicious Safia, as she moved around the house, cleaning, making their beds and feeding them, turned Antonio's mind to the women in his life, at least the women who occupied it nearly two years ago while he was in Madrid. They had, of course, at various moments occupied his thoughts while he had been on this mission. While he loved the many and varied physical aspects of his relationship with Carolina, she would never be his wife. Somehow, he could not see Carolina settling into that role. He and Carolina were almost too equal, both being keen and competent musicians, and while his personality was not of the kind which would demean a wife or treat her in some inferior manner, he could not see this professional person in the role of a child rearing wife. His conscience challenged his prejudices. Could it be because she was a little person, a dwarf? Was he afraid of what his colleagues and friends would think about him settling permanently with a dwarf woman and having children with her? He denied that view and its logic. After all, he had been seen with Carolina in public many more times than he cared to remember and felt proud of his relationship with her. But he could not see her in the role of his wife. A lover, maybe.

His views on Francisca differed markedly. He felt he was becoming attracted to her. His absence from her made him feel indirectly protective towards her. He often wondered how she was managing since the mysterious illness she suffered from, before he left Madrid. He had never come close to making love to her so there was a mystery about her. And she presented a challenge to him. He could not forget that she had asked him to marry her and he now felt he could agree, that is, if she had not found another in the meantime. He couldn't wait to see her to find out. Thinking about her made her irresistibly attractive. He was falling in love.

As he lay there on his bed, he had serious thoughts about his future. He'd enjoyed this mission immensely, not least the risk taking, the danger and finding ways out of the scrapes into which the two of them had manoeuvred themselves. And for a relative beginner, as compared with Tariq, he felt he'd made some major contributions to the mission. His most significant was to engage Fatima through the artful application of a little blackmail. That had paid great dividends, even if she had, they presumed, betrayed their trust in the end. But she had to be suspected when Tariq found that the door into her house would not open. Antonio had to decide whether to continue in this role as spy for the king, going on high risk, high reward missions or should he elect for a lesser role, one of simply spying on those whom he might meet in his profession as an itinerant musician. He'd have to think further.

Madrid felt so much closer now that they were in Anfa. The overseas voyage to Cádiz, as passengers of Captain Hernan de Porras, turned out mercifully to be uneventful, especially when compared with the voyage from Cádiz to Anfa. A few nights' beer swilling in Cádiz, a three day army relay to Madrid and they were ready to see Silva de Torres in his modest office at the palace.

Part VI

CHAPTER 29
Sworn to secrecy

'Welcome home, men. You each look so well. Tanned almost to blackness! No physical harm then, despite the time away!' said Silva as he burst from his office to greet them. Brondate almost fell over backwards in shock, not expecting such an immediate appearance of his master.

'Believe me, we are relieved to be back,' said Tariq.

'Come in and tell me the story. You can give me the information the king needs when we get to that point.'

All four stepped into Silva's office. Silva pointed Antonio and Tariq towards a chair each which he had placed in front of his desk. Brondate sat to the side in the typical position of a note taker. Between them, they related the whole story, probably in more detail than Silva wanted or needed.

Silva sat patiently with his eyes almost closed, his fingers touching his forehead, thinking and listening to each man contribute as the other began to flag. It must have taken two hours, if not longer to relate. The miserable Brondate scribbled furiously in his vain attempt to record it all.

'Tell me about the outcome! Are the Moroccans planning to build warships to attack us?'

'No,' they said in unison.

'What? Impossible!'

'They have no intention of attacking Spain,' said Antonio, looking straight and coolly into Silva's doubting eyes. 'They are not going to build ships for the purpose of attack. We cannot know how the Duke of Lerma or the king formed the idea that they would attack us by sea but the fact is they will not.'

'Every word of that is true,' said Tariq.

'They are fully aware of the *Morisco* problem but they regard that as an internal issue for Spain to deal with.'

'Exactly,' said Tariq. 'That's precisely what they told the Ottoman contingent. In fact they told them that their relationship with Spain was "not bad" and that they did a lot of trade with us.'

'Tariq is right. We'll have no trouble from the Moroccans, unless we provoke them, of course.'

'D'you mean to say we sent you all that way at such colossal expense to find the answer is "no". It'll leave the king vulnerable. Are you certain?'

'Absolutely,' said Antonio. 'Heard it with our own ears. Agreed, Tariq?'

'Dead right. That's what they told the officials from Constantinople. And why tell them a fabric of lies?'

'We'll have to tell the king, urgently. He is seriously thinking of building a new fleet, to be commanded by Admiral Pedro de Toledo. He won't have to do that now! Hector, go to see de Prada and fix a meeting urgently with the king. For tomorrow, first thing, if he's free.'

'Good as done, señor.' He sloped off.

'Much has happened here since you left for Marrakesh. Something in particular but I can inform you only in total confidence. I've been given express permission tell you because it may be a factor in your next mission. Just listen to this,' he continued quietly as if he didn't want anyone to overhear. 'The king in his wisdom has decided to eject the *Moricos* from Spain. They will be repatriated... if that is the word... to the Maghreb. My personal view is that the whole exercise is an inhuman mistake and will end in tragedy and disaster. I'm already ashamed that it will go ahead. I'm ashamed for Spain and our reputation in the world. But we must support the king's decision. We have no choice.'

'It's inhuman,' said Antonio. 'Thousands will die on the way. Others will be robbed and murdered.'

'I agree. It's a ridiculous idea. These people work the land. It will have a terrible effect on the economy,' said Tariq. 'Are you sure it's going ahead?'

'When will the expulsion take place? It will be a huge exercise,' said Antonio. 'How many are there?'

'No one knows for sure. About three hundred and fifty thousand. And the Valencians will be the first to go. Sometime soon.'

'And what about Reva my daughter? She is a *Morisca*? She cannot go to Morocco. She belongs with us here,' said Tariq, on the verge of tears.

'They won't all be deported,' said Silva. 'About two percent will stay. I am aware that your daughter is a *Morisca* and I've put a case to the king to excuse her. I cannot guarantee an exception for her but I'm doing my best.'

'Thank you, Silva. I'm so grateful. I cannot tell you how much. She means everything to me and Ishraq. Any idea when you will know? Does Reva know what's going on?'

'No and you mustn't tell her. The whole operation, from the decision itself to the detailed plan is a state secret. You must discuss it with no one, except on pain of death…and I mean that. Do you understand?'

'Of course, Silva. Totally,' said Tariq.

'I, too,' said Antonio, not quite sure of what to make of events. He suddenly remembered that Lupita, too, was a *Morisca*. He'd find some way of protecting her. He'd shelter her in Doña Marta's house, if necessary until the whole dirty business blew over. At least Carolina, a small person and a gypsy, couldn't be caught in this particular trap.

Silva politely dismissed them, saying that their next mission would not be for a month or two and that their bounty would be calculated and paid as soon as it was ready.

'Oh, by the way Antonio. Your old mare is pining for you. But she is well!'

'Thank you for some good news, Silva!'

Tariq and Antonio stood momentarily outside the palace, shook hands, hugged each other and went their separate ways. Tariq walked home to Ishraq while Antonio went to the palace stables to retrieve his long forsaken mare. She hardly recognised him and snorted disdainfully as the stable maid showed Antonio to her stall.

'Let's go home, old gal. You've been here long enough. Have you missed me?'

The horse looked at him as if to scowl. The aging mare seemed to have enjoyed her time in the palace stables and walked reluctantly back to their own modest stabling at Doña Marta's. He didn't want to ride her, so he slung his saddlebag over her back and led her by the reins. What could he expect to discover, now he was approaching the house? Silva had promised to pay the rent so he didn't expect any problems on that score. He just felt apprehensive, as if a shock awaited him, but he had no idea what, and when he thought about it realised that it could only be an irrational fear. He had, after all, never been away for that long before.

Having put his old mare in her stable stall and patted her tenderly on the neck to welcome her back, he unlocked the door to his rooms and stepped over the threshold. He noticed two letters for him lying on the small table in the hall. Doña Marta must have put them there. He picked up the first letter and opened it. It was from his father. He said that he and his mother were angry that he'd left a girlfriend to write to them about his visit to Morocco and wasn't impressed that she couldn't or wouldn't tell them why he was going. He said his mother hadn't stopped crying for days and had taken to her bed with a fever. He had to take on some more help with the farm until he was sure she had recovered. Apart from that he said, somewhat cynically, everything was fine and that it would be good if Antonio could find the time to visit them when he returned. Antonio smarted at this admonition. He stood there looking at it. Much as he loved his parents, he couldn't be ruled by them. He thought, probably wrongly, that he had done well to get a belated message to them and justified in not telling them the purpose of the journey. He decided to write to them to tell him of his return and promise them an eventual visit to the farm. There were too many things happening in his life to drop everything to go immediately.

So it was with a degree of trepidation that he picked up the second letter. He thought he recognised the writing: Carolina's. She had left town or found another lover, otherwise, why write to him? It read:

Dear Antonio,

I am in tears writing to you. I miss you so much. I haven't heard from you for nearly a year and nor has anyone who knows and loves you. I wrote to your parents only to receive a nasty reply from your father blaming me for your failure to write to them. It upset me to read it. Until then and from what you told me, I thought your father was a gentleman. But no more.

I have had enough of the insults I have had to endure in Madrid. Poor Lupita, as my colleague, has suffered them, too. Our band enjoyed some success after your departure but it didn't last long, especially as the insults and taunts against me, the dwarf, increased. Some people even spat at me. It was horrible. I can't help thinking that Iago the Bad was behind at least some of it but I have no proof. Sadly, Lupita and I have disbanded our little group. We couldn't find anyone to replace you and Lupita has found a job in the Príncipe theatre. She is a singer actress there.

So with some regrets and a plea from my father, I decided to return to Ávila. Who knows, I may return to Madrid at some time.

Please write to me to tell me you have returned safely. I will always have a place for you in my heart.

With many kisses,
Carolina

Antonio's mouth fell open. Now two unwelcomed missives. He deserved them. While he couldn't guarantee that a letter from Marrakesh would reach Madrid, he could have sent a message via Silva. And perhaps he should have written to his parents directly before he went. He would write to Carolina. This would be a difficult letter. First, he had to tell her that he had returned to Madrid and was safe and well. Second, he didn't want to provoke her into rushing back here to resume their relationship. Even as he came nearer to Madrid, he could feel his affections for Francisca increasing rapidly and he didn't want establishing a loving relationship with her to be complicated by Carolina's arrival. To that extent, her moving back to Ávila was a blessing. But he felt a pang of guilt in harbouring the thought, especial as he had enjoyed such intimate pleasures with her.

He decided that before settling in much further, he'd walk up to see Francisca. As he walked up the Calle de Toledo, he wondered what her reaction would be. Had she changed? Was she well? What were her feelings towards him? He turned to the right, into the Calle Mayor. Coming towards him was a man he recognised.

'Antonio, it is you! You haven't been around here for years!'

'Well, almost two years, Carlos. How are the Wandering Chordsmen? Are you still in business?'

'Yes, we are. Business is good!'

'I could be looking for work myself!'

'But you have a new career now. Something mysterious no one knows much about. You've been travelling a lot I hear. Someone said you were in Morocco. Sort of travelling salesman!'

'You could say that but I could do with some temporary work to tide me over until my next assignment, whenever that will be.'

'Can I get back to you on that, Antonio?' he said coldly, as if he didn't really want Antonio back in the troupe. 'I'll speak to Josep and Lupita.'

'Lupita? Lupita de Pastrana? The singer?'

'Yes, that's her. She's been working with us for over six months now. And on and off at the Príncipe.'

'We'll be in touch then,' said Antonio, shaking Carlos's hand.

Antonio rather enjoyed this short encounter. He never failed to be surprised at how much he could learn from the briefest of exchanges. So the Chordsmen were still active. They had not re-engaged Iago. And Lupita worked for them now. He walked further along to Francisca's house and knocked on the door.

A burly middle-aged, bearded man in a brimmed hat answered. 'Yes señor? Can I help you?' he said politely, looking Antonio up and down, as if he were a piece of furniture for sale at a market. Antonio had never met the man before. His reaction was to think that after all this time, the family had moved and this was the new occupant.

'Excuse me, señor. My name is Antonio Hidalgo. Can you please tell me whether Francisca de Polanco still lives here? If not, do… '

'So you are Antonio Hidalgo,' he said, shaking him vigorously by the hand. 'I'm pleased to meet you, señor. I've heard a lot about you. Come in. Francisca's in the kitchen.'

Antonio breathed a sigh of relief. He couldn't have wished for more. Francisca was still living here and he'd had a positive, friendly reception from her father.

'It's an old friend of yours, Francisca. Long lost Antonio! Quite a stranger, eh?'

'Antonio, it's you! After so long!' she said, throwing down a towel, rushing up to him and flinging her arms around his neck. Then she planted a kiss firmly on his lips. 'It's so, so good to see you. We've all been wondering how you were. You haven't changed in all that time. Except your skin is so brown, nearly black!'

'Let's leave them to it,' said Señor de Polanco, looking at his wife who was so surprised to see Antonio, she hadn't uttered a single word. She, too, went up to him and gave him a silent hug. Father and mother left them in the kitchen. They looked at each other, not knowing who should speak first.

'I love you, Francisca and I want to marry you,' he said.

She hesitated for a few moments before she spoke. 'I am sorry to disappoint you, Antonio but I am already betrothed.' He couldn't work out from the expression on her face whether she wanted to be married to her new suitor or whether her vacant look was designed to soften the blow to his pride.

He couldn't believe his ears. In total shock, he softly uttered the words, 'Betrothed… to whom?'

'He is a lovely man, a musician, like you. He was here only moments ago.'

Antonio's mind raced and his heart beat faster, almost in panic for what he had lost. He'd lost Carolina and he'd lost Francisca. To whom? He felt terrible, as if all his dreams had been shattered. The map of his future, sketch though it was, fell apart as if it had lain for too long in the wet. Suddenly he realised. Had she fallen for Carlos de Siguenza, the leader of the band? He was walking from this direction! What a fool not to realise! But surely he could never have guessed.

'Not Carlos? De Siguenza?

'Yes, Carlos. He is such a nice man and he likes you a lot too.'

'To me, that's a great tragedy. I wanted so much to spend the rest of my life with you. I have thought about you every day and I even worked out where we might live, here in Madrid, so you could be near your family. Are you really, sure, Francisca? I remember you so clearly telling me you loved me and I said I loved you. I did say I needed time to feel I was ready to settle and I think you were happy with that… and that you'd wait until my return from Morocco. I am distraught. I've never been so disappointed in my life. But I do respect you and respect you well. So I accept your decision and wish you every happiness in the future with my friend Carlos.'

She came up and hugged him again. 'You are a wonderful man, Antonio. You will make a great husband and father. I'm sorry. It's just the way things have worked out. If I had heard from you… and known more about what you were doing… well, who knows?'

'As I said, Francisca, I completely accept your decision. I think I should go now.'

'No, Antonio. I'd like you to stay. I can't let you go just like that. Please accept my invitation for some lunch. I'm in the middle of preparing it! It's my mother's pork dish, but in my style. One of your favourites!'

'You are kind, Francisca. I'll stay. I've hardly eaten since yesterday!'

Francisca directed her parents to sit at the dining table, as she went to dish up the meal. For a few moments the three glanced at each other in silence. Then the father started to converse with Antonio as her mother sat quietly listening.

'So you are a musician, too, Antonio. A musician with a second line of work, I understand. I play the guitar for my living and I don't do badly at it. I've been playing for over twenty years now and have five guitars.

What instruments do you play and how long have you been playing and with whom? And tell us about your other work!'

'I've played the violin since I took it up in my school in Pedraza. I was lucky in that the teacher encouraged me and only two of us wanted to play the instrument so it was like individual tuition. I play a few chords on the guitar but I can really play the violin. I worked in a touring group called the Wandering Chordsmen until I took on this other work. The Chordsmen were mainly itinerant and played with theatre groups around Madrid. We used to play as street musicians. I have a very special violin which I bought in Segovia a few years back. I'll play it to you sometime. The tone is beautiful!'

'Let's meet up and you can play it to me. How about tomorrow?'

'Love to!' smiled Antonio.

As he spoke, Francisca served up the pork dish, some carrots and some healthy sized chunks of bread and came to join them.

'That's enough of the music,' said Señora Díaz, speaking for the first time. 'Let's talk about something else. Have you heard the rumour about the *Moriscos*, Antonio?

'I haven't heard any rumours. What are they?'

'They are going to be sent to Morocco,' said Señor de Polanco. 'Expelled. You got back just in time! There's going to be much bloodshed. There and here.'

'I know about some problems. Very few have become genuine converts it seems. And there has been trouble in various parts of the country. Not all caused by the *Moriscos*, I think.

'You're right there,' said Francisca. 'Native Spaniards have stirred up trouble for them. In fact the clerics have been the worst. Ribera and his cohorts has been the main voice for getting rid of them.'

'But wouldn't it take a decision by the king to expel them?' said Antonio, knowing the answer better than any of them.

'Yes, of course,' said Señor de Polanco. 'But there's another rumour, too. It's that he's made the decision and won't announce it.'

'I can't see that,' said Antonio. 'D'you have any evidence?'

'Yes, indirectly. There are some odd troop movements. And navy ships are grouping around the Valencia coast. You can only believe that the *Moriscos* from Valencia will be the first to go.'

'It's horrible,' said Señora Díaz. 'Imagine losing everything, your home, your wealth and your living and being compelled to go to Morocco. You, your wife and your children… maybe even with a baby.

You don't know anyone there. You are just dumped on some alien beach. I can't think of anything worse. And we know a few *Moriscos*, don't we Francisca.'

'Yes, Carlos's colleague, Lupita, for one. She can't help it and why should she be thrown out of the country? She's a perfectly respectable woman. And I don't care whether she's a Muslim or a Christian.'

'Well, we've got deep into this one!' said the señor. 'This is such a good meal, Francisca. Better than your mother does!'

The señora stood up, went round the table and, laughing with the whole of her face, pretended to hit her husband across the head. 'Damn you, man. You don't know when you're well off!'

They each enjoyed the meal Francisca had prepared, the conversation and the laughter. Although Antonio felt badly upset at the loss of Francisca to Carlos, the gathering with her family served, at least to some extent, to soften the blow. Antonio declined the offer of a drink and decided to leave for his house, almost immediately afterwards. He and Señor de Polanco agreed to meet at the family's house at ten o'clock the following morning.

Antonio strolled back to his rooms in Doña Marta's place. While doing so, he felt quite miserable. Probably for the first time since he had left the farm in Pedraza, he became aware of his own solitude. Those close to him in Madrid had left, become attached to another or were no longer working in their previous roles - he thought of Lupita - and therefore unable to offer him work as a musician. Not that he needed to work. His work as an agent for the king, or more directly, for Silva de Torres, had made him moderately well off. And he'd yet to discover what would be credited to his bank account for the mission to Marrakesh. At least a few hundred *ducats*, he imagined, quite enough to keep him in his modest style of existence for a year, if not more. But he had no idea when a new mission would emerge from the desk of Señor de Torres. Surely, he wouldn't have to wait too long. If it were anything connected with the expulsion of the *Moriscos* and especially if the expulsions were to get underway before the autumn, he would not have to wait more than a month or so.

He unlocked the door of the house, went to his rooms and from a drawer in his desk, took out a quill, some ink and some paper and wrote two, not especially long but laboured letters. By the time he had addressed and sealed them he needed to rest. His bed beckoned him and while indulging in the memories of happier, less lonely times in or on that bed, he fell asleep.

He dreamt he was sleeping with a veiled woman in a mansion near the palace in Marrakesh, the most beautiful woman he'd ever seen. The woman placed a snaplock pistol in his hand and told him that he could do anything with her that he wished to do as long as it didn't hurt her. So he asked her what she expected him to do with the pistol. Surely, she did not expect him to kill her afterwards. She told him that that was certainly not what she wanted. That would be ridiculous. Quite the opposite in fact: she would have to kill him. She explained. He was an infidel and the only way she could justify making love to an infidel would be to kill him. He said he could not accept these terms, declined to sleep with her and left. As he closed the door behind him, he realised he was about to walk into a dark, narrow corridor. This puzzled him as he'd entered through a door off a large open landing and he remembered only one door into the room. He could barely see his way along the corridor which, after about twenty *pies* ended at another door. He pushed the door which crashed to the floor. The light from the opening almost blinded him. He realised that he'd entered another room through a wardrobe. The palace guards were about to shoot him. He woke in a sweat of fear, then realised that he was lying in his own bed and that the morning sunlight, stabbing through the window, had all but blinded him. The crazy dream seemed so real, despite its irrationality.

After he'd had a light breakfast of olives, some scraps of bread and a few tomatoes, he broke the seals on each of the letters he'd written the night before, made a few minor changes and re-sealed them. He'd been thinking that he should tell his parents that he still loved them and that the one to Carolina should mention the wonderful times they had enjoyed together, as colleagues and as lovers. He'd despatch them in the Plazuela de Selenque market on his way to see Juan de Polanco.

It wasn't long after ten o'clock that he was standing, his violin case under his arm, in front of the Polanco's and knocking on their door. It had to be Francisca who answered and let him in. She greeted him with a kiss on the lips, the kind that is usually reserved for a lover. Perhaps this was some form of symbolic compensation for her choosing to marry Carlos. The friendly greeting led her to escorting Antonio to her father's chair in the drawing room where he sat drinking some anonymous concoction that smelt like cabbage. As soon as Antonio entered the room, the señor stood, turned towards him and spoke.

'You can go now, Francisca. See if you can help your mother.'

Francisca glared at him and sped from the room, noisily closing the door behind her.

'I'm so glad you returned, Señor Hidalgo. I did wonder, after the bad news my daughter gave you yesterday. I'd have understood you not wanting to come here. It's probably the last place you'd want to be seen after she rejected you. Mind you, between you and me, I'm not too keen on this Carlos fellow. But, he's her choice so I'll put up with him. At least he's a musician!'

Antonio didn't expect that intimate observation from the father, given that he'd first met him only the day before. He didn't know quite what to say so he attempted to change the subject. As Antonio realised, you are most likely to be successful in doing that if you ask a question.

'So where do you go to play your guitar? Not just in Madrid, surely?'

'No. I play with theatre groups mainly. In the Príncipe and the de la Cruz. Usually accompanying plays. Usually Lope and Encina plays. It's good quality work and pays well! Occasionally, I go to other towns and play in theatres there… or even on the streets! That's an adventure! And I enjoy it!'

'You don't play the streets as a soloist do you?'

'Only sometimes! Usually, I join up with other players. I know so many now, I can usually find some to play with! Anyway, what are you going to play for me, Señor Hidalgo? I'm dying to hear you!'

'See if you recognise this one!' Antonio took his violin from its case.

'Don't play yet! Let me see that violin!'

Antonio carefully handed it to the Señor.

'It's beautiful, Señor Hidalgo! I love the colour of the wood. It's so light. Most violins I've seen are dark and miserable looking. This one looks so cheerful!'

'Less of the Señor, Señor. You can call me Antonio, if you wish!'

'In that case you call me Juan! Go on then. Play it!'

Antonio put the instrument to his chin, made sure it was properly in place, stretched his bowing hand over his head and placed the moving bow on a string. On his way to the Polanco's he'd thought about this commission and what he should play. He started with 'Roses for my mother', something that he would use to demonstrate his prowess as a violinist without wanting to be controversial or too provocative. He played a few verses and stopped.

'Recognise that, Juan?'

'Yes, it's "Roses".'

'Of course. You know it!'

'And you play it well, young man! Really well! When did you last play?'

'I'd have to think about that one. About a month ago, in Marrakesh. I took it with me and played it for practice, but not often enough. My playing is a little rough around the edges now. But I'll soon sort it out!'

'Call that rough around the edges? Sounded damn near faultless to me! You are a good player, I can tell you!'

'You are too kind, Juan!'

'Play something else!'

Antonio thought his way through his repertoire and decided to take a risk. After all, they were in a private house, around the back and couldn't be heard from the street. So he struck up, 'Woe is me Alhama'.

As soon as Señor Hidalgo identified the tune he reacted. 'For the blood of Christ don't play that tune here. Are you a *Morisco* sympathiser or something? We'll be slapped into gaol if anyone around here recognises that. It's a Moorish song. You know that much, don't you? But you play it damned well and it drips with emotion the way you do it. You've played it many times before. I can tell that straightaway!'

What a strange endorsement, thought Antonio. A condemnation followed by a compliment. 'I'm sorry, Juan. It's a song I've been compelled to play in some gatherings. I think I should explain. I was playing in an inn in Valladolid once which turned out to be a *Morisco* meeting point. I knew the song, of course, and was asked to play it. I say "asked" but the consequences of not playing it could have been painful. So I played it. The reaction was incredible. They were overjoyed. It made some of them cry. But that doesn't make me a *Morisco* sympathiser. I have my views of course and I don't agree with expulsion. It would be inhuman.'

Señor de Polanco hesitated as if he wanted to say something important but wasn't quite sure how to put it or how Antonio would react. He looked around the room until he felt compelled to break the silence where only moments before there had been so much sound. Then he spoke.

'I have an idea for you, Señor Hidalgo... I'm sorry... Antonio. I would like you to work with me. We'd make a good duet. Not only that, I know one of the theatre managers at the de la Cruz and he's been

nagging me for some time to find a partner. And as you play the guitar…
not very well… it has to be said. But at least you play it and I could teach
you to become much better. You are a natural musician.' He paused again
for a few moments. 'What do you think?'

'Hmm,' breathed Antonio. 'Thank you for making the offer. But I
have to be frank with you. I expect to be called to another mission soon.
Within weeks, maybe. Possibly months. I don't know and I can't say
much about it. So even if I did join up with you, it may not be for very
long. Once the mission is over though, I could re-join you, of course. At
least until the one after next.

'I know that the next mission will not be for anything like as long as
the last. Probably for a few weeks and I'm confident it will be in Spain.
Almost certainly in the south. If you are prepared to accept me on these
terms, the answer is, yes, provided we can agree on a daily rate.'

'Six *reales* a day, plus expenses. It's more than I'd normally give…
but you are a damned good violinist! I'm not worried about your other
work, secretive though it sounds, but we'll worry about that when you're
called away.'

'Agreed!' said Antonio. 'When shall I start?'

'How does tomorrow sound? I have a job in Guadalajara. Working
as an entertainer in the square. There's a play on there and we'll be doing
the entertaining in the intervals. Starts in three days' time, but we've got
to get there yet! The stage manager asked me if I could find someone to
make a duet and that's now you!'

Antonio thought about how this might fit in with Silva's next
assignment for him. He could afford to be away from Madrid for a month
and maybe a week or so longer but he didn't want to miss the new
opportunity, especially if there would be a *Morisco* connection. 'How
long is your contract there?'

'They aren't sure how successful the play will be but I would say
about a month or so.'

'I should be able to cope with that. How do we get there?'

'Horseback. You have a horse?'

'Yes, but she's an old one. She'll make if we can do it at a trot! And
we'll need plenty of breaks!'

'We've got loads of time!'

Despite having to rest his aging mare at frequent intervals, and
testing Señor de Polanco's patience in the process, the newly formed duet

arrived in Guadalajara the day before the stage production was due to start. The closer their approach to the town, the more Antonio felt attracted to his past lover, Jac. He hadn't seen her for years. He wondered whether she and her parents still worked in the inn. He'd try to convince Señor de Polanco that they should stay there.

'Where are we lodging tonight?' he said, looking across to him, still on their horses and walking them through the town towards the centre.

'There are plenty of inns. We'll soon find one.'

'I know a good place. Not far from the middle of town.'

'Been here before then?'

'Many times. Mainly with the "Wandering Chordsmen". Last time was when we did "Peribañez", about four years back. I thought I told you when we met at your place.'

'I don't remember,' he said, knowing that Antonio hadn't. 'Tell me more about the inn.'

'The beer is good. So is the food. And the landlady's daughter is a good friend of mine.'

'How good a friend?' said Señor de Polanco, smiling and giving Antonio a cheeky wink.

Antonio took a chance. 'Let's say lovers!'

'And you wanted to marry my innocent daughter!' he laughed.

'There's nothing like marrying an experienced man you know!' chuckled Antonio.

'I reckon you're making it up! You've never had her in your life!'

'Only if you say so!'

Señor de Polanco took Antonio straight to the central square, precisely where the Wandering Chordsmen had played. By then they had dismounted and were walking their horses by the reins. Antonio thought he recognised someone walking across the square towards them. As the man approached he realised it was Andres Moreno, the manager of the 'Peribañez' players. Moreno didn't recognise Antonio, probably because his skin looked so dark. He spoke to the señor.

'Hello, Juan. Good journey?'

'Apart from my new colleague's old mare which had to stop every half *milla*. Still we're here now! Let me introduce you to Antonio Hidalgo. He's quite good at the violin. Hopeless on the guitar!'

'Antonio. It's great to see you. I didn't expect you. And I'm sorry I didn't recognise you. How's life?'

'All is well, Andres. How about you?'

'Generally good. But the rumours about the *Moriscos* is causing havoc. Do you know about these whispers?'

'Yes, I know them well.'

'Two of my actors are *Moriscos* from Valencia. Decent men they are, too. They've heard that the *Moriscos* in Valencia are being expelled first so they've gone back to their families in Denia. I've had to change the play we are performing to Lope's "Madness in Valencia". Just to reduce the number of actors I need. It's ironic that that's the one we'll be doing. I'm rushing to get some notices out! See you tomorrow then.'

Antonio and Señor de Polanco made their way to Jac and her parents' inn. By then it was early evening but still light. Antonio went in first and saw Jac standing behind the bar, washing some beer mugs.

'Hello young lady! How are you?' said a smiling Antonio, naturally hoping relations with her would resume where they had left off, almost four years before. She quickly dried her hands, rushed from the bar and threw her arms around his neck in an unexpectedly emotional greeting.

'My darling, Antonio. I haven't seen you for so long. You look wonderfully well!' she said, but not sounding as bright as her actions were demonstrating.

'You don't sound right, Jac. Is everything all right?'

She broke into tears and sobbed uncontrollably. 'It's Father. He died two days ago. His poor lungs finally gave in. All that dust in the copper mines. It's so, so sad. So it's just me and Mother looking after the place now. We may have to sell up. We don't know if we can cope or not. We'll just have to see.'

Antonio put his arms around her and hugged her. 'I'm so sorry, Jac. I hate to see you in tears.'

'There is nothing you can do except say words of comfort. And we are distracted by what we have to do. The funeral is the day after tomorrow. Mother has gone to the funeral director to make the final arrangements.'

'Not on her own, surely?'

'With a friend. She left me to look after the inn.'

Señor de Polanco stood behind Antonio and slightly to one side as this intimate conversation took place. The look on his face betrayed his surprise at how well these two knew each other. In his own mind he had settled on staying at this inn, if only so Antonio could give some solace to his lady friend.

Antonio introduced Señor de Polanco to Jac. Antonio gave a limited explanation of his relationship with his new partner, saying only that they met some time ago in Madrid and that the Señor played the guitar like a musical god. They agreed to book for two weeks, to see how the rearranged programme that Andres Moreno had put in place would work out. The two men stabled their horses then took their saddlebags to their respective rooms and agreed to meet in the drinking area for dinner, after which a livelier Jac joined them.

'So what have you been doing since you left here the last time you came, with that woman... Lupita was it?'

Señor de Polanco raised his eyebrows until they twitched. He asked himself just how many women this former suitor of his virgin daughter had taken to his bed. He stayed silent but listened.

Antonio had to be careful in explaining his actions to Jac.

'I've been to Ávila, Segovia, and Valladolid, playing in music groups and, would you believe, I've spent the last year and more on a visit to Marrakesh.'

'What were you doing there?'

'It's a long story. Basically, working with a merchant friend of mine, selling his goods at the market!'

Neither Jac nor Señor de Polanco questioned Antonio's reason for going there but did ask about what it was like, the journey, what the people were like and what they wore and did. He told them about the range of goods they sold, to whom it was sold, not mentioning the palace, and, much to Jac's amusement, said how proficient he'd become in Arabic.

Antonio soon settled into his new work, providing, along with Señor de Polanco and a few other musicians whom Antonio had not met before, the musical accompaniment to 'Madness in Valencia'. Antonio didn't like the play anything like as much as 'Períbañez'. It seemed strange that two sane people, one a fugitive who believed he had killed a prince and the other a rich woman robbed by a blind servant, had found their way into a lunatic asylum and even odder that they'd fallen in love. He decided he'd just play his music, as directed by Señor de Polanco but do his best to make it fit the drama.

The routine of playing in the morning, a hasty lunch followed by a sleepy break in an inn or just lying in the square, an afternoon performance and then returning to Jac and her mother's inn, lasted a full month. The fact that audiences loved the play puzzled Antonio beyond explanation. Some of the women in the town saw it daily.

Antonio attended Jac's father's funeral. Sadly, her mother had only women friends who provided little cheer to the weeping widow. So Antonio, strong and youthful, sat with her and kept a firm and comforting arm around her waist during the ceremony. His handkerchief became wet with her tears. Their inn provided the obvious venue for the wake. Jac, her mother and some of their lady friends prepared a meal for the twenty or so mourners, only two of whom Antonio had met before, the *Morisco* doctor and his wife whose house Antonio had seen destroyed by fire.

Not surprisingly, the early but not entirely unexpected death of her father had its effect on poor Jac. While she continued to enjoy her relationship with Antonio, she found it difficult to give in to his several attempts at seduction. She felt even less inclined to consort with her other lovers. Antonio and Jac spoke nearly every day, usually after dinner and often over a beer, about his day's work and hers. The exhausted Señor de Polanco had usually adjourned to his bed by then. So had Jac's mother and most of their other guests. She laughed at some of the outrageous happenings Antonio had witnessed in the audience and he listened sympathetically at the problems she had overcome during the day. Some were created by her mother who, when the pressure of work became high, would burst into tears and rush to her room leaving Jac with everything that needed doing.

Eventually, after a good three weeks into their stay, the conversation turned to her disinclination to make love. So as not to be overheard they sat opposite each other in a booth and held hands across the table.

'It's difficult to explain,' said Jac, looking down at their clasped hands. 'I feel weighed down by a feeling of guilt even thinking about it. I'll tell you exactly what is going on in my mind. While Father was alive, I could indulge my lovers in private. He couldn't see me doing it. He may have had some idea but never said anything and I was always very discrete, as with you. But now he's gone, I think he can see me from up there.' She looked towards the ceiling. 'From heaven, where his spirit is resting.'

'I understand,' he said, squeezing her hand, not sure whether he understood or not. 'But you can't go on like that for ever. You might as well join a convent!'

374

The risk in making light of the problem paid off. She instantly responded with a quiet laugh. 'You are funny, Antonio. That's why I like you so much. At least one of the reasons!'

'I've an idea, Jac. We usually take all our clothes off when we make love. We could keep everything on... then, if Father can see you, he may not realise what you are up to!'

She looked unsure but suddenly her doleful expression vanished. 'Do you know? You could be right! Come on, Antonio, let's go to your room and try it out! Father won't even know I'm in there! And Mother will be sound asleep by now!'

They leapt up the stairs like a pair of frisky wolf cubs and quietly closed Antonio's door behind them. They gave in to a fond embrace, in the dark, just inside the door. Each tongue penetrated before they touched each other through their clothing. Their excitement grew to breaking point.

'On the bed or in?' said Antonio.

'I'm not getting into bed fully dressed!'

They quickly found a position with Jac on her side, her head on the pillow with Antonio facing her back. She lifted the hem of her skirt. He undid the top of his breeches. Holding her waist, he gently started.

'Oh, that's just lovely Antonio. You can be as slow as you like. But keep going. You are the best, you really are. It's so good. I haven't done this in months!'

'And you are an irresistible beauty, Jac. I haven't done this since Marrakesh.'

'Tell me more!' she said.

'You really wouldn't want to know!'

Their pleasure endured long after the ecstatic conclusion.

After their sixth week in Guadalajara, Andres Moreno decided to discontinue performing the Lope play. Audiences were dwindling and with the autumn just beginning decided to close the theatre until the following season. Señor de Polanco tried hard to talk him out of it but Moreno prevailed. He was losing money and that had to stop.

Jac pleaded with Antonio to stay, if only for a few days 'relaxed break' as she put it. Despite knowing full well what the lady meant, he said the two men would be safer travelling back to Madrid together. The two lovers hugged each other for too long. Then the men mounted their horses and were on their way.

CHAPTER 30
The exodus begins

They sat there in that cold, early October evening. The Duke of Lerma and the king, just the two of them, were enjoying a night of quiet drinking and eating. They dined in the main banquet hall of the Alcázar Palace, in the west wing. Despite the fire in the huge hearth and blazing braziers leaning from the wall, the cold had triumphed. Neither seemed happy in this huge, drafty room. Each wore a huge coat that reached almost to the floor. The king had donned a hat, a flat, broad brimmed construction that tipped his ears slightly outwards. The duke had perched his feathered headgear, a boat shaped object, on the side of the head at such a precarious angle, that a breath of wind would have landed it on the freezing stone slabs. Each concentrated on eating until the duke broke the silence.

'Things are going well in Valencia, Philip. Quite satisfactorily,' he said, his breath visible in the air.

'So they are on their way then,' said the king, peeling off a chunk of venison from the steaming joint in front of him. 'Excellent. There can be no retreat now. God is on our side. It will be good to be rid of them. It's a purge. A purification.'

'Not without its problems,' said the duke, downing a generous mouthful of the red wine, a tempranillo, which a footman had just poured into his glass.

'Tell me more. I want to be fully in the picture.'

'You remember that Mejía took your letters announcing the expulsion to Ribera and the Marquis of Caracena. I think you know he's our viceroy in Valencia.' The duke often had to remind the king, usually in diplomatic terms, of the names of his own officials. 'And much to our surprise, Ribera objected.'

'Yes, I remember you telling me. What's the matter with the man?'

'Hard to say.' He took another gulp from his glass. 'He's a fool. Suddenly he sees what a mess Valencia will be in without a hundred and fifty thousand vassals to clean his shoes, put on his cassock, perch his mitre on his head, grow his wheat, pick his grapes, tread them, fetch his water and wipe his ass.'

'Do you mind, I'm eating!' the king chuckled and almost choked on a chunk of over-cooked parsnip which he spat onto the table.

'It's true! They do everything for him. And now they're on their way!'

'He must have said more than that… or is Mejía covering something up.'

'Ribera wants the *Moriscos* in Castile to go first. He now argues that they are better integrated here. So more of a danger.'

'What rubbish! We've gone ahead anyway, I take it. We can't have that idiot getting in the way. Not now we are so far down the road!'

'Of course. The good thing is that he's cooled off now and realises he'd put himself out on an edge. In his latest missive, to me, he has the audacity to say he agrees with expulsion as long as we follow Valencia with throwing them out of the rest of Spain.'

'I suppose that's what we want to hear. We're going to do that anyway!'

'I've told Mejía to ignore him and just get on with the job.'

'So how far are we down this particular road?' The king took a hefty swig of wine.

'The best news I can give you is that they are on their way. Somewhere on the high seas.'

'Come on Francisco, tell me more. I'm quite excited now.'

'You are aware that two week ago, the first ships left Denia for Oran, on the Barbary coast?'

'Of course, you told me the day they went.'

'We've got more detail now. It's quite a story. They nearly all followed your edict. Only a few tried to escape. We hung them and left their corpses rotting on the gallows, right on the road. Must have discouraged some! Most of them capitulated and we now know that on the night of 2nd October three thousand, eight hundred and three left for our fortress in Oran. The first consignment! Well done, Philip! All credit to you!'

'Good decision I made on that boar hunt, eh?' the king laughed.

'For the good of the kingdom, Philip. No less!'

The king smiled blandly. He loved to receive little compliments.

'Another eight thousand left three days later! You'll never believe this, Philip. Maybe you will, but your barons distinguished themselves well!'

'What do you mean? Killed some off, did they? If they couldn't have them no one else could either! Is that it?'

'No! No! They went to the ports and helped them and their families onto the ships. Even found them the best accommodation on board!'

'Which of the barons did you say?'

'Denia for a start. He had most to lose. Twenty thousand of them. The Marquis of Albada, the Count of Alaguas, the Count of Bunol, the Count of Anna, the Count of Sinarca, the Count of Concentayna, and the Duke of Maqueda who went with the first embarkation to Oran.'

'Well beyond the call of duty, Francisco?'

'Totally. Not entirely stupid though. Denia will tell his vassals still here that Oran is a wonderful place and that those on the first contingent were well looked after, on the voyage and when they got to Barbary!'

'So what happened in Barbary, exactly?'

'It was a hell of a surprise to the local population when all these people turned up in Oran. But again, our commander of the garrison, the Count of Aguilar, distinguished himself. He managed to feed and water the first five thousand or so who turned up there. He even organised some escorts to take them inland. So Denia's man who'd gone with them reported back that everything was fine in Barbary.'

'Damned good for him! Can we honour him in some way? Is that a good idea, Franscisco?'

'I'll think about that one Philip. The bad news is that the latter reports haven't been quite so good. Oran has been completely overwhelmed by the influx. Poor Aguilar can't feed them. Many are dying of starvation or exhaustion. Many have been robbed of everything and are walking around naked... even with their children naked.'

'Not our responsibility now! They're in Allah's hands!' The king laughed aloud. The duke looked at him in dismay. 'Tell me about the ones who are still here. Are they just queuing up to get on the galleys?'

'Valencia is a disaster zone. So Mejía reports. *Moriscos* are selling anything they can't carry. The markets are awash with animals, wagons, furniture, linen, farming equipment. One of them gave his plough away... gave it! And the places they are leaving are being looted by the Christians. They are making a feast of it. Taking everything, even the windows and doors. *Moriscos* are flooding into the ports and they are being overwhelmed, too. They're not enough food to feed them all. Some are selling their own children for food and the soldiers are selling them for slaves.'

'That's illegal,' said the king, his head slightly bowed, as if he was becoming unsure of how he should react to the human misery that he himself had created.

'The *tercios* are selling the children into slavery. No doubt about it. And that's far from the end of the story. The Christians are robbing the *Moriscos* as they walk the roads to their port of embarkation. Some have been stripped of everything, their money, jewellery and even their clothes. Some are walking naked in the cold of autumn. Many have died of exposure or have simply collapsed by the roadside. Caracena reports that fifteen *Moriscos* were murdered by Christian thugs, not more than a few days ago. For their money of course, and many women and children have been raped. Caracena says no road is safe for them.'

From the twisted look on the king's face, the duke could see that the king didn't know how to react. Surely, he felt some degree of guilt, if only a smidgeon. 'We can't be accountable for crimes that others commit. But could we take the pressure of the ports we are using by engaging some more?'

'I think not, Philip. Ships are departing from Valencia, Denia, Alicante, Viñaroz, and even tiny Mancofa. There aren't any others close to Valencia we could use!'

'It all sounds bad to me.' The king sat holding his knife with both hands on the table looking dejectedly into his wine glass. He'd stopped eating.

'It's not all bad, Philip. Rest assured. Some of them are celebrating their leaving Spain. Women on the beaches of Alicante are dancing, clapping and singing their Muslim songs. They are thrilled to be leaving. They've put a band together and many men and women are going wild with excitement on the beaches. Women are dressed in their white *almalafas* and their jewels while their men are garbed in their best finery and even red caps and turbans. Many more waded into the sea, their hands held high in thanks to Allah for delivering them from us infidels. Us, infidels! Indeed! They just can't wait to get to Barbary!'

'I'm grateful to you for telling me that, Francisco. I feel better now.' The king took a sip of his wine, almost in peaceful celebration. 'But surely there must be some resistance. They aren't all going as lambs to the slaughter?'

'I was getting to that, Philip. No. We are beginning to see resistance, mainly near Denia. And we've plans to do something about it. And I want your approval, if of course, you agree.'

'Continue.'

'There are thousands of them up in the hills, off the Laguar Valley. Are you familiar with the geography, Philip?'

'I don't think so. Tell me...'

'It's high up in the mountains near Alicante but nearer Denia, I think. It's very high up so they have the advantage of elevation.'

'Are they equipped? Armed?'

'Heavily. They are armed and angry. It would be a major victory for them if they succeeded in staying there, or going further east or north. Imagine how a triumph for them would lift their cause. We want your permission to rout them, if necessary. Mejía wants to do the job. He'll succeed, I'm sure. But we want to try negotiating with them first. If not there's sure to be bloodshed.'

'Do it. Give Mejía my blessing. I will accept nothing but his triumph. He must win, whatever the cost.'

'Thank you, Philip.' The duke, still sitting at the dinner table, bent forward, as if to bow. He held up his glass and lifted it towards the king. The king did likewise. Their glasses clinked together.

'Here's to our victory, Francisco. I agree with negotiation before Mejía wades in. We should avoid bloodying the mountain, if we can!'

'We'll try, of course.'

'Keep me in touch, won't you?'

'Naturally.'

CHAPTER 31
The general

Antonio didn't know, neither did Señor de Polanco, nor did the people of Guadalajara that, by the time the two musicians left Jac's inn, the dreaded expulsions were already underway. Valencia reverberated with the fear of terrified *Moriscos* who were about to lose everything in the exodus. Many lost their lives as well as their possessions. The most inhuman of all imaginable atrocities had begun.

'So when does your new mission start, Antonio,' said the señor, raising his voice so he could be heard over the sound of their horses hooves clomping the hard road and wagons stirring up the last of the summer dust.

'It's hard to tell. Within a few weeks of our return to Madrid, I think. I don't know for sure.'

After a night's stay at an inn at the lower end of what was available on the road and a moderately paced ride, the two musicians arrived back in the Plaza Mayor in the middle of a Tuesday afternoon.

'Well, I have enjoyed your company, Antonio and so has Jac,' he laughed. 'Seriously, we must work together again sometime. Let me know when you are back from your next mission and we'll fix something. Try to learn the guitar in the meantime!' He handed Antonio a small purse. 'You've earned this!

'Thank you, Juan.' He hardly ever used his first name. 'And for the money. It's been a privilege.'

They shook hands, the señor walked towards his house and Antonio, still sitting astride his aging mare, walked her to Doña Marta's house. The poor horse neighed as Antonio closed the door of her stable stall. 'Thank you, sweetheart. You are the only girl I have left now!' He laughed to himself. 'At least you are good to me!' The horse looked at him and nodded, as if to agree.

Antonio entered the house then unlocked the door to his rooms. An envelope with a palace seal lay, address downwards on the floor. He bent over to pick it up, opened it and began to read it.

Dear Diaspora,
Where are you? I have been trying to contact you for days about your next mission which begins in six days' time on Thursday, 24 October.

Unless you can see me about it by first thing on Wednesday, you will not be permitted to go.
I am angry and disappointed that you have not informed me of your whereabouts. Kindly consider yourself seriously reprimanded for this shocking omission.
Sincerely yours,
Algebra, this day, 18 October

Antonio started to quiver. He could not believe what he was reading. At no time did Silva ask him to report his movements. Then he calmed down wondering if he should take immediate action. Yes, he'd go now, unannounced to the palace. He dashed out, locked up again and untethered his mare from the stall. 'Come on, gal! We're off to the palace. In a hurry.' He hadn't the heart to gallop the poor old mare, especially as she would have expected to rest after her journey from Guadalajara, so he trotted her all the way.

His greeting couldn't have been less welcoming. 'Where in the name of Christ have you been? We've looked everywhere for you. I've had the *corregidors* of Ávila, Valladollid, Segovia and Guadalajara hunting for you. We thought you'd been kidnapped. And now you turn up. Bloody hell, Antonio. You've got less than two days to prepare for the next one. So where in God's name have you been? And, wherever it was, why didn't you give me the courtesy of letting me know where you were going?'

Antonio felt seriously awkward, not to say embarrassed. 'I'm so sorry, Silva. I've been in Guadalajara playing the violin with a theatre group. Yes, I should have let you know. I thought I had about two months before the next mission.'

'I accept your apology. But don't do that to me again. I have a meeting with the Duke of Lerma in half an hour so I must be quick. Have you heard of General Agustín Mejía, commander of the king's army in Alicante?'

'Yes, you mentioned him when we met after Tariq and I returned from Marrakesh.'

'He's been given a new assignment. To flush a group of rebellious *Moriscos* out of the Laguar Valley, which is high up in the mountains, near Alicante. You will accompany him. I warn you now, he is a difficult individual. Don't try to befriend him. That will only annoy him. Do what

382

he says and listen to him carefully. He is a man of few words. He will not repeat an instruction. Any questions?'

'No Lusitano?'

'No! He'll be doing something on another front. I cannot tell you what.'

'What will the general want me to do?'

'I'm none too sure. You will be at his disposal. He may just use you as a sounding board. He might want you to spy on these people and help establish what resources he will need to crush them. I don't know.'

'From where do we depart? And when?'

'Front of the Alcázar, nine o'clock on Thursday morning. With four of his colonels and four escorts.'

'You say a group of *Moriscos*. How many?'

'About four thousand.'

'Further questions?'

'No.'

'I must go.' Silva stood, leant over the desk and coolly shook Antonio's hand. Then he said, with a stern look on his face, 'Just remember not to do that to me again. And if you get into trouble in Alicante, send me a message, via the army relay. Tell him about his horse, Hector.' Silva then sped from the room, not quite slamming the door behind him.

Brondate rubbed his hands together, and looked apprehensive, not knowing quite how Antonio would react. 'You may not take your horse. Bring her here in the morning and we'll look after her well. You'll be riding army horses. Is that all right?'

'I have no choice but just make sure my horse is happy in the palace stables.'

As Antonio arrived in the square, walking his aging mare by her reins, he inched closer to a number of soldiers, standing in a row alongside their frisky mounts. One of the soldiers, apparently the most senior, who wore a plumed morion, with red and white feathers, a bright red sash and a dazzling steel breastplate, held a rapier vertically as he inspected the other eight. The four colonels also wore morions but with no plume, half armour and grey baggy trousers that matched their dullish body protection. Each carried an harquebusier over his right shoulder, each at the same steep angle. The escorts wore brimmed hats and were plainly dressed.

As Antonio stopped, about ten *varas* in front of them, the senior looking officer shouted an order. 'Stand at ease. We depart in ten minutes.'

Antonio walked up to the senior looking one. Before he had a chance to speak, the officer said, 'Who are you?'

His abruptness quite shocked Antonio but it fitted Silva's description of General Mejía. 'I am Antonio Hidalgo. I believe I am accompanying you on a mission.'

'You are.' The soldier said sharply, looking Antonio in the eye. Then he turned away. 'Come and take his horse,' he shouted to a stable lad who was already walking a black stallion towards Antonio. The lad removed the pannier and saddle from Antonio's aging mare and, much to the animal's apparent disgust, placed them on Antonio's younger, sleeker mount.

Antonio stroked her neck. 'See you when I return, old gal! Be good!' The horse let out a short neigh as if to wonder and clacked her tongue in annoyance.

Antonio had never before travelled as fast. Not even on the relay that took him and Tariq to Cádiz. Using the army horse relay, the small group of men, including the general and Antonio, galloped as rapidly as their sweating mounts would carry them. They stopped overnight at miserable road side taverns in Ocaña, Las Pedroñeras and La Roda on their ninety *leguas* journey to the outskirts of Alicante. They rode this cold autumn road all the way to Albacete before they detected a sign of a *Morisco*. As they approached the town, whose towering church they could make out on the rugged, cloudy horizon, they saw a group of what appeared to be beggars coming towards them. As the men on horseback neared, the group stopped. The sight shocked Antonio. The ten or so of them looked emaciated. There were three women, five men and two children holding the hands of what Antonio presumed were their parents. One of the women was naked apart from a ragged blanket that barely covered her. Her face betrayed an uncommon agony as she constantly stared at a bundle in her arms. One of the other women wore a dress so shredded that she might as well be naked for what negligible protection it afforded. Even the men were in tatters.

'Who are you?' asked the general.

'We are Christians, escaping the *Morisco* onslaught,' said one of the men, failing to look straight at the general.

Still mounted, the general removed his rapier from its sheath and pointed it towards the man's heart. 'Now tell me the truth!' he bellowed, so loudly that his voice seemed to echo in the surrounding hills.

'You win. We are *Moriscos*. We have escaped from Alicante and are heading inland,' said another man.

'What's in that bundle?' said the general, pointing his rapier towards the woman's package.

'My dead baby,' the woman said and exploded into uncontrolled crying.

'Let me see,' said the general.

The woman, still sobbing, placed the package carefully on the road and slowly unwrapped it. Inside was the greying corpse of a baby girl, its eyes staring to eternity.

Antonio reacted by looking away. The mounted soldiers, except the general, did likewise.

'You three men,' instructed the general, pointing to some of the *Moriscos*. 'Take the baby and bury it over there.'

'We have no shovels,' said one of them.

'Use your hands,' said the general. Antonio was beginning to dislike this man. He vowed never to even attempt to befriend him but to treat him as a challenge. He would try to investigate the workings of his mind.

All of the *Morisco* men and one of the women started to dig. Three of his colonels, including one with an extravagant moustache, dismounted and helped the *Moriscos* to dig a shallow grave.

The mother, screaming in mental agony, placed her baby's body in the hole and stood. The other helpers used their dirty hands to rake the soil over her.

With the absence of any feeling towards these people, the general spoke again. 'Now turn about and walk back to Alicante. You know your fate. Do not attempt to escape it or you will all finish up in shallow graves.'

Whether they realised or not, there was nothing the general could do to carry out his threat, unless of course they openly defied him there and then. Nonetheless, and presumably because he represented the voice of a higher authority, they turned in resignation and walked back the way they had come. The baby's makeshift grave marked the end of their painful walk from Alicante.

There are certain sights or events in a person's life that, despite every effort to eliminate them from the memory, they persist indelibly. The more the mind attempts to eradicate them, the stronger and more permanent they seem to become. The staring eyes of the dead *Morisco* baby girl burnt itself into Antonio's memory as if it was a scar burnt into his flesh. Those dead eyes staring into the far distance haunted him like an ever present ghost.

While Antonio unintentionally recalled this grim and pathetic image, the general's group encountered another example of man's brutality to man. On the outskirts of Alicante, armed escorts were driving a group of a hundred or so men, women and children, most wearing clothes which were so ragged they were in effect naked. The escorts carried guns, swords pikes and cross bows. The guards shot, slashed by sword, stabbed a pike at, or shot an arrow towards any in their charge who attempted to escape. Many such groups had passed. The roadside betrayed the evidence: the dead or wounded that lay there. No one gave them a moment's attention. Anyone, a friend or relative, who wanted to help or bid farewell to the dying, became an equal victim. Antonio lost count of the number who had attempted to escape but had failed to do so. None of the general's company uttered a word in passing. These ghastly sights struck Antonio dumb. He could not believe or accept that the king's decision to expel these people would lead to such agony and heartbreak. These once proud people were totally destitute. A whole family of humankind was being punished for the crimes of the few and the faith of the many.

The sheer density of the crowds of *Moriscos*, walking towards their fate, increased gradually, the closer the general's troupe got to Alicante. The mounted troupe had to veer off the road to pass the crowd or simply follow where the road narrowed and where room to pass did not exist. Then suddenly they saw, approaching them from the direction in which they were heading, a soldier on horseback, carrying the flag of the Habsburgs, the red crossed laurel leaves on a white background. He had the same problem negotiating his jet black mount past the crowd of *Moriscos* approaching him. Eventually, he reached the general and his men and, while wheeling his agitated horse, spoke to him.

'Good afternoon señor. I presume you are General Mejía.'

'In that case, you are correct.'

'I am an emissary from Luis de Toledo, the Marquis of Caracena, the king's viceroy in Valencia. He is now in Alicante.'

'Out with it, fool. What does he want?'

'To meet you tonight in his office at the town hall. With your consent, I shall escort you there.'

'Lead on, my man.'

The emissary, despite the general's insult, smiled, turned his horse and led the way. By the time the troupe and escort reached the modest town hall, they must have passed thousands of pathetic looking *Moriscos* making their way to the docks at and around the town. At the centre they moved in waves towards the port of Alicante. Some walked away from the port. Others had stopped and didn't know which way to go. From high up they would have looked like a colony of ants swirling around a dung heap. Strangely, at least to Antonio's perception, some in the town sang out as if to celebrate a new life that awaited them over the sea. But the vast majority looked frightened, dejected, hungry, miserable and lost.

'I am meeting Caracena with Hidalgo. You others can find a drinking house. But be back here within the hour,' instructed the general, as his troupe tied their horses up outside of the building. He beckoned a gloved hand towards Antonio and the two of them, led by the emissary, walked into the main hall of the building.

'This way,' said the man, pointing towards a long corridor. 'The viceroy's office is down here.' Antonio walked two steps behind the general, the sound of whose boots echoed in the long, wide passageway.

'In here,' said the escort, knocking on a tall narrow door. They waited outside for all of five seconds before a private secretary let them in. The viceroy must have heard them and appeared, smiling and with his arms outstretched in front of him.

'My dear Agustín, welcome back to Alicante!' He walked towards the general and went to embrace him. The general held out a gloved hand.

'Steady on. I don't need that. A handshake will suffice,' he said, giving an abrupt rebuff. He then turned towards Antonio. 'This is Don Antonio Hidalgo. He is a spy. De Torres has sent him as my assistant. I've brought him merely so he can hear you at first hand. So what's happening in the Laguar Valley? I presume that is what you want to discuss.'

'Yes, over some food and a drink. Come through to my office. There is refreshment on the meeting table. Take a seat and help yourselves.' The marquis politely dismissed the emissary and closed the door.

'Let me tell you, Agustín. We still don't know how many there are up there. Could be ten to fifteen thousand. And the place is so high up, your men will have trouble getting them out.'

'Don't you believe it! If they can get up there, so can we!'

'We've tried to negotiate with them. But would you believe these accursed people? They want to negotiate in Arabic!'

'I have six thousand soldiers and none speaks that bedevilled tongue. Not one, I'm proud to say. So negotiation is out of the question!'

'Just a minute,' said Antonio. 'I speak Arabic.'

'That's just giving in to them. They'll have you over a barrel!' The general laughed.

'I disagree. If Señor Hidalgo is willing to speak to their so called "king", that would put us in a highly defendable position. We can at least say we tried. And the king wants to avoid bloodshed, if possible. We even found someone who speaks their language! Do you see what I'm saying?'

'Of course I see what you are saying. The damned language is illegal in this country. So we break the king's statutes to speak to them!' The general's face coloured purple with rage.

'Makes my point even stronger. The king will be delighted. Whatever happens, we can say we went to illegal extremes to comply with their wishes.'

'I agree with the viceroy,' said Antonio, calmly. He then took a bite out of a pear that he'd taken from a crystal bowl on the Marquis's table.

'Who asked for your opinion?' the general snarled. 'You have no opinion, as far as I'm concerned. You're here to do what I tell you!'

'Steady on, Agustín. Hidalgo is merely volunteering to do something for us that goes significantly beyond his terms of reference. It's up to us to decide and I'm sure he realises that.'

'All right! All right! With whom would he negotiate? How would we protect him? It wouldn't look good if they sent him back in a bag!' said the general, in a somewhat calmer tone. 'And we'd have to work out some terms for negotiation.'

'He would speak to their so called king, Mellini Saquien, at some neutral place. We would guarantee his return and we'd expect them to guarantee Hidalgo's. I suppose we'd give them the freedom to come down from the valley, unhindered and unpunished. We'd feed them and then escort them to the ports. Give them some time, say two weeks, to return to their houses and pack.'

'But they're up there because they refuse to be expelled.'

'Yes, but presumably if they didn't come down voluntarily you'd go up and rout them. That would be the other side of the coin and we'd put that to them as well.'

'Seems the terms are clear. Have you got that, Hidalgo, my man?'

'I follow, completely, general.'

Three days hard, cold ride later, Antonio met the *Morisco* king, Mellini Saquien, in a tavern on the road up to the Laguar Valley, twenty *leguas* from Alicante. The *Morisco* king had agreed to meet there provided the inn had been cleared of all its customers and that he and Hidalgo were the only ones in the drinking area. Antonio arrived first, leaving two of the general's escorts who had accompanied Antonio from Madrid, two hundred *varas* or so back down the road. He gave the dark skinned *Morisco* king a friendly greeting as the king walked in and ushered Antonio towards one of the tables. Saquien's confidence and presence impressed Antonio. The man seemed totally fearless and took the lead in the encounter.

'So what are you offering?' he said, in Arabic.

Antonio replied, also in Arabic, 'General Mejía is offering you free, fully protected passage down the valley, a full three weeks in your homes before an escorted walk to your designated port of departure.'

'Not good enough,' Mellini Saquien, laughed. 'Three weeks? What can we do in that time? Sell a few sheep? We need at least six weeks and want the army to bring us food and water. We are running low on both.'

'How many are there up there?'

'I wish I knew. Somewhere around twenty thousand. Maybe more.'

'A lot to feed and water. But I can agree to that,' smiled Antonio, shocked at the number. 'But not to more than three weeks at your homes.'

'In that case we cannot agree. I'm disappointed,' he said, standing up from the table. He made his way towards the door which he closed quietly behind him.

Antonio returned empty handed to the two escorts. They mounted their horses and carefully picked their way down the valley and eventually back to the town hall in Alicante.

'Stupid man. He's as good as dead now. We assemble our troops and start the march tomorrow,' said the general, quite delighted that he would be embarking on a military exercise against no more than twenty thousand civilians, however well-armed they might be. Even with the limited number of six thousand troops he couldn't possibly lose.

'Don't I have a say in this?' said the marquis, his voice raised and his face in tension. 'Whether you like it or not, these people are my subjects and I won't have them murdered by your army.'

'How will you stop me? I've complied with the king's wish to negotiate. Negotiations have failed so we attack them.'

'I insist you give them one more chance,' he said. 'What have you to lose by giving six weeks to sell up? They will agree because that's what they want.'

'I refuse. The terms we offered were better than I would have given. To that extent, Hidalgo exceeded his brief. Any more time would merely prolong the exercise and why should we reward them for being rebels. I'll assemble the troops and we'll leave tomorrow.'

'In which case, you can take full responsibility for the consequences. I disown you, your army and your decision,' said the marquis, reddening from the collar up. Antonio couldn't believe his ears. He didn't think the marquis would react so strongly. The marquis then glared at the general as if to drive him with his eyes out of his office. The general took the hint.

'I think I can detect when I am not wanted.' He turned towards Antonio. 'Let's go.'

The two of them made their way across the square from the town hall to the tavern in which they and the general's commanders would be staying.

'I want you to accompany me when I instruct my senior officers. You might learn something,' he said in all seriousness. Antonio laughed inside at the arrogance of the man while keeping any smile from his face.

'I'd be delighted, general.'

As they walked into the inn, the general's eyes alighted on one of his colonels, a large, moustached individual, drinking a beer with a woman showing an embarrassment of cleavage, apparently a *puta*. 'You can stop consorting with her. Go and find the other three. I want to meet you all here in ten minutes. Bring a couple of your men to protect our privacy. Pay her off,' he said, nodding towards the whore. The commander threw the woman half a *real* which she grinned at as she picked it up from the floor.

The general guided Antonio to a table in a booth at the back of the drinking area. They sat there until the moustachioed officer, with three colleagues behind him, approached. They each squeezed themselves onto the benches. Four uniformed army guards stood facing away from them to keep a look out. A plain looking barmaid brought a tray of drinks. No one dared smile, not even the woman.

The general began. 'We are going to march towards the Laguar Valley tomorrow. All six thousand of us. I want the swordsmen in front, pikemen next, followed by the harquebusiers. Cavalry at the rear. Got that? These people are rebels. Criminals. So our aim is to kill. It'll take four days to get there. We'll commandeer the churches for billeting on the way. Otherwise the men will have to sleep at the roadside.'

His colonels nodded in mechanical compliance. The general gave no room for questions. This seemed odd to Antonio who could see from the uniforms of these officers that they were of high rank and therefore highly experienced. The general then turned towards Antonio.

'I want you, Hidalgo, to go with Colonel Ortiz. He commands the harquebusiers,' he said, pointing towards the officer who had been talking earlier to the *puta*. The affable colonel leant over towards Antonio, didn't quite succeed in standing up straight in the booth and shook Antonio's hand for so long Antonio thought he'd never let go.

'*Encantado*, señor. We will work well together.'

Antonio reciprocated and wondered exactly they would be doing.

'Now sit down. I have further instructions... first Hidalgo, get another round of beers.' Antonio didn't ask who would pay and assumed it would not be the general. He came back with a laden tray and put it on the table. The general grabbed a cup and the others followed.

'I want a show of strength in the square early in the morning. All six thousand troops will assemble there at eight o'clock and face the town hall. It will look as if we will be attacking that building, but of course we won't.' He chuckled under his breath. Antonio understood well what that was about. 'On the left flank, I want the swordsmen. They will be arranged in files of fifty, in thirty rows. Then the harquebusiers, similarly arranged, then the pikemen, staves vertical, arranged as with the others. The cavalry will be at the rear, hundred in a file and fifteen deep. Got that?'

'Where do you want us?' said a thin, clean shaven one, wearing an open shirt and thigh length boots which folded over at the top. He uttered his words laconically, as if expecting a rebuke.

'At the Christ bleeding front of course. You won't be hiding tomorrow! No chance! You four will be evenly spaced along the front and I'll take the middle but just in front of all of you.'

'What about me?' Antonio dared ask.

'You'll be on your horse beside Colonel Ortiz, to his right,' he said, calmly as if realising his omission. 'Once we are all assembled, and at the stroke of nine by the cathedral clock, we leave the square and head for the valley, in the order I said before, but I will lead. You will be in the third group behind, along with Hidalgo. Is that clear?' he said, glancing at Colonel Ortiz.

No one replied. He repeated the question.

'Of course,' said Colonel Ortiz.

'In which case, good night!' The general stood from the booth and left the drinking room. All but Colonel Ortiz followed. He turned his ample frame in Antonio's direction.

'So how did you get yourself into this situation?' he said, curling the right side of his luxuriant moustache as he did so. 'Not the easiest of men, our beloved general.'

'I was warned but had no choice! It's a long story and I'll spare you the detail.' Antonio told him how, quite accidentally, he became an agent for the king and about his various missions, including his recent sojourn to Marrakesh.

'Holy Jesus, and you are still a young man. How old by the way?'

'Twenty four.'

'Amazing what you have done in that time and a musician into the bargain!'

'I'm afraid so!'

'I dread to think what we will be witnessing in the Laguar Valley. But those were his words: "our aim is to kill". So that is what we shall be doing. I hope you've a strong stomach! At least you've a few days to get used to the idea. I'm going to resume my pursuit of the *puta*. She can't be far away. Would you like to join me? After all we will be working together. We may as well play together!'

Antonio hesitated before he spoke. 'An interesting question! Yes, why not? Who goes first? You or me?'

'She's sure to have a friend, a partner. Especially, this time of night! Let's ask the bar lady!'

The two of them sidled up to the bar. The colonel asked the woman where the *puta* was likely to be. She said, to his surprise, that she had rented a room in this inn for the night. The colonel politely asked for the number but the woman refused, saying she'd go to the room and ask if she wanted to come down. Minutes later the *puta* was sitting with the two of them, discussing her terms.

'No. I'm the only one here. You'll have to take it in turns and I won't have one of you watching.'

'We'll toss a coin!'

'Here's your half *real*!' She spun it into the air.

'Tails,' said Antonio, laughing and before the colonel had chance to utter a word.

'You lucky swine! Tails it is!'

Antonio and the *puta* left the drinking area. She held Antonio's hand and dragged him behind her up the stairs to her room which reminded him of Fatima's in the Marrakesh *burdel*. Sparsely furnished, not well lit and with a badly worn carpet. She locked the door behind her. Antonio could already feel his excitement gaining pace.

'What exactly do you want?' she said. 'You'll have to pay in advance. I've been cheated in the past but not anymore!'

'Nothing unusual. I haven't had a woman in months so it will do me good but may not last long! How much?'

'For a handsome young man like you, half a *real* for a straight one. And the quicker the better. You know I have another customer!' she said, easing her dress from her shoulders and dropping it to the floor. She revealed a small but tightly formed body with firm breasts and buttocks. She could not have been older than nineteen years.

'You are beautiful,' said Antonio, loosening the belt on his breeches.

'Thank you, señor. You aren't dressed like a soldier. Or should I say undressed.'

'No, I'm supposed to be the general's assistant,' he said. 'I wish I knew what he wanted. Can we start? You lie on your back and…'

'Go on, young fellow. It's yours!' she laughed as if to anticipate mutual pleasure.

Antonio savoured her delicious perfume as he made love to the woman. As he enjoyed her, he wondered what tomorrow would bring. Would the general expect much of him or was he there as a witness. He didn't understand.

'Come on! Finish off. I thought you'd be quicker!'

Without saying a word, Antonio quickened to a conclusion.

'Damned marvellous!' she said. 'Thank you!'

'Thank you, young lady. Most enjoyable! Maybe we'll get together when I get back.'

'It would be a pleasure, señor. Until then. Would you mind telling your officer friend I'm ready now? Tell him I've spent his half *real* so he'll have to pay for my work!'

'I'll tell him but you can do the negotiation!'

CHAPTER 32
The Laguar

Antonio slept surprisingly well that night, considering that he knew so little about what might lie before him. He decided to arrive in the square at about half past seven so he could see the troops forming themselves into the parade in front of the town hall. There must have been at least a hundred local people, who happened to be passing through the square, to work or shopping maybe, and who had stopped to see the troops. They looked quite shocked to see this massive build-up of military strength. Antonio had no idea where the men had appeared from, where they had billeted or how they had arrived in the square. Three features of the event surprised him. First, the sheer discipline of the troops, which were guided obediently into their positions by what Antonio imagined were their corporals. Second the troops' dress. Very few wore anything remotely resembling a uniform. Most wore high boots and a wide brimmed hat. About a third wore morions. But there ended any uniformity. All carried weapons, including the swordsmen and the cavalry. Thirdly, the number of supply wagons. There must have been fifty, stopped behind where the cavalry were to form up. Men and women were loading the wagons with baskets of bread, sides of meat, bandages for the wounded, hay for the horses and spare clothing for the troops. A small band of soldiers was discreetly placing barrels of gunpowder, quivers of arrows and boxes of ammunition onto a heavy cart. They dropped a box and all ran away from it, as if it could explode. Nothing happened so they picked it up laughing and put it on the wagon.

The gathering of troops presented a frightening sight as they stood there, most on foot but fifteen hundred on horseback. The four colonels, each mounted, conducted a brief inspection, just before eight o'clock, the time they expected the general to appear. Eight o'clock came and went. No sign of the general. The four colonels walked their horses up to each other to discuss the situation. Where was he? Had he overslept? Had he been kidnapped? Had he been strangled in his sleep? No such luck: at about twenty past eight, he appeared on horseback from behind the town hall, duly dressed in his morion, plumed with red and white feathers, wearing a bright red sash over his steel breastplate, which glistened in the early morning sun. The four soldiers who had escorted him, his colonels and Antonio from Madrid accompanied him. He drew up alongside Colonel Ortiz.

'You and Hidalgo. I want you to join me on an inspection. Now and on foot!' The general led off and the two of them followed.

He started with the swordsmen and stopped about half way down the file. He walked along the row and kicked one of them in the heel. 'Your boots are disgusting. Where have you been with them? Jumping in a pile of shit? Get out of the formation and don't come back until they are clean.' The man cowered and sloped off. Then he checked the harquebusiers but could find nothing amiss. Similarly with the pikemen. He targeted the cavalry with the most acerbic of his criticism. He picked on a horseman so old he should have retired years before. 'You look foul,' he said. 'Your hair is a knotted mess, your horse is filthy and you need a damned good wash. Take your animal and go and sort yourself out. You've got thirty minutes. If you're not back by nine, we go without you.' The poor, chastened soldier kicked his spurs and trotted his horse out of the square, presumably to some stables nearby.

The general led Antonio and Colonel Ortiz back to the front of the parade. They remounted and walked their horses from one side of the square to the other. They stopped to speak to the other colonels. The troops in their command stayed in their positions in the parade. Just before the church clock struck nine, the old cavalry man appeared, a white towel in his hand, wiping shaving soap from his wet face. To the laughter and applause of those near him, he resumed his position in the assembly.

At the sound of the church bell, a drummer struck up a loud, persistent rhythm. A trumpeter at the rear blasted out a repeated triplet and the parade became a procession. The troops slowly, noisily and impressively began to leave the square, in exactly the order demanded by the general: him in front followed by the swordsmen, then the pikemen, the harquebusiers and then the cavalry. They were heading to the Laguar Valley. The chastised horseman failed to reappear.

The march almost exhausted the troops. Although they left in lukewarm autumn sunshine, the weather soon changed to being cold miserable and wet. The horses were as tired as the men, many of whom had suffered four nights in the freezing and wintery conditions. Eventually, they all arrived at the lower slopes of the Valley. Apart from a few hungry beggars who stood by the side of the road, hoping for a soldier to throw them a crust of bread, there was not a soul in sight.

'Tell your men we go up the Valley tomorrow. They can rest until then. We'll have the first choice of the tents and the men can draw lots for what are left,' directed the general. The troops, most of whom suffered a night of intense discomfort, were awakened by an overcast dawn and the smell of burning wood under soup cauldrons. At least a hot breakfast was nigh.

The march up the Valley was heralded by a trumpeter who blasted out three short notes followed by one long one, repeating the figure three more times. The general waved his outstretched arm towards the steep rise ahead of them and the swordsmen started out behind him. The disciplined soldiers in the square in Alicante transformed themselves into something that resembled a mob. They showed no sign of marching in step. Quite the opposite. Some walked, others ran and almost to a man, they shouted blood curdling victory cries before a single sword stroke, a shot fired or a lance thrown. The general managed to keep ahead of them on his mount. The hordes of soldiers climbed the Valley on two fronts as if to attempt to circle their foe or at least come at them from different directions. The pikemen followed. They too shouted and cheered as they did so. By the time the last of them left the night stop, there were three thousand troops climbing the craggy slopes of the Laguar. Then it was the turn of the harquebusiers, led by Colonel Ortiz with Antonio at his side.

'Look at that rowdy mob, Antonio. My men are more disciplined. They have to be to trust them with a gun.'

'Tell me, Colonel, why has the general decided to come with us? I'm surprised he hasn't left this to you senior officers to deal with.'

'Basically, he doesn't trust us. He's incapable of trust. We tried to bring them down without him... two weeks ago. He reckons we failed because we were too easy on them. Now he wants blood! And he'll make sure he gets it. I've never known anyone as ruthless!'

'Strikes me the same.'

'I'm going to stand here to direct my men to cover two fronts, just like the mob before us. Then we'll follow but we must stay in front of the cavalry! They'll be slow and will want to take up the rear from which they will protect us. You stay close to me!'

'Of course, Colonel,' smiled Antonio, welcoming some form of guidance and seeing the logic of the army's approach.

The harquebusiers followed their colonel's order. The sight of them, walking up the incline, with their weapons poised to fire, struck Antonio as incredible to behold. They had the uncanny knack of all having their loaded weapons aiming at the same angle, forty five degrees to the horizontal.

'We'll join here,' said the colonel after about twenty minutes and when half of his men had passed them. 'I can control them better from near the middle. Much harder from the rear!'

The two of them began to guide their mounts over the rugged terrain. The colonel shared the odd quip with his men who responded with a laugh. They clearly liked him and respected him.

'I still don't know why you are here,' said the colonel. 'I can't work it out!'

'I'm not sure either. My boss, the Corregidor of Madrid, told me to act as the general's assistant. That's hardly possible from here! And to be ready to perform any task he asked of me.'

'Has he asked for anything yet?' said the colonel, holding the reins by one hand and twisting his moustache with the other.

'Yes and no. I volunteered to negotiate with the *Morisco* king, Mellini Saquien, only because I speak the forbidden language and that's what he wanted to negotiate in.'

'So it was you who did that! You offered them more than the general wanted, I gather! He got quite excited about that... but, as I told him, the king didn't agree to anything anyway!'

'Yes, it was me all right. A strange meeting. Lasted all of two minutes and he left as soon as he realised he couldn't get his own way.'

'But he told you how many of them there were up there. We had no idea there were up to twenty thousand! Thought it was nearer six! So you did a good job. Well done young man!'

After they had been moving upwards for about an hour, Antonio suddenly thought he could hear shouting and screaming.

'What's that?' he said, looking anxiously towards the colonel.

'Sounds like the swordsmen and pikemen have engaged with the *Moriscos*. Let's go forward and see. You take charge until I return,' he said, looking down to his lieutenant on foot. The man nodded acceptance.

The colonel gently kicked his horse's flanks. Antonio did likewise and they sped further up the Valley. The shouting and screaming became louder as they rode. It became even louder when they turned a sharp corner beside an outcrop of grey rock. Antonio was appalled at the sight that befell them. On a fairly flat and open plain, the swordsmen were slashing to pieces hundreds of men, women and children. Most of those still standing had their backs to the soldiers as they attempted to escape this vile onslaught by fleeing back up the Valley. Women clutched babies to their breasts but the relentless slaughter continued regardless. The attackers shouted and laughed while their bloodied victims fell dead or dying to the ground. It was as if troops were taking pleasure in killing off the contagious victims of a fatal disease and had every right to do so. The pikemen also ripped into them, thrusting their staves into heads, chests and limbs. They too cheered and laughed as they perpetrated this obscene violence against the almost completely defenceless. It was an horrific onslaught. Some of the *Morisco* men attempted to defend themselves with kitchen knives, makeshift bows and arrows and pikes made out of tree branches but succumbed to the superior strength of these callous and merciless troops.

Antonio and the colonel stopped. Antonio had never seen anything as shocking, disgusting or depraved. His glaring eyes focussed on a woman who presented her baby to a pikeman in a gesture to save it. Without a moment's hesitation, the swarthy man, laughing as he did so, thrust the pike straight into the baby's chest. The woman let out a deathly scream and dropped to the ground pointing to her own chest, begging them to kill her, too, and to follow her child to its death. Another pikeman pushed his pike between her ribs. He killed her and spat on her twisting corpse. A swordsman, modestly threatened by a man with a sling, swung his sword so hard at the man's neck, he almost decapitated him. A child of about ten, who was running away with a pike stuck in his back and dragging on the ground, collapsed with blood pouring out. Antonio presumed he was dead. A family group of four was surrounded by swordsmen. They made the parents watch as they beheaded their children. They forced the crying parents to stand next to each other, alongside their children's remains.

Antonio, in a pointless gesture shouted, 'Stop!' but nothing was going to prevent the multiple executions.

'A waste of breath,' said the colonel. 'Once these animals have a taste for blood, there's no stopping them. My men are of a different breed. Chosen because of their restraint.'

'That so?' said Antonio, still in shock at these hideous events running uncontrolled before his eyes.

'Correct. You'll note that I've given no order to fire. And the men will simply continue to march forward until I say otherwise.'

'I see.'

'But we have to continue to move up the Valley or the mob in front will lose any protection my men may have to provide.'

As they approached this field of slaughter they could see its devastating horror. The uneven terrain ran with blood. The human redness had stained the ground under the horses' feet. There was blood everywhere. Not only blood. Corpses, some whole, many dismembered littered the scene. Broken, robbed of their lives by military thugs. There were legs, arms, even eyes and intestines, littering this bloody field of death. Not only were these individuals deprived of life, the men who had destroyed them were now ripping rings of the dead fingers, tearing bracelets off arms, even slashing off wrists to make the plundering easier. Pockets bulged with what had been taken from the bodies.

Standing next to the colonel, Antonio's mind could hardly bear to be in this most hideous of places. Hell could not be worse. He wondered why he had agreed to this mission. Why had he come here? Silva had told him that the general was being sent here to crush these people. He should have known what 'crush' meant. It meant to kill them, if they didn't agree to come down. That was so obvious now. If he'd have thought harder then he surely would have reached that ineluctable conclusion. But here he was surrounded by death: death by military execution. Not as the result of a court martial or trial but summary death at the hands of marauding, bloodthirsty monsters. Spaniard killing Spaniard. He couldn't understand it. Thoughts of his earlier life attempted to push those of this open brutality from his mind. His career as a musician seemed so far away. He hadn't played his new violin since playing with Señor de Polanco. Would he still be able to play? How would witnessing this death field influence his playing? There were no answers. Only questions.

'Have we seen enough of this?' said Antonio.

'My men are right behind us now so we should move forward, further up. God knows what will happen up there.'

By then the plundering on that flat land had all but reached its end. The swordsmen and pikemen were beginning to abandon the bodies they had robbed and, obviously delighted with their spoils, had started to move further up the Valley, hoping for another hopelessly one-sided confrontation.

'I dread to think,' said Antonio. 'My heart tells me I should get off my horse and fight for the *Moriscos*. But my head tells me I would be dead in an instant.'

'Totally right,' said the colonel. 'We'll have to see what's up there.'

They moved on about half a *milla*, only to be confronted by another scene of devastation. Some of the swordsmen and pikemen were engaging a huge number of *Morisco* men in open battle. The general was nowhere to be seen. Antonio estimated that at least a thousand *Moriscos* were fighting the troops. Although the *Moriscos* had the tactical advantage of being higher up than the soldiers, their weapons were so pathetic that they were forced to fight by hand. The soldiers took advantage. Swathes of *Moriscos* were lying dead and injured on the ground. Bodies were piled on bodies. Blood spilled everywhere and even flowed into the narrower crags. The confrontation generated less noise than the slaughter of the defenceless, further back down: the troops seemed to take this battle more seriously than simply killing and plundering.

'I can't believe I am seeing this,' said Antonio. 'Those men have no real weapons. Why can't we get them to surrender? There's been enough slaughter on these hills.'

'I'll try but I doubt that I'll succeed. Stay here!'

With that, Colonel Ortiz rode quickly forward to the battle front. He raised his arm and shouted as loudly as he could. 'Hold back, men! Stop fighting! I want to give the enemy a chance to surrender.'

He then turned towards the men they were fighting. 'Who is your leader? I want to speak to him.'

The proud figure of Mellini Saquien stepped forward. 'I am the leader, señor. I am the *Morisco* king!'

Still mounted, the colonel shouted across at Mellini Saquien. 'I want to offer you a chance to surrender. It will be your one and only chance. Surrender now and this battle is over. There will be no more fighting here!'

The man paused. He was thinking. How could the king surrender? If he did, the whole mountainside of *Moriscos* would have to follow.

'I categorically refuse,' said the king. He turned and walked back to join the men on the battle front, in particular a group who were protecting him.

'Re-engage, men!' said he colonel after giving Mellini Saquien time to re-establish his position. He returned to join Antonio.

'It had to be worth a try. You saw the result.'

'Yes and I recognised him. Why did you instruct our men to re-engage? You could have made them stand off and guard the route down.'

'Out of the question. We've a lot of troops up here but not sufficient to encircle the whole mountain. If the general wants to trap them up here, it'll have to be higher up!'

The animated soldiers attacked even more aggressively than before. They seemed to thirst for the sight of blood and death. Within minutes of the recommencement, tens if not hundreds more *Moriscos* lay dead or dying. More blood flowed. Not only did they kill, the troops mutilated the dead and wounded in front of their fellow *Moriscos*. Arms were hacked off and heads removed by repeated sword strokes. One group of rabid pikemen stripped one of the *Morisco* bodies and cut off the man's genitals which he threw into the few hundred who were still standing. Antonio saw the anger on Mellini Saquien's face as he witnessed this atrocity. He escaped his protectors and ran towards the men who had committed it and attempted to attack one with a make shift pike. A swordsman lashed into him and soon he lay dead on the ground. 'We've got their leader,' shouted one of the swordsmen. Let's cut him up!'

Antonio couldn't bear to witness the horror which was about to be perpetrated. As the troops lashed into the dead or dying body, a shout went up within the *Moriscos*. Antonio interpreted for the colonel. 'Now he's dead, they are going to withdraw.'

The *Moriscos* turned and ran as fast as they could back up the hill. The soldiers gave chase but weighed down with their arms and plunder, failed to catch a single one. Soon the two hundred or so who had survived were out of sight of the troops, probably hiding in the rocks or in their enclaves further up the valley.

The troops continued to move further up the mountain, vaguely in the same formation, with the swordsmen and pikemen, by now completely integrated, at the front with the harquebusiers behind and the cavalry at the rear. The pockets of the swordsmen and pikemen bulged with what they had stolen from those they had killed. Some had even filled sacks of loot which they had proudly slung over their shoulders.

As Antonio and the colonel rode further up behind the swordsmen and pikemen, and amidst the harquebusiers, the colonel responsible for the cavalry approached them with one of the general's escorts.

'Colonel Ortiz,' said the mounted escort, whom Antonio recognised as one of the four who came with them from Madrid. 'General Mejía wants to meet all four of you colonels in half an hour. Please follow us and I will escort you to him. He wants to see Hidalgo as well.'

The escort turned toward Antonio, realising that he had not been quite as polite as their relative positions demanded, and said, 'Is that alright, señor?'

'Of course,' said Antonio, and the three sped off, to find and inform the other two colonels of the meeting.

The general and his colonels met in a craggy glen which Antonio estimated was well past half way to the summit. The troops had stopped advancing, Antonio assumed on the orders of their sergeants because he hadn't heard Colonel Ortiz give one. From the look on the faces of those Antonio could see, the men seemed to be awaiting further instruction. Most were chatting and joking with each other, some standing but many were sitting to give their weary legs a rest.

'Gentlemen, well done for all of your efforts. I estimate that we have killed at least fifteen hundred of these people. We've left hundreds, probably a further thousand fatally injured and maimed. And I'm not aware of one casualty amongst our forces!

'I have been pondering our continuing strategy. We are going to stop here and wait. These people need food and water and once you men have encircled the mountain at this height, there will be no escape. They will have to surrender, or die. Preferably the latter,' he laughed.

'We need to inform the king that the end of the *Morisco* rebellion is in sight. For this purpose, I am sending Antonio Hidalgo back to Madrid with this letter. He will be accompanied by the four escorts who brought us here.

'I want you to organise your men as follows. You will work in groups of eight. Two swordsmen, two at the pikes, two harquebusiers and two cavalrymen. Optimally space youselves around the hill. Just make sure there is no means of escape. You will patrol night and day. Do you hear that? While four sleep the others will be awake. I am going to billet here with your lieutenants as my protectors. Any questions?'

'Only one, general. It will be far easier as less wasteful of the horses' food if we kept the cavalry separate,' said the colonel responsible.

'I don't agree. It will be good exercise for their riders to get the food themselves. Anymore?'

No one replied.

'In which case, Hidalgo and his four escorts must prepare to go and the rest of you can sort out your men's positions. Here is my letter, Hidalgo.'

Antonio walked forward to accept the letter. He didn't know what to say in bidding the general farewell, so said nothing, but held out a hand. The general gave him the letter which took the form of a sealed scroll. He shook Antonio's hand and simply said. 'Give this to the *corregidor*. Tell him it's for the king.' No wishes for the future, thanks or anything else, not that Antonio expected anything of this strangely cold, brute of a man.

Antonio turned and went over to Colonel Ortiz who was smiling and twisting at his moustache. Antonio returned the smile as they shook hands in a friendly farewell. 'Thank you, Señor Hidalgo. I've immensely enjoyed your company and I sincerely hope we meet again. May I wish you the best for your future career! I wish I'd heard you play your violin. You will be brilliant at it, I'm certain!'

Antonio said goodbye to the colonel and stepped towards his four escorts, one of whom was holding his horses' reins. He climbed on and turned to wave to the general and the four colonels as the five of them began their descent.

CHAPTER 33
A change of heart

Antonio reached Madrid far later in the day than he expected and too late to see Silva. So he bid farewell to his escorts and went back to his rooms in Doña Marta's house, deciding to take the general's missive to Silva first thing in the morning.

Antonio was generally a cheerful sort of individual who always looked at the positive side of most situations. However, he then felt desperately low, lower than he had felt for years. He simply could not eradicate the images of those dead and dying *Moriscos* from his mind. The flowing blood, the smell of it, the severed limbs, the dead children, that man's severed genitals thrown through the air to the glee of the thrower, but most profoundly the staring eyes of the dead baby in its mother's arms by the roadside, on the way to Alicante: it all affected him badly. Nor could he see any justification in committing those acts of extermination on those people. He could just about understand an execution of an individual who had been tried for a serious crime, even if the trial was by the Inquisition, but the wanton slaughter of all those innocents simply could not be justified.

Not only did he feel for the *Morisco* victims of the mindless killings, he harboured a terrible sense of guilt. He had just stood there watching while these atrocities took place. He asked himself why he hadn't done more. He could at least have searched out the general and pleaded with him to stop the slaughter. Even if he had been unable to persuade him, he could have tried his colonels. Colonel Ortiz seemed decent enough. He had, at Antonio's suggestion, attempted to convince Mellini Saquien to surrender. Antonio reluctantly gave himself credit for that, even if it ended in failure, Saquien's death and that of more of his *Morisco* cohorts.

He decided he had to eat before he went to bed. So he walked around to The Silversmith's, off the Platería. He pushed open the door and walked to the bar in the drinking room. He asked the pretty bar lady for a beer and to tell him what he could eat. He settled on some beef stew, chick peas and some bread.

'Go and sit down. I'll bring it to you,' said the girl. Even in his current state of misery, her mere appearance gave him spurious pleasure. Not feeling that he wanted to speak to anyone, he went towards the back and sat at a table in an area where only a few others gathered. He glanced around the room. To his profound relief, he recognised no one there.

'Why do you look so miserable?' said a voice to his right and a little outside his field of view.

He looked around. 'Iago, I didn't see you. How are you?'

'You didn't answer my question.'

'I was just thinking. I haven't paid my taxes yet. I was thinking about how much I owe!'

'Why should that make you look so miserable?'

'Maybe I was looking serious rather than miserable,' said Antonio, annoyed at Iago's probing. Up to then, he had avoided telling Iago about his job as a spy and that was not about to change.

'You must be earning good money then,' Iago said, hinting that Antonio might want to tell him more.

'Quite good,' said Antonio, without elaborating.

'Did you know I've rejoined the Wandering Chordsmen?'

'No. I thought they said they'd never have you back,' said Antonio, chuckling as if to make a joke of it and welcoming a change of subject.

'They did, but that wore off. They so badly wanted a dulcian player.'

'I'm glad,' said Antonio, not sure whether he meant it.

'Francisca de Polanco's father is also a member - or was - but only two days ago, he had an almighty row with Carlos and left. And Carlos is betrothed to Francisca. Did you know that?'

The question unsettled Antonio. The woman he had fallen in love with promised to another. It reawakened those awful feelings of rejection and jealousy. 'Yes, I know. What was the row about?'

'No one is saying. But they almost came to blows. The rumour machine says that Carlos tried to cheat him out of some money.'

Antonio listened intently. He couldn't believe that Carlos would swindle anyone, especially a colleague working in the band. There had to be another reason.

'Are you sure it was about money. I can't imagine Carlos doing that.'

'Yes, fairly sure. They have quite different personalities and Señor de Polanco sometimes thinks he's funny when he just isn't.'

'Hmm,' said Antonio, still wondering. The bar lady brought his beef stew and smiled as she placed it in front of him. 'Are you eating, Iago? You can join me if you wish.'

'No. But only because I'm meeting Hector Brondate, here in about fifteen minutes.'

'It's good that you became friends. By all means tell him you've seen me.' Antonio didn't really want to see Brondate, at least not then so he ate his meal a little quicker than he might have otherwise, bade Iago farewell and went back home, wondering all the way what the row between Carlos and Señor de Polanco could be about.

Antonio wanted to be at the palace early, not least because he wanted to see his old mare and hopefully the old girl wanted to see him. He walked into the outer office only to be greeted by a smiling Hector Brondate, as if his lugubriousness had vanished at least for a minute or two.

'Señor Hidalgo. I saw Iago last night and he said he'd seen you. How are you?'

'I am fine, thank you. I've brought a letter for the *corregidor* to give to the king. It's from General Mejía,' Antonio, said coolly.

'Señor de Torres is not in the office yet, but I'm expecting him any minute. Please take a seat. Would you like something to drink?'

'No thank you. I had a drink before I came here.'

Antonio sat there watching while Brondate shuffled through some papers. Some he filed in folders and others he carefully labelled and put in order in a single folder, as if they were the papers he wanted de Torres to see that day. Then the man appeared, bursting into the outer office as if he was making up for his lateness.

'What are you doing here?' he half smiled at Antonio. 'The battle for the Laguar Valley cannot be over yet, surely?'

'Not when I left... but let me explain. The general gave me this letter for you to deliver to the king,' said Antonio, taking the scroll from his bag.

'What does it say?'

'I wasn't with him when he wrote it. But I can tell you how it was when I left, five days ago now.'

'Let's go into my office. Come in, Hector. You can take notes.'

All three stepped in. Silva sat behind his desk and put his hands on the back of his head and waited for Antonio to begin.

'I won't bore you with the journey there... or back. But I will tell you that the general seriously upset the Marquis of Caracena.'

'How, exactly?'

Antonio told him how he'd been up the valley and failed to reach an agreement with Mellini Saquien. He explained why the marquis had become so angry that he had virtually thrown the general out of his office.

Silva was surprised that the normally placid marquis could have become so agitated.

Antonio continued from the time the army started up the Valley. He reached the point where he and Colonel Ortiz witnessed the killings and mutilation of the *Morisco* women and children and paused.

'What's the matter? Can't you continue?'

'What I witnessed then was the most inhuman thing I could imagine. I can't get it out of my mind and I am plagued with guilt about it.'

'Please tell me. I'm sorry to put you through this but I have to know. Especially, now that I have to deliver the general's letter.'

Antonio related every detail of these horrific scenes. He had difficulty at certain points in putting his thoughts into words but, with a few more pauses, managed to complete his story, right up to the point where the general handed him the letter and dismissed him.

'I don't understand why he sent you back. He could have sent a messenger. He should have continued to use your services until the end of the rebellion. I thought I'd agreed that with him. You recorded the agreement, Hector, didn't you?'

'Yes, señor, it's in my notes.'

'Get them!' said Silva, angrily.

Brondate soon returned. 'Yes, here it is.'

'Show me... Yes, it's clear enough, "the general would retain the services of Diaspora until the rebellion had been quelled". I don't understand it. Did you upset him somehow?'

'I don't think so... but I don't think I impressed him either. I admit, I was relieved to get away from the man,' said Antonio, slightly with his head down as if he was to blame for something but wasn't sure what.

'Well, you're back here now and you don't have to concern yourself about him. I'm intrigued to know why you harbour these feelings of guilt. I can't see what you've done that's wrong,' said Silva.

'I feel I should have begged the general to show some mercy or at least persuaded Colonel Ortiz to approach him. Ortiz was a reasonable man and I liked him a lot.'

'I'm glad you said nothing,' said Silva, as reassuringly as he could. 'The general was acting on the orders of the king and you would have infuriated him if you tried to stop him. You can rub those thoughts from your mind. So what does this letter say?'

'I've not seen it. Probably that his troops killed upwards of fifteen hundred Moriscos and that there are about twenty thousand trapped on the mountain. And that he is starving them out. They'll have to surrender or die.'

'I see,' he said, suddenly realising the number. 'Twenty thousand?'

'Yes, at least that's what Mellini Saquien told me when I was negotiating with him.'

'Well, done, Antonio. That was crucial information. Just what we sent you there to find out!'

'Thank you. You've cheered me up!'

'I'm glad.' He paused and came around the desk and held Antonio's hand. 'But I also have some bad news I'm afraid. Your horse fell ill, the day after you went. Three days later, it died. The stables did everything they could but it simply passed away. I'm so sorry.'

The news struck Antonio like a thunderbolt and he visibly recoiled. 'That is bad news. I don't know what to say, other than to thank you for telling me. I feel I should go now.' By that point he had trouble in holding back his tears and all he wanted was to leave.

The three shook hands in what had become a gloomy end to the meeting.

'Do come back soon and we can talk again. I'll let you know the king's reaction,' said Silva, trying to bring some hope.

Antonio began walking back to his rooms in Doña Marta's house. He had never felt worse. First he'd lost Catalina then, even worse, Carolina. He then fell in love with Francisca. She had shattered his dreams by rejecting him in favour of Carlos. He loved her and had truly hoped to settle down with her and care for her the rest of his life. But that was not to be. Now he had lost his treasured old mare, which could, it seemed, understand his every word. He had lost everything and felt miserable and alone.

He stepped dejectedly into his rooms and wondered quite what he should do. Silva had made no indication of another mission. In some ways Antonio was glad. Another like the last could finish him. He still found it difficult to prevent those images, especially the dead baby's eyes, from flooding into his mind. He sat in his favourite chair and thought. He needed to consider his future. What should he do with his life? Did he want to continue on these missions? Should he resign his status as a special agent? After all, he was appointed to that position only because of a freakish combination of events. Should he tell Silva he wished to end that job? Should he seek to go back to working with the Wandering

Chordsmen? It was a simple life and one he could enjoy again. He really had no idea.

His thoughts turned to his poor mare. Once again, he felt guilty. The old girl had taken three days to die and he hadn't been there with her. She had looked at him strangely when they had parted before he went to Valencia and made a strange noise. Perhaps she thought he would be away for a long time, as long as he was in Marrakesh. If so, she might have lost the will to live. Silva never did say what she died of. Antonio wasn't going to ask.

He spent the next few days in a more positive frame of mind. He would take a little time away from Madrid and go and visit his parents. He said he would the last time he wrote to them. They were all he had left now so he needed to stay in touch with them. He made some other important decisions. He would not return permanently to Pedraza but would continue living in this great city. He would engage himself as a professional musician, playing full time and he would ask Silva if he could change his status as a spy. He would, if Silva agreed, become an observer, simply reporting any suspicious activity that he saw and suspected could threaten the king or state. He started to practice on his new violin and by the end of the second day he performed quite to his own satisfaction.

It was during an afternoon of practice that there was a loud knock on the door. He carefully put down his violin and bow and went to answer. He expected no one so was puzzled and surprised when he saw Señor de Polanco standing by the threshold.

'It's you, Señor de Polanco... Juan. You are the last person I expected. Do come in!'

Antonio led the señor through to the drawing room before they shook hands. Antonio sat in his chair and the señor sat in the one diagonally opposite. The señor looked quite doleful, as if he had come to say something Antonio didn't want to hear. But he had seen and heard so much lately that he didn't welcome, another disaster wouldn't make much difference, unless it concerned Francisca. Then he remembered how ill she had become, what three years before? Had he come to tell him she had died? He suddenly felt the colour drain from his cheeks.

'To what do I owe the pleasure, Juan? It's some time since we've spoken. Is everything all right?'

'Yes, all is fine. Iago told me he'd seen you. I saw him a couple of days ago but I need to tell you something.'

'Please do!'

'It's about Francisca but I'll start at the beginning. Iago told you that I have had a big row with Carlos. True?'

'True,' said Antonio, still wondering what this was about and how it concerned him.

'Well, I joined the Wandering Chordsmen and I'm glad I did. Just over two weeks ago, after you left, we went to perform for a touring theatre in Toledo. It was quite a lucrative job and we were there for about a week. We stayed in this cheap, run-down inn, not far from the theatre and near the cathedral. At the time, there were four of us, Carlos, Lupita, Iago and me. After the first day, spent in rehearsing, we all went back to the inn for a meal and a drink. We all became a little jolly, but not drunk. I decided to stay down and chat to Iago while, first Lupita and after about ten minutes, Carlos went upstairs to bed. Iago and I chatted for about half an hour. Then he went up. I stayed down to finish the last of my beer and then I retired, too.

'I went upstairs. Because I was a little merry, as you might say, I opened the door to the wrong room. I always try the door before I unlock it. Well, the door opened and I innocently walked straight in. And there in the light of a couple of lamps, I could see before my eyes, Carlos frantically screwing Lupita. I was heartbroken. Here was the man betrothed to my daughter having his way with another.'

Antonio interrupted. 'Lupita? I'm amazed. She was always so innocent. I cannot imagine her doing that, especially knowing Carlos was promised to another.'

'It was her all right. I cursed the both of them and went to my proper room. I just couldn't sleep that night and couldn't decide what to do. Should I just let it go or should I tell Francisca? The two of them just about broke me with that act of abandon.

'By the time the dawn came up, I had sorted it out in my mind. I would stay with the group just for this job and then I'd leave, but most importantly, I'd tell Francisca and advise her not to marry him. I thought, if he was capable of being unfaithful this close to marrying my daughter, what would he be like when married to her.'

Antonio tried to interrupt again.

'Just let me finish. I'm getting to what's really important. Anyway, Francisca broke down when I told her. That must have been three or four days ago and she sobbed her heart out, poor lass, for two whole days. But now she's seen the light. And you, Antonio are that light. She realises that she should never have refused your offer of marriage and wants to marry you!

'She would have told you herself but didn't want to hear you say no. Anyway, I told her I was coming to see you and agreed I'd tell you myself. I understand that this will have taken you completely by surprise… and I don't want you to make any hasty decisions. But all I ask is that you think about it. My belief is that she genuinely loves you. This isn't a reaction to being cheated by Anyway, what do you think?'

'You have completely taken me aback, Juan. I don't know what to say. I've loved Francisca for a very long time, and even after she refused me. I have, I admit, made love at least once to another but that was in Valencia and I was not betrothed then.'

'That doesn't count,' said the señor, emphatically.

'I need time to think about it but I promise to let you or Francisca know in a day or two,' he said, still in utter shock.

'Another thing I wanted to say. If you haven't teamed up with any other musicians since your return from Valencia, would you join me? I'll teach you to play the guitar because I need a second guitarist!' he chuckled, now in a less serious vein.

'Let's do that, Juan. We got on so well in Guadalajara.'

'Let's shake on it then!'

'When do we start?'

'You've got a big decision to make but any time after that.'

Señor de Polanco did not tarry and made his excuses to go. Having showed the señor out, he went back to his chair, sat in it and began to ponder.

He loved Francisca and could not escape from the fact. His love for her had grown all the time he had been on the mission to Marrakesh and right up to the time he had gone to propose to her. What he was unsure about was whether she loved him. He didn't want to feel that she had been thwarted along the path to marriage and that all she needed was the hand of another, any other, to continue down that path. It was true that before Carlos appeared, she did say loving things to him and there was a strong sense that he had rejected her. He had to find a way of testing her, just to see her true motive.

He didn't want to rush into this new relationship so spent the following day and the day after sorting out his financial affairs, practicing his violin and generally thinking about Francisca, his renewed love. He decided to go to the Polanco's house after lunch on the third day after he had seen the señor.

'We thought you'd given us up,' said the señor, after letting him in. Then he whispered, 'Well?'

'I'm very nearly decided,' said Antonio, as the señor took him to see Francisca. Francisca's mother came out of the kitchen and planted a kiss on Antonio's cheek. As on other such occasions, she didn't utter a word.

'I'll leave you with Francisca,' said the señor, showing him into the drawing room where Francisca was sitting at a table embroidering a leather purse.

She immediately put down her work, dashed over to him and kissed him firmly on the lips. 'My dear, Antonio, I love you. I really do. I want to say "yes" to your offer of marriage.' She then dropped to his feet in tears.

'We have to talk, Francisca. I truly love you but do you truly love me? Your father told me the story of Carlos and I can understand you rejecting him. But are you turning to me merely as a substitute? I have to know because I want to make a life with you, to protect you and be the father of your children.' By then, Antonio had joined Francisca on the floor and was holding both her hands.

'I do love you, Antonio. I truly do. I only wish I hadn't been taken in by the charms of Carlos. I regret that I hadn't been more patient and waited for you to come back from Marrakesh. And equally, I want you to be my lover and father of my children. I would do anything for you. I love you. Can I say more?'

Antonio decided that this was the time to test her. 'I must tell you one thing, Francisca. I want to go to Lupita. I have some unfinished business with her.'

'That's the woman Carlos betrayed me for?'

'That's her.'

'I don't want you to see her. I hate her. If you have unfinished business with her, why not write to her. She might make a play for you, Antonio and I cannot be sure what will happen. We are just beginning down this road and although I love you, I don't know yet if I can trust you. Trust comes later, after the marriage vows. I wouldn't want you to go with another woman. If you did, I wouldn't believe you loved me and I would have to start again. It's a matter of honour.'

'Let me tell, you, Francisca, I have no intention of seeing her. I have no business with her. I just wanted to test your reaction and you have passed with distinction! I am convinced you love me! I will marry you! If your father agrees!'

Francisca cried again - tears of pure joy - and Antonio had difficulty containing his. Then they stood and hugged each other. They stayed in each other's arms and bathed in the soft eternal comfort each gave to the other. The time came for them to stop this passionate embrace.

'Can I tell my parents that we are betrothed?' said Francisca.

Francisca's parents were delighted. At first her mother could not speak and simply kissed each of them. Her father made light of it.

'But he hasn't asked me yet and I may refuse.'

'You wouldn't dare, Father. Knowing what I've already been through!'

'You are right, of course. Congratulations, the pair of you.'

Her mother then spoke. 'Now we need to arrange a wedding! Where would you like to get married?'

'Where you were married, in the church of San Ginés!'

'Do I have a say in this?' said Antonio. 'Maybe not!'

Preparations for the wedding began apace and the two of them were married not two months later. A few days after the betrothal, Antonio rode up to Pedraza to tell his parents about the forthcoming event. They were delighted and both of them came. The two mothers seemed to compete over who could shed the most tears. Antonio and Francisca started their married life in Doña Marta's rooms but it wasn't long before they moved into a larger place in the Lower San Ginés, not far from the church in which they were married.

Francisca's father, true to his word, taught Antonio to play the guitar and within a year of tuition and practice he had reached a high professional standard. Antonio and Señor de Polanco worked well together as a travelling duet. They joined up with many different local groups or just played together, often travelling to towns around Madrid, just as Antonio had done with the Wandering Chordsmen. The Polancos only had two daughters so Señor de Polanco would, as he said, be able to pass the family guitar playing business on to Antonio.

Before the wedding, Antonio went to see Silva. He explained his new domestic situation and Silva was pleased to enable Antonio to change his status to observer. He would never have to go on one of these missions again.

Carlos and Lupita were married only a few months after Antonio and Francisca both of whom went to the wedding. The circumstances were, however, slightly different. Although Carlos protested that he had made love to Lupita only once, on the occasion when they were so rudely interrupted by Señor Hidalgo, Lupita became pregnant. So whether he loved her or not, he did the honourable thing and took her hand in marriage.

The purge of the *Moriscos* continued right up to 1614. It became the turn of the *Moriscos* of Castille to be expelled. However, because so many were in key positions in government and business, the king took a more lenient view about them. He therefore did not expel Lupita, a *Morisca,* but instead compelled her to go back to Ávila to join her family there. Carlos felt compelled to go, too. So the Wandering Chordsmen were disbanded.

Reva, Tariq's stunningly beautiful daughter, did not enjoy such immediate fortune. Despite Silva's petition to the king, she became the subject of an expulsion order. Tariq lodged an appeal but the strain on Reva's mother was too much for her to bear and she died of a heart attack. The day after her funeral, which Antonio and Francisca attended, the king granted the appeal. Tariq eventually recovered and rebuilt his life as a spy and businessman. He sacked his deputy, whom he had never really trusted, and installed Reva instead. She was the only woman in Madrid who held such a prestigious position. She eventually married and gave up the job to care for her flock which eventually grew to seven.

Catalina, of course, became Antonio's sister-in-law. She delighted in attending the wedding with the nurse friend she lived with to the east of the town. Catalina became a reliable and trusted friend of the newlyweds and often joined them for a meal and a chat. Her past relationship with Antonio became a fading memory.

Eventually, Francisca became pregnant and on 28th of September 1614, produced a son. The birth almost killed her but within a month she had fully recovered. Antonio and Francisca called the baby Juan, Juan Hidalgo de Polanco. They named him after Francisca's father. When he was about three years old, his grandfather put Juan on his knee and gently strummed his little hand across the strings of a guitar.

'You can play, Juan,' said Francisca.

'That's brilliant,' said Antonio.

They all wondered where those first notes would lead.

The end